EMBER DAYS

EMBER DAYS

Margaret Wander Bonanno

Seaview Books

NEW YORK

Manufactured in the United States of America.

FIRST EDITION

Designed by Tere LoPrete

Library of Congress Cataloging in Publication Data

Bonanno, Margaret Wander.
    Ember days.

    I. Title.
PZ4.B69745Em   [PS3552.05925]   813'.54   79-3629
ISBN 0-87223-590-4

For my grandfather,
who always read his newspaper backwards

BOOK I
Sunset Park, 1930–1945

Outside the kitchen window the rain was sheeting against the sooty yellow bricks of the row houses. The knotted draggle-end of the clothesline sawed back and forth in the raw October wind, sometimes banging against the window-pane and driving Helen's heart into her mouth. Through the long gloom of the railroad rooms that led into the front parlor, she could hear the robust, unflagging voice of the priest intoning the first half of each Hail Mary, and ragged low murmured responses from the women hunched kneeling on the faded flowered carpet. From time to time her mother's voice rose above the others—half-sighing, half-keening: a plea for sympathy and attention.

Helen's grandmother, her mother's mother, was being waked in the front parlor.

"We don't get many that's waked at the house anymore," Mr. Kelly, the scrubbed and sanguine little mortician, had remarked, bustling into the house and bringing with him an incongruous odor of bay rum. "Still, we tries to make 'em as easy as the parlor wakes. It's harder on the staff, you understand, running back and forth, but you being just down the street from the parlor. . . ."

He was in there now, patting Helen's mother's hand, trying to keep her calm for the sake of the unknown life swelling beneath her middle-aged abdomen.

"It's up to you ter take the load off yer mother, then, miss," Helen's father had said when he left for work that morning. "Don't be after lettin' her get upset. Too much of grievin' will mark the baby."

"*Hail* Mary, fullofgrace, theLordis withthee," the priest went on, with his curious habit of emphasizing the word "Hail" as if to startle from sleep any of the weary, black-clad, lumpy figures who might consider dozing between beads. Helen kicked the heel of her penny loafer back against the leg of the kitchen chair every time he did it.

She didn't believe what they'd all said, all her aunts and cousins and what-have-you's, as they'd clumped down the long hallway in their wet galoshes, leaving puddles and covered dishes filled with broth or baked beans or corned beef or codfish cakes or rice pudding all over the shadowed dining room where the only male relatives, two of her father's cousins, were getting progressively drunker on a flask of Irish whiskey and arguing in increasingly louder voices about whose goat had gotten into whose vegetable garden in a boundary dispute begun in Quidi Vidi, Newfoundland, some thirty years before. Helen didn't believe that too much grieving would mark the unborn baby, her soon-to-be brother or sister. She believed her mother thrived on grief, welcomed it after fifteen years of caring for an aging parent and struggling to raise a family of her own at the same time. The louder she grieved now, the more the relatives might remember how she'd suffered in silence before.

"I'm glad the old crow's dead!" Helen kicked her heel back viciously against the chair leg again. "I wish she'd died ages ago, before I was born even! I wish I'd never seen her!"

Her younger brother, Danny, struggled to speak past the

mouthful of pound cake he'd filched from a parcel brought
by some relative. He washed it down with a mouthful of milk.
"Mom'll tan your backside if she hears you say that" was his
solemn opinion.

"I don't care!" Helen said sulkily, picking absently at the
beginnings of a pimple on her otherwise pretty fifteen-year-old
chin. "And you're gonna catch it for stuffing your face before
supper, you big pig!"

"When're we gonna eat, anyways?" Danny whined, wiping
the milk off his upper lip with the back of a fat, prepubescent
hand. "Why don't they lay off their praying and clear out?
When's Pop coming home?"

"I don't know," Helen sighed, peering again down the
long hall that led to the front door, past the bathroom with its
light bulb on a string, the only illuminaton for the hall since
the front foyer light had been removed by the air-raid warden
during the blackouts (it had not been replaced, even though it
was now months after the end of the war). Whenever somebody had to use the toilet and closed the door, the hall became
an endless black tunnel, with only the faintest glimmer from
the street lamp through the white gauze curtains of the foyer
door. When *was* Pop coming home? "I'm only waiting it for
him. We're gonna end up feeding the pack of 'em anyways."

"Aw, cripes!" Danny exhaled, the closest he could get to
swearing. "I wisht it was all over and they'd throw the dirt
on her box and get it done!"

"Mud more like, if the rain keeps up tomorrow." Helen
sighed, dragging herself up from the chair and lighting the
gas oven with a big kitchen match struck off the safety strip
tacked to the wall. She was wearing her school uniform, even
though she hadn't been to school since her grandmother finally
died just before dawn yesterday. There were simply no other
clean clothes, and the endless parade of relatives through the
house since the word got around the neighborhood yesterday
morning had precluded the chance of washing anything in the
old hand-crank machine, just as the wretched weather made it

impossible to hang things anywhere but in the kitchen to dry. And of course it wouldn't do to have laundry hung about the kitchen with company in and out. Her head ringing from the stuffiness of the overcrowded flat and the vicious circle of the laundry problem, Helen began filing to and from the dining room to put some of the lukewarm covered dishes into the oven to heat. She didn't know or care what was in half of them, or whether there would be enough to go around. She slammed the oven door shut on another of the priest's "Hail Marys."

"Jeez, won't it be funny not having her around, though?" Danny marveled, meaning their grandmother. "Not having to creep about because she's napping, or keep out of her way when she's rampaging."

"You'll have to be quiet for the new baby soon enough," Helen reminded him, jumping suddenly as the knotted end of the clothesline slammed against the window again. She peered, agonizing, down the hall. She thought she'd heard the front latch click. Could it be Pop at last?

A figure—no, two figures—were thrown into sudden relief as they passed the light from the bathroom door. It was Aunt Ag, their mother's older sister, and her little snot-nosed adopted son, Alistair.

"Children"—Aunt Ag nodded grandly, slipping off her other elbow-length black glove (she'd started on the first one as soon as she'd entered the hall) and shrugging her furpiece onto·the back of a dining room chair; the minks' little artificial bead-eyes glinted sadly at Helen in the near-dark, their limp paws swinging leadenly—"how's your poor mother holding up?"

"As well as can be expected," Helen replied, tossing the brown hair up off her pale forehead with the effort of such a mature opinion, as well as an ingrained resentment toward this woman for never taking the burden from her mother's shoulders even for a little while. She heard Danny's snort of laughter behind his fat fingers and couldn't look him in the eye. "Father Flaherty's been saying the beads. I think that's helped some."

"Your father home yet?" Ag took off a little veiled black hat and set it on the sideboard, spreading the veil with her fingers to keep its shape.

"No'm. He's on overtime this week," Helen said. "I'm holding the meal for him, but them inside'll be getting impatient."

"You'd best feed them, then," Aunt Ag said reasonably. "Set out the plates and the silver, sure, and when they're through with the rosary they can eat. You can hold something back for your father."

"I guess so."

"Fine," Ag said, the matter settled. She was good at settling matters. It came of always having to make decisions alone. "Alistair, stay in the kitchen with your cousins. It's too much of gloom in the parlor."

"Right, mum." Alistair spoke for the first time, the pervasive Liverpool accent escaping from him even in those few words. It set Danny snorting again. Helen gave him a poisoned look.

"Take off your raincoat, why don'tcha?" she offered Alistair awkwardly, never knowing how to handle this new addition to the family.

"Yeah, why don'tcha—Alice?" Danny asked maliciously.

"Me name's Alistair," their new cousin said sullenly.

They were supposed to be nice to him, even though he was not family in the strictest sense. He was an orphan; his parents had died in the London bombing. Through a strange series of events, their Aunt Ag—Irish as far back as her illiterate ancestors could tell—spinsterish, aloof, and in her middle forties, had adopted this English boy, even though she'd never expressed the slightest interest in children before. But then, Aunt Ag had always puzzled the rest of the family. It was hard to believe that she and Helen's plain, comfortable mother had sprung from the same womb, that both were daughters of the withered old harridan laid out in state in the front parlor.

"Shut your trap!" Helen hissed at her brother. "And help me lay the table."

"Women's work," Danny sneered. "Let Alice help you."

"Me name's Alistair," the boy growled. He was a year younger than Danny, small and thin, whereas Danny was big-boned and heavy. Still, if it came to a fistfight, Danny would always back off sniveling.

"Go on!" he whined now. "Somebody's got to clear out the boozers first, anyways."

He was right. As if in dreadful parody of the fights of boys, the argument in the corner of the dining room had been escalating to where the two men had staggered to their feet and squared off, each willing to swing first if only his double vision would clear.

Helen somehow found herself on their side of the room, standing as close to their elbows as she could, not daring to touch either of them for fear the sudden contact would set off their fists like a spring mechanism.

Fortunately her Uncle Alf's vision cleared first. His was the more even temper of the two. "And sure, why are we after takin' on like this?" he began to slobber. "What with this poor mite havin' lost her grandmother in this very house, and her lookin' like an angel itself in her little school uniform. Ain't yer ashamed now, Petey?"

"Me, is it?" Uncle Petey was swaying slightly, the wooden leg he'd earned in the Great War only barely supporting him. "And who was it started the whole row? Me, is it? I been as good as gold all evening. And whose whiskey might ye've been drinkin' to get yer in such a state?"

"Ar, yer old miser, and didn't I go in halves with yer?" Alf's eyes reddened with sudden emotion, and he fumbled in his pockets for some change. Pressing a quarter into Helen's hand with his weather-hardened one, he leaned down to look her in the eye. "Here yer go, girly. Buy something for yerself and the lads there. And tell yer Dad we'll be at Murphy's later should he be so inclined."

Helen stood rooted to the spot, having broken up the battle without so much as a word. She watched the two men weaving down the narrow hall, first one then the other leading as their broad shoulders caromed off the walls on either side.

God, had it always been like this? And when was Pop coming home?

"It's gone ter be a girl," the old woman said, catching hold of the button describing solemn circles from the end of a string as it dangled over her daughter's swollen abdomen. She shook her head, and the iron-gray hair straggled out of the knot at the back of her neck and frowzed about her face. "Circle is a girl. A boy is straight up and down. So a girl it is. And yer gettin' yer just reward. Wasn't I after tellin' yer not to bend and stoop and reach over yer head and get yerself so excited? Now ye've brought it on early, and it's yer own fault. The moon's all wrong for birthin' this week. Ye've brought it on yerself."

Mary Kathleen bit her lower lip to mask the pain of the contractions. "The doctor was after sayin' it might come early," she gasped when the pain let up enough to allow her to speak.

"Doctors!" her mother snorted.

Mary Kathleen's mother's single experience with a doctor had not been a positive one, to her way of thinking. She had managed, like many poor women of her generation, to birth several babies and take care of over sixty years of minor ailments without the interference of one of these strange, muttering individuals. It was not until she had arrived on her newly married daughter's doorstep over a year ago, announcing that she intended to die within the year and would need special care, that her trouble with doctors began.

Her new son-in-law, of whom she'd never approved, did not take her self-imposed death threats seriously, and immediately packed her off to a man he referred to as the "family doctor"—a term unknown in their native Newfoundland. The doctor had come to the same conclusion as the son-in-law. There was nothing wrong with Helen Blake that a good hard kick in the bloomers wouldn't cure.

Mary Kathleen's mother had gone back to her room in her daughter's apartment and complacently waited for death all the same. There had been no love lost between her and her son-in-law since.

"Let her be, then, Mrs. Blake," he said now, with the exaggerated politeness that drove her mad. He sat in his favorite chair next to the table with his smoking paraphernalia, reaming out his pipe to disguise his nervousness. As far as he was concerned, his wife should have been on her way to the hospital by now, and the sooner he put a stop to this foolishness—

The old woman diverted her rage from her daughter and directed it at him. "Doctors is it, Mr. James Daniel Manning?" she shrilled, hands on her hips, her sharp-lined face twisted with a scowl. "There's things in this world that doctors can't do nothing about, and half of them not believin' in God as it is. You mark me words—I've been after warnin' her time and again, but she's been like a madness all the week, hangin' curtains and scrubbin' and cleanin' and up and down ladders. She's got the baby all twisted up inside her, and it's gone ter be a hard time birthin' it now. She's brought it all on herself."

"Enough, goddamn it!" her son-in-law roared, his face turning suddenly as red as the flame-colored hair that gave him his nickname. "Have done and be quiet about it! Who's to do all the work if not herself? Have I seen yer lift a finger or do aught but bostoon about yer aches and pains all day long? Let her be!"

"Shush, Red, don't!" Mary Kathleen pleaded. Their voices jangled her already tight nerves. Neither of them seemed to remember she was there.

"Sure, who does all the cookin', I'd like ter know?" the old woman whimpered, quelled always by the first evidence of mastery in any man. "Who is it is up first thing in the morning, even though I can't hardly move my legs for the artheritis, and I'm gone ter die any time?"

"Stow yer artheritis, then! And if yer gone ter die, by all means be me guest!" Red growled. His voice softened as he looked at his wife. His face lost its flush and became suddenly pale. "Kat? Is it bad, then?"

Kat shook her head, unable to speak for a moment. Her

small, strong hands gripped the arms of the big chair ferociously. "I don't know how it is," she gasped finally. "It's like pieces of me are breakin' up inside."

"Oh, oh, oh!" her mother began to wail, wringing her hands in despair. "And isn't it how I was with the first one, and didn't he die before the priest could cross the bay ter baptize him? And the second, the little girl, who never so much as took her first breath—"

Red brought his hand down on the tabletop with such force that the little porcelain cats and dogs his wife loved so much rattled violently on the shelf above his head. It was enough to drive his mother-in-law out of the parlor.

"Damn her!" he growled. "Damn her and her ugly idears! She's no right to rag yer so!"

"She don't mean it, Red, sure she don't," Kat gasped. "It's just she birthed so many, and all but Ag and me died before they could talk. She can't help it."

"The hell with her!" Red murmured, but his temper was over as soon as it had flared up. He got up and crossed the room to crouch beside his wife, holding her work-roughened hands in his scarred and mangled ones. "You're a marvel, you are, to put up with her. Let's leave her cry and get yer to the hospital."

Kat nodded, pulling herself up from the chair with one hand pressed to her side. "Sure, it'll not be after goin' away by itself," she agreed.

Helen Mary Manning cried before she was completely born. As her creased and mottled bald head breached the birth canal, she let out a yell, and the doctor laughed so hard he could hardly hold on to her to ease her the rest of the way out.

"A girl." He smiled behind the mask, holding her aloft like a kosher chicken and watching her small rib cage heave with the effort of her bellowing. "And I'm not surprised. Only a woman would open her mouth before she'd even arrived in the world."

"Me husband," Kat murmured, a little giddy and very tired. "Must tell—me husband."

"We'll let him know in a moment, Mrs. Manning," the nurse said over her shoulder, swathing the baby in a blanket and holding her close to her own body for warmth. "She's small—not over five pounds, I'm sure. But listen to the lungs on her! It's the little ones that are the fighters. She'll do just fine!"

"Happy . . . so happy," Kat murmured, the drugs they'd given her beginning to send her under. "So afeared I'd—lose her. . . ."

"She's a fine, healthy baby, Mrs. Manning," the nurse assured her, as the struggling bundle in her arms calmed a little, emitted a single shuddering yawn, and slept. "Try to get some rest now."

When the nurse found the time to walk down the hall to the waiting room to tell Red Manning about his daughter, he had run out of pipe tobacco, thumbed through every magazine twice over, pared his nails down with his pocket knife to where they almost bled, and was haranguing the other two men in the room with him about his particular slant on politics and the social order.

"I've only been in this country ten years—that's but a third of me lifetime, now—but I've seen the lay of the land, so to speak. And I'll be after tellin' yez straight off—it's the unions'll be the salvation of the workingman. Don't get me wrong, mind yer—I ain't no bloody socialist—but I'll give yez an example. Now, where I come from, which is a bare bone of a place called Newfoundland—first dwelling place of the white man in this part of the world, and don't forget it—there's not much a man can do to earn his keep only sit in a little boat waitin' for the fish ter see it his way. Now, the rich fellers (merchants and middlemen and such) that lives in the capital at St. John's—they knows how a man is dependent on the way the fish is bitin', and they keeps the fisherman (who's usually an illiterate s.o.b.), they keeps him under their thumbs. Makes sure he can't sell his fish independent, but has ter go through them. They also sees to it that he has ter buy his supplies from their stores—fishing gear, clothing, and the like. So they got him goin' from both ends. He don't know the first thing about organizin', formin' a union, so they got him screwed. That's why every third winter they're starvin' up there. That's why I came ter this country, where even an ignorant s.o.b. can keep body and soul together. That's why I say it's the unions, brothers, the unions that'll—"

When he saw the nurse in the doorway, he grew quiet, knowing somehow she had come to speak to him.

"Your wife just had a lovely baby daughter, Mr. Manning," she said with a smile.

"And how is me wife, then?" Red asked soberly. The moment frightened him more than anything ever had in his eventful life.

"Just fine," the nurse assured him. "She's resting comfortably. You can see them both tomorrow."

Red Manning rose solemnly to his feet, sucking thoughtfully on his empty pipe. "Thank God for that, then," he said quietly. "And thanks to yerself as well, Sister."

"Oh, but I'm not—" the nurse began, then stopped herself. Most of the workingmen in the area were employed at the Navy Yard or the Bush Terminal; they came from Ireland and Devon and Newfoundland. No matter how long they'd been in the States, most of them still called a nurse "Sister."

"You're welcome," she said instead, and disappeared down the hall.

Red was about to leave. The other two men had been in a state of nervous agitation since the nurse had come in; neither had the courage to ask about his own wife. At the moment they seemed relieved that their talkative companion was on his way out.

Red looked at each of them in turn—business types, shirt-and-tie men. He'd give them something to chew on. "The next time you have a good fish dinner," he said to the nearer of the two, holding his scarred hands out for inspection, "remember that the man who brought them fish in had hands that looked like mine."

He nodded to them both, then went on his way. The sleeves of his flannel shirt were rolled above his elbows, despite its being mid-fall, cold enough to wear a jacket at least. Newfoundlanders never felt the cold.

Red walked some half-dozen blocks from the hospital, but in the opposite direction from home. He was heading down toward the waterfront, toward where a friend of his cousin Alf's had once owned a pleasant enough seaman's bar during the boom days of the Great War. Murphy's Bar and Grill had been boarded up for over a decade. A big, faded "For Rent or Lease" sign was tacked over the sheets of rotting plywood that covered the shattered plate-glass storefront, destroyed during a celebration of the signing of the Armistice, when a few of the boys had gotten out of hand. Within a few months of that memorable night, the Eighteenth Amendment had made it unprofitable for Murphy to bother with the window.

Murphy still lived in the pallid two rooms behind the boarded-up saloon, though he could easily afford to live elsewhere. Murphy was a bootlegger, one of the best independents in the city, with a direct line on Irish whiskey, smuggled into the States by way of Labrador Bay (except in the coldest months, when the only way over was to skate across) by any of his seven brothers, who'd never left Newfoundland. Murphy could well afford to buy himself a house in Park Slope, where the lace-curtain Irish lived, or even Bay Ridge, where the rich Scandinavians were grudgingly accepting the spillover from Sunset Park, but he stayed in his two rooms behind the bar, sitting atop the biggest cache of Irish whiskey in the borough of Brooklyn.

"It's real simple," he would explain to anyone who asked him. Very few did anymore, since the only ones who drank with him were old friends who'd already heard his explanation. "Down here I'm me own man. Ain't nobody can boss me. Most of the world don't know I exist. The minute I starts buyin' real estate somebody's goin' to get nosy. Bad enough

I'll have the cops on me back, and maybe even the government itself, but some of them wops from that there Mafia starts pushin' in on me and I ends up workin' for them or cookin' in me own juices in some alley. No, sir, not me. It may not be the best of neighborhoods, but it sure is peaceful."

So he haunted his two stale little rooms, used the Gents in the saloon, slept most of the day, entertained his friends at night. He was not married. Some said it had something to do with a freak accident with a fence post in his teens; there were those among his maligners who said he favored little boys. Whether or not either was the case, he lived alone and didn't seem to mind it. Everybody wondered what he did with his money.

Red Manning was heading for Murphy's that night, which was unusual in itself. Red was not a drinking man. He saw nothing wrong with a shot of medicinal in his morning coffee during the winter to help him brave the driving wind from the Narrows as he walked to work, and when he was younger and in the merchant marine he had gotten mildly drunk in some of the famous port cities of the globe. But he was thirty now, and a family man, and there was this incidental known as Prohibition. Personally, he thought it was nonsense to tell grown men what they could or could not drink, and felt superior in the certainty that such a law wouldn't stand a chance in his home country, but there was no point in running counter to the law unnecessarily.

But tonight was different. Tonight his first child had been born. Red was glad it was a girl. He did not subscribe to the notion that a man could not rest easy until he had fathered a son. In this country there were doctors and hospitals, and babies didn't have to die with the alarming frequency that they did where he came from. In spite of the Depression and periodic layoffs, his job was steady, and his income didn't depend on the tides and the weather and the St. John's merchants. There were no luxuries, but he and his wife and the new little one, and even his sour old mother-in-law, could live comfortably. There was plenty of time for more babies.

It was late, nearly midnight, when Red tapped softly on the alley door at Murphy's. He had no intention of getting up at five to go to work *this* morning. It was his sole desire to sit at Murphy's battered kitchen table in the blue haze of pipe smoke and cigarettes, getting pleasantly drunk and telling everybody about the new baby daughter he hadn't so much as glimpsed yet.

"She's bald as an egg, sure, but a joy to look at. She'll be fair and blue-eyed like my people, but she's already got Kat's features," he told one well-wisher, and to another, as he grew progressively drunker, "Sure, she's got masses of dark hair like the Blakes, but she don't favor either side. She's one of a kind, I tell yer."

It was nearly three when his cousin Alf helped him up the stoop of the two-family row house, fishing the key out of his pocket for him and fumbling it into the lock.

"You'll have a word—a word with the foreman, then—when yer goes in terday?" Red asked in what he thought was a whisper, holding himself up against the doorjamb. Alf was the kind who could drink all night and still show up for work the next day. "You'll speak ter McCoohey, then, and tell him how I was after walkin' the floor with worryin' about the missus all night—"

"Sure, Dad, sure. Only keep yer voice down," Alf hissed, patting him on the shoulder and nearly tipping him over. "Get yer to bed now and hush yer blather."

"You'll tell McCoohey I got no phone is why I couldna call in meself. Sure, he's no way of knowin' I've not missed a day in five years—"

"Whisht, man! He knows it well enough. Stow yer noise and get ter bed before yer after havin' the old grumpus up and raggin' yer."

None of the Mannings envied Red his live-in mother-in-law, and their sympathy was free-flowing, if hard on a man's pride.

"Yer right, lad." Red considered it, clapping his hand over Alf's, which still rested on his shoulder. "Yer right at that. Bad enough listenin' ter the old bitch in the morning with me head like a balloon."

They parted company, and Red made his way down the long dark hall, avoiding by instinct the boards that squeaked. He stopped in the bathroom to relieve himself of the effect of all that whiskey, and a thought occurred to him.

"And why shouldn't I wake the old bitch, then?" he wondered aloud as he buttoned his pants, ending up with an extra button at the top of his fly and an extra buttonhole at the bottom. "And why shouldn't I?"

He crept with exaggerated softness through the maze of rooms, ending up just outside his mother-in-law's door. A less-than-genteel sound of snoring reached his ears.

"The gall of her!" he muttered indignantly. "Snoozin' away while her daughter is after sufferin' the pains of Hell itself!"

He raised a powerful scarred hand and rapped sharply on the door, turning the big glass knob at the same time. The snoring ceased abruptly, and the figure in the bed emitted a muffled shriek.

"Holy Mother of God!" the old woman cried.

Red had to laugh. Before she flashed on the bedside light, she had pulled the covers up to her chin, as if anyone could possibly catch a glimpse of the shriveled old body swathed in yards of flannel nightgown. Her hair hung past her ears in frowzy gray braids, and her mail-order teeth sat in their glass on the dresser, next to the statue of the Infant of Prague and the bloodstained picture of the Sacred Heart of Jesus in its dime-store frame. Red's whisky haze cleared at the sight of her. God, she was a mess! Would Kat look like that in another thirty-five years?

"Well, missus," Red said loudly, "thought I'd give yer the courtesy of lettin' yer know ye've got yerself a grand-daughter."

"Thanks be to God!" Helen Blake croaked. "And how is she, then?"

"Doctor says she's fine and healthy," Red reported, putting

emphasis on the word "doctor." "She's a grand baby, he said. And Kat's pulled through something wonderful. Doctor says it was a right short labor for it bein' her first. So all yer signs and omens was for nothing."

"Then thanks be to God again!" The old woman released her death grip on the blankets and groped for her ever-present rosary—a worn one of black wooden beads like the ones the nuns used. Blessing herself with the crucifix, the old woman suddenly had a thought. "And if she's after havin' such a short time of it, then where might yer have been till this hour? Oh, as if I couldna smell it on yer from here! Hangin' around with them evil, dirty scuts down by the piers, and that ugly mother's son Murphy! Sure, I ought ter call a constable on the lot of yer. Fine business it would be if they knew what really went on down there—"

"And would yer have the sole support of yer daughter and granddaughter—and yer worthless self, I'd add—thrown into the jug and out of his job?" Red was losing his patience. "I'm thinkin' yer wouldn't. Good-night to yer, Mrs. Blake, and be grateful it's turned out right."

He had silenced the old woman. She watched him fade from the doorway and was about to turn out the light when she thought of something else. "Sure, what name are yer givin' her, then, James Manning?" she called out to him in a milder voice.

Almost immediately, his fiery-red head reappeared in the doorway. "I thought I was after tellin' yer," he said mischievously. "It's Helen Mary—after yer gracious self."

Possibly the first word Helen Mary Manning became conscious of in the midst of the kaleidoscopic impressions of infancy was "don't."

"Don't put the baby's basket so near the window, then," her grandmother would say. "Sure, she'll be after catchin' her death of cold."

"Don't be after lettin' her suck her thumb, Mary Kathleen.

It spoils the shape of her teeth. And don't be after buyin' her one of them vile, filthy pacifiers, either."

"Don't let the child crawl on the floor, then. There's no tellin' what she might pick up."

The second prohibition—the ban on pacifiers—was harder on Kat than it was on the baby, who was high-strung and jittery, and who cried unceasingly from six in the evening until nearly midnight every night until she was five months old.

"Gas," her grandmother pronounced indifferently, taking a turn at rocking the child, which seemed to help a little. "She'll outgrow it, sure."

Kat couldn't help wondering if a pacifier or the freedom to suck her thumb might not help the poor thing—ease the cramps that distended her small stomach, provide her with some satisfaction of an infant's desperate need for mother-comfort. But Kat didn't dare contradict her own mother. Instead, she ended up giving the child the breast far more often than the once every four hours the doctor insisted was normal, and a little more frequently than she herself found comfortable. The whole process dragged her down and made her feel exhausted. There were days when she didn't know if the sun was out or if it was teeming rain, days when it seemed that the only thing that mattered was fitting in a handful of chores and possibly getting dinner on the table before the incessant howling began.

But there was something so self-indulgent about lying in bed after Red went to work and having her mother bring the baby to her. Mother and baby would lie there in among the blankets and the big homemade quilt, sometimes dozing until nearly ten. The more Kat thought about it, the more she discovered that most of the memorable moments of her life had taken place in that bed.

The ban on crawling did Helen Mary the most damage. She was an alert, active child, small and wiry and full of unchanneled energy. Under her grandmother's vulture eye she had to spend the first year and a half of her life caged in a wood-slatted playpen, or carried from room to room like royalty. Her father's attempts at liberating her from her variety of prisons were short-lived. Her grandmother would swoop down on the two of them, shrieking and lamenting, and the guilty, frightened look on Helen Mary's face plunged Red into deep remorse. So he surrendered, only getting around the ban by taking her out alone in the big padded perambulator on his days off. He would wheel the pram to the nearby park, spread a cautiously concealed blanket on the damp grass, and put Helen Mary down in the center of it. He would bring the child flowers and leaves and blades of grass to fondle and study and sometimes put in her mouth. He let her suck her thumb, too, but only outside the house where her grandmother couldn't see. At home he joined the opposition, for Kat's sake, and solemnly removed the thumb from the baby's mouth when he found it there, even going to the druggist for paregoric to put on the offending digit. And while he took her to the park and sat her down on the blanket as often as weather permitted, he always kept her confined to the limits of the blanket, stopping her adventurous creeping as soon as she threatened to crawl onto the grass itself. He had unwittingly fashioned for her a different kind of prison, though at least it had no bars.

As a result of this systematic confinement, Helen Mary was eighteen months old before she attempted to stand and take her first hesitant steps. She had been thinking about doing it for nearly six months, but there didn't seem to be any point. How was she to know that it was possible to escape from prison simply by adopting the upright posture of her elders? But she did walk eventually—awkwardly, stiffly, on tiptoe, as if she was afraid to let her heels come in contact with the floor, lest that bring the wrath of the old vulture on her as so many other things did. Kat became terrified that she might have polio, and badgered the doctor for explanations as to why the child walked so oddly. The doctor gave Helen Mary a thorough examination, and not understanding the restrictions of her environment, shrugged his shoulders and said she'd probably outgrow it.

The last of Helen Mary's problems was her name.

Helen Mary had been named after her grandmother, and

having two women under the same roof bearing the same name drove Red to distraction.

"Is Helen asleep, then?" he would ask Kat when he came in late from overtime at the Terminal, thinking of how pleasant it would be to spend some time in his own house without the constant presence of his mother-in-law.

"Sure now, Mom or the baby?" Kat frowned at him in exasperation, her brown hair tumbling down over her forehead as she fussed with his kept-warm dinner. This sort of mix-up happened half a dozen times a day.

"Yer mother, of course," Red would say. "I've no objection ter spendin' the time of day with me daughter. But herself I could live without in any weather."

"Well, they're both asleep, then," Kat said with the irrefutable logic that he loved about her. She set the plates down on the table and indicated that he was to sit down. "I saved my own to eat with you. We've the house to ourselves till the baby wants nursin' again."

"It's a pleasant enough thought," Red considered, rubbing his red-stubbled chin and wondering if he ought to shave twice in one day to spare Kat's having her skin rubbed raw later when they. . . . "Is there some reason we've got to eat it this moment? I'm not terrible hungry."

Kat caught his eye and saw the gleam in it, and her pale skin flushed slightly. "Sure, you're a rogue itself, you are." She smiled shyly. "Wantin' ter work up an appetite, was yer?"

"The thought had crossed me mind." He grinned.

And for an hour or more the two of them were able to forget about babies and mothers-in-law and warmed-over suppers.

But the confusion over names continued, until Kat's irrefutable logic arrived at a solution. "She was baptized Helen Mary, and that's what we'll call her," she said. "And Mom we'll call just Helen."

And Helen Mary grew up not knowing that even her name had been tainted by her grandmother's influence.

Her ventures into walking were short-lived. She had been

practicing for less than a month, inuring herself to the chorus of "don'ts" that followed her every time she strayed down the hall toward the front door or touched one of her mother's precious knicknacks. Then a disquieting series of occurrences transpired. The first was a sudden and frantic attempt on the part of her mother and grandmother to toilet-train her. This led to balking, fussing, sleepless nights, and an attack of colitis that brought the doctor to the house with dire warnings about dehydration and the dangers of excessive discipline. Helen Mary was allowed to keep her diapers for another six months.

The last in the series of occurrences was the arrival of her baby brother, christened Daniel Peter Manning. The day her mother went to the hospital to birth him, Helen Mary sat on the floor and howled for an hour. The day her mother came home with the strange-smelling, overweight bundle, Helen Mary went back to crawling. She was put back into her wood-slatted prison and lectured about jealousy on the part of a big sister who ought to be *proud* to have a new baby brother. Red stood it for as long as he could.

"Be quiet, then, the pair of yer!" he bellowed finally at his wife and mother-in-law, setting his new son howling and making Helen Mary look up at him with that pitiable expression of guilt. "Sure, she's not yet two years old, and she don't care for the little turd, and you'll not make her by blatherin' at her the whole day long!"

With that he swept her up out of the playpen, stuffed her little arms into the hand-knitted sweater, and carried her outdoors to where it was almost summer. He didn't bother with the perambulator—which was now fitted with blue pillow shams and a blue carriage cover, whereas before it had had pink—but walked the several blocks to the park with his daughter in his arms. He didn't bother his conscience with having called his son a turd, either. The three weeks he'd had to observe the boy had shown him that young Danny had about as much personality as a blob of shit, and a Newfoundlander called it as he saw it. Let his mother-in-law rant and rave and tear at her frowzy gray hair; he'd be gone long enough for her to get it out of her system. As for her aiming it at Kat, Red was beginning to think that maybe Kat deserved most of what she let her mother get away with. It was high time that a woman of nearly thirty, with two children of her own, learned to stand on her own two feet.

Red stopped walking just inside the park. He set Helen Mary down in the grass—*right in* the rain-damp, broken-glass, dog-shit grass. He didn't care if she caught a cold or soiled her dress or tracked mud from here to Byzantium. He set her down in the grass, and backed up a few steps.

"All right, then, Miss Tish," he said. "Let's see yer walk."

Helen Mary began to crawl, found the grass too high and wet and her progress impeded. She began to whimper, holding her arms out to Red so that he would pick her up.

"No, sir, yer ladyship," he replied. "Get up off yer padded arse and walk."

She stopped her noise abruptly and looked at him with reproach. He did not alter his position. Slowly, ass-up and stiff-legged the way toddlers do, Helen Mary pulled herself to her feet. She took a step, then several all in a rush. For the first time in her life, she let her heels touch the ground. She found she could balance better, discovered she didn't pitch headlong into things as often. With open arms, she ran the last few steps, tumbling into Red's legs and clutching him around the knees.

"God love yer!" he whispered, picking her up and swinging her over his head in the way that his mother-in-law claimed would damage her brain. "God love yer—yer a fighter, you are!"

And she walked home beside him, her small soft hand curled inside his scarred and mangled one. Helen Mary never crawled again.

Helen Mary didn't like her younger brother, but she never actively disliked him either. As long as nobody in the house prodded her into being nice to him—sharing her toys, keeping him amused when he was cranky—she managed to ignore him. By the time she was almost old enough to start school, she had evolved into a bright, inquiring little wisp of a child, who needed less sleep than the doctor thought was normal, who learned to read by sitting in Red's lap while he read the funny papers to her, and who had as many dolls as a workingman's daughter could own, all of which had handmade clothes she had learned to stitch herself.

It was also around the age of five or six that her uncanny power began to manifest itself.

There had been signs of it as early as infancy, but Helen Mary's grandmother was the first to mention it aloud. "She's as smart as a bee, sure," her grandmother would say. "But it's a quare habit she's got of starin' till yer think she'd burn a hole in yer."

This staring, unconscious on Helen Mary's part, had the effect of neutralizing any argument that took place within her hearing. Any verbal battle in the making—usually between her father and grandmother, less often between mother and grandmother, and almost never between mother and father— brought her into the room with the combatants, where she would stand as close between them as she possibly could, turning the intense light of her huge brown eyes on each of them in turn, until her presence permeated their anger and made them stop, embarrassed at how ridiculous they suddenly appeared. It got so that they could only argue at night, after she was asleep, and more than one nocturnal battle had been halted at the sight of the little figure in the white flannel nightgown looking on solemnly from the doorway.

Her power became more uncanny as it reached out even to affect her brother, Danny. He was at this time not quite four, already overweight, a whiny, mulish child overindulged by his female relatives, secretly disliked by his father. While Helen could not prevent him from bullying her—he was bigger and stronger than she, and not attuned to the subtleties of chivalric behavior—she could stare him into submission when his attention was fixed away from her, as when his whining drove their mother to near-distraction. She had more than once saved him from a hiding with the razor strop when he pushed Red's temper to the breaking point.

Finally, Helen Mary's power was able to control total strangers. Red never tired of telling about the time she'd slipped away from him on their way home from mass on the Feast of the Assumption and somehow gotten into the thick of a crowd watching a brawl between two men. Both had been drinking home brew, and were more than a little out of their heads. Helen Mary slipped through the legs of the onlookers, and before anyone could think to grab her out of the way, had calmly stood staring at each man in turn. No one remembered how it happened exactly, but the two men dropped their fists almost simultaneously, and both went home looking sheepish and ashamed.

"It's quare, that's all," her grandmother would say, slopping tea into her saucer and supping it noisily, toothlessly. "It's the work of the Devil, I tell yer, that evil eye of hers. Someone ought ter speak ter the priest."

"Leave the child be," Red growled menacingly, slapping at Danny's fat hand, which was groping too far across the table in search of yet another biscuit.

Kat said nothing. Helen Mary looked down at her plate, absently kicking the leg of her chair.

"She's an odd duck, sure," her grandmother sniffed. "I pity the man'll get her."

"He'll be a right privileged character, Mrs. Blake," Red said grandly. "That is, supposin' there's a man good enough for her."

Helen Mary came home in tears on the day in June when she got her final report card. From the redness of her eyes and nose and the state of the balled-up handkerchief, freshly ironed only that morning, it looked as if she had been crying most of the day.

Her grandmother met her at the front door. Helen Blake managed to drag herself from her bed of pain every day—or so she described it to Mrs. Conroy next door—in time to catch sight of her little namesake in her parochial-school plaid, lugging the too-heavy leather satchel full of books that made her tilt to one side, as if her thin small arm would pull loose from her shoulder, and trudging across the avenue and a third of the way down the block to her own home in the line of undistinguished yellow brick row houses. Of course, Helen Blake didn't really come out to the brownstone stoop solely to look out for her granddaughter, who could hardly come to any harm on such a short walk home, but to catch up on all the local news that traveled up and down the street and throughout the neighborhood from stoop to stoop and clothesline to clothesline, all the way down to the little "Eye-talian" fruit market on Fifth Avenue. Miss a single day on the stoop, and one missed a wealth of gossip.

So it was that while clucking with Mrs. Conroy over the influx of Ukrainians into what had once been a solidly Irish and Scandinavian neighborhood, and shaking her head over the antics of that no-good Tessie O'Shea down the block—and her half-gone with the child and no man in sight—Helen Blake caught sight of the frail green-plaid figure and noticed something different in the way her granddaughter walked. The old woman stopped snapping the green beans she had in her lap, nodded perfunctorily at Mrs. Conroy, who never *would* stop talking, and studied the litle figure's progress. Ordinarily Helen Mary hurried home from school, striding along jauntily, though stiff-legged with the weight of the book bag, eager to be home and tell about the day at school. Today the book bag was empty—the children had turned in all the musty, ink-stained textbooks for use by next year's first graders—and Helen Blake could see by the way it swung aimlessly in her hand that Helen Mary's burden was almost nonexistent. Why was she dragging her heels, then, and scrubbing at her eyes with her free hand as she walked? Helen Blake scooped the green beans out of her apron into the colander beside her on the step, and stood, hands on her hips. The gesture brought Mrs. Conroy to an abrupt stop in both her knitting and her conversation.

"Sure, what is it?" Mrs. Conroy, who had a true Irish brogue and not a bastardized Newfie one, demanded in alarm.

"Somethin's after ailin' the child," Helen Blake said, and said no more until the little figure reached the wrought-iron gate at the foot of the stoop and pushed it open.

"You're a sight, then," Helen Blake greeted the girl, always fearful of being too soft on her. Life was hard on a woman even in the new country, and the sooner a girl learned this the better. "What's the trouble?"

"I'm not telling to you," Helen Mary sobbed, her voice all quavery from crying. She pushed past her grandmother and slipped into the house. The sound of her small, impatient footsteps echoed hollowly in the hall.

Helen Blake was simply stunned. Her granddaughter had never been fresh. Backed into a corner, she could fight like a wet cat, but her everyday personality was meek to the point of submissiveness.

"Well, can yer top that?" Helen Blake exhaled in disbelief. "As soon's I get ter the bottom of this, I'll be after takin' the brown soap to her brazen mouth. Did yer ever!"

"Must be something powerful is eatin' at her," Mrs. Conroy opined. "Last day of school, too. Don't suppose she got hurt or nothing?"

Helen Blake shook her head in confusion. "Sure, I couldna tell yer," was all she said.

"Poor mite!" Mrs. Conroy clucked. "She bein' small for her age—maybe the others picks on her. But if it was me was her grandmother, I wouldn't mix in it. It's for the natural parents to take care of such things."

Helen Blake gave her a narrow look. The remark was obviously directed at her; she was less than silent around the neighborhood in her belief that grandparents knew more about the raising of children than the parents did. She picked up her colander of string beans and headed up the steps toward the house.

"Good morrow to yer, then," she said shortly, going inside.

Mrs. Conroy did not look up from her knitting. She had managed to raise her brood without benefit of a third generation in the house, and she pitied Kat Manning no end. But then, unsought advice never went far.

Helen Blake found her granddaughter curled in a tight, defensive ball in the middle of her bed in the all-but-windowless room—there was one window in the corner, but it overlooked an air shaft—that she shared with her younger brother. An invisible line of demarcation ran down the middle of the room separating her territory from his, her dolls and prayer books from his trucks and cars and shoehorns. The carpeting in this no-man's-land was worn thin, because the other two bedrooms led off from this one through one door and the parlor was at the other door. Privacy was a concept Helen Mary had never heard of. Until she was fifteen she would never be able to dress or undress anywhere except in the bathroom, would always have to be fully clothed and sitting demurely with her knees together under her skirts even in her own bedroom, because it was not completely hers. Her brother Danny's snorting, fat-boy sleep patterns would become part of her subconscious, and he would waken sometimes and listen to the quarrels she had with herself in *her* sleep, taunting her about them when she awoke. It never occurred to Helen Mary's parents that having siblings of the opposite sex sleeping in the same room might be considered abnormal. In Newfoundland, entire families sometimes slept in one room. That married couples found the time or the space to beget as many children as they did was a miracle in itself.

Helen Blake stood in the doorway of the stale-smelling, dingy room, tapping her foot on the worn carpet. Her unbending spirit was almost moved by the tragic quality of the child's muffled sobs. Short of death itself, what on earth could the little mite find to cry so intensely about?

"You'll have ter be tellin' me about it, then," Helen Blake said stonily, knowing no other way to begin. She sat on the edge of the girl's bed, her back like a ramrod. "Yer ma's out ter the market with Danny, and yer can't keep up this yowlin' all afternoon. Out with it, then."

Helen Mary sat up and looked at her grandmother. She couldn't speak for several minutes because she was shaking too hard with violent hiccups.

"Won't-tell-you," she hiccuped finally. "You'll-only-yell-at-me."

It had to be something terrible, Helen Blake thought, to make the child so fiery. This was the closest she'd come to actual defiance in her entire life.

"I wouldn't either," her grandmother said solemnly, raising her right hand to emphasize her sincerity. "True as the day I was born."

Helen Mary considered for a minute. "Cross your heart and hope to die?" she blurted out suddenly.

"Whisht, child!" The old woman was horrified. "Don't tempt the Devil!"

"It's just a 'spression," Helen Mary whimpered, her lower lip trembling as if she would break into a fresh bout of tears. "Everybody in school says it."

Children's games, Helen Blake thought. Was it possible that she herself could have been a child once, could have engaged in anything as frivolous as a game? It couldn't be. Life was hard where she came from. A child was an adult as soon as she could speak. No, it couldn't be.

"All right, then," she said, softening a little. "Cross me heart and whatever all else. I'll not be after yellin' at yer. Now tell me what it is that's ailin' yer."

Helen Mary sniffled grandly and settled herself more comfortably on the bed. "We got final report cards today," she began.

"Yes, sure, I knew that." Her grandmother nodded, biting her tongue to keep from saying more.

"An' last week Sister said she's only gonna give the highest grade of ninety-eight, as ninety-nine is too close to perfection, an' only God is perfect," Helen Mary recited all in a rush.

Her grandmother nodded, in perfect agreement. Thanks be to God, the nuns were just as strict in this lax and evil country as they were at home.

"An' she—Sister, I mean—only gave out a single ninety-eight, which was to Mary McConnell, who's not nearly as smart as me."

"And what were you after gettin', then?" her grandmother demanded, unsmiling in the face of her granddaughter's self-importance. Sure, wasn't pride the first of the Seven Deadly Sins?

"Only ninety-seven!" the girl burst out, starting to cry again. "And I worked so much harder than Mary McConnell. I wanted to be the best!"

Her grandmother threw up her hands in exasperation. "Well, if I didn't think I'd heard everything!" she said. "You are the living end, child, you surely are!"

She was going to lecture her on the pride that goeth before the fall, but saw this as a hard-core case that her simple powers of rhetoric could not hope to penetrate. Let Kat handle this one, and if she couldn't, the girl ought to be sent to the priest.

Helen Mary had been what Sister Misericordia, her first-grade teacher, had on more than one occasion referred to as a "model child." She was intelligent without being arrogant, obedient without being subservient, alert and inquiring and motivated by some inner drive to work just a little harder than everyone else. Had the nun given her the lower grade in order to teach her the meaning of humility? If so, her plan had backfired.

On the first day of school, Helen Mary had been assigned a seat near the front of the room because she was smaller than most of the others. There was only one child in front of her—a pinch-faced towheaded boy who seemed to have a perpetual runny nose. No sooner had everyone been seated at the cramped, battered, bolted-to-the-floor desks than he began to cry.

Helen Mary leaned forward and tapped him on the shoulder. "What's wrong?" she whispered, knowing instinctively that talking would be forbidden.

The boy's hair was so blond it was almost colorless. His face had turned a mottled pink the minute he started crying. He looked at Helen Mary and started to wail. "I wanta go home!" he howled. "I want my mother!"

Sister Misericordia, who had been straightening the big brown-paper window shades, turned in alarm at this outburst.

"Michael Francis Kavanaugh, what is the meaning of this?" she demanded, though there was a smile lurking behind her sternness. She was a generously built woman just entering middle age, and she loved all children, as long as someone else took them home at the end of the day. "Your brother Patrick never cried in my class!"

"I wanta go home!" the boy howled again.

Within moments his sentiments had affected nearly everyone in the room, and among the other small people who couldn't eat breakfast for the churning in their stomachs that morning, or who caught a chill in the seemingly friendly September sunshine when they stepped out of their homes, the mood soon spread. Most of them began to sniffle and whimper. Only Helen Mary seemed unaffected.

The damp, green-painted auditorium Kat had brought her to that morning was the biggest room she'd ever seen outside of church. The sight of all those other children, all shapes and sizes and temperaments, perched restively on the rows of folding chairs in their green-plaid uniforms filled her heart with happiness. And this classroom, with its dusty yellow sunlight and the so-ever-present-as-to-be-invisible crucifix at the front, was a place of wonderment to her. It was the first time in her life she'd realized that the universe need not be contained within a squalid collection of railroad-flat rooms.

"You're a terrible gommil!" she hissed at the boy in front of her, borrowing a term she'd heard Red use often, though she didn't know what it meant. "School is a fair wonderful place!"

Fortunately, Sister Misericordia heard only the latter statement, and while her Boston-bred ears winced at the Newfie accent, she was at once endeared to the child who'd uttered it.

"School" was writing huge, wavery graphite letters on sheets of yellow, splinter-studded paper, or watching them slide off to one side as you scratched them squeakily on the chalkboard. School was Reading—a skill Helen Mary had acquired prematurely thanks to Red and the Thimble Theatre—and discovering the wondrous worlds imprisoned between the covers of a book. School was Arithmetic and Spelling, and tracing cardboard holly wreaths or bunnies or silhouettes of Lincoln and Washington and coloring them with the prescribed crayon. This last activity was known as Art. And there was Music—mostly the memorization of hymns—and something called Citizenship, which meant you never used the words "mick" or "wop" within a nun's hearing unless you fancied the taste of soap.

But school was, first and most importantly, Religion.

By the time a child was of school age, it was understood that he or she knew the difference between right and wrong. This was referred to as having "reached the age of reason," at which time one became responsible for all sins committed: the little venial sins, like forgetting to say your prayers or lying about who ate the last piece of cake, and the grievous mortal ones, like missing mass on Sundays or murdering your father. Both of the latter carried the weight of eternal damnation to Hell and a permanent loss of grace.

To insure against this dire tragedy, children like Helen Mary were steeped in their religion from the moment of birth. Kat's endless recitation of the rosary in the labor room had been the only thing between her and the pain. The first day Helen Mary had been put in her arms in the hospital, she had requested the chaplain to come and pray over the child—not lest some ill befall her body, for that would be the will of God, but to protect her newly unfolding soul, already tainted, as was every newborn infant's, with the Original Sin of Adam and Eve.

Helen Mary's first complete sentences had been the lines of a prayer:

> Now-I-lay-me-down-to-sleep-
> I-pray-the-Lord-my-soul-to-keep-
> If-I-should-die-before-I-wake-
> I-pray-the-Lord-my-soul-to-take-

She dutifully repeated this after her grandmother—who had reserved the privilege of teaching it to the child for herself— not knowing what she was saying exactly, but sensing somehow that the word "die" was one that made adults cringe in ordinary conversation. The thought lodged itself unanalyzed in Helen Mary's brain for well over a decade.

And so she found nothing extraordinary in what she heard from the nun at school, or heard repeated by the priest at the special mass for children at nine on Sunday mornings. Good was good and bad was bad. Nearly everything a person could think of doing was bad, and the few things that were good were carefully delineated and easy to understand. Life was quite simple, if rigorous and usually unrewarding, but then Helen Mary had been learning this from birth.

There was only one thing about Helen Mary's religion that startled, and in a way she did not understand, excited her. She never tired of hearing stories about the lives of the saints, particularly those brutally tortured and martyred for the Faith. St. Agnes's horrible mutilation because she refused to surrender either her religion or her virginity, St. Cecilia's miraculous ability to survive burning at the stake, and the slaughter of St. Ursula and the Host of Virgins affected Helen Mary most peculiarly. As if these were not enough, there were the stories the nun loved to tell of contemporary martyrs—nuns and priests slaughtered by the godless Protestant Huns in the Great War, missionaries tortured and imprisoned by ignorant, dirty pagans in places like China and Africa.

"Did you know," Sister Misericordia would hiss at them, her eyes bulging in a kind of fervor, "did you know that in some parts of the world, at this very moment, there are living saints suffering torment and deprivation for the love of God and His Church? In some countries in this world, at this very moment, saintly Sisters and priests and lay people are herded into filthy prison cells half the size of this room—dozens of them, barely able to find room to stand, much less sit or lie down or kneel in prayer. They must stand there in their own filth, starving on moldy bread or rice and a cup of dirty water. Sometimes their guards will spit in the cup before their very eyes, and yet these poor, brave martyrs for Christ must drink it anyway. Oh, think of it, children, and be grateful that you are here in this blessed country of ours, where we are free to practice the one, true Religion. . . ."

By now Helen Mary would be only half-listening. Nearly swooning from the exquisiteness of the horror of it, she was aware of a thrilling sensation down her spine, and of a strange, damp, tingling sensation in her underpants. She felt as if she had to urinate badly, and yet she enjoyed the feeling. What did it mean? Why did it happen to her every time the nun launched into one of her stories? Why was she able to sit and listen, entranced, while the other children squirmed and made noises of disgust?

It wasn't as if she were a novice to horror stories; she heard them all the time at home. But her grandmother's stories did not affect her in the same way. Her grandmother managed to find something bad to say about nearly everything, but news coming out of Newfoundland since the Depression held nothing good in it. The Depression was one thing in the States. A quarter of the work force might be idled, but for those like Red who could depend on their jobs things were tight but not unbearable. Helen Mary had never gone hungry, though she found baked beans four nights a week to be a little trying. But she steeled herself with thoughts of the missionaries and their moldy rice, and ate the beans with a smile, even though she belched for three hours afterward. There were times when she wished she had more than one Sunday dress, but the thought of St. Ursula's students—all of them beheaded or pierced with arrows when they were scarcely older than she was—made her grateful for what she had. But her grandmother's stories from Newfoundland were something else again.

A letter or two would arrive at the house every week from cousins or friends of her grandmother, written traditionally by one of the few lettered people in the outports who wrote for the illiterate. Helen Mary's grandmother, who couldn't recognize her own name on a piece of paper, would hand the letters over to Kat to be read.

"It's from yer cousin Patricia, then," Kat said cautiously one night, sitting at the kitchen table and contemplating the outside of the envelope.

Her mother sat across from her, peeling potatoes. It was Friday, the night Red always brought fresh codfish home from the open markets down on the piers. Codfish and potatoes and boiled turnips, and slices of white bread with sugar sprinkled on them in place of real cake, which was too expensive—it was a feast compared to the rest of the week.

"Aye." Helen Blake nodded. "Sure, she always has Ted Gosse from Torbay to write the letter for her. I recognize the hand."

Kat looked up from the letter. "Are yer wantin' me to read it out?" she asked carefully. "Comin' from her, there can't be good in it."

Mother and daughter exchanged looks. There had been times before when Kat tried skipping over some of the endless accounts of poverty and sickness and death that the cutback in fish processing had brought upon the Old Country in recent years. Her mother sensed the hesitation in her voice and made her begin from the beginning. Kat was not about to try skipping anything again.

"My life's been naught but tragedy since yer father's passin', Lord have mercy on him!" Helen Blake said dramatically, the paring knife poised in her hand as if only the grace of God and her own iron will kept her from plunging it into her breast. "Get on with it, then."

Kat tore open the envelope and began to read—slowly, hesitantly, sounding out the words phonetically the way she'd been taught in the six short years of her schooling. There was contained on those two yellowed sheets (written on both sides for economy's sake) an unending lament about shortages and men idled by the lack of markets for their catch; about malnutrition and slow death among children and the elderly—for in an economy where the principal, the only, resource was fish, what was an uneducated population to do?

Kat's melancholy tone continued, detailing every horror, while her mother clicked her tongue and went on peeling potatoes. Neither was aware that Helen Mary hovered in the doorway, absorbing every word.

And neither wondered why the child spent much of her free time—what little she had between school and homework and the endless mending of socks and shirts that had fallen to her because her grandmother's eyes were bad, her mother was too busy, and she used such tiny stitches for a six-year-old—playing at funerals or Martyrdom of the Virgins with her precious dolls, or simply sitting for an hour at a time lost in morbid thought.

"Sure, ye'd best be after finishin' them potatoes, child," her grandmother would scold at dinnertime. Helen Mary had always been a delicate eater. "Didn't yer poor little Cousin Annie die of the malnutrition down to Newfoundland, and her not even old enough to go to school yet?"

It didn't matter that Helen Mary's "cousin" Annie was not really a blood relative, but a cousin of a cousin of an in-law, like many members of the endlessly extended families of small-town Newfoundland. Nothing mattered except the profound misery that engulfed Helen Mary at the thought of anyone— *anyone*—starving to death. Her misery was fueled with the graphic pictures supplied by her relatives' letters of the particular form of slow starvation that plagued them; it wasn't a matter of having nothing at all to eat, which would have made the ending quicker, but of running out of the imported foodstuffs like flour and fresh fruit and milk and eggs and living solely on the catch, dying off with endless slowness from scurvy and rickets and low-grade infections. And it was the anatomy of this ordeal that destroyed the taste of food in Helen Mary's mouth, made her stomach heave at the sight of a plate heaped with food, when far away where it was dark and cold there were children her own age and younger *starving*.

It only proved that what the priest said at mass was absolutely, frighteningly right. This life was transient—a stopping-place on the road to Heaven, the priest had said—and the only way to get to Heaven was to do one's very best.

"I wanted to be the best!" Helen Mary sobbed again, and her grandmother stormed out of the room in a temper.

"She ought ter be sent ter see the priest," she greeted Kat, who came down the hall just then, arms full of bundles, an irritable Danny whining behind her, her figure beginning to soften into the third month of a new pregnancy. "She may be too young for confession, but I never heard the likes of it! The brass on her!"

Kat put the bundles down and pushed Danny out of the room. She sat heavily on a dining room chair and listened to her mother's version of what had happened.

"I'll see to her," she said finally, wearily. "Would yer put on the beans for me, though, and see if there's bacon enough for the flavoring?"

It would keep the old woman occupied and unable to eavesdrop. While Kat could never openly defy her mother, she was proficient at blocking her attempts at interference whenever possible.

"Yer grandmother's been after tellin' me yer troubles," Kat began, sitting on the bed and smoothing the tangled brown hair up off the girl's pale forehead. "Yer don't need to take on so. I'll not scold yer. I'm right proud that yer smart enough to get the ninety-seven. Sure, I was never that good at school. And yer father—well, but the poor man never had but the single day's schooling in his life."

Helen Mary sat up suddenly, startled by that piece of news. "But how could he?" she asked, awed. "Sure, Pop can read an' do figures and everything. Only one day?"

Kat smiled, glad the child's mood was not so deep she could not be distracted temporarily. "It's what he's always told me, sure," she said warmly. "Although you and I both know the way he has with words."

Helen Mary giggled, her face like sunshine from behind dark clouds.

"I'm thinkin' it might have been more than the single day," Kat said with a smile, feeling well for the first time that day. This pregnancy was making her sick earlier than the other two had. "But we wouldn't want to spoil his favorite story."

Helen Mary giggled again, but the sun was beginning to be engulfed by the clouds again.

"What *is* it, child?" Kat demanded, clutching at her. She had never seen the girl so terrified. "What could it be to worry yer so?"

"I'm a-scared," the litle girl said, shivering from it, beginning to cry again. "I'm a-scared God'll think I wasn't trying my best, an' maybe then I'll get sick an' die of the malnutrition like Cousin Annie—"

The rest of her outburst was smothered as Kat hugged her fiercely to her breast. She clutched the little form against her until the sobbing stopped. Too exhausted to cry anymore, Helen Mary lay weakly against her mother's shoulder, hiccuping softly from time to time.

"Now, you listen to me, and listen hard!" Kat said in a low tone, harshly, as angry at the child as she was hurt for her. "That is the worst blather I've ever heard! Ye've done yer best, and that's all there is to it. There's no God alive would punish a girl as good and pure and hardworking as you are. And there'll be no more talk of Cousin Annie in this house, from you or yer grandmother!"

She got Helen Mary into her nightgown, and washed the tear-stained face. Tucking the child into bed, she went to the kitchen to warm some milk to help her sleep. In all this time she spoke not a word to her mother, who fussed about making supper, sneaking bits of brown sugar from the bean baking into Danny's open mouth as he sat swinging his fat legs in the corner by the pantry.

"Well?" the old woman demanded sullenly when Kat finally emerged from Helen Mary's room the second time.

"Well, nothing!" Kat snapped, surprised at her own nerve. She was so caught up in her fury that she didn't hear Red click the latch or come down the long hallway, didn't know he would hear and applaud her words to her mother. "There'll be not a word about death in front of that child from now on! Keep yer morbid idears under yer own scalp!"

Helen Mary was sleeping soundly in the early-morning hours, and did not hear the commotion in her parents' bedroom. She did not know that Kat had to be rushed to the hospital with a miscarriage. When she finally did get up the next morning to find her mother gone, she was told by a somewhat-chastened grandmother that Mom had a stomachache, and had to rest for a few days. Assured at the first sign of alarm that Mom's ailment bore no resemblance to the malnutrition, Helen Mary went back to playing Martyrdom of the Virgins, without having to know the truth about this or her mother's subsequent miscarriages. Procreation was a subject a young girl needn't know about until she got married, after all.

"Always read a newspaper backwards," was Red's advice. At that moment he was carefully ignoring the headlines and the UPI dispatches from Berlin on the front page of his *Daily*

News, flipping deliberately to the back to see what was happening with the Dodgers. "After ye've studied the sports and had a little laugh at the funnies, yer might have the stomach for the news."

Danny looked up from his baseball cards and snorted derisively. He was seven, and had recently discovered that his old man wasn't perfect, that in fact he was pretty ignorant about most things. But an occasional quiet snicker was all he was allowed in his father's presence. Outright disagreement usually earned him a sharp smack across his fat backside.

Not so with Helen Mary, who was allowed the privilege of inquiry. At the moment she was winding yarn for her mother— the crinkly unravelings of last year's too-small sweater, which by some magic would be re-knitted into one that fit. Her father started to read the sports page aloud, as anyone who grew up with illiterate parents learned to do at an early age, and Helen Mary listened intently. She was not terribly interested in baseball, but she loved the sound of her father's voice. He read far better than her mother did, with no hesitating over the long words. He did not stop at the end of a line the way her mother did, cutting phrases in half until her eyes found the next line and continued, disjointed. Helen Mary's father read extremely well, almost as well as a teacher, and the question she'd wanted to ask him for years finally had to come out.

"How come, Pop?" she asked, the ball of yarn poised in her hands. She would have to question his pronouncement first, before she asked him what was really on her mind. "How come you should read the sports page first? Isn't that like eating your dessert first? Suppose then you couldn't finish the meal?"

Red looked up from the paper, annoyed. But he thought about it, and laughed out loud. "Yer a corker, you are!" he chuckled. Was there a Newfie who didn't have a sweet tooth? "Sure, I never thought about it that way. Shirkin' yer responsibility, isn't it? Avoidin' the harsh realities of life and losin' yer head in the funnies. I never thought of it like that!"

"Maybe because they never had time to teach it to you at school," Helen Mary said carefully. The plunge had to be taken now or never. "If it's true you only went the one day."

Red put down the paper and stared intently at his daughter. His blue eyes penetrated her brown ones. Why was it she looked so much like Kat only when she frowned? She was frowning now, embarrassed by what she'd said, afraid he'd be angry.

"And where were yer after hearin' that?" Red demanded softly.

"I—I heard you telling Mom once," Helen Mary blurted out nervously, never able to lie outright.

Danny snorted again, rolling around clumsily on the faded flowered carpet. "What a crock," he wheezed. "Imagine him only—"

Red's expression silenced him.

"I only meant her!" Danny pouted, pointing at his sister. "I meant she was lying, not you!"

"Stow yer noise, then!" Red growled, dismissing him. The boy whimpered for a while, but no one noticed him, so he sought refuge in the kitchen, where his grandmother would comfort him. Red looked at his daughter again. "And don't yer believe it, then? That me old dad sent me to school for the single day and told me to learn all I could because he couldn't spare me from the store?"

Helen Mary said nothing. Her passion for truth told her she couldn't accept it. Her love for her father told her she didn't dare challenge him.

"And aren't yer after believin' I'm that smart enough to learn to read and write and figure in the single day?" Red demanded. "Don't yer believe it, then?"

Helen Mary opened her mouth, but nothing came out. There was no way out of the situation she had instigated. She would have to answer him. "No," she said finally, drawing upon the courage of the Virgin Martyrs. "No, I don't."

Red continued to stare into her eyes, though something that

could have been amusement had control of the corners of his mouth. "And yer might be right at that," he said, turning at last to the headlines. The news on the first six pages, before the store ads began, was filled with the names of places in Poland and Czechoslovakia that even a great scholar like himself couldn't pronounce.

There were two influences upon Helen Mary's later childhood that fell outside the immediate family. One was her very closest friend, whose name was Loretta. The other was Aunt Ag.

Loretta was tall, whereas Helen Mary was short; had flaming red hair with a natural wave, whereas Helen Mary's hair was a nondescript brown and straight as a string. Loretta was allowed to say "ain't," and could whistle through the space where her front teeth used to be. She was the only girl on her block to own a bicycle—a genuine third hand, two-wheeled, repainted Royce Union bicycle. That was why she didn't have any front teeth. A week after her permanent incisors had grown in, the front wheel of her bike struck a loose cobble at the end of the street, and Loretta was flung headlong over the handlebars and into a telephone pole. The bike got away without a scratch. Loretta's father, who had six other kids to worry about, shrugged and said it was a good thing it wasn't her nose. A man might marry a girl with no front teeth and think it was cute. He might even spring for bridgework if he was rich enough. But a girl with a broken nose. . . .

Helen Mary adored her. They were in the same class in grammar school and sat across the aisle from each other. For the first time in her life, Helen Mary broke a school regulation and began passing notes to her friend. If they were ever caught, she promised herself, she would take all the blame upon herself. She admired Loretta's brashness, even envied it. She could never aspire to as much spirit herself.

Aunt Ag's effect on her was a different matter.

Helen Mary's grandmother had given birth to seven children. Only her two youngest girls had survived past five years of age. Her husband died at sea. But she accepted her lot as being no worse than that of any other woman she had ever known. Life in Newfoundland in her time had been hard, and she had no more right to sympathy than anyone else. She did not complain about her past, only about everything else under the sun.

The elder of her two surviving children, baptized Agatha Mary, had come to the conclusion at an early age that the life of her mother's generation was not for her. She was barely eighteen when she announced her intention of moving "up to America."

A Newfoundlander's sense of geography differed sharply from that of a cartographer. Newfoundland was, for all he knew, the center of the universe, overshadowed perhaps by a vague race memory of the particular county in Ireland or the west of England from which his clan originated. Newfoundland was always referred to, regardless of one's geographical location at the moment, as "down to the country." Any other part of the globe, therefore, became "up," whether in a geographical or a social sense. The most frequent objective of the young emigré, fearful of the sameness and poverty of fishing people's lives, had always been the United States, approached either by way of the Saint Lawrence and Montreal or down the coast by way of Boston, Bridgeport, and Brooklyn. But the journey was always referred to as "up to the States," and the few who got homesick and tried to return to Newfoundland were going "down to the country."

Ag's mother had squelched her plans to emigrate almost immediately. Too many young people were drifting away from the outports, and while a young man might benefit from sowing his wild oats abroad, the same did not hold true for young girls.

"And where might yer be thinkin' of takin' off to, then?" her mother demanded when Ag first voiced her intentions.

"I suppose yer think yer can support yerself in a strange country—a young girl alone and beset by a multitude of evils? Are yer out of yer mind, then?"

Kat had watched her sister's face in the flickering light from the open hearth. Kat was sixteen, and a homebody. She had no desire to go anywhere, ever.

Ag was different. Ag was wild and rebellious and had never been satisfied with anything. Ag was handsomer than Kat, and she was never at a loss for young men to buzz around her hoping for a chance. She sneered at them; told them outright that they smelled bad. She was not going to be any fisherman's wife.

"I'll not be after goin' alone," she told her mother, with that perpetual sarcastic twist to her voice. "I'll be stayin' in Boston with Peggy Mulavey's sister-in-law and them. They've a room to let, and they'll be after givin' me references for to go for a shopgirl."

It was a common practice. While the young men were free to ship out on passing merchantmen or simply hitch a ride on the ferry, with no need to explain where they were going and only the promise to send money home from time to time, an unmarried girl of whatever age could not leave her parents' house without being chaperoned by relatives or former neighbors in the new country.

As it turned out, Ag's mother managed to hold her elder daughter at home for nearly two years more. It might have been better for all concerned if she had let her go the first time she'd asked, but then, no one could foretell the future. The spring after her twentieth birthday, when the last icebergs had floated out of the harbor and it was safe to travel, Ag was gone.

Helen Mary would learn these things, and more, about her aunt as she got older. All she knew as a little girl was that Aunt Ag was strikingly pretty for a woman her age (her age at the time being only her middle thirties, but to a little girl this seemed a great antiquity), and that she worked in a department store and lived by herself and owned a furpiece. Helen Mary's mother, on the other hand, was plain and work-worn and looked older than she was. She wore an old cloth coat, and never seemed to have a minute to herself. It wasn't the fact that she was married that made the difference as Helen Mary saw it. The difference was that Aunt Ag had refused to take any responsibility for the care of their mother.

In school, Helen Mary was taught that there were three roads a woman could take to reach the Kingdom of Heaven. The first and most blessed, of course, was the religious life, though it was understood that this was open only to a chosen few. The most common route—and the nun could not help help sneering a bit as she said the word "common"—was the choice of marriage-and-motherhood, in that order and inseparable. The last, and apparently the most lonely and unrewarding, was referred to as the "life of single blessedness."

Helen Mary studied Aunt Ag, who managed to appear for Sunday dinner twice a month, though without a reciprocal invitation to her own flat. Aunt Ag did not seem the least bit lonely or unrewarded.

Of course, Aunt Ag wasn't a bad person. She had been working for the Red Cross even before Pearl Harbor. She spent a great deal of her free time rolling bandages, packing cast-off clothing for relief boxes, and, recently, giving lectures on civil defense in the church basement in the evening.

And she had adopted Alistair.

Alistair didn't fit into the picture somehow. In the first place, if it hadn't been for the desperate situation of orphaned children during the Battle of Britain, he almost certainly would never have been placed with a single woman. And Aunt Ag had always been so freewheeling and independent, it didn't make sense for her to tie herself down with a child all of a sudden. Even if he was almost eleven, and matured by his experiences in the bombing, he was still a child, someone who needed clothing and schooling and proper supervision. Why should Aunt Ag suddenly burden herself with that?

And of course, Alistair's being English drove the family to distraction.

"Sure, wouldn't it be after makin' more sense to adopt one of yer own kind?" Ag's mother had demanded at one of the Sunday dinners just before Alistair arrived on the boat from London. "What with all of the little ones down to Newfoundland dying of the mal—"

She got no farther. It was hard to say which of the trio of Red, Kat, and Ag was glaring at her hardest.

"Or sure there's kids from Ireland want adoptin'," the old woman sniffed, more subdued. "One of yer own kind is all I'm sayin'."

"It was this particular child needed adopting at this time," Ag said grandly, her speech made more precise from working in department stores and adapting to American speech. "And he's Irish on his mother's side, Mom, so don't be after talking nonsense. Besides, the Depression's over, if you haven't noticed. The kids down to the country eat as well now as they do here."

Kat watched her older sister from her place at the foot of the table. As always in Ag's presence, she was torn by several emotions. The first was an admiration for the way Ag could put their mother in her place, something Kat seldom dared. There was concern for Helen Mary, whose delicate appetite evaporated completely at even the half-mention of malnutrition, and who had since excused herself from the table. And there was a secret understanding, which only Red shared, of why it was so important for Ag to have a child who was at least part English.

Helen Mary meanwhile had drifted into the room she shared with Danny, empty now because her brother was still at the dinner table, still stuffing his shining pink pig's face. She savored the semisilence, broken only by the murmur of voices and clank of dishes in the next room. But there was an oppressive odor in the perpetual twilight of her room, an odor of corned beef and boiled turnips, that nauseated her slightly, and she felt a bout of self-pity coming on.

She thought of that frightened little boy somewhere out there in the Nazi-infested ocean, sailing away from the only home he'd ever known, to a country where people spoke differently and ate different things and had different customs. She tried to imagine how she would feel if her whole family was suddenly blown away by a bomb; the nuns in school lately were full of descriptions of disembodied hands lying in the rubble.

And if a bomb hit my house, Helen Mary thought. . . .

And if the Nazis blitzed America and the bombs started dropping on the Navy Yard and the Bush Terminal where Pop works on the boilers of the LSTs and the smaller destroyers, and up from the waterfront past the tenements where the shanty Irish and the new influx of Spics brawl over their beers all night, past the Gowanus Expressway, Fourth Avenue, Fifth, Sixth, up to my house, and if a big bomb reduced us all to rubble in an instant and I somehow survived, how would I feel? . . .

And if Mom and Pop had married in Newfoundland instead of here, and if I had been born there, and died of the malnutrition when I was six. . . .

And when I grow up I'm going to be like Aunt Ag and lead the life of single blessedness and adopt not one but a dozen Alistairs. . . .

"Well, it's funny, don't you think?" Loretta asked her again, cracking her gum and blowing huge, improbable bubbles through the gap where her front teeth were supposed to be.

"I don't know what's funny about it," Helen Mary said irritably, being as quiet as she could in the noisy subway station. It wasn't the sort of topic she liked to discuss in such a public place.

They were waiting for the train home from school. They were high school freshmen, skittish and awkward in their uniforms, wary of their conspicuousness in this irreligious society they were part of. Loretta stood craning her long neck to see

past Helen Mary's head down the whole length of the platform, watchful in case any of the nuns—or worse, the senior
class monitors—might happen along to reprimand her for the
bubble gum or the lipstick or the fact that her skirt was rolled
three times at the waist to expose a little more of her rather
fine legs. She'd been in so much trouble already this year that
any one of these infringements of school regulations would be
enough to have her thrown out on her large freckled ear, but
Loretta kept up her small private rebellion all the same.

"I mean it's funny her having just the two of you, and
getting p.g. this late in the game," Loretta said. "Here you are
fourteen, and how old's the Pig?"

"Twelve," Helen Mary mumbled, not even smiling at
Loretta's favorite name for Danny. She wished the train would
come so that it would be too noisy to continue this conversation. It was embarrassing.

Helen Mary, as always, conformed strictly to school regulations. She never chewed gum or wore lipstick or rolled her
skirt up, because such things were as stringently forbidden at
home as they were in school. Her grades were always among
the highest in her class, though she understood now, as she
had not in first grade, that pride was a greater sin than sloth,
and she no longer cried if someone else did better than she.
Except for her friendship with Loretta, which could easily be
construed as consorting with evil companions, she was considered by all the nuns at Bishop's to be a docile-natured and
promising child.

"Twelve years' difference." Loretta whistled. (How she
could whistle with no front teeth was a mystery, but she could,
and did, frequently. The old saw that went "A whistling
woman and a crowing hen are neither good for God nor men"
apparently didn't bother her.) "Boy, do you think maybe
your mother was trying not to all these years and then she
slipped up? Boy oh boy!"

Helen Mary looked at her in absolute horror. She could
not speak.

"Well, there's ways not to," Loretta pointed out, exasperated. "Holy Moses, don't you know *anything*?"

Helen Mary began to blush indignantly. Of course, she knew *some* things about sex—most supplied by Loretta herself. But what could this business be all about?

"Your mother had Timmy less than a year ago!" she pointed out. "She's not that much younger than my mother."

"That's true." Loretta nodded, cracking her gum again and flinching at what might have been the shadow of a nun's habit descending the stairs at the far end of the platform. It wasn't, and she relaxed again. "But she's had the four more between him and me, and then I was number three. So she didn't slip up—she wanted to. My mother don't know what to do with herself only keep having babies."

It made Helen Mary think. Why was her mother pregnant, or, as the women in the family always said, "expecting," after so long? Six months ago Helen Mary hadn't had the vaguest idea how a woman went about having a baby. She'd thought it was something that just happened once you were married, and now Loretta was telling her there was such a thing as freedom of choice in the matter. But then, Loretta had two older brothers, and one of them was even in the navy. If Helen Mary had her facts straight, it was men who started the whole business anyway, so maybe they knew something about preventing it. How *did* one prevent it?

The train roared in just then. Helen Mary crammed in beside Loretta, and they rode in silence for forty-five minutes because she didn't dare ask such a question in such a place, even though she was dying to know the answer.

When she finally got around to asking it, as they stood by the wrought-iron fence in front of Loretta's stoop, she was horrified anew.

"That's disgusting!" she half-shouted. They both cringed simultaneously, expecting heads to appear at the venetian-blinded windows to see what was going on. Helen Mary lowered her voice. "I never heard such a disgusting thing in my life! It's bad enough a man's got to go around sticking his whatsis in a girl just to give her a baby, but wearing one of those things so she won't get a baby—that's too disgusting for words!''

Loretta roared until her face turned red and a flock of heads appeared in several windows to shoo them both home. Helen Mary knew, even as she spoke, that she'd have to confess it on Saturday afternoon under the category of "impure thoughts" if she wanted to receive communion on Sunday. Still, she felt justified in her inquiry. A girl had a right to know what sort of vile, perverted things her future husband— whoever he might be—might try to do to her once they were married. Mary Helen was sure such a repulsive device had to be an occasion of sin, if not a sin in itself.

Six months ago she'd known nothing about any of this, had not yet been initiated into this new world of sinister implications and fresh opportunities for temptation. Sex had not reared its ugly, bloodstained head until the afternoon when she'd had that fight with Danny. . . .

The two of them engaged in verbal battles almost constantly now. It was unavoidable considering the disparity in their temperaments and the cramped quarters they had to share. More than anything else in the world, Helen Mary wanted her own room. Pragmatically speaking, she knew this would not be possible until her grandmother had the good grace to croak. This apartment, this drab hodgepodge of railroad rooms full of lace doilies and holy pictures and gauze curtains and mouse-traps in the pantry—this apartment, Helen Mary knew instinctively, would be her home until the day she married. In Newfoundland, she knew, families built ramshackle wood-frame houses on the little shelves of thin-soiled ground that sloped down to the harbors, the outports where the little one- or two-man boats put in and out seven months out of the year. The same families, she knew, lived in the same house for generations, adding on rooms when grown children married or change-of-life babies were born, closing off rooms when old folks passed on or grown children failed to marry. It was not unusual for a fisherman's widow—who had perhaps been granted so few years with her husband before the sea's envy-green grasp snatched him away that they had produced no children—to wither away alone in a house of twenty rooms or more after her parents and siblings had all died and her nieces and nephews gone up to the mainland or the States.

Here in Brooklyn, the row houses were immutable: two-family structures on one side of the street, four-family houses on the other. Rooms could not be added on to an architectural concept that did not encompass the Newfies' way of life. Helen Mary accepted the fact that as soon as her grandmother died, the back bedroom with the two windows overlooking the clotheslines and the ailanthus trees would be hers. She more than half wished it would happen soon.

It wasn't that she hated her grandmother. She certainly couldn't love the old shrew, any more than she could develop an affection for the drippy faucet in the bathroom or the latch on the front door that always slammed shut on her hand no matter how quickly she slipped through once the buzzer rang or how often Red complained to the landlord. Helen Mary's grandmother was one of life's chronic petty annoyances. Her entire life force seemed aimed at making the rest of the family miserable. The older Helen Mary got, the more she saw the old woman's irritating effect on Red and her interference in the workings of the household. She became convinced that this was more than a case of bearing one's cross in life. This sort of thing simply shouldn't be.

The fight with Danny had nothing directly to do with their grandmother, though it was possible that if Helen Mary had had her own room it would never have started.

Danny's only obsession, aside from eating, was the construction of model airplanes. His only response to the magnitude of the world events that transpired around him was an overwhelming desire to own a model of every American, British, German, and Japanese plane that ever was. He hoarded his allowance, and actually went so far as to acquire a paper route so that he could amass enough wealth to purchase and construct these horridly replicated balsa-wood and paper concoctions. He put them together in his corner of the communal bedroom at every possible waking moment. The fumes from the airplane glue always made Helen Mary feel sick.

"Can't you do those things in the kitchen?" she asked him. She'd been slightly nauseous all day, and right now she had a terrible headache. She was trying to do her homework; the little algebraic formulas had begun to dance around on the page.

"Mom says I can't," Danny replied complacently, too lazy to move at the best of times, and mulish about taking suggestions from his sister. The glue made him stuporous, but he rather liked the effect. It also took the edge off his appetite, which was a very good thing. The other boys in the seventh grade had started calling him "Fat Ass"; his figure was beginning to worry him. "Open the window if it bothers you."

"You know Mom won't let us this time of year," Helen Mary said crossly, wanting suddenly to hit him. Her mood was strange. She almost never wanted to hit anybody, particularly Danny, who was about forty pounds heavier than she. "The landlord told her the fuel bills are going right through the ceiling, and the coal company put him on C.O.D. If we don't conserve heat he's going to shut us off completely."

"That's tough," Danny grunted, without much feeling. His fat and the glue would keep him warm.

"Can't you lay off for a while?" Helen Mary kept at him. "Just till I get my homework done?"

"Fuck your homework!" Danny said with uncharacteristic vehemence, his speech slurred by the vapor of the glue. "Rotten little brownnose! All you do is homework all the time."

"And you're a fat, disgusting pig!" Helen Mary burst out wildly, jumping up from her desk and knocking her algebra text on the floor. She was so dizzy she could hardly stand. "Loretta's right—Danny the Pig! Fat Ass!"

"Don't you call me that!" Danny said ominously, getting

up from the bed languorously so as not to disturb the fragile pieces of his model. "I'm warning you—"

His fat fists were clenched, but Helen Mary defied him, sticking out her chin, her own small fists on her hips. She wanted to strike out at him, to bloody his nose and pound on that shiny lard face of his until his eyes got puffy, but she didn't dare. Anger, occasion of sin; thou shalt not kill—besides, he's bigger than me.

"Even you wouldn't hit a girl!" she sneered at him, daring him to defy the code even the shanty Irish lived by. Women were sacred. Models of the Blessed Virgin, bearers of the next generation. "Fat Ass!"

He hit her. Punched her hard in the stomach so that she doubled over and turned very white and had to bite her lower lip to keep from crying out. Red was in the next room, she knew; a sound from her would bring him rushing in, and he might actually kill Danny this time. Helen Mary had seen the look in her father's eyes when he looked at Danny sometimes, and even her peacemaking powers were beginning to lose their effect on him. Red hated his son, and only a fool couldn't see it.

So she bit her lip, making little choking sounds back in her throat until the pain ebbed away into her extremities and left her winded and gasping. She straightened up slowly and looked at her brother with fire in her eyes. He began to whimper, knowing what she could do to him if she only told their father.

"You'll never do anything like that to me again," she gasped, barely whispering, still out of breath. "That's on your soul until the day I die, because I'm not going to forgive you for it!"

Her fury made him cringe though he sneered at religion usually, and he stumbled and wheezed and had to rush to the bathroom. He found excuses to stay away from the room, away from her, until he went to bed that night.

And Helen Mary woke up for no particular reason at four in the morning to feel her nightgown sticking to the backs of her thighs. She felt flushed, thought she must be sweating a lot to make it stick to her like that. She threw off the covers and flicked on the light. The nightgown was sticky with blood.

When he hit me, she thought with horror—when he punched me he must have broken something inside, and now I'm going to die. Going to die in the flower of my youth, struck down by the infidel like one of St. Ursula's Virgin Martyrs.

She turned off the light and settled down in the bed again, vaguely aware of a trickling sensation in that forbidden territory between her legs. She was aware, too, of that strangely pleasant-irritating feeling she'd experienced so long ago in Sister Misericordia's class, listening to the stories about the missionaries.

I'm going to die, Helen Mary thought, barely disturbed at the idea. She fumbled for the little blue rosary—bits of sky-blue glass, the Blessed Mother's own color—she always kept under her pillow, and began to pray calmly, wondering if she'd be granted the grace to finish before she ran out of blood.

Now I won't have to take that algebra test tomorrow, she thought, beginning to drowse off. I am going to die, and I'll probably have to spend only a short time in Purgatory because I went to confession last Saturday and the sins I've committed since then have been little ones.

Except for calling my only brother "Fat Ass." Poor Danny! Now at least he can finish his planes in peace.

O my God, I am heartily sorry for having offended Thee. . . .

Helen Mary pulled herself to a sitting position again and turned on the light. With what strength remained to her, she reasoned, she ought to change the sheets, perhaps even drag herself out to the bathroom to sit on the toilet so that her poor, brokenhearted mother would have less of a mess to clean up afterward. It would be hard enough on her, losing a daughter this way.

She tucked her nightgown between her legs so she wouldn't drip on the floor and fumbled the slightly stained sheet off the bed. Gathering it into a bundle in front of her, she glanced in Danny's direction. He was curled on his side with his back to her, snoring rhythmically.

Poor Fat Ass! Helen Mary thought irrationally, wanting to laugh loudly. O my God, I am heartily sorry. . . .

She brought the sheet and her rosary with her to the bathroom. It was there that Kat found her half an hour later when she got up to use the toilet.

"Jesus, Mary, and Joseph!" Kat exclaimed softly at the sight of the girl. She was sitting on the toilet, her forehead resting wearily against the cold tile, her right hand working the beads of the rosary though she was barely awake.

"Sure, what's the matter with you?" Kat demanded.

Helen Mary told her, as coherently as possible considering her exhaustion and her resignation to death. Kat listened patiently, shaking her head and clucking her tongue in disbelief. When her daughter's tumbled words ran out, Kat sighed deeply.

"And I guess I've no one but meself to blame," she said wearily. "I was meanin' to tell yer soon, but I was near fifteen when it happened to me, so I thought there was time yet. It's not an easy thing to be after explainin' to a girl."

Helen Mary looked up at her blankly, not comprehending. Was this supposed to happen? What could it possibly mean?

Later, dressed in a clean nightgown, her womanly secret secured in one of Kat's sanitary napkins, Helen Mary sat with her mother at the chipped enamel kitchen table, drinking weak tea with lots of milk and sugar, watching the winter sun peek feebly between the row houses, and listening to Kat's explanations. Kat's words were unschooled, but her tone was soothing, and what little information she could supply was awesome news to the girl who had been certain she'd be dead by now. Helen Mary said nothing.

"What is it, then?" Kat asked when she had finished, seeing the troubled look on the girl's face. She'd almost seemed happier thinking she was going to die.

"If this has to happen every month so that I can have

babies," Helen Mary said hesitantly, "well—what if I don't want to have babies?"

Kat looked shocked. "Well sure, every girl wants to have babies!" she said, thinking wistfully of her lost ones and of the two she'd been permitted to keep, especially this one who had so suddenly crossed the threshold from girl to woman. "That's only natural!"

"Aunt Ag doesn't have babies," Helen Mary pointed out. "I'd rather adopt kids, like she did with Alistair. I don't want to get married."

Like you did, she almost said, but held her tongue to keep from hurting her mother. But she didn't want to end up like her mother, with her rough, reddened hands and her shapelessness. She wasn't just physically shapeless; she lacked character. She was so used to living through her mother, her husband, and her children that she had all but faded into their personalities, losing her own. No, Helen Mary wanted to be like Aunt Ag, and keep her figure and her personality and own a furpiece.

"How come you have to be married to have babies, Mom?" she asked out of the clear blue. The presence of a man had something to do with it; she could see that. But what was it exactly?

"Never you mind about that just now," Kat said abruptly, growing suddenly agitated. It was past six o'clock; the house was beginning to stir. Old Helen's slippered feet could be heard shambling down the hall toward the bathroom. The sound of the toilet flushing meant their private moment to-gether—the first Helen Mary could recall in a long time—was about to be intruded upon. "Yer just take care of yerself with this business now. There'll be time enough for them questions when yer get a little older. Ye'd better get back to yer bed before yer grandmother comes in."

Helen Mary looked at her mother, puzzled. Back to bed? She ought to be getting ready for school.

"I'm after lettin' yer stay home for today," Kat said brusquely, busying herself around the kitchen. "You'll prob-ably be feelin' pains in yer back the first day, and it's best to stay off yer feet. But don't be gettin' idears, now. It's only for the first time. Now shoo!"

Helen Mary was awestruck. She hadn't stayed home from school since she'd been quarantined for scarlet fever back in the fourth grade. This was an unheard-of luxury.

Kat rummaged around for her pots and pans, making breakfast, savoring the moments she'd had with her daughter alone. She wanted to go into the girl's room and throw her arms around her, tell her how wonderful those moments had been, but she could not. She might have had an impetuous, loving nature at some time in the past, but it was stifled now under too much convention, too great a necessity to keep others from knowing how she felt. But by the time her toothless, frowzy-looking mother in her man's bathrobe shambled into the kitchen, Kat was humming softly to herself, something she only did when she was extremely happy. Had her mother been less nearsighted, she might have noticed that tears sparkled in her eyes.

By the time Helen Mary noticed the change in her mother's figure some four months later, she had already acquired whatever information she needed from Loretta.

Kat was pregnant, for the sixth time in her marriage, for the first time in nearly a decade. She was forty, and had had three miscarriages. The prognosis was not good.

When old Helen Blake was informed that her daughter was pregnant yet again, she took to her bed full-time.

"Sure, it's the last year I'll be seein' on this earth!" she lamented loudly any time someone passed the bedroom door, which was always wide open. Should anyone be thoughtless enough to close it, she would let out a wail so pitiful—accusing the lot of them of wanting to forget her before she was even in the ground—that someone would be obliged to open it again. "The Angel of Death is after comin' for me this time for certain!"

"I'm thinkin', missus," Red remarked with great solemnity,

after a week of this kind of talk, "I'm thinkin' we heard this same tune fifteen years ago."

"God has spared me this long!" the old woman cried. "He has given me eighty years and allowed me the sight of me grandchildren. This is the last year I'll be after seein' on this earth! God has called me to Him!"

"If God is wantin' the likes of her," Red growled when she was out of earshot, "sure, He's out of His mind!"

"Whisht, man! That's blasphemy!" Kat hissed at him. "And there'll be storms a-brew if she should hear yer."

To her own surprise most of all, Kat kept her baby past the third month, that mysterious deadline that had claimed her other three. She seemed to blossom with this pregnancy as she had not with the others, even the two that had produced Helen Mary and Danny. Her other pregnancies had drained her, made her nauseous and headachy for the entire nine months. By contrast, this one seemed to bring her new strength and a glow of health. And as she grew stronger, her mother grew weaker.

"Sure, I'm dyin' and there's nobody cares about me!" she would wail. "It's grateful I am to be seein' me dear Petey again, but sure, it's hard when nobody's after carin' about yer!"

Kat somehow found the resources to nurse the old woman, carrying trays of food into her room because she was too weak to come to the table, changing sheets and giving her sponge baths, helping her down the hall to the toilet, cleaning up after her when she couldn't get there on time. It drove Red into a frenzy.

"If she was me own kin I'd have her out on the street by now!" he raged, standing in the hall just beyond the old woman's door to be certain she heard. "The old faker's as healthy as a horse, sure. If it was me I'd be after callin' the doctor this minute and showin' the old faker up. She's like a child that's jealous of the new life comin', and she ought ter be straightened out about it!"

He gave vent to his anger in this manner only when he could

stand it no longer, knowing that as always his rage would fall on Kat's head because it was the only way the old woman dared strike at him. He did go so far as to call the doctor, who, though he was not a Newfoundlander, had found in his twenty years of practice that the wiles of the elderly spanned ethnic distinctions.

"There's nothing definite that's wrong with her," he said softly, emerging from her room with the stethoscope still in his hand. "She's at an age where she could talk herself into dying any day, or turn around and live to be a hundred. But in my experience, if she really wants to die, she'll eventually talk herself into it."

Whatever the truth happened to be, the old woman either could not or would not rise from her bed. Kat soon had to turn the housework over to Helen Mary, and neglecting to consider the fact that she herself ought to be off her feet as much as possible in this stage of her pregnancy, spent most of her waking hours fetching for her mother.

Helen Mary would rush home from school as soon as she possibly could, her ear glued to the big radio in the dining room for news from Europe in these last days of April 1945, as she peeled potatoes and got the supper ready—although what she'd rather do was sit on the stoop with Loretta, talking and hoping and reading the *Daily News* frontwards for a change, because someday soon this war was actually going to end. When the supper dishes were done and she'd finished her homework, she tackled the laundry she'd hung on the line before she left for school that morning at seven-thirty and stood in the kitchen ironing, the radio still on, long after she should have been in bed. Her innate paleness became a mushroom's pallor; dark-blue smudges formed under her eyes and made her look tubercular.

All that Helen Mary lived for in this blurry and exhausting time, her only distraction from the concern for her mother and growing hatred of her grandmother, was the knowledge that the war would soon be over. Like all of the good things in her short life, this knowledge carried with it a great sadness. Helen Mary rejoiced with the greater part of the world at the news of Hitler's death, but news from the neighborhood tinged this information with melancholy. Loretta's oldest brother left the navy with burn scars on his face, neck, and chest and partial deafness. His ship had been blown out from under him off Guam; only a fraction of the crew survived. The next-oldest brother had raving nightmares, and his daytime moods were unpredictable. He could not keep a job, and eventually became an alcoholic. A neighbor's boy died of malaria in the Bataan Death March; a boy on the next street disappeared during the Battle of the Bulge and was never accounted for. The Gold Star banners hung in front of the venetian blinds in the parlor windows brought no swell of patriotic pride to Helen Mary's breast. Instead, they afflicted her with an attack of the shudders every time she had to pass one of these houses.

On V-E Day, Red took her and Danny over to Manhattan on the subway to see the excitement in Times Square, but the crowd was so huge they couldn't get out of the subway station. Danny consoled himself by wolfing down three hot dogs and throwing up in the street on the way home.

In the months that followed, the newspaper accounts of the liberation of the death camps had the same effect upon Helen Mary that the missionary stories had once had. She read them voraciously, the paper propped against the dish drainer as she cooked, the wasted faces pressed against the barbed wire contrasting horribly with the smells of food in the steamy kitchen. The faces filled her dreams at night, when she was not too exhausted to dream.

Summer was a little better. Helen Mary did not have to think about school. She was able to stretch the household chores out over the length of the day, squeezing out an hour or so to sit in the yard under the ailanthus tree, knitting horse-reins or reading, listening to the frenzied buzz-saw of the cicadas in the heat. It hurt her more than a little to watch Loretta and the other girls on the block heading for Coney

Island and the beach almost daily. There were boys in the group as well, those too young to be in service, and there was a great deal of laughing and innocent foolishness that made Helen Mary wonder. Of course, she wasn't going to get married, so she really didn't have to worry about going out with boys, and the other girls weren't allowed to date this young, only to go out in a group. But she stared at the whiteness of her thin arms and legs, unconsciously perhaps comparing them with the pallor and thinness of the faces pressed against the barbed wire, and wondered what she would look like with a tan.

But school began again almost immediately, or so it seemed, and the round of homework-housework-exhaustion began as well, evaporating her self-pity. And the joke was that Loretta, with her fair skin and freckles, fell asleep in the sun on that August day when several thousand civilians were incinerated at Hiroshima, and nearly died of sun poisoning. Nearly a month later, she was still itching and peeling under her school uniform.

In October, Helen Mary's grandmother died, though not before raging and howling like a madwoman for one entire day and night, foaming at the mouth and tearing up the bedsheets with almost superhuman strength. Red would not let Kat, who was two weeks from her time, go near the room where what was left of the old woman was being ministered to by the priest and the doctor and finally sanguine little Mr. Kelly with his aura of bay rum. When they had her in the casket at last, it was Red who gathered up the tattered and stained sheets, the blankets and pillows and the mattress cover, and dumped the lot in the garbage can at the side of the stoop.

"I'm after openin' the window to let the stink of her out," he told Kat, who was slumped in the kind of half-stupor she would retain for the next two days, breaking out of it only during her histrionic wailing. "If the landlord opens his mouth about the heat he's goin' to get it from me. After the waking's over I'll be throwin' the mattress out as well. Then yer can go in and sort through her kit to yer heart's content. But no one's to go into that room without my leave. Whisht, the stink on her, though!"

Helen Mary was sitting in the kitchen chair, listening to the rain sheeting against the window, when she heard the front-door latch click again.

Her father was home at last.

"How're yer holdin' up, then, miss?" he greeted her, his joy at shedding a mother-in-law only vaguely disguised by the required solemnity of the occasion. He'd been drinking a bit, too.

With the end of Prohibition, the boards had come down from the shattered front window of Murphy's Bar and Grill, and the glass had been replaced. Business went on as usual, as if all the dry years and bootlegging had been a figment of someone's delirium tremens. Murphy's was legit again, and a man could stop for a few on his way home from work with a clear conscience, especially if he had a wake facing him in his own front parlor.

Red had taken off his shoes and mackinaw just inside the front door so as not to track up the floor, noticing as he trod the hall in his stocking feet that others had not been as considerate. It was not their house.

"I'm okay, Pop," Helen Mary replied, in a quavery voice that belied her statement. "Really."

"Sure, I know," he said, putting his newspaper down on a small clear space on the kitchen table. "It's a terrible mess, and the sooner it's over, the sooner we can start livin' like human beings again. Sure, it'll be nice not havin' to listen to the old grumpus, then, won't it? She didn't go a minute too soon for my likin'."

Helen Mary could not say anything, though she allowed herself a small smile. She was not as secure as her father was about his personal salvation; she felt certain that maligning the so-recently dead was not recommended for her soul.

"Are the lot of them here, then?" Red asked her.

The murmured prayers from the parlor told him before Helen Mary did.

"Gutless sheveens!" he muttered, shaking his head in disgust. "And where were they at when yer mother was after needin' a hand with the old baggage? I've a mind to go in there and clear them all out. All they're wantin' is a free meal."

Helen Mary laughed, the first time she could remember doing that since her grandmother had begun to die in earnest. She bit her lower lip and looked up at her father, embarrassed.

"Sure, but that's a lovely sound!" Red grinned at her. "Don't be after squelchin' it down for me. You and me can be honest on one thing—there wasn't a thing the old bitch was good for except trouble. Only she gave birth to yer mother, she never did a good turn for anybody. Am I right, then?"

Helen Mary gasped. She'd never heard her father use the word "bitch" before, and his expression of her own opinions lifted the sense of guilt from her shoulders just a little.

"Right as rain," she told him with a nod, unconsciously using one of her grandmother's favorite phrases. It sobered her for a minute, then reminded her of the one thought that had kept her sane throughout the past seventy-two hours. "There's something I've been meaning to tell you," she said.

Red looked at her oddly. Talks between father and daughter had become remote over the past year, as if Helen Mary's reaction to her mother's pregnancy, or perhaps to her own budding maturity, had made her wary of him, of men in general. Though heaven knew what other men she knew anything about, with her all-girls school and her restrictive upbringing. He wondered what it could be that she wanted to tell him before she told Kat.

"What is it, then?" he asked cautiously.

"Now that she's d-dead," the girl said, her voice quavering a little again, "I don't want to be called Helen Mary anymore. My name is Helen, and that's what I want people to call me."

Red thought about it for a moment, then burst into a grin.

She had told him first because he would understand the significance of it, of having and holding her own identity. It was a concept beyond Kat's grasp.

"Right enough!" He smiled, allowing his scarred hand to rest on her head for half a minute. Theirs was not a demonstrative culture. "Yer entitled to as much."

The moment embarrassed both of them, and Red sought a way out first. He squinted into the parlor, where the droning of voices continued. It was too much for him. "It's time I'm after routin' the pack of them," he decided.

He strode into the dining room on his small, stockinged feet—a short man, stocky and powerful, unafraid of anybody, least of all a priest and a pack of wailing women. He stood in the doorway that led to the parlor, and cupped his hands at the side of his mouth as if he meant to shout. "Them as wants to eat," he called loudly, bringing the praying to a mumbled standstill, "it's about to be put on the table."

BOOK II

Harmony Bay— The Years Before

The trip home from the cemetery in the hired car was a dreary one. The rain had not let up from the previous night; the steady downpour ensured difficult walking over the sodden grass to the grave, and even those with umbrellas were uniformly drenched from the knees down. Kat slumped heavily in the middle of the back seat of the limousine between Ag and Red, a ruined handkerchief pressed against her upper lip, her eyes glassy. The two flanking her wore identical expressions of controlled boredom, and relief that it was almost over. Helen Mary perched on one of the fold-out seats behind the driver, sneezing sporadically. By tomorrow she would be in the throes of a full-blown cold. Danny sat in the other seat, staring morosely out the window, his fat backside hanging over on either side of the seat. Only Alistair, who'd been sent to sit up front with the driver, had managed to find some joy in the day. He'd discovered that the driver was a transplanted Aussie who'd played professional rugby in his day. Since after two years in the States Alistair had still not fathomed the mysteries of football, this information delighted him. He and the driver talked continuously, as if they were the only ones in the car. Death was a commonplace in Alistair's short life, but the discovery of a fellow rugger. . . .

Helen Mary's prediction had been correct. The dirt they had thrown ceremoniously on the old woman's coffin had in fact been little clumps of mud. There had been much surreptitious use of handkerchiefs and tissues afterward. No one had been paying attention to Kat, nor could they have anticipated what she was going to do.

She had thrown herself on her knees in the downpour and flung herself on her mother's coffin, beginning anew that crazed keening she had kept up throughout the wake. It had taken Red and two of his brawny cousins, sober now, to haul her back onto her feet, where she continued to wail. They stood holding the bulk of her, half-suspended because her legs refused to support her, looking helplessly male and at a loss to stop her from carrying on. It was Ag who brought her to her senses.

"Quit squalling now, will you?" she demanded, her eyes flashing and her right hand clenching as if she would strike her younger sister as she hadn't since they were girls. "At least think of the baby. Do you want to lose this one, too? Think of the future, and to hell with the past!"

Kat had quieted then, watching Ag apprehensively as if she would really hit her. Ag gave her a final disgusted look, turned on her heel, and stormed back toward the car, defying anyone to do anything else but follow her in out of the rain.

They did eventually. The immediate family clumped wet and muddy into the one car; everyone else cramming into the cars of the few wealthy enough to own them. Once outside the cemetery, they splintered off in various directions, honking their horns in muted good-byes. Kat had wanted to have everybody come back to the house; Red and Ag had vetoed that. They wanted it over.

When the driver let them off finally in front of the row house, the rain had stopped. A quick October wind had begun to clear the clouds away; there was a suggestion that the sun might make an appearance. The light was a strange orangy-yellow, something that had captivated Kat the first time she'd come to this new country as a girl. Winter always came with a bang in Newfoundland; there was never enough time for autumn and its strange tricks of light. As she stood on the stoop for a moment, with Red supporting her elbow and the rest of them crowding behind her to get inside and change their sodden clothes, she felt a warm wetness rush down her legs.

"Jesus and Mary!" she inhaled softly, watching it run down over her shoes and blend with the rain-wet on the stoop so imperceptibly that the children below her on the steps never noticed a thing. "Sure, it's gone ter come today!"

This labor did not feel like the others. With Helen and Danny there had been short, urgent labors, the contractions closing in on her with unbearable pain within the first three hours. Kat had always been drugged, but never to the point where she'd lost consciousness altogether. This time she lay on her side in the labor bed, yawning and drowzing, while a series of uneven and mildly annoying contractions plagued her for nearly eight hours. The sun had gone down, the doctor was out to supper, the nurses had changed shifts, and no progress was reported.

Belching slightly with the aftereffects of his dinner, the doctor returned, examined Kat, and went out to speak to the floor nurse. "I'm going home for a few hours," he said. "If there's any change, have them call me. If not. . . ."

He paused, and the nurse waited. The doctor sighed. "Why the hell do they have to keep having babies?" he demanded of no one in particular. "This girl's a bad risk to begin with, and her age hasn't made it easier on her. If she's still the same around midnight—and I'd be willing to make book on it—put her under. I guarantee you I'll come in at eight tomorrow morning and there'll be no change. This is going to be a thirty-six-hour labor, and if that baby gets out alive I'll start going to church again."

At five minutes past twelve, the night nurse gave the near-comatose Kat a shot of something that sent her under completely. Her only connection with reality was a vague seasick awareness of the continuing pulsation of the useless contractions running counter to her heartbeat. She ceased to be a person then, becoming nothing more than an involuntary reflex, a reaction to the hormones that triggered this squeezing of her uterus, too weak to propel the baby outside where it belonged. Kat was no longer Kat, but a series of reflexes. A strange moaning issued involuntarily from her throat—the anesthesia had relaxed her vocal chords—every time she exhaled. Women in labor in adjoining rooms measured the duration of their own contractions against the number of times they heard this melancholy sound, which would continue throughout the night and into the following day.

Kat was no longer Kat, only a series of reflexes. She had her reflexes, and her memory.

It was the summer of her sixteenth year, and Kat sat on the large, smooth rock where her late father's property abutted the inland road that led north from the capital city of St. John's past Torbay, the next-closest town, to their own out-port of Harmony Bay. This far north it was just a dirt road, used mostly by travelers afoot, since few were wealthy enough to own a cart, and no one from these parts had ever seen an automobile. Kat was not usually permitted the luxury of an entire morning to herself, but her mother and Ag had gone into Torbay to market, and she had done her chores as quickly as she could. There was a reason for her being out by the road on this particular day, and it was an important one.

The night before, which was Midsummer's Eve, Kat had taken an egg from the larder where she emptied her basket every morning after collecting from her mother's half-dozen hens. She had taken a cracked china cup she'd been hoarding for months under her bed in the room she shared with Ag, had broken the egg into it, and had returned the cup to its hiding place. And this morning, with everyone else in the house gone, she walked down the short graveled path that led from the kitchen door to the road, with the precious cup clutched in her hand.

It was a custom still practiced by most girls in Newfoundland, though no one could explain its origin. It was believed that the egg, thus mystically prepared, when poured into the roadway had special powers. A girl had to ask the given name of the first man who stepped over the egg, and that would be the name of the man she was to marry.

Most of the girls her age or a little older confessed to Kat that they'd tried it, though they laughed and said they really didn't believe in it. Still, she would notice them being exceptionally polite to young men they knew who had a certain first name. Kat herself wasn't sure what she believed, and that wasn't the only reason she had to be careful not to be seen about her errand. Her mother didn't approve of a girl her age being interested in men, and was quite harsh on the subject. Then there was Ag, who was two years older, prettier, and quite superior in her opinions. She thought most outport men were ill-smelling clots, and if she caught her sister mooning after a particular one, she'd never let her hear the end of it.

So it was that Kat took her time, sitting on the big rock with the blue china cup all but hidden in her two hands. The houses were close together, and some old biddy was always peering through the kitchen curtains. Any unusual activity would be reported immediately to Kat's mother. Kat steeled herself for what she was about to do. As casually as possible, she put the cup down between her feet and tipped its contents into the roadway.

There was a good chance that someone would happen along soon. Though most travel between one outport and the next was done in the small boats, the road between Harmony Bay and Torbay was inland enough to be passable for six months out of the year, as long as there was no snow. Once the boats had gone out for fish in the early-morning hours, anybody who had business to do would have to do it on foot.

Almost immediately, Kat could see the figure of a man walking in the road. She watched him curiously, shading her eyes against the summer sun with one hand, the other clutching nervously in her apron pocket. He was too far away yet for her to see his face, and she didn't recognize his gait. He did not walk like a fisherman, that was for certain. Any man who spent his days sitting in the small boats waiting for the cod, even the boys in their middle teens who'd only done it for a few years, developed a rheumatic, bowlegged gait. It was the hours they spent crouched in the bow, the barbed bultow line sawing back and forth between their fingers as the fish struck and then struggled for what could be an hour or more— the endless sawing of the line scarring the men's fingers down almost to the bone—it was the endless sitting in one position that did it. If a lad spent his youth in the small boats, he would walk like an arthritic crab all his days, no matter if he eventually rose above his lot and abandoned fishing for another way of life. Whoever this man was, then, he was no fisherman.

Kat stared down the road at him, on her feet now, rocking nervously heel to toe, toe to heel. Let the neighbors poke their noses through the curtains if they liked. She had already spilled the egg on the path undetected, and for all anybody knew she was only looking out for her mother to come home from Torbay.

Torbay. As she thought the name, she caught the flash of sunlight off the stranger's hair, which was the color of flame on a night when there was frost. Kat knew who he was then, though she didn't know his first name and had never spoken to him. There was a store in Torbay—the only store excepting the bait shop—a big dry-goods store where the families from Harmony Bay went to buy because their own outport was too small to boast a store. The store was owned by a fellow named Manning, a surprisingly dry and taciturn man for a shopkeeper, whose only distinction was that he and his dun-colored wife, who was even homelier than he, had produced eleven children, ten of them female, all of whom had flaming red hair. It was their only son, plagued by an equal number of older and younger sisters, who was coming Kat's way.

Now, it was common knowledge that a woman with red hair crossing your path was a sure sign of ill luck, and the Manning girls had had difficulty catching husbands, though some said it was for other reasons. But what happened if a red-haired man crossed one's path? And did it have any effect upon the enchantment of the egg?

As he came closer to where she stood, Kat began jigging nervously in the path. She might stand over the place where she'd dropped the egg, so that he couldn't step over it. Would that break the spell? It would mean she'd have to wait until next summer to do it over again, and by then she'd be an old maid of seventeen. The thought was unbearable, and Kat vacillated until he was nearly face to face with her, at which point she hopped over to where the egg was, straddling it awkwardly.

The young man, who'd been striding rather quickly with his eyes on the road, nearly collided with Kat before he saw that she was there. He drew in his breath and stopped abruptly. "Good mornin' to yer, miss," he said, blushing a little.

Didn't he have a grand voice? Kat marveled, remembering her manners just in time. "And good mornin' to yerself, sir," she gasped, breathless.

"Did yer lose somethin', then?" he inquired pleasantly enough, and when she looked puzzled, he went on: "Yer after standin' about in the road so, I thought yer might be after lookin' for something. Was it a ring, then?"

"Nooo," Kat said carefully, still dancing around over the egg, but wanting to hear him talk again because his voice charmed her. "I'm—I'm after waitin' on someone."

"Are yer?" He relaxed a little, backing away a few steps as

if to get a better look at her. Something about her pleased him, though he was hard put to say what it might be. "It wouldn't be a sweetheart, would it? Yer kinder young for that I'm thinkin'."

"I am not!" she said crossly, surprised at how important it suddenly seemed that she impress him. "But I've no sweet-heart. It's not me age, mind yer, only me old mother."

"Binicky, is she?" he asked, trying to take her arm and in-duce her to walk a way with him. She pulled her arm away and would not budge. "What is it, then? I only wanted to walk a bit. Yer neighbors are after seein' us talkin'; there'll be no sly business if that's yer worry."

"It's not," Kat said, standing her ground. Something pe-culiar was happening to her insides, like the time when she was ten and she and Ag had gone out berrying and stuffed themselves with bague-apples, those deceptively sweet goose-berries that made you feel all stuffed and woozy at first but gave you violent cramps and three-day shits when you got home. This was a similar feeling, only pleasanter, and Kat could not help but wonder what it meant. If the feeling was that much pleasanter than eating gooseberries, how much more awful might be the retribution that followed? Half-crazy from the sound of his voice and the twinkle of blather in his sky-blue eyes, she tripped over her own feet and backed away. As he tried to come closer to her again, he stepped not over but right in the spilled egg.

"Ouf, what's this, then?" he exclaimed, trying to scrape the mess off his boots onto the dirt of the road. "How did that get there?"

"I—I dropped it only this morning. I was a-gatherin' them from me mother's hens and I—dropped that one on the path and was afeared yer'd step in it—" Kat heard herself blather-ing, bit her tongue to stop.

"All yer had to do was tell me to mind where I walked, lass," he said, suddenly older than she and that much superior. It made Kat wonder how old he really was—twenty at the least—and how many girls he had chasing him, and how much a fool she looked to him. Did the girls chase him, in spite of his red hair and all the rumors there were about the Mannings? Kat despaired, and wanted only to escape the situation her own awkwardness had caused.

"Mom'll be after comin' by anytime now," she said a little wildly, all but envisioning her mother and Ag coming down the road. "And she don't care to have me talkin' to the boys, then, for a fact. Good morrow to yer, then, Mr. Manning."

"Me name is James," he called after her as she hurried toward the house. "James Daniel, though me friends call me Red, for a reason yer can see. And what might be yours?"

"Mary Kathleen Blake!" she called back, stopping in the gravel path and turning back to look at him in spite of herself, and thinking all the while: James, James Daniel Manning. So the man I marry will be called James, unless his havin' red hair somehow breaks the spell. And sure, it isn't a hard name to like. "Though *my* friends call me Kat!"

That night Kat lay in the handmade bed one of her uncles had constructed out of fir logs bound together with hemp rope, listening to Ag's steady breathing across the room and fingering her rosary indifferently. When she finally managed to sleep, it was to dream of small children who had her features, but flaming red hair.

A girl of sixteen summers—a marriageable age among her people—lay on a bed of soft balsam branches cut from the very tree she lay under, clutching the caribou-horn amulet she had worn on a thong around her neck to ensure a safe childbearing. It had been so. The child drowsed against her small, light-brown breast, sated after its first meal. The sun had moved only a little since she had squatted on the balsam branches to bring him forth, alone and silent against the pangs of birth, as was the custom among her people. Like a number of the unmarried girls whose lives had changed since the gods had come to live with them, she had birthed a child whose hair would grow in to be the color of fire.

Her people, like most of the aboriginal peoples of the wooded north countries, referred to themselves simply as "the Human Beings." In their tongue the word was *Beothuk*, which distinguished them from the Naskapi, who had driven them east across the treacherous water from the Great Woods. But that was long ago, as the great burial ground just to the south of where the young girl lay under the balsam tree suckling her baby, the place where the gods had come to live, could testify. The bones of the ancestors had been interred in this sacred place, smeared with red ochre and accompanied by their tools and weapons and good-luck charms to ensure safe passage to the spirit world, for more than three thousand summers. This the young girl knew from the elders of her tribe, just as she knew that it was no disgrace, but a privilege, to give birth to the child of a god.

The gods had come over the water when she was a small girl, their boats looking like great sea birds with monstrous heads and many legs that thrashed in the water, propelling them along. Even the bravest of the men, those who bore the scars of battles with great black bears, hid behind the trees when they saw these strange beasts approaching. The girl remembered peering between the branches where she stood, inland a bit and sheltered with the other children, to see that they were not monstrous birds at all, that their many legs were nothing more than oars propelled by men—oars longer and more powerful than those her own people used to propel the bark canoes, but oars nonetheless, driving nothing more fearsome than great canoes with monsters' heads carved at the front. It was with this knowledge that her people began to make themselves visible from behind the trees, preparing to meet a race of men who, like their canoes, were surely superior.

And the inhabitants of the canoes proved to be as strange, and in a way monstrous, as their boats. There were similarities between them and the Human Beings, of course. They walked on two legs like men—unlike the seal gods and the whale gods, who could transform themselves into man-shapes but who could not stray far from the sea, and unlike the bird gods, who always preserved some semblance of their wings no matter what form they chose. For the most part these new gods wore furs and tanned hides as clothing, though it was taken from animals unknown to the Beothuk. There were similarities in their weapons, though they did keep in their possession the Spirit of Fire, imprisoned in a little stone. The Beothuk could only capture this spirit by dint of much labor with sticks and the chanting of prescribed prayers. But this was where the resemblances ended.

Perhaps it was their great height, or the pallor of their skin—some were even speckled and blotched like the belly skin of the trout—or the great bushes of sun- or flame-colored hair that sprouted on their heads and faces and over much of their bodies. Perhaps it was the strange tongue they spoke, or the amulets they wore that seemed like liquid sunlight, or the thunderous way in which they laughed over the least little thing (the Human Beings did not laugh aloud at all once they had passed into adulthood, although some giggling was permitted in lovemaking or religious trances), or the euphoria-inducing potion they carried in skins and kept under guard in their monster-headed canoes. Whatever it was about them, the Beothuk concluded that they were probably gods, who, like the indigenous gods of the sea and the forest that they had coexisted with since the day the sun was born, were best to be propitiated.

So it was that when certain of the god-men singled out some of the young girls among the Human Beings, offering them pieces of liquid sun and showing their big teeth in wide smiles, the girls went willingly, flattered to be among the chosen. There was some grumbling among the men of the tribe at first, but since no married woman was endangered, and since the gods' weapons were obviously more powerful, the grumbling came to nothing. Besides, other monster-canoes soon brought more of these god-men, and many had women with them, women who also had flame- or sun-colored hair and trout-speckled skin.

The young girl under the balsam tree sighed and stirred slightly on her bed of branches. Night would come soon, and one of her mother's sisters would bring her food and start a fire, and one of her brothers would stand guard some distance away, lest the smell of blood and birthing bring a bear or other predator into the clearing once it grew dark. By tradition, a woman who had given birth had to remain outside the enclosure of the *mamateek* walls for one full night after her child was born, lest evil spirits follow her back to her village and cause plague and disarray. Usually it was the woman's husband who stood guard during that lonely night, forbidden to cross the magic circle surrounding his wife, where only women could enter, but close enough to see his child and speak words of joy and endearment to its mother. In the case of those chosen by the gods, however, things were done differently.

The one who had chosen the young girl had come with the later arrivals, bringing with him to the strange settlement of sod-and-branch huts two storeys high—incomprehensible to the Beothuk, who migrated from winter to summer and summer to winter, and were content with the smaller, tentlike structure of the mamateek—not only a woman but several children, two half-grown and one but recently weaned. For this reason the girl had been particularly flattered that he had chosen her, for what possible charms could she possess beside the towering god-woman whose hair was flame like his?

She had not been frightened the first time she went with him. Life in the mamateek did not lend itself to privacy; she knew what it was that men and women did in the shadows on winter nights, and did not feel threatened by it. But the way he took her that first time, in a little clearing just up from the shore, was not what she'd expected. It was brutal and rough, with no pretense at offering her pleasure for the pleasure he took. It was the same each time she went with him, and her body often ached all over from the bruises he inflicted—striking her seemed to excite his passion—but she continued to follow him, for to be chosen by a god was not something to be taken lightly.

He had made no move to keep her when her people began to gather their possessions for the trek to the winter grounds inland. She did look at him meaningfully once, as she passed with the others the place on the cape where the land gave out and there was nothing to be seen but ocean, the place where the god-men and their women stood before their huge sod houses to watch the Beothuk depart. She had placed one hand on her abdomen as she passed him, to tell him in her own way, since she could not speak the god-tongue, that she carried his child. But he looked right through her, as if she did not exist, or as if she were indistinguishable from the many who walked with her—for the god-woman with the hair of flame stood beside him, and her belly, too, was beginning to swell.

And when the river ice had melted and the Beothuk returned to their summer grounds near the cape, some of the god-men had taken their monster-canoes, braving even the icebergs in the harbor, and returned to wherever it was they had come from. The girl of sixteen summers—a marriageable age among her people—carried in her belly the child of a flame-haired man she would never see again. Back in his own land, he would someday in the long future take his flame-haired grandchildren onto his knee beside the slate hearth, and tell them stories about the quaint customs of the dark-skinned skraelings he had encountered over the water when he was a younger man and had journeyed with Eiriksson, who was called "the Lucky."

Red stood on the deck of the little green Brooklyn ferry, brushing a few wayward strands of hair out of his eyes and staring out toward Staten Island. He had been riding back and forth on the ferry for most of the afternoon, paying the nickel only once, and sneaking through the turnstile or hiding in the men's room on the boat on the return trips. Once he varied his route by taking the ferry to Manhattan, but it was a longer ride and the boat was bigger, not as close to the spray as he liked it, and he was almost caught and thrown off. So back he went to the Brooklyn ferry, which was where he'd ended up after he left the hospital. They had told him that Kat would have a very long labor, and that he ought to go home for a few hours.

Red didn't want to go home. Ag was there with the kids, her conscience possibly bothering her over how little she had participated in her own mother's wake. Ag would make dinner and see to it that the kids got to bed at a reasonable hour. There was no necessity for Red to go home. He wanted to go back to the hospital and be near Kat, even if he had to wait all night. They wouldn't throw him out, would they? Back at the apartment the old woman's ghost lingered—and would linger for the longest time despite his efforts to rid the place of her. Until they could give or throw away her rusty black dresses and elbowless sweaters, she would continue to haunt them. ("Don't be after buyin' anything new for me!" she would lament every Christmas and birthday, opening the presents greedily just the same. "Sure, I don't know why yer bother when I'm not long for this world!" And the new sweaters and nightgowns and crisp blouses would be stuffed into the bottom drawer of her dresser, while she went on wearing the old rags until they all but rotted off her. The new clothes were still there, wrapped in the original tissue paper, yellowed now. The drawer bulged open from the density of them.)

No, Red was not going home until he had to. It was almost dark now. Red still leaned against the rail at the back of the ferry, watching the gulls reel and screech and plunge for the garbage left in its wake. He was alone out here; native New Yorkers found October nights too cold on the ferry's deck and clustered together in the overheated cabins. He would return to Brooklyn one last time, walk from the Sixty-ninth Street pier past Owl's Head Park and the army installation, the blocks of warehouses, and the train yards until he got to Murphy's. He would have some sandwiches, perhaps a beer, and go back to the hospital. He would wait. He knew that this baby would be hard on Kat, knew with the kind of resignation his background had ingrained in him that the baby might be stillborn, that Kat herself might be in grave danger. Whatever happened, he was going to be as close to her as he possibly could at the outcome.

At the back of the boat, the wind swirled backward, blowing the few strands of hair remaining on his head into Red's eyes with annoying frequency. He should have worn a cap, had forgotten it in the mad rush to get Kat to the hospital. He kept brushing the hair back, realizing as he did so how little of it he had left. He'd started balding in his middle twenties, and now, at forty-five—but there wasn't a gray strand in the lot. He still lived up to his nickname.

The ferry pulled into the slip at St. George, on the Staten Island side, and the thin-blooded types streamed out of the cabins and down the gangplank. Red pushed the hair out of his eyes and sighed, blending in with them as well as he could. Once more through the turnstile and back to Brooklyn, and Kat.

A wedding is a great event in any society, and the smaller the town or village the greater the enthusiasm, for if the bride and groom are both locals, chances are everybody has known them since the day they were born, and it is perfectly permissible for the older generation to nod and smile and say they knew it all along. In the smaller outports of Newfoundland there were added touches that brought the mood of the wedding day, when it finally arrived, to a fever pitch bordering on hysteria.

In the first place, rare was the couple who could simply arrive at the conclusion, strictly on their own, that they ought to marry. Tradition dictated that a younger daughter shouldn't be betrothed until her older sisters had had at least one offer of marriage, whether or not they accepted. Young men often had widowed mothers or a half-dozen younger siblings to support, and the drain on their meager incomes might make the support of a wife and children next to impossible. It was not uncommon for a couple to be engaged for upwards of five years, waiting for time to remove such obstacles.

Even for the couple who had no difficulty along this line, all was not smooth sailing. Chances were they couldn't afford to set up housekeeping on their own, so a spare room in some relative's house had to be found, in the hope that bigger quarters might be available once the babies started coming. Quilts and bed linens and a hodgepodge kind of hope chest had to be saved up for; a girl's first bit of sewing when she was barely five or six was apt to be the embroidery on the pillowcases that would grace her marriage bed. A bride had to make her own wedding dress, which meant a journey to the nearest outport that had a store, praying all the while that there hadn't been too many engagements since the last shipments came up from Halifax and North Sydney, so that a certain lovely bolt of white brocade might still have a few yards left on it.

Only the bigger outports boasted a church, most often a clapboard chapel with no pews, and even this close to St. John's there weren't enough priests. No one got married in the winter, because the harbors were blocked with ice and the overland roads were snowed over sometimes twenty feet deep, and even a priest with a dog team couldn't get through. Many a lass had cooled her young man's ardor with "Whisht! And what if yer gets me *that way* now, and the priest can't get past the ice till May?"

By the time Kat was sixteen, she had been to twice as many wakes as weddings, and the announcement that a distant cousin on her father's side was going to wed her one true love on the first week of September—after having been engaged for only two years at that—filled her with absolute joy. The flurry of activity accompanying Kat's trip to Torbay to buy goods for a new dress rivaled that at the bride's house.

The cousin's wedding ceremony itself was not unlike a wake, with the priest intoning long passages about the hardships of life and the enticements of temptation, and a great deal of muffled weeping among the women. The only difference was that the usual pine box in the middle of the church had been replaced by two warm young bodies, huddled close to each other in defense against the life that awaited them. He was a great gangling lad of twenty-three, already possessed of the arthritic gait and scarred hands of a fisherman; she was a slip of a girl of twenty, youngest child and sole caretaker of an ancient mother whose house they would live in. Kat, watching them, trembled with them in their helplessness, and was soon crying along with the others. This merited a sneer from her sister, Ag, who yawned through the service and swung her legs nervously under the bench. She had only come for the dancing, after all.

And the dancing was worth the wait, for the best reel players in the vicinity had come all the way overland from Topsail to grace this wedding celebration. The fiddler began the second the chapel bells let up, and would not stop, except once in a while to wet his whistle, until nearly dawn. It was to be a memorable evening.

It was mostly young people who did all the dancing, though there was more than one matronly type in her thirties or early forties—some of them big with a fifth or sixth child—doing a reel or two with the best of them. The days following a wedding dance almost always saw the onset of premature labor, which was a good thing, for then the baby could be baptized before the priest went across the water again. As for those who were too old to dance, they came to eat and drink and gossip, though not necessarily in that order. Because the dining table was seldom big enough to accommodate more than a dozen, and since there might be as many as a hundred guests packed into the house, it was customary for the family to invite people to come and eat in the order of their importance—immediate relatives and local bigshots first, then close friends and neighbors, more distant cousins, and all the way down to poor relations and those invited out of obligation. Each group would be seated at the table with great ceremony, and would eat with great gusto and slowness, ignoring the wistful stares of those who hadn't eaten yet. Only when the last member of that group had risen grandly, belched politely, and excused himself from the table, could the next group be seated. Meanwhile, the dancing went on.

Kat simply had to stop. She was out of breath and had a stitch in her side; her pale forehead was clammy with sweat and her eyes were feverish. She was not as good a dancer as Ag—few were—but she made up for it with her vitality and stamina. Even so, she was winded and would have to rest. Besides, she saw no reason to make a further display of herself, for the lad she'd set out to impress had not shown up at all.

The dancing always started with the girls, who would begin a reel in orderly groups of four and dance with each other until the less awkward of the young men, steeled with a shot or two of the strong stuff, chose to join them. By the end of the night, when it came time for the young people to have their turn at the dinner table, all but the homeliest of the girls and most backward of the men had paired off, if only temporarily.

Already Ag was holding court, bestowing her opinions upon half a dozen lads whom she really had no use for, while the unclaimed girls made catty remarks behind her back. Although she had attended the same convent school in Torbay for the same six years as the other girls fortunate enough to go to school at all, Ag was somehow more brilliant and interesting. Not only that, but she could play the piano, and since her father's house was the only one in Harmony Bay to boast such an instrument, Ag was an impressive catch for any fisherman's son. But tonight, as always, she would walk home arm in arm with her sister, declining the eager company of any of the men.

Kat, for her own part, was as dejected as anyone could possibly be in the midst of this furor and gaiety. The dirty jokes had begun now that most of the older women had gone home and the men had gotten looser with the flow of whiskey. The newlyweds would have no privacy this night; the groom's friends would see to that. They would be stationed under their window the entire night, shooting off rifles and tossing pebbles at the glass, howling like wolves until the moon went down. Wedding nights were a form of madness, but a madness prescribed by tradition, and usually taken in the spirit of fun. No matter the grimness of daily life; there was no excuse for misery tonight.

But Kat was miserable, because she'd spent the greater part of two hours craning her neck over the heads of the crowd, praying for a single glimpse of a man with red hair. The Mannings were distant cousins of the groom, and by rights at least some of them ought to be here. Some of them were. Kat's heart had leaped into her mouth at the sight of someone with flame-colored hair earlier that evening; it had turned out to be one of Red's older sisters, who, when asked somewhat circuitously if her brother would be attending, shrugged and said she didn't think it mattered to anyone.

He wasn't coming, then, Kat thought, and wished she could go home right that minute, the better to nurse her misery in the quiet of her room. But her mother was long gone with the other older women, and Ag had no intention of being among the first of the young ones to leave. And it was unthinkable for a girl her age, even in a society where doors did not have locks, to go out in the dark alone.

"You hain't crying now, har you?" A male voice behind her in the kerosene-lit room made Kat jump. He had a strange accent. An outlander, here at a hometown party? She turned sharply.

"I am not!" she snapped without thinking, wiping the telltale moisture out of her eye with the back of her hand. "And it wouldn't be yer business if I was!"

She feigned disinterest, but her curiosity was aroused, and she had to know who he was. It was probably the cut of his sandy hair, more than the Devon accent (which could simply have meant that he came from the west of Newfoundland), that gave him away. He was a British soldier, one of the troops garrisoned near St. John's since the beginning of the Great War.

"Yer must be a friend of Ted's, then," Kat said with a weak smile, referring to the groom. She was sorry she'd been so rude. "Sure, I didn't mean to bite yer head off, only yer came at me at a bad time."

She knew many of the local boys often befriended the British enlisted men, awed at their stories of the world beyond the horizon, dreaming of the chance they themselves might have to escape the fishing boats by joining the military. Young Ted had fully intended to join up; his new bride had talked him out of it.

"No skin off me nose," said the young soldier with a shrug, pleasantly enough. "Yeah, the lad an' me used ta drink together a bit. Thought he was gonna enlist, only the missus had a word with him. Har you a relative?"

"First cousin twice removed on me father's side," Kat said grandly, with the flawless genealogical skill of a member of a close-knit and often-illiterate society. She clarified it for the puzzled outlander, who was frowning. "The bride's mother and me father was first cousins. That means if she had a brother I could marry him without a dispensation."

The young soldier shook his head. "Phew!" he said. "It's too much for me. But answer me this question—why were you crying?"

"It's nothing, sure," Kat said loftily, shaking her long brown hair back over her shoulders. The curls she'd set in rags the night before were a wilted mess by now. She must look a fright. Even if Red did come by this late, he'd hardly look at her. The thought made the tears start again.

"Boyfriend didn't show—is that it?" the stranger asked

sympathetically, giving her elbow a friendly squeeze. "Tell me about it, and I'll cheer you up if I can. Not to worry that I'd steal you from 'im."

No such thought had entered Kat's mind. "I'd be after thankin' yer for leavin' me in peace!" she said irritably. The lad was to friendly; in the mood she was in it was grating.

"Excuse us!" the young soldier said, pretending to be insulted. "I guess you're near as stuck-up as your sister. Runs in the family, does it?"

"Who said Ag was me sister?" Kat scowled at him. So that was the real reason he'd spoken to her. "We don't look a bit alike!"

"Like enough to know you're sisters," the young man argued, cocking his head to one side. "An' what'd you say 'er name was?"

"Agatha Mary Blake," Kat said, deciding he'd be just the type to fix Ag's wagon. "And she's eighteen years old and cold as a mackerel. She'll not bother with the likes of you!"

The soldier considered it for a moment. "Even a mackerel can cook if the fire's 'ot enough," he said, nodding slyly. "'Ave a 'appy!"

When he'd left her alone, Kat wanted to laugh, until she remembered how miserable she was. Her eyes clouded over again, and she almost missed the man she'd waited for.

Red had come in at last, probably while she'd been involved with the soldier. He was talking right now to the bridegroom. Kat's heart started to flipflop.

But surely he won't even speak to me! she thought. I was not a bit civil to him that day in the road. What would he do if he knew I was after thinkin' of him every blessed day for the three weeks since? Will he so much as remember me? she wondered, seeing him slap Ted on the back and head in her direction.

The dancing had stopped for a while; the musicians were having a few drinks. The room was crowded and stuffy and full of pipe smoke. Kat could see that the blond soldier had managed to talk to Ag; Ag's proud head was tilted just a bit to hear what he was saying over the noise. Every so often she laughed her special and not quite genuine laugh. What would be the outcome of that? Kat wondered.

"And how's the egg business, then?" Red was standing directly in front of her, and Kat was struck dumb.

"The what?" she managed to say, blushing hot and furiously.

"Yer know, I was after forgettin' that business with the egg," he said, grinning at her embarrassment. "One of me sisters set me straight. We're a bit too modern for the like of that over to Torbay. Well, and have yer caught him yet?"

"Caught who?"

"The lad with me first name, sure!" Red teased her. "Yer after havin' three weeks to do it in. Come on, then, where's he at?"

"There's no one," Kat said soberly, forgetting she didn't entirely believe the old superstition. "Unless it's yerself," she blurted out in spite of herself.

Red was surprised as well. "I'd no idea the both of the Blake girls were as forward," he said. "Sure, everyone knows about yer sister, but I was after thinkin' you were the shy one."

"There's times when it don't pay to be shy!" Kat said, almost making a plea, looking him square in the eye. He might as well know how she felt; there was nothing she could do about it except tell him.

"Aye," Red nodded, thinking about it. "So we're both of the same mind on that. Are yer after wantin' ter dance, or would yer take some air with me and have a bit of a talk?"

"I've had me fill of dancin'," Kat said.

The water was cold even to a seasoned sailor, and in spite of its being summer. It was bitterly cold, and the solitary swimmer's teeth chattered until they tore involuntarily at his blue, shaking lips. The old scars on his back from the floggings ached from the cold and the salt water, and if he did make it to shore he would be stiff for days. It did not matter. At the times that he could force his eyelids open against the brine, he kept his glance fixed on the bobbing, mist-shrouded light that meant the shore and safety, perhaps even a fire and warmth and something to eat. It might also mean death at the hands of red savages or pirates, he knew, but a quick dispatch was preferable to the slow life-in-death he had known in Her Majesty's Navy.

His name was O'Muir, which in his native Gaelic meant "of the sea," and which was significant in view of the course his life had taken. He'd been born on the Isle of Man, one of many children of a couple who harvested kelp. They'd sold him to the captain of an English man-of-war that limped home after the battle with the Armada, a third of its crew depleted by a strange typhus-like disease, the result of the tight-fisted queen keeping her men on short rations even during the battle. The captain needed a cabin boy, and paid for the lad with a handful of coins his parents neither knew the value of nor were likely to need in their barter-based economy. He had been twelve then, almost an adult, since the harsh life of the shore people made anyone over thirty an old man.

The life was exciting to a lad who'd thought the universe ended at the horizon, and before he was twenty he had sailed all of the known world. Only now and again would he get homesick—though all he had known of home had been a mud hut and cold and never enough to eat—and would drink too much and mutter to himself in Gaelic and jump over the side at the nearest opportunity, to swim for the shore of whatever place he was near. He was inevitably brought back and flogged.

This was another of those nights. But he was thirty now, well past his prime, and he'd sworn on the souls of St. Patric and his family gods that they'd never take him alive. He'd garnered as much information as he could on this desolate place they were passing en route to the New World, had heard it was mostly inland marsh and a rocky coastline, sparsely populated.

It sounded almost like home. He knew this much and also the name of the place—New-Found-Land; in French, Terre Neuve. Armed with this much information, he had slipped over the side for one final try.

O'Muir kept swimming, his limbs like lead now, only the pains from his back keeping him conscious. When he thought he could go no farther he trod water and felt his foot strike something solid. He groped with both feet until he found the bottom, then let the surf propel him onto the steep, pebbled beach.

The lights he had seen shimmering vaguely from his ship had come from a series of bonfires just up from the beach, sheltered against the prevailing wind on little shelves of rock along the coast. O'Muir could distinguish structures—mound-like huts of animal hides or what could be sail canvas, some of them heaped about with sod for insulation. Were they the dwellings of red Indians? he wondered. Surely they looked no more menacing than the hut he'd been born in.

Better to die from a well-aimed arrow than to shake apart from the cold, O'Muir thought. He let out a shout, and was immediately answered by the appearance of some half-dozen men from the huts. All of them had muskets, which they quickly trained on the shadowy figure just beyond the fire-light. All of them were bearded, and O'Muir had heard that Indians wore no beards. Pirates, then? Had the bonfires been set to lure ships closer for plunder? O'Muir offered a quick prayer to St. Patric and his family gods and waited.

Suddenly one of the bearded figures let out a laugh like the bellow of a bull and lowered his weapon. He spoke—God be praised—in a rough version of the queen's English.

"It be's another washin' up fro' the tide!" he roared. "Anon a bloody liveyer!"

Later, gorging himself on a stew of fish and boiled roots inside one of the huts, O'Muir listened in turn to each man's tale of woe, all of them remarkably similar to his own. All of these men were outcasts, renegades mostly from fishing boats, forbidden by English law to form permanent settlements on this island lest they multiply overmuch with the native women and create an independent fishing population that would threaten England's claim to the waters. They stayed just the same, clinging to the barren rocks, starving most of the time, freezing to death in the ominous winters. They called themselves "Masterless Men" or "liveyers," which meant simply that they "lived here."

"Yer shipmates mought be a-lookin' for ye," the leader of the tiny colony advised O'Muir. "It be's best t'appear yer here awhiles. Another name'd do yer as well. I'll not ask yer true name. Where be yer from?"

"Innis Mannan," O'Muir blurted out, giving the Celtic name of the Isle of Man. He was feeling sleepy from the warmth of the fire and the sudden fullness of his gut—too sleepy to lie. What did it matter?

"Like enow." The bearded one nodded. "We'll clep ye O'Mannan."

It was about ten degrees centigrade, not unusual for an early autumn night in coastal Newfoundland. Kat had a shawl about her shoulders; it had been so hot in where the dancing was that she was all perspired. She sat, very ladylike, her feet together, on an empty keg on the wharf, while Red sat with his feet over the side, idly watching an extraordinarily high flow-tide creeping in. There was a full moon, after all, and that would explain the behavior of the tides. More than one careless fisherman would find his towlines fouled and his lobster pots in a snarl come morning from not putting in closer to shore this night. But it wasn't expected that much would get done the day after a big wedding anyway.

Kat had been chattering away like a magpie for what she guessed to be about an hour, but now she was silent. The sounds of the rowdies leading the procession of the bride and groom to the wedding chamber had disrupted her talk, and a shudder had passed through her when she thought of what that other young woman had in store for her tonight. She and Red sat in utter silence under the moonlight, even though the sounds of gunfire were only sporadic now.

"Then yer father's been dead since yer was four." Red broke the silence, sensing perhaps the mood she was in and what had caused it. Outport girls were funny. They all wanted babies, but they seemed so terrified of the little they knew about making them. He could not see her face because she was looking down at the water, and the side toward him was thrown into deep shadow by the moonlight.

"Aye," Kat said with a nod, looking down at her hands. She could not remember talking this much since she'd left school over two years ago. She had been able to talk that way among the girls at school, though the appearance of a nun always silenced her. She never spoke much to her mother, and while she and Ag whispered to each other sometimes in the darkness of their room, it was usually Ag who did most of the talking. As for men, the only men Kat knew to speak to were relatives—uncles and cousins and such—and once they exhausted the weather, that day's catch, and their rheumatism, they would lapse into silence. Where could she have found the courage to talk so long to a man she hardly knew? And what must he think of her for being such a yapper?

"I remember the night the *Nancy Todd* went down," Red was saying thoughtfully. "I was about nine, I guess, and helpin' out at the store. Everyone for miles around was after stoppin' by to talk about it and figure would there be any survivors. There seldom was in a hurricane, sure, but sometimes the big whalers'd founder so clean a man could live through it, if he was a strong swimmer. I didn't know yer daddy was on her."

"He was, then," Kat said, wanting to talk about it all in a rush, because all her life she'd been only able to listen to it from her mother and all the other relatives, none of whom cared to know her feelings about the vague, mustached figure who stood by her bed in his oilskins every morning before he went out on the boats, sweeping her out from under the comforter to hug her until the oilskins squeaked and all the breath was wrung out of her. No one expected her to miss her father; she'd been "too young to remember him, sure." But she did remember him, and she needed to talk about him. "Mom didn't want him to go for a whaler, sure, because she feared him bein' gone as many months. But the catch was poor that year, and he was after needin' the extra comin' in."

"Aye." Red nodded, knowing what she meant. "But he was one of them they never found, wasn't he?"

"A Bridegroom of the Sea," Kat said grandly, using the local expression, her voice catching a little. "Mom is still of the notion he's alive somewheres, wanderin' around with no memory in some other outport. She's half-daft about it most of the time."

Red shook his head. "It's a cryin' shame!" he commiserated. "But yez were all right on the money end of it, then?"

"Aye," Kat said. "Me uncles was mostly working for Dad anyways, so they just took over the boats and kept Mom and Ag and me. That's why we were after goin' to school instead of let out to work that young."

"Ag's older than you," Red observed, and for a moment of panic Kat wondered why he had to know. Was he, like the British soldier, only talking to her in the hope of meeting her sister? If so, he'd been extraordinarily patient for over an hour.

"Two years," she gulped, feeling her heart sinking into her shoes. Closer to yer age than me, she thought, and that much smarter and prettier. "What's it to yer?"

"She's an awful binicky lass, then, ain't she?" he asked. "Is it losin' her father makes her like that, yer think? How comes it she's so different from you?"

Kat blushed, grateful that he couldn't see it in the moonlight. It was not Ag he was interested in, after all.

"She's not happy," she explained. "She's not after wantin' to be a fisherman's wife. She's for leavin' Harmony Bay."

"Leave here?" Red repeated. "For where, then—St. John's? There's none but rich people there; they'll not have her except for an upstairs maid. She's better ter settle for a fisherman. What does she want, then?"

"Farther than that," Kat replied, wondering again what made Ag tick. Why would anyone want to leave Harmony Bay? "She's after wantin' to go up to the States."

Red whistled softly. "Sure, and isn't that an idea we've all had more than once? I've been thinkin' toward the Merchants meself."

Kat's heart jumped violently. Would he join the merchant marine, really? What would she do without him? "And why's that, then?" she asked, trying to sound casual. "Yer no fisherman, but a shopkeep's son. Is yer life that hard, then?"

He would have answered, but a sound attracted his attention and he stopped to listen. Kat frowned and listened too. There was laughter, that of a man and a woman, coming from somewhere nearby. Nothing moved in the moonlight, but the wind was tricky here on the point, playing in and out among the rock ledges where lovers often sheltered on a night like this, and the sound could be coming from a few yards or as much as a mile away.

"Someone's after enjoyin' theirselves," Red grunted, pleased at the sound. He'd never had time for the rock ledges himself.

"It's dirty, what they're doin'," Kat snapped, though as she said it, she wondered. Could it be so bad if it afforded them so much pleasure?

"No dirtier than what the new couple'd like to do if they got the chance," Red observed. "It's only the priest's allowin' it that makes the dirty clean."

Kat was horrified. She jumped to her feet with as much dignity as she could muster and pulled the shawl close about her. "It's a shame!" She scowled. "A shame yer had to go muck up a lovely time with such dirty talk! I'm after lookin' for me sister. It's time I'm gettin' home."

She could see only part of his face in the moonlight, and

what she saw was amused at her abruptness. His hair was spun copper in that light, all ginger and fire. It made her heart jump.

"I'll walk a ways with yer," he offered, taking her elbow like some grand gentleman in a book. A thrill ran through Kat, and she did not pull away. "Until yer find yer sister."

Kat suffered his touch as she picked her way over the rocks up from the waterfront, stepping over and around the wooden frames, or "flakes," for the sun-drying of the salt codfish before they were shipped to St. John's. Neither she nor Red could smell the clinging, half-rotten stink of the fish; it was part and parcel of the air they'd breathed all their lives, and they'd grown immune to it. When they came up parallel to the rock cliffs, they heard the laughter again, intermingled with sounds of scuffling and snatches of dirty talk. Kat froze, not wanting to look at the two shadowy figures in the cleft of the rock, so busy with each other that they heard nothing, but she was glued to the spot, mesmerized. She'd recognized the laugh as Ag's.

"Well, I guess yer after findin' yer sister," Red whispered close to her ear. He began to pull her away. "Come on. It's me'll be takin' yer home, then."

O'Mannan, née O'Muir, adapted readily to the life he had chosen when he flung himself over the side that summer night. As a boy, he'd been deft in the shaping of curraghs—the squat little flat-bottomed boats of hide used for fishing and the harvesting of kelp—and found the skill returning to him after so many years. He fished alongside his companions, playing out the lines of braided straw rope barbed with hooks of caribou horn and baited with entrails to entice the prolific cod. He shared with the others the dangers of the life, and when times were bad they pooled their catches and distributed them evenly, for every able-bodied man was needed, and if one was to starve they might as well starve together.

O'Mannan—dubbed *Aedh*, or "flame," by those who knew

Gaelic, because of his bright-red hair—learned to build a hut of cured caribou hides, imitating the native mamateek. He hunted caribou and small game with the others in the winter, using native weapons. When he had survived two winters without starving, he came to the conclusion that it was time to get himself a woman.

Most of the liveyers were on friendly terms with the Beothuk, and had married native women according to native customs, adapting their consciences somehow to the religions of their upbringing as they did so. Though they themselves chose to make permanent settlements on the coast, they did not interfere with the Beothuk custom of migrating with the seasons, and took care not to settle on ancestral land. The Beothuk way of life would continue undisturbed for yet another century, before the steady influx of white settlers deprived them of their coastline settlements, setting a pattern of slow starvation and disease that would decimate the entire native population within two hundred years. But for now, liveyers and Beothuk coexisted in peaceful symbiosis, exchanging cultures and making babies.

It would be easy enough for O'Mannan to acquire a woman. He was inured by now to the stink of the bear grease they used in their hair, and figured he smelled no better, what with his hands up to the elbows in fish guts most of the time. All that was needed was for him to approach one of the elder braves who had marriageable daughters, offer him a winter's catch of caribou hides and the handful of ha'pennies he'd had in his pouch the night he swam across, and the bargain would be made. The obstacle was that O'Mannan, in his thirty-two years, had never known a woman. Because of his small stature and flaming hair, and his forced service at a young age, he'd been easy prey for his shipmates on the long, womanless voyages. In his youth he'd been pretty enough to have officers vying for him, but the last years of his sailing life had found him victimized by anyone on board who was larger and stronger than he. His encounters had been exclusively homosexual, frequently violent, usually loveless. He would not know how to go about it with a woman.

So he watched for the first two years, seeing the native couples pairing off in the balsam woods on summer nights, hearing the grunts and murmurs of his companions and their women beyond the walls of the mamateeks. He was startled one night, as he lay on a mat in his own desolate hut, sleeping fitfully because it was fall and blowing up a gale, which always made him think he was back at sea and heading for rough weather, to hear a scream—a hoarse sound as of a man in sudden pain—coming from the next hut.

O'Mannan sprang through the doorflap of his hut. He had built it on this very spot because he got along so well with the man in the next hut—a brawny bloke with one eye missing who went by the name of Tim. He had taken a new bride only the week before, his first wife having died of a fever the previous winter, leaving him with three exotic but unkempt children. O'Mannan had not seen the new woman, who stayed inside the mamateek day and night, scolding the children in the mixture of English and Beothuk they understood. The scream had been Tim's. What could have happened?

O'Mannan tumbled into the hut and found Tim clutching his left arm, which was dripping blood from an open slash in his hide shirt. In the dim light of the low-banked fire the faces of the children could be seen; they were rubbing their eyes and clustering together in fear. O'Mannan could not see the woman's face, only her shadowy form, crouched in a heap against the side of the hut.

"What is't, man?" O'Mannan demanded of Tim, who by now had twisted the sleeve of his shirt into something of a tourniquet with his free hand and was laughing wildly. Others had come running when he screamed, though not as quickly as O'Mannan. They crowded around the doorflap, curious.

"It be's nought! Nought at all!" Tim roared at them when he could take the time from laughing. "It's only her ladyship refuses me the honor!"

O'Mannan peered closer, trying to get a good look at the woman, wondering. Was it possible she'd lived in the hut an entire week without Tim's demanding his rights as a husband? Was Tim that patient, to wait on the whims of a woman? Or was it the knife that had kept him at bay? Did she hold the knife even now?

He did not have long to wonder, for the woman suddenly sprang to her feet and began to talk feverishly, gesturing at O'Mannan and then raising her hands to her own hair. O'Mannan knew only a few words in Beothuk; its grammar was complex and lacking in personal pronouns. He caught the word "god" and the word "flame" and scowled at Tim, who understood perfectly and was doubled up with laughter.

"What is't?" O'Mannan cried, puzzled and a little fearful. "What says she about me?"

Tim shook his head, out of breath and unable to speak. He waved his injured arm, still bound with the tourniquet, at the woman.

"Go ye with him, then!" he wheezed finally, still laughing. He eyed O'Mannan with glee. "Ye've wooed and won a bride, me good man, though I've no doubt it was the furthest thing fro' yer mind. Take her and go, then! Children of the gods, me arse!"

Before he knew what it was all about, O'Mannan was being led back to his mamateek by the Beothuk woman, who was a head taller than he, but was at least weaponless. When they got inside where the firelight was stronger, he gasped.

"God's bones!" he cried, crossing himself for the first time in twenty years. " 'Tis a red-haired Indian!"

"Helen Mary," her Aunt Ag said over her shoulder from the armchair. "Put the kettle on, there's a dear. A cup of tea wouldn't harm us, for a fact."

It was ten o'clock at night, nearly twelve hours since Kat had been bundled off to the hospital to have her baby. Ag was staying with the kids, not because she felt they needed supervision, but because it was a way of forgiving herself for recent behavior. It did not bother Ag that she had seen so little of her mother when she was alive—the bad feeling between them went back to the earliest days of her child-hood—but that she had done so little to help Kat once the old woman finally died. But then, Kat had wanted it that way.

So Ag sat now in Red's favorite chair, her dainty stockinged feet with the painted toenails propped up on the coffee table to prevent varicose veins, and told herself she was taking a load off her younger sister's mind by looking after the kids. When Helen came back from the kitchen, yawning a little from the tensions of the past few days, Ag was feeling mellow.

"Where're the boys at?" she asked indifferently, leaning her head back carefully against the cushions so she wouldn't crush her permanent. She had wavy, chestnut-brown hair with a single chic gray streak in the front—it would be a year or two before Helen caught on to the fact that neither the wave nor the color were genuine—and, with judicious use of powder and lipstick, managed to look five years younger than she was. Still, even Helen could see that there was something brittle and cold about her.

"In Danny's and my room," Helen answered. "Playing checkers. Probably for money, or they wouldn't be so quiet."

"Whose idea was that?" Ag asked, though she really didn't care. She didn't know how to talk to her niece, or any young person for that matter, and had been filling in the long hours of cleaning up after the wake and making supper and doing the dishes with aimless chatter.

"Alistair's," Helen said, with a little more animation than her aunt. "Danny cheats, but he doesn't know Alistair's on to him. He's been losing all night."

Aunt Ag laughed—a little, calculated laugh—and was silent.

"Wish I knew what was keeping your father," she said finally. "You'd think the doctor'd send him home if she was having a long time of it."

She watched her niece's face to see how this remark was received; there was no change in the girl's expression. At what age did children learn the facts of life these days? Ag wondered. Did the girl have any idea what it was her mother was going through right now?

"Your mother might be having a hard time with this baby," Ag said cautiously. Helen looked at her, unflinching. "You do know what I mean, then, do you?"

Helen nodded. "Yes," she said. "Mom's kinda old for having babies."

"You know all about it?" Ag asked, rather relieved. "How a woman gets a baby, and all that?"

The girl blushed. "Pretty much," she said. "Some of my friends—we gab a lot. They've got married sisters and all."

Ag laughed again; it was more real-sounding this time. "You kids today are something!" she said. "Is there anything you don't know?"

Helen took the remark seriously. She started to speak, then thought the better of it. But her aunt saw the sudden animation of her face and picked up on it.

"Go ahead, say it," she demanded, forgetting instantly that her mother was dead and her sister in the throes of a dangerous labor. She felt an intelligence in this girl that she hadn't found in most women; it was why she always got along better with men. "Come on—tell me what you were going to say."

"I changed my mind," Helen said, looking away, pouting like a child. "It was a nosy question. I have no business asking it."

That was enough to make Ag sit up in the chair. She swung her feet off the coffee table and groped around for her high heels, as if she needed to be well armed before they went any further. "I can't let you get away with that, and you know it," she said, glaring at Helen. "Tell me, sure!"

"Nothing," Helen tried to assure her, but Ag was having none of it. "Only I've always wondered why you—well, why you never got married or anything."

" 'Never'?" Ag repeated, amused. "Whisht, child, I'm only forty-two. There's women older than me getting married every day. Am I over the hill, d'you think?"

"I didn't mean it that way," Helen said with great difficulty, wishing she'd kept her mouth shut in the first place. "It's just that you came to the States when you weren't much older than me, and you went straight out to work. You've been working ever since. Didn't you ever have a—you know—a sweetheart or something?"

"And if so, why didn't I marry him and have a houseful of brats, you mean," Ag finished for her. "That wasn't my way of seeing things, that's all. I never wanted to be tied down, sure."

"But—" Helen began, and not knowing how to say what she wanted to say, shrugged and looked down at the pattern on the faded flowered carpet, feeling foolish.

"I'm no more or less happy than your mother is," Ag pointed out. "She thinks she and your dad have the life of Riley here, and she pities me my loneliness. I'm not the one to contradict her. We've different personalities, that's all. She's a hard time of it, and so have I, but in our own ways. But I don't envy her the suffering over the babies and the endless meals to cook and the mountains of washing."

Ag studied the girl for a long moment, wondering if whatever advice she could give her—poised as she was at the place in adolescence where love and romance and poetry were all of existence—would spare her the pitfalls of dealing with men, or only frighten her and poison her mind. Did she have the right to say anything at all?

"And another thing," Ag said finally, after the longest pause. "I did have a sweetheart once, and I'd've done anything in the world for him. Anything in the world."

Helen looked at her aunt with awe, startled by this information. Adults never said such things to children, never allowed them to see this much of the soul beneath the conventional facade. Helen was only certain real people said such things because she'd read them in a book somewhere. What should she say?

Ag looked at her niece sadly, leaving the door to her psyche open for one more moment. "Only he went away and never came back," she said. "And if you must know, it's why I've never gotten married."

Helen was struck dumb. Had her upbringing been other than it was she could have commiserated with her aunt, delved deeper into the subject, or, embarrassed as she was, at least had the resources to change the subject. But it wasn't; she couldn't.

The door to Ag's soul slammed shut with finality. "Mind the kettle!" she said to Helen, who bolted for the kitchen to stop its whistling.

In the wee hours of the morning after the wedding in Harmony Bay, Kat lay awake for the longest time waiting for Ag to come home. She had no idea what time it was; knew only that she'd been so deathly tired when Red Manning left her at the kitchen door without so much as a handshake that she'd tumbled into bed without taking her clothes off. And now she couldn't sleep. She lay in the darkness punctuated with her mother's snores from the next room and wished and wondered and prayed. Wished that she would see Red again and soon, that she would find excuses to shove Ag aside and accompany her mother when she went to the store at Torbay, where she might catch a glimpse of his flame-red hair, watch the twinkle in his eyes, and listen to his blather. Wondered, though she dared not dwell on it too much, what Ag and her soldier boy were about up there on the rock ledges, and wondered how long it would take for the cold to drive Ag home. Prayed, because her rosary was under her pillow anyway, and because it gave her something to do while she waited.

She was almost drowsing when she heard furtive footsteps, as of stockinged feet moving cautiously across the plank floor. She could see Ag's silhouette thrown across the dormer window by the moonlight as she crept across toward her bed.

"Ag?" Kat said, propping herself up on one elbow. Her voice sounded like thunder in the silent room.

"Jesus and Mary!" Ag gasped, dropping the shoes she'd clutched carefully in her hand. They clattered hollowly on the wooden floor, and both girls stopped breathing. For some reason, Kat felt as guilty as she thought Ag ought to feel, as if she were somehow implicated in her sister's behavior. The two of them froze, listening as the snoring in the next room broke off abruptly, stayed suspended for a moment or two, then went on as before.

"Yer gave me such a fright!" Ag hissed at her sister, plopping down on the side of Kat's bed. "What's the matter with yer?"

"I was asleep when yer came in, sure," Kat lied. "I wanted to be sure it was yerself."

"And who else might it have been, then?" Ag rolled her eyes in the dark. "Yer the living end sometimes, for a fact!"

"I'll not tell Mom yer was after bein' out this late," Kat offered, willing to risk that much complicity, but no more. She offered it as a bribe, to get Ag to tell her what went on.

"Yer can tell her if yer like," Ag said, throwing her hair over her shoulders in an arrogant way she had. "Yer can tell her what we was about too, for all I care!"

Kat's eyes widened in horror. She'd been scanning her sister's face, what she could see of it in the graying dark, trying to see if there was some change, some evidence of newly acquired knowledge, or sin. Was Ag a sinner? How far had they gone, out there on the rock ledges?

"I'd not know what to tell her," Kat said cautiously. "Sure, I only heard yez laughin'. I never seen what yez were doin'."

Ag's spine stiffened; Kat could feel her straighten up in the way that the mattress shifted. "It's not yer concern what we was after doin'," she said grandly, immune to possible threats of blackmail, which she thought Kat might be hinting at. "It's nothing would get me a baby, anyways. Yer can rest on that."

"Ag!" Kat's voice rose to nearly normal volume. She subsided under Ag's glare, apparent even in the dim light. "Sure, I'd not tell her anything. It's a matter between you and yer confessor."

Ag let out a laugh, a wild crazy laugh that still sounded false. Was there a real person under the many masks Ag wore? The laugh was reckless, defying the old woman who snored so complacently in the next room, daring her to wake up.

"My confessor!" Ag repeated, shaking her head in disbelief. "As if I'd be tellin' the likes of tonight to some frozen old priest! No, I'll tell yer," and she lowered her voice to become quite serious. "It's this way: I have got to get away from here, away from the old woman, away from the gossip and the smallness of the place. Can yer understand that? Freddie may be English and all, but he's got through high school and he's a corporal in the army, and when he gets out he's going for a carpenter. He'll have a trade, yer see, and an education, and a chance to make his mark in the world. And I've got to let him know that he's important to me, and I've got to give him what he wants so I'll be that important to him. I've got to be after makin' him want to come back for me when he's out in six months, and we'll marry and travel the world over if we've a mind to. If I don't go with him I'll end up toothless and daft and talkin' circles like her ladyship yonder. She'll not let me emigrate; then I'll find me own way out."

Kat listened, dumbfounded. The careful calculation that had led Ag to this course of action was beyond her. If she were an old maid of eighteen and had never set eyes on Red Manning, if she didn't love the very air of the place where she was born, could she even then be as cold-blooded and certain of her goal as Ag? Kat knew she couldn't, and shivered as she thought of Ag's raw nerve.

"How can yer be so certain he'll be after sendin' for yer?" Kat asked, without malice. "Six months is a while, sure, and there's bound to be girls where he's goin' to. Suppose he forgets yer?"

"He'll not forget me," Ag said grandly, again using her wild laugh. "Not after tonight. And we've another two weeks before they move his unit out."

Kat's heart jumped. What strange seductive tricks did her sister know, and where had she learned them? It was enough to make her risk sounding like a fool just to ask her. What had worked for the soldier boy would surely work for Red Manning. Was there a way to make Red remember her all his days? Blushing wordlessly in the dark, Kat realized she was treading thin moral ice, and all but crossed herself. Magic charms with an egg were one thing, but this—

"And yer not doin' half-bad yerself," Ag broke into her thoughts. "How's the carrot-top?"

"He's all very well," Kat snapped, annoyed at this casual characterization of the man she loved. "We only just talked."

"Aye." Ag nodded, smug and superior. "And a great lot of talkin' it must have been. Freddie and me was after watchin' yez from time to time. I never seen such a shy and moonstruck pair."

The news elated Kat somehow. Could it be that Red really cared for her, but was too shy, as she was, to do anything about it? Why hadn't she seen it for herself?

"And if yez hurry, yez could catch the priest before he crosses the water," Ag taunted, more cruel than she needed to be. She was not nearly as certain of her future as she pretended to be, and her emotions had been strained to near the breaking point by the events of the night. "Sure, he's waitin' on Betsy Dowd to have her baby, so he can baptize it before he goes back. Unless all that dancin' tonight brought her on early, yez ought to have a week or more yet."

Kat was angry. She hadn't a cruel bone in her body, and she had as much right to a sweetheart as her stuck-up sister.

"I'll thank yer to shut yer yap!" she blazed suddenly. "Don't rag me for lookin' out for meself as well! Ye've a lot of nerve, and not the brains to go with it!"

It took Ag by surprise. "All right, then, don't get huffed!" she snapped, secretly pleased that her sister could show some spirit. "It's only yer feelings I'm thinkin' on. Mom don't approve of the Mannings, and yer ought ter know it. She'd stand between yez if yer was that taken with him."

"She don't mind buyin' from 'em!" Kat retorted, tugging her fingers through her hair the way she did when she was angry. She hadn't bothered to put it up or even to brush it; it would be all mops and brooms by morning. "They're decent people. What's she got in it for them?"

Ag looked at Kat as if she had three heads. "Ye'll sit there as cute as a rat and tell me yer don't know why," she said.

It was nearly dawn; they could see each other's faces clearly. Kat shook her head. "If yer mean that business about them bein' Indian," she said, "sure, and isn't that pure blather? There's none of us in the whole of the island that's just one thing. Some is part Eskimo, I've heard. And we know Daddy was Irish, but Mom's never said much about her people. Have yer even wondered on that? It's all a great lob anyways. People is people."

She thought about it for a moment. "And yerself spendin' the night with an English lad who ain't even Catholic!" she scolded Ag. "Yer think she'll be after likin' that arrangement? Ye'd better think on that a bit once he's gone. By the by, does he know where they're after sendin' him?"

Ag looked thoughtfully at her small, pretty hands in the gray light. "Belfast," she said.

Ag's English lad would stay in St. John's for another two weeks, but it would not be as easy for them to be together as she had thought. It would have been different if it hadn't been fall. In the spring and summer, she and Kat—now that they were beyond school age—spent most of their days down by the flakes with the other girls, salting the fresh-caught cod and turning them in the sun so that they would dry evenly. It was messy and tedious work, lightened only by the constant chatter among the young women, and the occasional flirtatious talk with the unmarried men when they came in off the boats of an evening. The winter months were more subdued because of the cold, spent mostly indoors cooking and baking and cleaning, and engaged in the seemingly endless knitting of mittens and scarves and sweaters that passed as cottage industry in the outports. Handmade items brought a good price in St. John's or over the water, but most of it went to the middleman. Ag had learned piano at the convent school and showed enough aptitude to take in a handful of pupils, and this lightened the dreary, dark afternoons.

In the spring or summer, it would have been simplicity itself for Freddie to hang about the flakes to talk to her, and never mind the gossip. After all, there was no accounting for the young people when they stopped to have their midday meal. He might even have stopped by the house in winter under the pretext of learning the piano, especially since the old woman often napped when Ag had a pupil. But September was harvest time; time to take in the potatoes and turnips and other hardy varieties that grew in the tiny, thin-soiled kitchen garden. It was the only time of the year the old woman ventured outdoors for prolonged periods—the summer sun being too strong and the rest of the year too damp for her arthritis—to keep an eye on her daughters as they grubbed up tubers and lopped off beet tops and wasted nothing. Ag was trapped, and she knew it.

So while Kat, who was dutiful and methodical and could think while she worked, scrounged away at the dusty potatoes and dreamed up excuses to get to the store at Torbay on her own, Ag, who had lately become dreamy and inept and prone to dropping dishes, leaned against the makeshift wooden fence and plotted a way to get to Freddie, until even her daft old mother began to grow suspicious.

"Agatha Mary!" she shrilled so loud that Ag dropped the

trowel on her foot and nearly knocked over the part of the fence she'd been leaning against. "Sure, yer after starin' down that road so long it's a wonder yer don't grow roots. What's ailin' yer?"

"Not a thing, Mom," Ag snapped back, scrambling for the trowel, suddenly attentive. The answer had come to her in a flash; if she could only get word to Freddie. "I'm after gettin' a crick in me back from bendin', is all. I didn't know I was starin', sure."

She gave Kat a warning look, and Kat shrugged as if to say it wasn't any of her business. Ag never considered her advice worthwhile anyway.

It was Friday at supper that Ag made her move.

"I'll be after stayin' the weekend with Maudie Brown's people," she announced, clearing away the dishes. She waited for her mother to open her toothless mouth in objection before she went on. Kat kept her eyes on her plate. "Sure, she's still in the dumps over losin' the baby, and her husband's after goin' up to St. John's for the week to get the dog sledge fixed. There'll be none in the house but her old mother, and her too weak to climb the stairs but once in a day. Maudie's asked me to come stay with her; it'll be after cheerin' her up. We can while away the time gabbin', sure, and she'll feel that much better."

The old woman squinted at her elder daughter. Ag was not noted for her acts of charity. She seldom mixed with her school chums once they got married, once their lives took on the tinge of tragedy that was indigenous to outport life. What was Ag up to?

"Yer'd stay at Maudie's house, then?" the old woman ruminated. "And sleep with her, in her bed—her husband bein' gone, I mean—and there bein' only the one bed in that end of the house to my way of knowin'. That's it, then? Yer'd stay the night?"

"Aye," Ag said without the slightest flutter. Kat seemed to be having trouble swallowing, but nobody was paying atten-

tion to her. The old woman began mumbling something about
needing Ag around the house.

"Sure, we're after takin' all the vegetables in this week,"
Ag said impatiently. "Ye've Kat to look after yer, and I'll
only be across the yard ter the next house. It's only the two
days. If yer'll not let me emigrate, yer might give me a taste
of the free air now and again."

It was a sore point, and a weapon Ag had used with im-
punity for nearly a year since her mother had refused to let
her move to the States, and all her uncles had gathered around
the kitchen table to offer her solid reasons why she must stay
and be a comfort to her old mother in her declining years.
Ag had succumbed then, but not without gaining leverage,
which she never hesitated to use. She and her mother both
knew that the issue would come up again, when Ag was
older, and that this time Ag would win.

"If yer mind's set on it, go then," her mother grumbled.
"But sure, I can't see the point of it. A fat lot of comfort
yer'd be to a woman's lost a bairn. Yer as cold as a mackerel,
Agatha Mary. Ye've not a drop of real blood in yer veins."

"That remains to be seen," Ag said grandly, tossing her
head and setting the plates down in the washtub a little too
forcefully. An observant eye might have seen that her small,
perfect hands trembled as she picked the pieces of a broken
plate out from the bottom. "Jesus and Mary!" she sighed.
"Well, at least yez'll have no broken china while I'm gone.
I'll be after packin' now, and I'll see yez in church of a Sunday, can I get poor Maudie to come."

Kat sat on her own bed, watching silently as Ag threw
some clothes into a big knitted shawl. Nobody in Harmony
Bay owned a suitcase; when one went away for more than
overnight it was usually forever. Kat was weighing the seriousness of the sin of complicity, though if she'd wanted to
tell the old woman what Ag was about she wouldn't have
known how. She knew Ag had wooed Maudie into her confidence—Ag could be very persuasive—and Maudie, in spite

of her recent sorrow over her stillborn child, could appreciate
the joy of a man and a woman, and would try to help. It was
even rumored around the outport that she and her Georgie
had done some playing about before their own marriage, and
that it was God's punishment that the baby had died. Whatever was the case, Ag had plotted her way most carefully.
Somehow she'd managed to get word to Freddie in St. John's,
though any boatman transporting a letter from Ag to the
garrison would surely have told the old woman. Kat was
miserable. How was Ag clever enough to arrange the impossible when she hadn't figured out, in nearly a week, how
to get as far as Torbay to see Red?

So she said nothing, watching with some embarrassment as
Ag paid particular attention to the condition of her best
underwear before she folded it and placed it in the shawl.
Ag's conscience was as clear as her intent.

Ag even managed to get out of doing the dishes, using the
excuse that she'd have to hurry over to Maudie's before the
sun went down completely. Kat heard the door slam as she
bent over the washtub, almost wanting to tell on her sister
for the sake of the dirty dishes. But to call someone back
after they'd started a journey meant bad luck, she knew, and
Ag would do what she liked no matter what.

Red came home from the hospital around midnight,
amazed to find Helen and Ag still awake, talking softly in
the front parlor. The floor nurse had told him Kat's labor
would be long, and they could expect nothing to happen
overnight. He was better off at home.

"Ye've school tomorrow, Lady Jane," he said to Helen.
"Shouldn't yer be in bed?"

"I'm not tired," Helen said. The circles under her solemn
brown eyes were chronic now; it was possible she was beyond sleep. "Anyway, I was worried about Mom."

"Yer mother's comin' along fine," Red said, trying to sound

convincing. "They're after givin' her a shot of something, so she's in no danger, and no pain. Baby'll come tomorrow. Get yer to bed."

"Aunt Ag and I were talking," Helen objected, bordering as close as she could on actual rebellion. "I want to stay up longer."

Red sighed. Whatever else might be said, *he* was tired, too tired to argue with his daughter, who was fifteen after all, an age beyond which a woman couldn't be convinced that anything was for her own good.

"Suit yerselves." He shrugged. "But ye'll clear out of here, anyways. I've got the sofa this night."

Everything had been arranged in frantic exchanges while they waited for the cab to come for Kat that morning. Alistair and Danny would sleep in the children's bedroom, Helen and Ag would share the big bed in the "master" bedroom, and Red would have the parlor. Since he'd stopped in the bathroom on his way down the hall, there was nothing preventing him from taking off his trousers and rolling himself up in a blanket at that very moment. As he sat on the edge of the couch and bent to untie his shoelaces, Ag took her feet down from the coffee table, picked up her shoes, and made her exit.

"Come along, then, Helen Mary," she said. "We'll talk inside."

Later, Ag stood before the mirror in the bedroom, in her flannel pajamas—she didn't believe in nightgowns—putting her hair up in vicious metal curlers that preserved the permanent wave, and wondered what was taking her niece so long in the bathroom. Putting a net over her hair, Ag went to look for her, and found her standing in the open doorway of her dead grandmother's room.

Helen's hand was poised on the light switch, as if she'd forgotten to remove it, so entranced did she seem with what she saw in the room. The room was virtually unchanged, except for the stripped-down mattress—Red's handiwork. It looked exactly the same as it had all the sixteen years the old woman had inhabited it: a mess of holy pictures and devotional prayers, ugly little knickknacks crowded onto dusty hand-crocheted doilies, faded rose-covered wallpaper, blinds and curtains drawn tightly to create an aura of perpetual gloom. There was the smell of her, too—camphor and Sloan's Liniment, Dr. Brown's Herbal Salve—and the rotten-sweet smell of death. There was a pall of dust over everything. The place was a tomb. Repulsive. When Ag put her arm around Helen's shoulder, the girl shuddered.

"What's the matter, then?" Ag whispered, giving her a squeeze. "She's gone."

"I know," Helen whispered back. "It's just that I was thinking—this is supposed to be my room now. But it's so ugly I don't think I want it!"

Ag glanced at her sideways in the light from the dusty overhead fixture. There was something she'd been meaning to ask the girl, but she was afraid of putting ideas into her head that had not been there before. However, Ag was not one to pull her punches.

"You're not terrible upset that she's croaked, then, are you?" she asked. "It's my guess you'd be almost glad."

"I am!" Helen blurted out before she could think. She turned to face her aunt in a flurry of anguish. "Maybe it is a sin, but she was a horrible, ugly old nag, and she took all her misery out on Mom. It's not so much for me I'm glad but because she can't bother Mom anymore."

Ag nodded, pleased with the response. "Aye," she said. "Only sometimes you're too honest for your own good, you know that?"

The girl looked embarrassed at this, and Ag tried to cheer her. "Come on," she said, giving Helen's shoulder a final squeeze. "Tomorrow you and me can pass the time while we wait to hear about your mother in clearing out this place."

Helen looked alarmed.

"We can't expect your mother to come home with a new

baby and have to worry about this shambles," Ag pointed out.
"Sure, if it's to be your room, you ought to help clean it.
And it'll do your mother no good to have the old nag's
clothes and such about. Morbid memories are bad for the
baby."

They had to pass through the room where the two boys
snored to different rhythms in their beds. Alistair lay, as always, hunched in a ball, defensive against the bombs that still
dropped in his dreams, twitching slightly. Ag stopped for a
moment to smooth his forehead and adjust the blanket around
his shoulders.

"She was an orphan, you know," Ag told her niece as they
lay in the dark, curled away from each other in the double bed,
awaiting sleep. "Your grandmother, I mean. Did you know
that?"

Helen popped her head up from the pillow and stared into
the darkness. "I never knew that!" she said, shocked.

"Aye." Ag sighed, resettling her head so that the curlers
wouldn't pinch so. "Maybe that's why she was always so
sour. Sure, it wasn't old age. She was always that way."

Helen was wide-awake now. "Tell me about it!" she
pleaded.

"Some other time, sure," Ag murmured, dozing. "I don't
know why I brought it up. I'm plain wore out tonight, thank
you."

It was deathly silent in the house with Ag away, Kat
thought. Ag had never been gone overnight since her sister
could remember, and while she always talked about the things
only she was interested in, and interrupted anyone else, there
was a great deal of life missing without her there to chatter
and fuss and pick out little melodies on the piano. Kat sighed
for about the fifteenth time, put down the dress-pattern catalogue she'd been poring over, gave the fire a useless poke, listened to the endless creak of her mother's rocker in the

semi-gloom for as long as she could stand it. She saw that her mother was staring at her.

"Ye've a fair idear where yer sister's at, don'tcher?" the old woman said so suddenly that Kat jumped, though their eyes had met nearly a minute ago.

"Sure, she's after tellin' yer, Mom. She's gone ter Maudie's," Kat said a little too sharply. "Honestly, yer gettin' wonderful forgetful lately."

"Aye." The old woman nodded knowingly. "Keep on with it, if yer like. I'm sure she's after lettin' on to yer, and that makes yer as guilty as herself fer lyin'. Sure, it ain't like yer to lie, and I could scrawb it outta yer if I wanted ter, but I'm thinkin' I'd be better off not knowin'."

Kat did not answer, but had to look away from her mother's piercing eyes. Her mother began to moan just then, out of nowhere, frightening Kat out of her skin.

"Sure, and what's wrong with the girl?" the old woman wailed, her rocking chair becoming more frenetic with her grief. "Didn't I raise her right? Was it bein' without a father made her go bad? Don't she realize there's nothing in this world as pitiful as an unwanted child?"

Kat watched her mother orchestrating her little scene for its audience of one. She wanted to shout, wanted to scream that a young girl growing up needed approval and assurance and the warmth of a mother's arms around her, needed love. How many nightmares and nameless fears had she confided to Ag because their mother belittled them for falling prey to such nonsense, and never offered a word of comfort? Ag had been Kat's surrogate mother for all these years, but to whom could Ag turn for the love she craved? Was it any wonder that Ag was cold and bitter and rough as the back of a dogfish? Kat wanted to shout, but couldn't because her tongue was stuck to the roof of her mouth and her words would have done no good anyway.

"Don't she realize," the old woman went on—unaware of the anguish on her younger daughter's face, recognizing her only as a pair of ears to absorb another variation on the endless tale of woe—"don't she realize what she's after lettin' herself in for? Supposin' she does get a child, does she know what she's lettin' it in for? Yer don't have to name the man— I can tell yer he'd not lift a finger for her once she gets that way, and then what'll she be after doin'? Men are all of a piece, exceptin' yer father, God rest his soul! But as for the child, she only needs to ask me. I'd tell her what becomes of a child nobody wants."

Kat stared at her mother in amazement. What was she talking about? Had she finally gone completely daft?

"Aye," her mother said, braking the rocker suddenly, seeming to think her daughter had understood her. "Have yer ever wondered why I'm after tellin' the two of yez over and over about yer father's people and never a word on me own? Yer know all about the Blakes—how they was barons to the west of the Shannon till the British drove them out; how yer father's father came here at the time of the Famine; how he started with nothin' and ended bein' one of the wealthiest men in the outport. Have yer ever wondered why all of the uncles and cousins is on yer father's side and yer never hear tell of anyone from mine? Have yer ever heard me breathe a word about me own?"

Kat forced herself to speak. "Well, why didn't yer, then? Sure, Ag and me was after wonderin', but we didn't know how to ask yer."

The rocker was motionless now. "It's because I have no people," the old woman said histrionically, gripping the arms of the chair. "It's because I was a few days old and left on the steps of the Portuguese mission church in St. John's, wrapped in a dirty old blanket and the cord still on me. No one ever come ter claim me. I grew up with the nuns in the foundlin' home!"

It would have seemed natural, instinctive, for Kat to jump up from her place on the hearth rug and throw her arms around her mother, but she did not. She had been taught differently.

"I never knew," she said solemnly, her voice breaking a little.

"Aye," the old woman replied, pleased that she could show one of her offspring, at least, how cruel life had been to her. Her voice sounded hollow, as if she were far away, closer to the relived past than the living present. "We worked, the lot of us. They had no books for to teach us anything, so all we did was work. We worked at the convent until we was old enough, then we was farmed out to the rich ladies in St. John's. We was on our knees at mass of a mornin' before the sun was up, and on our knees scrubbin' the rest of the day. When I was twenty I was sent for to cook for a merchant's wife—the first time in me life I remember gettin' up off me knees—and yer father, God rest him, was after steppin' in one day with a load of lobsters he was wantin' ter sell. He and the merchant was after talkin' prices for so long it got ter be noon, and the wife was after sendin' him ter the kitchen for somethin' ter eat. He was at the level with the help, sure, and had ter eat in the kitchen. I was so shy from bein' treated like a stick of furniture all me life I didn't know how ter begin ter talk to him. But he talked ter me, and we got started. He was twenty-two then—as handsome a man as ever held an oar—and just after comin' inter his father's property. He bought me from the lady of the house with a five-dollar gold piece, and we was married that same afternoon."

Kat blew her nose as quietly as she could, preserving the respectful silence she felt this narrative deserved. But her mother was not finished yet.

"He gave me the only home I ever knew, God rest his soul! I don't know why I'm after tellin' yer this now, for it's in the past and can't be made over, but maybe it's so one of me daughters at least will keep in her mind what it is that happens ter unwanted babies."

Toward the middle of the morning of her second day of labor, the nature of Kat's contractions changed. She was still heavily sedated—it was the only way with high-risk patients in those days—still emitting those pitiful high-pitched sounds, half-sigh, half-shriek, that would fray her vocal chords and leave her hoarse for a week after. But her contractions became stronger, as if her uterus, bored with the manner in which things were being handled from the outside, had made a decision on its own. Her labor began to resemble normal transition, with a hint that the outcome might be a healthy, living baby. The doctor, groping for a fetal heartbeat between the thundering contractions, finally took the stethoscope out of his ears.

"We may actually get a baby out of all this," he told the nurse dryly. "How long are the contractions?"

The nurse looked at her clipboard, where she'd been keeping some sort of record for about half an hour. "Fifty seconds' duration, three minutes apart," she said.

"Dilatation?"

"Five centimeters."

"Son of a gun!" the doctor exclaimed, as if he were doing all the work. "That's one more than last night." He shook his head. "Christ, these Irish Catholics! If she makes it through this alive, it's going to be her last."

Loretta had called for Helen at seven-thirty that morning, as she always did on school mornings. They walked down to the subway together, the newly risen sun spinning long, thin shadows out in front of them on the sidewalk.

"Whole neighborhood heard about your mom," Loretta said, a fresh piece of gum busying her lower jaw even at this hour. "Jeepers, is that strange!"

"Is what strange?" Helen asked vaguely, her head buzzing from lack of sleep.

"Her going into labor the same day as her mother's funeral," Loretta explained, as if anyone would know what she was talking about. "Don'tcha see, my mother says dreams always mean the opposite of what you dream—like dreaming of a wedding means death, and dreaming of a funeral means good luck. So she figures if you actually go to a funeral, particularly someone's in your own family, then it's double lucky if you go into labor the same day. Like life leading out of death, or something like that. See?"

"I don't know," Helen murmured, getting a sudden chill. She'd been half-listening to her gabby friend, more concerned with the fact that they would pass near the maternity wing of the hospital on their way to the subway. She tried not to think of what was happening to her mother somewhere inside those dirty brick walls. "They sent Pop home from the hospital last night. I don't think she's going to have that baby."

Loretta's eyes widened. "You think it's gonna die? Or that your mom'll maybe—Jesus!" She clapped a freckled hand over her missing incisors. "Cripes, was that a dumb thing to say! I didn't mean it—swear to God, cross my heart and hope to die!"

"That's all right," Helen said without emotion, fishing in her pocket for a subway token. She was halfway down the steps when she realized Loretta was not beside her. Helen stopped and looked up at her friend, still poised on the top step, looking taller than usual from this perspective.

"Cross my heart and hope to die!" Loretta was shouting, gesticulating toward the blue and indifferent sky. "Holy Mary, Mother of God, if any part of what I just said comes true, may my tongue turn black and burn in Purgatory for a thousand years!"

"Come on, will you?" Helen demanded, storming up the steps and grabbing her friend by the elbow. Loretta's sudden display of religiosity embarrassed her.

In the now-empty railroad flat, Ag was undergoing a disquieting experience. She had gotten the boys up and ready for school, and was startled to find her brother-in-law awake and smoking his pipe in the kitchen. He'd apparently been up for some time, though he'd neither washed nor shaved, nor had he made any effort at breakfast. Mildly disgusted, but not surprised at what she considered typical male behavior, Ag clattered around the unfamiliar kitchen searching for the right pots and pans, evidencing her disapproval in facial expression if not in words.

Red ignored her, continuing to sit and smoke until she put his breakfast in front of him. He ate in silence, the only sign of life other than the movement of his jaws being the time he cracked Danny on the knuckles with the back of his knife for some infringement of decorum. When the boys finally rattled out the front door, Red got up from the table with a grunt and shambled down the hall to shave.

Ag put down her fork just then—she was only picking at the eggs anyway—and realized what it was that was bothering her. She had never before in her forty-two years seen a man sit down to breakfast unshaven. She supposed her father might have, but she'd been six when he was lost at sea and she couldn't trust her memory. All of the various uncles and male cousins who drifted in and out of the house at Harmony Bay throughout her girlhood had always appeared at the table scrubbed till their wind-reddened faces shone—chins shaved, mustaches trimmed. And Freddie . . . well, she hadn't known Freddie long enough to discover his morning habits, but she was certain he would never have come to breakfast in yesterday's beard.

With a queer feeling in her stomach, Ag threw away the rest of her eggs, though it pinched her thrifty soul to do so, and began to wash the dishes. She was drying up when Red appeared in the doorway.

"I'll be goin' back to the hospital," he said solemnly. "If I get any word I'll give a call upstairs and the landlord'll be after lettin' yer know."

"Aye," Ag said stoically. "I'll have to ask him for the use of the phone to let my employer know I'm out for the day. Sure, it's a shame you can't spare the money to put in your own phone."

Red gave her a cold look. How he spent or didn't spend his

money was his business. Any other day he might have taken the trouble to inform Ag of this in no uncertain terms, but he didn't have the stamina for it this morning.

"I'll be on my way," he grunted, and that was that.

It was later, after she'd made the beds and dusted a bit and gone upstairs to use the landlord's phone and leave a nickel on the table for the courtesy, that the queer feeling came over Ag again. She'd decided to spend the greater part of the day sorting through her mother's belongings, throwing out the rusty old dresses and elbowless sweaters, saving the heirlooms to be divided up later. There had been no question of her illiterate old mother's leaving a will; the few pieces of jewelry and religious articles that were worth anything would simply be divided evenly between the two sisters. Ag was for giving her share to Kat or Helen—they'd earned it, she figured—and she wanted no particular reminders of her mother for herself. That was why she'd wanted Helen to stay and help her: to let the girl choose whatever trinkets she might want for herself, and to witness the fact that Ag took nothing, so there'd be no possibility of bickering later. But Helen said she wanted to go back to school that morning. Midterms were coming up soon, and she'd been trapped inside the apartment for too long already.

So the task was Ag's alone, and she made quick work of the clutter in the closet and the bureau, but when she got to the jewelry she lost her momentum. In the midst of a tangle of broken rosaries and tarnished pearl necklaces in a rosewood box on the bureau, she found her baby ring. She and Kat, in honor of their surviving the fatal first year of life, had been given tiny rings by their relatively affluent father—small circles of ten-carat gold with the smallest chip of a gemstone: opal for Kat, who was born in October, and garnet for Ag, who was a January baby. The stone was missing from Ag's ring, the result of some mad clambering over the rocks near the harbor when she was five and the ring could hardly be squeezed onto her chubby, growing finger. She'd been twisting it to lessen the discomfort when it slipped out of her hand and ricocheted off a large stone, nearly disappearing into a crevice. She'd scrambled to retrieve the ring, but the gemstone was gone forever.

When their fingers had grown too big for the rings, Ag and Kat had given them back to their mother for safekeeping. Kat had asked to have hers back when Helen was born, also in October, and the girl wore it still on a small gold chain with the crucifix she'd gotten for her First Communion. Ag had forgotten about her ring until this moment, and was shocked to find that her mother still had it. She'd expected the vengeful old crow to destroy it or give it away, as she had with everything else Ag left behind when she emigrated to the States.

But here was the ring, the little hole that had held the garnet looking greenish and dirty the way cheap gold always did after a number of years; and Ag sat in a heap on the stripped-down mattress and began to sob, because the thought of that tiny chip of blood-red gemstone glinting secretly in the rock crevice for nearly forty years, assuming some crazy gull hadn't found it and swallowed it and shit it out over the open sea, brought back with a rush the past she'd been running from since she was eighteen and she spent the night with Freddie. Freddie, who went to Belfast that very week and who never. . . .

Ag's rebellious weekend actually did Kat a good turn, for while nobody acknowledged aloud what Ag had really been up to those two days, a cold and ominous silence ensued between Ag and her mother, which, though neither knew it at the time, would never really be broken. The upshot of it was that when the old woman wanted to go to Torbay she no longer took Ag with her, but Kat.

Kat was ecstatic, though she hid her joy well beneath her usual placid nature and her wariness of the state of siege between her mother and her sister. She spent half the night before, and all of the morning, practicing what she would say when she saw Red Manning.

As it turned out, they barely got a chance to look at each other at first, for both understood without saying as much that secrecy was of the essence. Kat's eyes adjusted quickly to the dim light inside the low-ceilinged store—actually an extension of the rambling frame house that sheltered the prolific Manning clan—and she searched among the stacks of boxes and bolts of dress goods for a glimpse of flame-red hair. Her mother, in a more crabbed state of mind than usual, tugged impatiently at her arm.

"Mary Kathleen—sure, whatever are yer about?" she whined. "I'm after wantin' ter look at the curtain stuffs. Stand still, would yer, and quit starin' about like a calf! What's ailin' yer, sure?"

Kat had to stand by her mother's side like a child, though she continued to stare about the place, hoping. What if he weren't here today? He'd told her he worked on the boats during the summer and parts of the fall, had shown her the new scars on his first two fingers from the towlines. She'd never realized before how painful they must be. All the men she knew had been fishing so long that the scars were ancient, a tougher variety of leather than the rest of their skins, but the sight of the fresh cuts on his unmarked hands—so recent they'd been oozing blood the night they'd talked on the pier—had filled Kat with pity. And now, what would she do if he were out on the boats today, after she'd walked the three miles to the store at her mother's snail-slow pace? Could she go back home without seeing him?

But he was there, in the back by the bait tubs, jawing with some old-timers and doling out bloody chunks of cut-up herring into their bait pails. By some miracle he glanced in Kat's direction just then, and she caught the glimmer in his eyes even at that distance. She danced impatiently from one foot to the other while her mother seemed bent on examining every length of cloth on the entire counter. She watched as Red finished his business at the bait barrel, wiped his hands on his disreputable apron, and started toward the front of the store where she was.

"Ho, Jim boy, there's the flour wants unpackin'!" came the voice of a crow from behind a stack of tinned goods, and old Ed Manning, skinniest shopkeeper on the Atlantic Coast, stood with his hands on his hips to be certain he got the last ounce of work out of his only-begotten son.

"Aye, Dad. In a minute, then."

"One minute's as good as another!" the old man croaked. "Get on it, lad, and don't be after rilin' me!"

Kat's cheeks burned with the indignation she knew Red felt but could not speak. She might almost have said something sharp to the old man herself, shy as she was, if her mother hadn't chosen that moment to poke her in the ribs.

"Sure, where's yer manners?" the old woman hissed. "Say yer good mornin' ter Mr. Manning, and say it right!"

Kat stood out in the aisle and self-consciously bobbed in the little half-curtsy the nuns had taught her at school. "Good morning to yer, Mr. Manning," she said and smiled, though she loathed his very guts for the way he treated his son.

His wizened, stingy face broke into a dry grin. "And good mornin', yerself, young miss. And to yer gracious mother," he said with a nod, and a brief smile twisted old Helen's mouth like a tic. "Can I get aught for yez, ladies?"

"We're after lookin' about a bit, thank yer," Kat's mother snapped, and moved away from him down the aisle. She considered herself a step above the Mannings. Red hair or no, there was Indian blood in them for a fact, and if she had had her choice of buying anywhere else. . . .

Kat knew her mother's opinion about the Mannings as well as she knew her own name, but she wasn't thinking about that now, was thinking of nothing at all except that if she managed to be dragged out of the store without a chance to talk to Red she would simply explode. She watched him heaving fifty-pound sacks of flour onto the shelves near the confectionery and had an idea.

"Will yer twack about here the entire morning?" she asked

her mother impatiently. "Sure, I'm not a child, yer know. Yer can trust me to walk about without breakin' things."

"What're yer after?" The old woman squinted at her. "Ye've ants in yer pants this day, for a fact."

"I'm fancyin' some candy," Kat said, knowing her mother's weakness—like her own—for anything sweet. "I'll be after pickin' it out now for to save some time."

"All right," her mother said, still vaguely suspicious. "Get me some of that licorice, then. Sure, I can't chew 'em with me teeth gone, but they're after soothin' me throat in the winter."

Kat bolted toward the confectionery with the eagerness of a child. When she was certain her mother's attention was elsewhere, she cleared her throat and rapped on the counter.

"Mr. Manning, sir," she addressed Red's back in a timorous voice. "I'll be after purchasin' some sweets, if yer please."

"Be right with yer, miss." He grinned, wiping his floured hands on the selfsame dirty apron he had worn at the bait barrel and playing along with her. He rattled the lids of some of the apothecary jars that held the peppermint drops, molasses taffy, licorice allsorts, and horehound sticks. "What's yer pleasure?"

"Quarter-pound of the licorice, and maybe a chunk of the rock candy—the dark stuff, thank yer," Kat said airily, businesslike. She couldn't maintain it long for watching his eyes dance. She lowered her voice. "Sure, herself yonder's got me fair distracted! I was wantin' to talk with yer."

"Well, so yer are," Red said complacently, doling the candy into the scale with a small metal scoop. He was better than she at masking his true feelings. Surrounded at home by eleven women from ten to fifty, he had to be. "Pour out yer heart to me, lass. I'm all ears."

"It's that—well—" Kat groped. How could she tell him what she truly felt without sounding forward? "It's to tell yer how much I was after enjoyin' yer company this Saturday past, and if ye've ever a need to pass through our way again—"

She couldn't continue. This line of talk was not only forward and downright brazen, but it put her in grave risk of telling him too much before she knew his true feelings. For all she knew he didn't care a herring about her. However he felt about her, Kat did not feel strong enough at the moment, what with worrying over Ag and keeping her mother pacified, to know about it. More emotional turmoil had been packed into the past few weeks than in all the sixteen years that preceded them. That was why she was halfway home before Kat fully understood what Red said to her.

"As a matter of fact," he began, wrapping the candy in paper parcels and making change, "I've been workin' out a bit of a business enterprise up your way. I'm after plannin' a delivery service out of the store—bringin' things to folks as can't get here regular. I've got me a boat for as long as the weather holds, and who knows but I'll buy into a dog team for the winter, if the idear turns a profit. It's anything to get out of the store and away from himself now and again. And I'm thinkin' a cup of hot tea or a home-cooked meal at the end of the route might make the trip that much easier."

Kat had nodded vaguely, not connecting his plans with herself in any way. She took her parcels, thanking him with dignity and as little show of emotion as she could manage. She went to join her mother, who had finally abandoned the idea of making new curtains, her arthritis being what it was, and had set about gathering canned goods and tea and a five-pound bag of sugar. When Red's plan finally penetrated Kat's beclouded brain, it was all she could do to keep from turning cartwheels in the road.

Red would be making deliveries in Harmony Bay, and he would need a place to stop and refresh himself, particularly in the winter, with it down in the minuses and ten-foot drifts about. What better excuse to hang around the kitchen and make small talk, for even a lad who was part Indian couldn't be turned away in the cold of a Newfoundland winter!

Kat was beside herself with joy for days, only stopping to

wonder from time to time if he'd thought up the idea before he met her or if it really was an excuse to see her more often.

The only damper on her mood was Ag. Ag hid her sadness over Freddie's departure remarkably well, and seemed to thrive on her mother's hostility. But as the days following her fateful weekend lengthened into a week, then two weeks, then three, a change came over her.

"I'm after missin' me friend," Ag said quietly one night when she and Kat were getting ready for bed.

Kat stopped battling the rats' nests in her hair and looked at her sister in alarm. "Are yer sure?" she asked, the hairbrush poised in mid-stroke.

Ag shrugged. "I don't know. I'm never terrible regular, but I've not been this late before."

"Mother of God!" Kat whispered, dropping the arm with the hairbrush until it hung helplessly by her side. "What'll yer do, then?"

"Sure, I don't know that either!" Ag snapped. "Did I think about that three weeks ago, I might not be in such a mess!"

Kat searched desperately for something comforting to say; there wasn't much. "Will Freddie be after writin' to yer?" she asked.

"He said he would." Ag's voice was muted. She stood by the window in her nightgown, searching for some stars in a cloud-studded sky. The first snow of the season would fall that night. "He'll be sendin' them to Maudie's house, care of her, but with another envelope inside for me. Providin' he gets to it. Sure, it's been three weeks! And a fat lot of good *that's* gone ter do me anyways!"

She flapped the curtain shut and threw herself into bed. "Sure, I wisht I was dead!" she sobbed. "I wisht I'd die in me sleep this night and have done with it!"

Kat looked down at her hands and said nothing.

"And it's all her fault!" Ag raged suddenly, shaking her fist at the wall that separated their room from their mother's.

"Sure, if she'd given me my freedom I'd've had no need for this!"

Kat opened her mouth to offer the opinion that some of Ag's predicament might be her own responsibility, but decided against it. Her sister had already rolled over to face the wall, and she wouldn't listen anyway. Feeling suddenly selfish for her own happiness, Kat got up to put out the kerosene lamp. As she lay in her bed in the dark, she thought she could hear Ag crying.

But Ag was not pregnant. Her bleeding started three days later, and two days after that she got a letter from Freddie.

Freddie was not one for writing letters. The one he sent, written on one side of a sheet of plain paper, consisted principally of an address where Ag might write to him and a handful of terse sentences on what it was like to do a night patrol in dirty old Belfast, still in limbo after its civil war. There were rumors, he said in closing, that all British troops would be pulled out by Christmas, the better to let the Irish finish the job themselves. The note was signed, "In fond remembrance, Your Freddie."

In fond remembrance, Your Freddie. Ag folded the letter carefully and put it under her pillow. She reread it every night before she went to sleep, even though there was scarcely anything to it. For now, it was all she had.

On the eve of the final troop withdrawal, Freddie and another sentry were picked off from a rooftop by an IRA sniper. The other soldier got by with a leg wound. Freddie caught it in the back of the skull, and was dead before he hit the cobblestones.

Ag did not know for several months. She wrote to Freddie the same day she got his note—an impassioned three-page epistle reminding him how much she loved him and outlining their plans for the future. When he did not answer, she chalked it up to the fact that men didn't care to write letters, and that Freddie had more important things on his mind just now. She had no way of knowing that her first letter and several subsequent ones, which she gave directly into the hands of the ferry pilot who brought the mail to St. John's, were intercepted and given to her mother. The pilot was a Harmony Bay man, who had know the Blakes all his life. What if his own daughter had gone bad? he would have said if anyone had accused him of tampering with the mails. It was the least he could do to let Ag's mother know.

Ag's mother kept the four letters her daughter wrote over a period of several months. She did not open them at first; only tucked them into a drawer and pondered what she ought to do. When her curiosity became unbearable, she thought of having Kat read them to her, but knew she could not trust Kat to keep silent. Determined, old Helen took one of her nephews—a lad of fourteen who had gone to the Christian Brothers' school at St. John's—into her confidence. The outpouring of emotion that issued from those pages under the boy's hesitant and embarrassed reading sent the old woman into an absolute rage.

"Was there ever a worse evil daughter born inter this world!" she shrilled, dismissing the red-faced boy by pressing a coin into his hand and pushing him out the door. "Mother of God, somethin's got ter be done!"

Whatever she had in store for Ag was nothing compared to what actually happened. That very afternoon Red Manning's creaking new dogsled, leased on time payments from a dealer in St. John's, arrived in Harmony Bay with deliveries from his father's store and that month's mail. It was January; the harbor had been frozen over for three months. Every boat from L'Anse au Meadow to Halifax was moored for the winter. Dogsled was the only means of transportation this far north of the railroad, which couldn't get through anyway if the snow was too deep. Red Manning's appearance was doubly welcome because he brought the mail.

Had he known what was contained in the official-looking

envelope with the British army letterhead that he dropped at
Maudie Brown's house that afternoon, he might not have been
so eager to deliver it. As it was, his mind was on other things,
particularly his last stop, at the Blakes', where Kat would
have dinner for him. Already the sky was lowering; it might
snow again, meaning he'd have to stay the night, tucked onto
two kitchen chairs with his feet nearest the stove, carefully
segregated from the women of the house. The prospect pleased
him. He did not know he would be the unwilling witness to
a scene between Ag and her mother that would be the principal topic of conversation in the outport for the rest of the
winter.

Red left the letter in the custody of Maudie's purblind
mother, who brought it to the kitchen where her daughter
was baking. Maudie's life had brightened somewhat since Ag's
fateful weekend. Inspired by the pure and uncomplicated love
Ag had for Freddie—at least as she interpreted it—Maudie
had gotten pregnant again, and was already three months gone.
This one would live, she promised herself, and there would be
more to follow. When her mother handed her the letter, she
wiped the bread dough off her hands and frowned at it. What
on earth would the British army want with her? she wondered,
never connecting it with Freddie and Ag. Her Georgie had
served in the Great War as a volunteer, since Newfoundlanders were not citizens of Canada and did not have to serve. Was
it something to do with that? Bewildered, Maudie tore the envelope open and went white as a sheet.

"I've got ter go ter Ag's!" she shouted to her mother, who
was nearly deaf along with everything else. Ignoring admoni-
tions about catching her death of cold and harming the baby,
she slipped into her sealskin boots, threw a blanket around
her shoulders, and waded across the well-trodden snow to
the Blakes'.

She went around to the parlor entrance, knowing they ate
supper early and would be in the kitchen, and wanting to be
certain she could speak to Ag with some measure of privacy.

She was immensely relieved when Ag herself answered the door.

"Jesus and Mary!" Ag exclaimed, pulling Maudie in from the cold by the elbow. "Are yer courtin' disaster, then, Maudie Brown? What brings yer here in such a state?" When Maudie could not answer, Ag took her by the shoulders and began to whisper. "Is it a letter, then? Have yer got a letter from himself?"

Maudie shook her head, swallowing hard to gather her courage. "It's about him, then. Only it's—Mother of God—it's from the army itself—they've wrote ter tell yer—oh, I can't say it, Ag! I can't!"

"Jesus and Mary!" Ag whispered. She wanted to scream but couldn't; wanted to rend the air with the loudest sound to echo off the rock cliffs since the British guns had driven out the French in 1762. But she couldn't, because every living soul in Harmony Bay would be at the door in minutes wanting an explanation. "Jesus and Mary!" she said again, even more softly. "As if I wasn't after knowin' that anything I ever wanted in this world would be taken from me! Everything!"

"If there's aught I could do for yer—" Maudie began, anxiety itself.

"Not a blessed thing!" Ag shook her head, her second skin of arrogance and superiority tightening around her. "Only get yer home out of the cold before yer harm this baby too. Go on!"

She pushed Maudie unceremoniously out into the snow and slammed the door. Then she sat in her mother's rocker and slowly read over the letter she'd snatched from Maudie's hand. She finished it the third time just as her mother shuffled in from the kitchen, wondering what could be keeping Ag. She and Kat had been busy greeting Red, who had arrived in the kitchen while Maudie was in the act of reading the letter in her own house, and there had been much banter and laughter while he took off his coat and boots and helped them unload the groceries he'd brought on the sled. They'd lost track of Ag all this time.

"Who was it after knockin', then?" the old woman demanded, wondering who'd have the brass to come into her house and leave without so much as speaking to her. The rest of what she'd planned to say was cut off in mid-breath by Ag's scream, bubbling up in her throat like vomit, and needing to be let out.

Ag screamed. Then she screamed again. Before she found breath enough for the third scream, Kat and Red had rushed in from the kitchen to restrain her. Both of them had a fair idea what Ag was screaming about.

Between sobs, Ag told them about the letter, while they held her down in the rocker, Kat on one side and Red on the other, to be certain she wouldn't harm herself. Only in grief could a girl of her background let her true feelings out of the dark corridors where they were usually kept hidden by convention, ethnic stoicism, the Church, and what-will-the-neighbors-say. Local lore was sprinkled with tales of young women hurling themselves into the sea to be with a husband or sweetheart who had drowned. Ag had to be restrained in any case.

"If he'd only—got through the—the last day!" she sobbed, clutching her hair at the temples as if to tear the images of his death out of her brain. "He'd be out in the spring—he was gone ter come back for me—he said—"

"And just as well, then!" her mother yelped, getting into the act at all costs. It was only her daughter's sins coming home to roost, after all. Vindictively, stupidly, misjudging Ag's passion, the old woman hissed at her, "A fine pair yer'd be, with all that filth yer was after puttin' in them letters! A fine gurry pair yer'd be, then!"

Ag tore free from Kat's grasp then and hurled herself at her mother. Only Red's strong arm kept the scene from bloodshed; he actually heaved Ag off her feet and back into the chair.

"Steady, then!" he soothed her, refusing to release her until her spine fell slack against the back of the chair. "It's yer old mother yer after goin' at. Can we be civilized, then, or is it a brawl yer want?"

"What letters?" Ag shrieked. "How comes she ter know about letters?" By now every light in the outport was on, and people were gathering at the Browns' and nearer to hear what was going on, and to get the lowdown from Maudie. "What kind of dirty schemin' has she been up ter?"

The old woman backed down, finally grasping the range of Ag's fury. "What letters, then?" she whimpered. "Sure, what would I know about letters when I couldn't read me own name on a paper? 'Twas yerself mentioned letters, not me!"

Such a torrent of abuse came from Ag's mouth then as had never been heard from a woman in the history of Harmony Bay. Every dirty word that every fisherman used to bully himself and his boat through a sudden gale, but that no woman ought to let on that she'd ever heard, much less used, in her lifetime, Ag leveled at the three of them, for in her blind reaction to the betrayal of one member of her family she considered them all traitors. When the poison was finally out of her system, she became quite calm. She rose from the chair with her characteristic grandness of gesture, seeming to loom taller than her five-feet-one, invincible.

"Ye'll hold me till the spring," she told her mother in a voice like stone. "But when the harbor ice breaks ye'll see the last of me!"

The rest of that winter was the worst time Kat could remember in her entire life. There might have been other times that were as bad—the year her father died, the time she got scarlet fever from God knew where and had to be quarantined and nearly died—but they were vague and undisturbing memories. The absolute silence between her mother and Ag drove her mad. While Ag stayed in her room most of the time, at first in abject silent mourning, later in a kind of forced gaiety that consisted of making stacks of things to take to Boston with her and humming snatches of songs, their mother's ap-

proach was aggressive and head-on. Ag had no need to talk
to anyone now, but her mother needed to talk that much
more.

"Would yer be so kind as to inform yer sister we'll be after
eatin' our supper as soon as she lays the table," the old woman
would say quite loudly to Kat, while Ag sat in the same room.
It happened a hundred times a day, until even placid Kat
could stand no more.

"Let me be, would yer!" she shouted one afternoon. She
had never raised her voice to her mother before. "If she must
be told, tell her yerself and leave me out of it! I'll not stand
it anymore!"

The weeks dragged into months. The harbor would be
clear by the end of April, or early May if it proved a hard
winter. Ag would stand in the kitchen flipping over the pages
of the calendar until she got to May, counting the days aloud.
It drove her mother mad.

Ag was going this time; there was nothing anyone could do
about it. She'd written to the Mulaveys, friends of the family
who'd emigrated to Boston years before, giving the letter
directly into Red's care to be certain it got to St. John's un-
molested. She trusted no one else. Mrs. Mulavey wrote back
to tell her welcome. It was all arranged. There was no meeting
of the uncles this time. Ag was overage, and adamant. Her
mother knew she was defeated.

No matter which side she studied it from, Kat felt depressed.
She would welcome a relief from the terrible tension once Ag
was gone, but she couldn't accept the fact that she and her
sister were going their separate ways. By rights they should
have married local boys and set up housekeeping in adjacent
houses, if not under the very same roof. Their children should
have grown up together. Now Ag was going away, and there
was no telling about the future.

Kat leaned more and more on Red, pouring out her sorrows
to him on the few occasions when he could spend the night,
and the three of them—Ag could be heard upstairs pacing

around and singing—sat by the fire. The old woman, weary
from the war of nerves with her elder daughter and the need
to chaperone the younger one, nodded and began to snore.
Red and Kat did nothing to disturb her. They sat as close
to each other as they dared by the roaring fire, talking in
whispers, sometimes reaching their hands across the foot of
space that separated them and allowing their fingers to inter-
lace. They never did anything else, though they might have
had they been quiet about it. Kat would sometimes find the
courage to reach across with her other hand and trace the
scars, healed now and no longer horrible, on Red's fingers.
Their understanding of each other—neither dared the word
love—grew deeper.

The state of siege between the old woman and Ag had one
advantage: She never noticed what was going on between
Kat and the shopkeeper's son. Was she so preoccupied with
Ag that she couldn't see the way they looked at each other
across the supper table, the way they laughed over things no
one else thought funny, the way Kat passed him a plate or
a cup after filling it and held it for a lingering moment before
she would let it go? Or did she refuse to see, because she
dreaded losing her second daughter as well?

Kat's life continued to be a series of ups and downs. Ag was
the principal cause of the downs, she told herself, and everything would be fine once she was gone. Once she and Red
could be together without worrying about Ag. . . .

In the second week of April, a slow thaw began. The ice
in the harbor began to break up with loud crackings like gun-
shots day and night. Icebergs, silent and ominous, floated
regally past in the open sea, rising over the horizon like great
white ships, tinted green and blue and pink and orange by
the strengthening sun. Sometimes they rolled sedately on their
sides with a great rushing, booming noise, sending oversize
waves toward the shore and swamping some of the less-secure
boats. They were awesome.

In the last week of April, Ag slogged the three miles to the
shore at Torbay alone, ankle-deep in mud from the thaw,

coming back with a brand-new cardboard suitcase—empty—
that she'd ordered especially from St. John's. She'd saved
every penny she earned from piano lessons and knitting, and
had just enough for the suitcase, the six-hour ferry trip from
Argentia to North Sydney, Nova Scotia, and the series of
trains and ferries and yet more trains that would eventually
bring her to Boston. With absolute confidence that she would
survive the journey and arrive at her destination unscathed,
and equal confidence that she could support herself once she
got there, Ag showed no signs of backing down.

On the first day of May, just at dawn, she stood at the edge
of the inland road that led through Torbay to St. John's, at
the exact place where Kat had stood last summer with the
egg in the cracked china cup. So many things had happened
to both of them since that day, Kat thought, standing beside
her sister, shivering more from emotion than from the morning
air. Ag intended to walk the three miles to Torbay, lugging
her precious suitcase. Once there she could hitch a ride in one
of the small boats going to St. John's, or, with real luck, find
someone who was going the entire distance overland, or
around Cape Race and Cape St. Marys to Placentia Bay and
Argentia, where the ferry was. It was accepted, in a land
where automobiles were only a rumor, and where horses and
oxcarts were not everyday occurrences, for those on foot to
"borrow" a ride with strangers. Chances were that the passers-
through knew somebody from the outport anyway, and an
unwritten code of honor protected these travelers, even unescorted young ladies. "Sure, what if she were one of yer
own?" went the argument.

Ag might even have caught a boat from here to save her
the three miles to Torbay, but the fishermen of Harmony Bay
had arrived at one opinion of her. She was a fallen woman and
an ungrateful daughter—sins of equal weight in such a society—and to a man they sided with her mother. Let her walk,
they'd decided. It was good for her soul.

The two sisters stood side by side in the still-muddy road,
not daring to meet each other's eyes. Ag ought to be going

now, before the entire outport was up and about, peering through their curtains to watch her long-anticipated departure. But for all her disdain for the place, Ag knew as she stood there that she was never coming back, and the knowledge caught at her like a stitch in her side that made her want to sit very still someplace instead of walking such a distance. Her mother was still in bed, refusing to recognize the event that transpired outside her front door. For the rest of her days in Harmony Bay, she would speak about Ag as if she'd died that previous winter.

"Yer after bein' so stubborn!" Kat broke the silence at last, terrified that her sister would pull away suddenly and start to walk before she could say what was on her mind. "Ye'll not wait for Red to come take yer to Torbay. At least take the sandwiches. They're not poisoned, sure!"

"I'll not wait the day out," Ag said, looking away. "And I'll not have yer and Red mixin' in it. There's enough accused of sin as it is—poor Maudie's after takin' all manner of grief from her people on my account, and I'll have no one else in trouble over me!"

"Take the sandwiches, then," Kat repeated, almost pleading.

Ag gave her an annoyed look. "I'll not be wantin' 'em. Sure, there's places to buy food in St. John's—restaurants and such. There's got ter be, in a place as big," she reasoned, but her voice quavered a little. She wasn't sure. St. John's was no more than fifteen miles from where she'd lived her entire life, yet she'd never been there. She'd pored over her old geography books and begged information from the people she was going to live with, but she had no accurate picture of the mainland, or Boston, or anywhere. "Anyways, the butter was after turnin' two days ago, only Her Stinginess wouldn't part with it. I'm hatin' ter think what them sandwiches'll smell like come noon."

Kat shrugged, clutching the small parcel against her thin chest, pretending she wasn't hurt. Her eyes stung anyway, and she started to sniffle.

Ag turned toward her. "Sure, it's mean of me, I know. But can't yer see I'd only learned ter love the one time, and they're after takin' him from me? I don't dare get close ter another soul as long as I live!"

Kat nodded, understanding. It was what she'd needed to know before Ag left.

"Yer did love him, then?" she asked quietly. "All that blather about gettin' free of this place—it wasn't just that, then? Yer did love him?"

Ag's smile was vague and sad. "Does it make me sin any less? I wonder. Aye, I loved him—though it's a queer thing, me knowin' him only the one week. But it was as if, even without the dirty business, as if we knew each other all our lives—like we'd grown up across the yard from each other, instead of half the world away. We didn't just scrawb about, yer know. We talked. Jesus and Mary, how we talked! And when I was after findin' out I didn't have his child in me I sat down and cried. If I had it in me ter love, it was him, and none else."

Morning sounds were beginning to reach them—sounds of human activity in the kitchens and the harbor superimposed over the endless screeching of gulls. If Ag was to go today, she must go now. The sisters hugged quickly, and Ag did something extraordinary. She rested her hand against Kat's cheek with great tenderness, with an affection she had never shown before nor would again.

"I'll write yer," Ag gasped, and her eyes were not entirely dry. "Best of luck to yer and yer redhead. Maybe herself'll leave yez in peace after she realizes what she's done ter me. And if she gets too much for yer, come along after me. Sure, she'll not be at rest till the day she dies, and there's no need for yer to suffer guilt for leavin' her to herself."

Kat said something unintelligible, but Ag had already grasped the handles of the suitcase and set off down the road. As a last awkward attempt at comforting her sister, she turned back and snatched the parcel of rancid sandwiches from her, hurrying away so Kat couldn't see the dampness on her face.

"He'll not let me make the deliveries now," Red said to Kat. "He says them that's able-bodied can buy for them that's laid up, same as they did before. He wants me by him all the time. Sure, I think he's after workin' out why I come here so often."

It was Sunday, the only day Red was able to get out from under his father's miserly thumb. The old man had come to the conclusion that his only son must be courting a girl on his many excursions to Harmony Bay, and was doing his best to put an end to it.

Red and Kat walked hand in hand along the stretch of green that surrounded the usually priestless chapel on the rise above the outport. The villagers came at dawn, on the three Sundays a month that the priest was over the water, and held a rosary service; it bound them together and tided them over until the priest could return. Now it was nearly dinner time, and the chapel and its environs were deserted. A courting couple could walk among the gravestones in peace.

Holding Red's hand and walking beside him came naturally to Kat now, after the long winter nights by the fire and the unsettling time in the spring before Ag left. Life with her mother alone had turned out to be less harrowing than Kat had expected, and whenever she and Red could snatch some time together she thought of how utterly satisfying it would be to spend the rest of her life with her hand in his, walking, walking. And now this.

"He's after givin' me a choice," Red went on, kicking at the number of small stones that always worked their way up through the thin soil. "Either I make up me mind this very week to take on the store in me own name and promise never to sell it outside the family or I go to work on the boats and stay there. He's so powerful worried about his womenfolk he don't give a gull's ass about me!"

He was speaking words he'd kept down for years, words he dared let out now in the silent churchyard. Kat listened in silence—a little awed at his temper, which she'd never seen before, aching for him in his dilemma.

"Sure, is it my fault or his I'm the only son?" he went on. "The five girls above me is pretty much took care of: Three's married, one's about ter be, and the other's for the convent. It's the five younger ones he's rompsed about. They're too young yet to know if they'll all get husbands. And that's supposed ter be my concern! He's too bleedin' sly to trust me sisters' husbands with any part of the store, so he lays it all ter me. I don't want no part of it!"

They had passed through the churchyard with its smattering of whitewashed crosses and graves marked out with stones—half of them empty for the men lost at sea; many of the rest filled with stillborn babies and women dying young. This far above the harbor there was a stretch of beach—not sand, but more of the same small, round stones—rolling gently down to water almost warm enough to swim in if you'd grown up here. Today it was overcast, and a bit of a wind teased at them; it was a safe bet no one would be swimming. They had the beach to themselves.

"I'd almost go along with it," Red mused, half to himself. Kat still said nothing. "If it wasn't for the conditions he's settin' down with it. Not that he's said as much, mind yer, but he'd not want me ter marry. It's a fine thing for me sisters 'cause it gets 'em out of the house, but he'll not have me bringin' in any extra mouths ter feed. That's why he's put a stop ter the deliveries. He's a mind of what I'm after spendin' me time at up here."

"And yer risked comin' up here to tell me ye've made up yer mind," Kat said quietly, looking down at the stones surrounding her small feet.

Red looked at her. "I was wonderin' would yer talk at all," he said. "It's like what I'm sayin' is nothin' in it for yer. Do yer realize what I've been tellin' yer? It's me whole future. Ye've not said a word."

"Ye've obvious made up yer mind beforehand," Kat said,

not daring to think that his plans could include her. "There's nothing I could say would change it."

Red had to admire her. "Yer think that, then? That I'd not consider what yer'd want? Yet yer came out to walk with me and listen ter me blather all this time, thinkin' I wasn't carin' for yer own needs?"

"Aye," was all Kat said, when she only had to keep breathing to say "because I love yer." But she held her breath.

"It's thinkin' on your needs had made it that hard ter decide," Red said, squeezing her hand for emphasis. "Yer know I'm fond of yer."

"Aye." Kat nodded sadly, bracing to be let down. "'Only there's things a man in yer place has to do to think he's a man. I'd not stand in yer way now and have yer hate me for it later."

He'd never heard such courage come from a woman, and it brought a tightness to Red's throat. He stared out toward the horizon for some moments before he could speak.

"There's something else I'm thinkin' on," Red said carefully. "Yer know about my mother."

Red's mother had tuberculosis, principal cause of death among post-childbearing women in their society.

"Aye," Kat said. "She's got the consumption. Bad, too."

"She'll not see through another winter," Red said, almost indifferently. His tone startled Kat, and she gave him an accusing look. He became defensive. "Sure, it ain't my fault! And no use pretendin' there was ever any hope for her. She's ready to go when it comes for her. I'll be glad to see her free of the pain and the coughin'."

Kat considered his viewpoint. "I'd not looked at it that way," she conceded. "Poor old dear! And it's for her yer stayin' on."

"Partly," Red acknowledged. He brought his eyes away from her and back to the horizon, which glimmered faintly in a shaft of sunlight penetrating the cloud cover far out at sea. "Will yer hear me decision, then?"

Kat nodded without speaking.

Red pulled in a breath. "I'll work the boats this summer,"
he began. "Me hands'll get used to it, and I don't care if it
kills me. I'll not truck with his bloody store another week.
And when herself finally goes to her rest, I'm for the merchant
marine."

Kat's hand tensed in his, and she pulled away in a kind of
horror. This was not what she'd expected. She thought he was
going to say he'd go for a fisherman; she could live with that.
But how could he leave the outport for two years or more
and leave her here?

"Oh, don't yer see?" he cried, anguished, grasping both her
hands and peering hard into her eyes. "Yer but a lass—only
seventeen—and yer mother'd not let us marry this year. I've
not a handful of change to me name, and no place ter live.
I'll hitch up for two–three years and get me a skill, and I'll
save every penny I make. I'll come back for yer. I'd swear
that on me life!"

Kat shook her head in confusion, unable to speak past the
jumble of emotions that battered at her.

"Tell me what yer thinkin'," Red pleaded. "It's what I've
got to do. If yer won't give me yer blessing on it, then I am
lost."

"I'll—I'll not stand in yer way," Kat gasped finally. "Sure,
go or stay, yer all there is for me."

Red worked the boats that summer, until his skin burned to
the same color as his hair and creases formed in the back of his
neck. His back ached from the hours of sitting in one position
and he began to stoop when he walked. The raw skin on his
hands never did heal completely, though he poured brine over
the fresh scars every morning till the tears stood in his eyes.
Sometimes the joints of his fingers became infected, and he
ran a light fever most of the time. Still, he was no worse off
than any of the few hundred thousand men from the age of
twelve to nearly seventy who plied the small boats on all four

coasts of Newfoundland, and whose fathers and grandfathers had done it before them. In all those months of his initiation, Red never set foot in his father's store except to get fresh bait of a morning, and to pass through on his way into the house at night. His father and he never spoke; he spent whatever hours he could stay awake with his mother, watching over her labored breathing, waiting for the inevitable. On Sundays he walked to Harmony Bay to be with Kat.

In the middle of September, as the first frosts were beginning to settle in at night, Red's mother died in her sleep. On the very afternoon she was buried, Red set out on foot for St. John's, empty-handed, and with nothing in his pockets but a handful of change, his clasp knife, and his baptismal certificate to offer as identification when he shipped out. He had to hurry. If the harbors began to ice over, he might not escape until spring.

Kat waited nearly a year. Red wrote to her dutifully twice a week from wherever he was; it might take weeks or even months for some of his letters to get to her, and very often two or three arrived at once. Kat wrote too, and sometimes her letters crossed his on the way, and questions might go unanswered for months or stories be repeated because the writer couldn't remember if they'd been reported the first time or not. Kat's life was calmer. It slowed into a predictability she had missed since the day she met Red. Her existence had an immediate goal, and the steady repetition of days filled with menial chores and her mother's endless complaining meant only that she was that much closer to the day she and Red would be together again.

She never mentioned his name to her mother, who surely must have known where she'd been those Sundays—even deserted churchyards had eyes—and while her mother couldn't read them, she must surely have wondered at the number of letters with exotic stamps and postmarks that arrived for her younger daughter, who had never gotten mail of any description before. Kat considered: Should she say something to her mother about her plans for the future? Was she being deceitful in remaining silent? If she couldn't say anything now, what would she do when Red came back and they decided to marry?

Her mother knew well enough what was going on. She had only to look at her daughter's face each time a letter arrived. And for all her distraction over Ag, she wasn't so stupid that she couldn't figure out who Kat's young man was. The neighbors had been sly in their inquiries, wondering if they could expect another scene like the one last winter. The old woman kept silent for as long as she could, but the seemingly endless flow of letters brought her to the breaking point.

"And when's the date, then?" she demanded, watching Kat's face glow as she slipped the most recent arrival into her apron pocket to be devoured over and over in her room later. "How soon does he come back—assumin' he will—and when's the wedding? And will yer be wearin' a white dress is me next question, or have yer been up to yer sister's tricks?"

Kat blushed and stammered.

"We've not done anything to be ashamed of," she managed finally, unconsciously adopting some of Ag's arrogant manner and finding it made excellent armor. "And we've nothing certain for a wedding yet. It's too soon to plan, with him bein' so far away and no tellin' how long."

"Aye." Her mother nodded shrewdly. "And yer so certain I'll let yer. Yer know what's said about the Mannings, then."

Kat had been waiting for this, had been rehearsing in her head for months what she would say when her mother brought it up.

"It's no disgrace havin' mixed blood," she said flatly, without the anger she'd practiced. "And we'd be the ones ter talk if it was!"

"I'm not talkin' mixed blood, only Indian!" her mother muttered peevishly, stung by her daughter's remark. "It's that heathen way of them. Them girls is all sluts what can't keep a house proper, and half the time none of 'em goes ter church. And all that red hair! Every one of 'em with red hair. It's a bad sign, I'm tellin' yer. Yer fine young merchantman's got a fearsome temper under all that blather. He'll beat yer sure as day, like his old man beat that sickly wife of his. It's bad blood in the lot of 'em, mark my words!"

"At least the Mannings knows what they are and ain't ashamed of it," Kat said mildly, strangely unaffected by her mother's mood. "I couldn't begin ter tell what I am."

It struck her mother to the bone. Was ever a poor, defenseless widow cursed with two such headstrong daughters? The old woman sighed, defeated.

"I know better than ter try and stop yer," she said. "It's already cost me the one daughter. What will yez do, then? Will yer sit about and wait for him for God knows how many years? Are yer so certain of him that yer know he'll come back to yer? There's plenty of heathen women in them Chinee ports he's sailin' for would give him as much as a wife and not ask a Christian marriage for it. It'd be like blood meetin' like blood, and no remorse in it."

Kat's temper flared, but she was not a shouter like Ag. "Mother of God, yer a cruel one!" she whispered. "But he's comin' back for me, sure. Only I'll not wait for him here. I've wrote ter Ag. I'm goin' up ter the States with her. I'll wait for me young man there."

She expected a scene, expected loud lamentation and wringing of hands that would go on for weeks until she could finally leave. Instead, her mother narrowed her eyes at her in stony silence, as if she were not worthy of a reply.

"I'm after thinkin' it out, Mom," Kat explained, placating. "I can go for a shopgirl, like—like Ag did. Then I can save money, too, so when Red comes back we'll have a bit of a nest egg for the future. Sure, I can't sit here idle the whole time he's gone. I'll go out of me mind!"

Her mother sighed. "And what's ter become of me? Does anyone think on that, or care? Sure, what's ter be my future?"

Kat had expected this, too. "Sure, there's family all around can take care of yer if ye'll not be stubborn about it. All Dad's brothers has offered yer a place more than once—yer can take one of the nieces in ter live with yer. Or close the house entire. It's too big for yer alone anyways."

"I'll thank yer not ter tell me what ter do with me own house!" her mother shrilled, rousing herself at last. "The only happy years I've ever known were lived in this house, and if I have ter die alone I will die in this house!"

"Aye." Kat nodded, strangely indifferent. She had saved her trump card for this moment. "Sure, if yer that determined to keep me with yer, yer welcome to come to the States once I'm settled."

She knew she had her mother there. They'd have to go to Boston to stay with Ag, at least for a while. Ag had her own apartment now, and Kat knew her mother would rather die than acknowledge that her elder daughter was still alive and had actually made something of herself.

The old woman appeared lost in thought, weighing decisions that seemed never to have occurred to her until now. Had she been so certain Kat would stay with her forever? She gave a final, profound sigh.

"All the young blood is leavin' the outports," she said wearily. "Soon there'll be none but us old ones. Yer too restless, all of yez. Yer can't but think there's somethin' better for yez just because it's somewheres else. Go, then. I can't hold yer any more than I could hold yer sister!"

Kat went to live with Ag in Boston. With her sister's help, she got a job as a shopgirl in one of the posher department stores. Ag had already been promoted to having an entire counter to herself, but she was on her feet all day the same as Kat. They worked seven and a half hours a day, six days a week—longer during the Christmas rush—and with no overtime. They earned the lowest hourly wage the store could get by with under the law, and they got a three percent commission on every item they sold. Ag, who was aggressive and could pounce on a customer the minute she stepped off the elevator, managed very well. Kat was shy and reticent and got customers by default; when every other girl in her department was busy, the customer had no choice but to go to her.

When Ag had been there for two years and Kat almost one, the management of the store laid off all its "non-American" employees the week after Christmas. The steady influx of personnel from Canada and Ireland filled the store with unfamiliar accents, which the customers found disturbing. In order to restore the store's image, management had decided only to employ local girls with broad Massachusetts accents. Other stores around Boston gradually followed suit. Undaunted, Ag moved to Bridgeport, Connecticut, where a small number of Newfies had gotten a toehold in the working-class Irish neighborhoods, dragging her reluctant younger sister with her. When things got tight in Bridgeport they moved again, this time to New York, to Brooklyn, to a tight-knit neighborhood of multifamily, yellow brick row houses called Sunset Park. The few acres of greenery that gave the place its name faced west over the Narrows, and boasted a swimming pool, horseshoe mounds, and enough flat, grassy space for the men and boys to play soccer. Ag and Kat settled here for good.

Despite the rigors of the working week, there were wondrous things to experience in their new, chosen country. There was the magic of being able to flood a room with light at the flick of a wall switch—no mean pleasure for those used to the dimness and the bother of kerosene lamps. There was the new sensation of walking on sidewalks: long, smooth paths of concrete alien to feet accustomed to gravel paths or rutted dirt roads. There was the noise, the hurry, the endless montage of automobiles-trolleys-trucks, the amazing underground world of the subway. The greatest joys of Kat's day were the twenty-minute trolley rides to work every morning and back again in the evening. No matter that she had to stand after a long day at the store; it was as much a wonder to her to travel in something with wheels as it would have been for a New Yorker to travel to work in the small boats she took for granted.

Life was not all work, either. The transplanted Newfoundlanders had their own organizations and social clubs, where even in the darkest days of Prohibition it was possible to get spirits. It was understood that even an unescorted woman could sit in a back booth with a small beer or a Guinness and be treated courteously or left in peace, whichever she preferred. It had been Ag's idea to hang about these places; she dragged Kat along with the same adamant persuasion she'd used to get her to move from Boston to Bridgeport to Brooklyn. Kat didn't drink, not even beer, and she didn't think she should be in such places. They were plainly illegal, and besides, the unmarried men might get the wrong idea.

Ag enjoyed being with men now, as she hadn't back home. Many of the younger men had been in the merchant marine or the navy, had seen something of the world, and liked to talk about it. Ag became a good listener. She would pal around with these rough-hewn types, sharing their blather and laughing as loud as they did. She began to wear lipstick and rouge, and to smoke cigarettes, though only on Saturday nights in the local club. Still, she never went farther than friendship.

Kat, meanwhile, sat in the back of the room with the beer she refused to drink sitting flat and warm on the table before her, and thought about Red. The few other women who came regularly became her friends; they respected her for waiting for her young man, and did not consider her the threat that her feckless sister might be.

Kat sat at the same table every Saturday night, glad at least to be off her feet and in company, rather than alone in the tiny apartment she shared with Ag. She'd tried that for a while, but without someone to talk to she had nothing to do but worry at her knitting and daydream about Red. It made her sad. If she could only fill up the evenings of the few months that remained before he came back. Letters found her in Brooklyn now—letters from Hong Kong and the Mediterranean and the Virgin Islands. Just a few more months.

Kat did not know then that she would wait for Red nearly six years in all. A few weeks before the end of his three-year hitch, the disasters began to strike.

He was sitting in a seamen's pub in Sydney, fending off the dryness of the climate with a couple of pints and avoiding the enticements of some of his shipmates who knew the local girls. He intended to keep himself clean for the woman he loved. A fight broke out between some of the crew of his ship— mostly Newfies and French Canadians—and some English merchantmen. Red Manning was not one to let all hell break loose around him without somehow participating, so he turned on his bar stool and calmly selected his own particular British sailor. They traded a few slugs, and Red found himself flung under a table against the wall with a singing in his head. Too dazed to move, and suddenly drained of his temper, he lay calmly watching the outcome. Nobody noticed him. When the local constabulary finally broke things up, one of the Frenchmen had been stabbed in the chest. He died the following morning.

Every man in the place was impounded for questioning. Most denied seeing anything, and were eventually released. Red made the mistake of telling someone about his view from under the table, and mentioned that he'd seen two men from his ship, who had some sort of personal vendetta against the dead man, slipping out just as the brawl escalated. The magistrate told him he'd have to remain in port as a material witness until the case came to trial.

This took nearly eight months. Red's ship sailed without him, bringing the Frenchman's body back to Quebec. The trial dragged on for six weeks, and the case was finally dismissed because Red was the only witness, and a doctor's testimony that he'd suffered a concussion undermined his credibility. Steaming but powerless, he hung around Sydney another two months until his ship came around again so he could finish his hitch and go home.

He'd supported himself for nearly a year washing dishes and doing odd jobs. When he'd come to under the table in the pub his pockets had been rifled. The money he'd scrounged for three years, carrying it with him when he went ashore so he wouldn't worry about its safety aboard ship, was gone. He had to start all over again.

When he finished that hitch, Red shipped out again for a year on another boat, this time sending the money directly to Kat for safekeeping. His father died suddenly and unexpectedly of pneumonia that winter. The old miser had stinted himself worst of all in his chronic stinginess. He'd caught a chill from keeping the store unheated until it was so cold his breath blew out in vapor before him, the price of paying a lad to go inland to cut firewood for the stove being more than he was prepared to pay. He refused to see a doctor, though he need only have gone to St. John's to do so. Doctors, as he pointed out, gasping for breath, only took your money and killed you anyways. Within two weeks he was dead, leaving no will, his accounts in chaos, and his ten female offspring totally unstrung. Red shipped home as soon as he could.

It was another year before he could get the mess straightened out, the store left in the custodianship of his two eldest sisters' husbands, and himself extricated once and for all from the situation. He took not so much as a penny from the old man's estate for himself; sound money did not eradicate bad blood as far as he was concerned. He kissed his sisters good-bye and headed for the States, never looking back.

It was an older, more settled redhead who appeared on Kat's doorsill after all that time. He had put on some weight; it looked well on him. The flame-colored hair was thinning on top, and he'd begun to smoke a pipe. He was still a virgin, though Kat would not need to know that just yet. He had learned boiler repair and riveting during the years at sea; he proudly showed Kat the foreshortened index finger of his left hand, the tip of it smashed by a faulty rivet and amputated at the root of the fingernail. Kat wept over it and kissed his hand and threw her arms around him, the first time she'd done so in their seven years of—in a manner of speaking—courtship. But they could make up for lost time now.

Red studied the changes in Kat as well. She'd rebelled against the long, flowing hair her mother made mandatory in girl-hood as soon as she'd arrived in Boston years ago. She'd had it bobbed to just below her earlobes for so long she'd almost for-gotten the feel of its weight swinging behind her every time she moved her head, but to Red the effect was new and he was entranced by it. She looked older, though he could hardly say how, except that in some way the girl of seventeen had been transformed into a woman of twenty-four, without any spe-cific alteration in her features. Whatever it was about her, she was more attractive than ever.

Red brought news with him from Harmony Bay. Kat's mother had finally taken in one of her nieces to keep up the big house, and seemed none the worse for wear despite her endless complaining.

"And what about yerself, then?" Kat demanded of him, searching his face for clues to the sadness she found there. He'd been secretive about the events in Sydney, and she wondered about that. She knew about his father, but considered that a cause for relief rather than sorrow. "Am I still the one yer want, or did yer find them foreign girls more interesting?"

"And wouldn't yer just love to know?" he teased, some of the old twinkle coming back into his eyes. "I hate ter disap-point yer, but there hasn't been a one. It's for you I've waited. Turn me away and I'll be a bachelor all me days."

"Sure, I'd never do that!" Kat cried, taking him seriously, flinging her arms around him again. "As soon as yer wrote me yer was comin' up ter the States I went right ter the priest. He's for talkin' to yer as soon as yer settled in. He's after knowin' yer cousin Alf, and said if yer was as good a man as him I'd made a good choice. We can get it settled and announce the banns right away. Sure, we're both of age; there's none can stop us."

"Aye." Red nodded, pretending to give it serious thought. "And it's a lovely idear, then, isn't it?"

Red led Kat away from the rectory after his interview with the priest with a tremendous grin on his face. The marriage banns were announced before the congregation at mass on three consecutive Sundays. On the following Saturday Red and Kat were married, with Ag as maid of honor and Red's cousin Alf, wooden leg and all, standing as best man. Kat wore her mother's wedding dress, shipped reluctantly down from Harmony Bay because, as the old woman put it, at least one of her daughters ought to have the use of it. She matched it with a short veil she'd fallen in love with at the store where she worked, and which she'd managed to soil a bit at the hem—the only dishonest thing she ever did in her life—so it would be marked down.

The newlyweds spent their wedding night and the next two weeks in the tiny apartment Kat and Ag had shared up till then, sleeping in the twin beds in the one small bedroom, while Ag tossed about on the sofa in the sitting room and tried to stay out of their way. After that they found their own apartment, a large railroad flat on the first floor of a two-family yellow brick row house just down the block from the church. They used their hard-earned money sparingly, buying the few bits of furniture they needed. Red went to work at the Bush Shipping Terminal, within walking distance of home, and Kat quit her job in the department store without a qualm. She spent her days with her feet tucked up on the chintz sofa, crocheting fine-work doilies for the backs and arms of the armchairs.

The day after the last of the furniture arrived, a letter came for Kat from Harmony Bay, written by a literate neighbor in the name of Helen Blake. She had closed up the big house, Kat's mother announced, and was coming to live with her married daughter.

Thirty-six hours after she'd gone into labor, thirty-seven hours after they'd lowered her mother into the ground, Kat Manning was delivered of a baby boy. His head was enlarged as a result of the prolonged labor, and the forceps left two noticeable impressions in the skull just behind his temples that would never quite go away. He was remarkable both in color and reflexes, considering his long ordeal, and the only thing that disturbed the delivery-room nurse was that he steadfastly refused to cry. His throat and nostrils were cleared of mucus and his respiration was normal, but he simply chose not to cry, only stared around contemplatively when they removed the membrane covering the top of his head like a skullcap.

"My mother always said that was lucky," the nurse remarked, tying the cord and fussing with him.

The doctor raised an eyebrow. "What?"

"Being born with a caul," the nurse said. "People always said that made you lucky."

"All it means is that the placenta was deteriorating during delivery," the doctor grunted. "If he's lucky it's only because the thing didn't jut out in front of him in the birth canal and suffocate him."

The nurse gave him a look that he couldn't interpret, put the baby in the waiting isolette, and started to wheel him down toward the elevator.

"Wait a minute," the doctor said, and she stopped in the hall. The baby still looked around, yawned, made no sound. "Get someone else to bring him down. I want you to prep her for surgery."

The nurse looked at Kat, drugged and immobile, unknowing. Then she looked at the doctor.

"I'm going to jump the gun on Mother Nature a little," he explained. "When she comes around I'll tell her it was an emergency procedure to save her life. In the long run it is, because if she conceives again it'll kill her, but these Catholics can't see that."

The nurse was Catholic, and wanted to say so, but she agreed with him in principle. "Do you want me to scrub?" she asked.

The doctor gave her a whimsical look. "May as well," he said. "We're fellow conspirators in this thing already."

The last of the Mannings dozed unconcerned in the isolette as it was wheeled down to the elevator.

BOOK III
The Broken Chrysalis, 1945–1960

"So your mother's had a new baby. Isn't that nice!" the neighbors clucked with that smug look about their eyes that made you wonder what they really meant. Why did they act as if they thought there was something dirty about having a baby at forty? Helen would blush and mumble when they cornered her after mass or in the stores, as if she and not her mother were the guilty party. The priests always said it was a woman's vocation to bring life into the world. What were the rules of the game?

Kat was kept in the hospital for two entire weeks after Johnny was born, and when she did come home it was to leave the baby in Helen's arms and go into the big bedroom to cry. Aunt Ag was around a great deal, and there were whispered conversations in which the word "operation" kept cropping up. Helen pieced it together as well as she could, but it bothered her that no one took the trouble to tell her. Finally Red set her straight.

"Yer mother's a shy one about tellin' yer such things," he began, his face the color of his hair, indicating that he wasn't all that comfortable with such topics either. "But it's that she can't have any more babies."

Helen put down the bottle of formula and swung Johnny to her shoulder for a burp; he was beginning to doze in her arms. "Oh," she said, not knowing what to say next. "I sort of figured that. Only, I don't see why it should bother her. I mean, she's forty years old and she's got the three of us. And this one's close to perfect. I thought she'd be happy that he's all right."

Red pondered it, unable to comprehend Kat's behavior any more than his daughter could. "I'm after thinkin' it's that she couldn't decide for herself. Like the matter was taken out of her hands," he said, sucking on his pipe. "For all the trouble she had this time, she still hates ter think himself is the last she'll have. Sure, her own mother was forty when Kat herself was born."

The two of them were silent for a moment, studying the instigator of this conversation as he nuzzled into the crook of Helen's elbow and snored lightly. Helen was right. Except for the marks of the forceps, he was close to perfect. Helen at this age had been thin and colicky, Danny fat and lethargic. Johnny was not only physically perfect, but he had a sunny disposition. He was a delightful new toy for Helen to play with when she came home from school and her mother was in a mood. She fed Johnny, changed him, rocked him to sleep, spent hours petting him and running her fingers through the mass of dark hair he'd been born with, which grew thicker and darker almost daily.

"It's queer," Red mused, laughing a little behind his pipe. "Yer mother married me to have redheaded kids, and look at yez. One's darker than the next."

Helen knew he was teasing and did not feel offended. She smiled and fingered Johnny's hair again.

"Do yer like him much?" Red teased her. "How can yer care for something that can't only eat and sleep and piss all day?"

"I *love* him!" Helen squeezed the baby so hard he jumped in his sleep. "He smells so nice! I think babies are wonderful."

"Aye," her father said, pleased at her enthusiasm. "Yer'll want a few of yer own someday, I imagine."

Helen blushed. "Well, I've got to get married first, Pop. I'm kind of young for that."

"Aye." Red nodded, thinking that Kat had been only a year older the first time they met. "Only I'm thinkin' ye've two years of school left. I was wonderin' how yer saw the future."

Helen started to say something, but had trouble phrasing it. She looked down at Johnny's sleeping face and said nothing.

"Sure, I know it's a bit of deep thinking for yer age," Red said, misunderstanding her silence. "But it'd not hurt yer to give it some consideration."

Helen had given it a great deal of consideration. It was the idea of verbalizing it, of being presumptuous enough to think that anyone in the family wanted to hear about the plans she had for her life, that brought her to silence. When she and Danny were younger, people always asked him what he wanted to be when he grew up. When they got to Helen, they told her how wonderful it was to be grown up and have a husband and babies. Helen had never doubted that this would be her life, and it had only recently occurred to her that she might be shortchanged. Still, as far back as she could remember she had wanted babies, so perhaps the other options, if there were any, were not that important.

Last week her sixteenth birthday had come and gone, largely unnoticed in the chaos of her grandmother's dying and her mother's giving birth to Johnny, but it had made Helen's thinking process more acute. She saw her future quite clearly, and it was only a matter of explaining it to her father.

"I thought about it a lot, Pop," she said quietly. "I think I know what I'm going to do once I graduate."

"I'd like to hear about it if yer'd care to tell me," Red said with the careful hands-off attitude he had evolved over the years toward a daughter who was more of a woman than a girl, a phenomenon he found disturbing.

"I'm going for secretarial courses," Helen said, trying to evince some enthusiasm at the prospect. "I'll start typing and shorthand next term. All my teachers say my grammar and handwriting are excellent, and I'm very efficient. I think I'd be a good secretary."

Red watched her face, saw that she was trying too hard to say what she thought he wanted to hear. "Is it what yer want, then? Truly?"

Helen could not lie to her father. With him, she could not force herself to express an emotion she did not feel, nor disguise one she did feel. "It's something I know I can do well," she said.

"Aye," Red assented, fussing at emptying and refilling his pipe to mask his uneasiness. "And ye'd not be doin' it all that long, I'm thinkin'."

Helen frowned at him, bewildered.

"Sure, yer pretty enough!" her father said, annoyed that he had to spell it out to her. "I see no reason why yer wouldn't have a husband before yer well into yer twenties."

"Oh," Helen responded, watching Johnny's face again, not knowing what to say. Was she pretty enough? Was that all that mattered?

"Well, Jesus and Mary, child! Isn't it what yer after wantin'?"

"Of course, Pop!" Helen said vehemently, making Johnny startle in his sleep again. "I do want to get married. But suppose I don't meet the right person until I'm—say, thirty? Or even older. It's the idea of working in some boring office all that time that scares me."

"What would yer want, then?" Red asked patiently, his pipe relit and his disposition evener. "Yer know we've little money. Between you, me, and the wall, no one expected this baby to live. I know that sounds cruel, and it don't mean I don't love him, but it's a fact. And don't breathe a word of it to yer mother or she'll kill me, sure, for all her bein' down in the dumps. But now we've not only another to feed and put clothes and shoes on, but it's another boy as well, and a boy is after needin' more education in this man's world than a girl does. When I was a lad, a man's worth was measured by the strength of his hands and his courage. Nowadays any weakling can survive if he's gone to college."

"I know that, Pop," Helen said, a little out of breath, holding back her resentment. There was another meaning behind his words, and she was slowly beginning to grasp it. She would sacrifice anything—her very life—for Johnny. But why should Danny go to college, solely because he was a boy?

"Another thing," Red began, hesitating as if on the verge of revealing a great secret. "Also between you, me, and the wall. Yer brother Danny hasn't half a brain in his head, and even less a drop of humanity or character in his soul. I'm thinkin' he'd be after starvin' to death if he didn't have a college educa-tion to hide behind. I'm even wonderin' if that'll save him. But do yer see my point? You, lass, are brightness itself. Yer a scrap-per, in yer own quiet way, and if yer weren't there'd always be a husband to get yer through. But the lads've got to have some help."

"It's okay, Pop," Helen said, seeing that he was upset, trying to soothe him. "I probably wouldn't like college anyway. High school's boring."

It seemed to Red that she was sincere. "It's that yer brighter than most of them," he said, feeling burdened by the need to make decisions so important to her future. "Sure, if we could spare the money—"

"Pop," Helen dared to interrupt, taking charge of the con-versation before it became more than either of them could handle. "Grandma couldn't write her own name. And Mom's only had six years of school. I'll have a high school diploma, and my kids'll go to college. That's the way it should be. I'm not complaining."

"It might do yer more good if yer did, sure," Red mumbled vaguely, wishing there were no need to deal with these things. He changed the subject abruptly. "And shouldn't His Nibs be in bed? Jesus and Mary, but yer've got him spoiled rotten!"

Helen's first job paid twenty dollars a week. It seemed like a fortune. She was hired as a junior secretary for a petroleum company near Rockefeller Plaza. For six months she worked in a typing pool with fifteen other girls; then her efficiency and cheerfulness earned her a promotion. She had her own desk in the executive suite, complete with wall-to-wall carpeting and piped-in music, and worked for only one man. There was, however, no change in salary. Helen accepted this as her due. At least it was quieter here, and no one jostled her. She even got an hour for lunch instead of a half-hour.

She kept half of her salary for herself. It paid for subway tokens, the one cup of tea she allowed herself at midmorning—lunch came from home in a brown bag—and an occasional lipstick or afternoon at the movies. Major purchases, like a new dress or shoes, were made with great caution and much debate. At the end of the week there might be as much as two dollars left over. That went into Helen's savings account. The other ten dollars she gave to Kat, voluntarily, to pay her room and board. Kat never refused the money. Without saying anything to Helen, she was putting it aside for Danny.

Danny didn't want to go to college. He made it clear that four years of high school had been absolute torture, and he had no intention of prolonging his suffering. He had no immediate plans for vocational training, either. The thought of getting his hands dirty gave him the shudders. He did not bother planning for the future; whining about being forced—as he saw it—to go to college monopolized all his time.

Helen said nothing, listening to her brother's lament at the supper table nightly, but Red took her silence as a reproach. He searched his daughter's face for signs of discontent, but found none. She seemed satisfied with the future he had offered her, and never complained. She spent most of her free time reading by herself, or playing with Johnny. Some of her happiest moments were spent with her baby brother, tickling him and letting him roll on the floor the way she had been forbidden to do as a baby. Johnny tolerated the attention of the rest of the family, endured the cooing and fussing of relatives and neighbors, but his face lit up when he heard Helen's footsteps down the long hall in the evening, and the rest of the day was for her.

But Red continued to watch his daughter and wonder. Was Helen happy? Would marriage and babies be enough? He amazed himself in thinking such thoughts. Marriage and babies had been enough for his wife and his mother. What made his daughter any different? And what if she didn't marry until she was thirty, or at all? What kind of future would she have then?

There were a few boys from the neighborhood who took her out now and then—a privilege she'd been granted once she graduated from high school—but it was usually a double date with Loretta and nothing very serious. They went to the movies, stopped sometimes for a late snack at Schrafft's or Junior's, but Loretta always got the giggles and talked too loud, and Helen grew quieter and quieter. She had known these boys since grammar school. How could she possibly take them seriously? Helen liked to believe she was no romantic. She shook her head over Loretta's passion for Errol Flynn, remembered sitting with her while she cried every night for a week when Leslie Howard was killed during the war. Helen didn't fall for movie stars. But when she thought of marrying a boy from the neighborhood, she despaired.

So she tried not to think about getting married at all, tried to keep from smiling at every good-looking man she saw and then glancing down at his hands to see if he wore a wedding ring. Most married men didn't wear wedding rings, she reminded herself, and of those a good portion would not mind lying to a single girl in order to mislead her. Helen might have been naive about some things, but even she knew that much. No, she thought, before she even allowed herself to become interested in a young man, she would have to know a great deal about him.

She prided herself on having all of her emotions solidly buttoned up. She would be, for now at least, a career girl. If the right man didn't come along for a while, it didn't mean she had to stay a humble typist all her life. Riding up in the ornate elevator every morning, she imagined herself like Kate Hepburn, the consummate Career Woman. She would be like the newspaperwoman in *Woman of the Year*—brilliant, successful, fashion-conscious—and she would catch Spencer Tracy in the end. But then she would get off the elevator, punch the time clock, and break another fingernail at the typewriter before it was even ten o'clock; and by five o'clock the burning behind her eyes and the pain in the small of her back, and the spot on her pinkie from scooping the dregs of her cheap worn-down lipstick out of the tube, reminded her that she was neither brilliant nor succesful, that it did her no good to be fashion-conscious on her salary, and that she probably wouldn't catch Spencer Tracy in the end.

But, of course, Kate Hepburn was a lot older than she, Helen reasoned, taking the ornate elevator down to the subway in the evening, so she had had longer to get to the top.

Helen would go home to a predictably dull evening; unless Loretta came over with some magazines and gossip, there was nothing to do but read, listen to the radio, take up the hems on her dresses, and go to bed. Sometimes she had to baby-sit for Johnny as well.

Her parents were going out often in the evening lately. There was always a wake or a novena for Kat to occupy herself with, and Red would not let her go out alone, so in spite of his yearning for his chair and his pipe and his newspaper, he would have to put on a tie and go with her. Then, too, he tried to keep her interested in other events in the parish, to prevent her slipping away from him into hopeless gloom. He even—God admire his fortitude, Helen thought, watching her parents getting ready to go out—began taking Kat to Monday-night bingo.

On those nights Helen took care of Johnny, feeding him, giving him a bath, reading to him, and putting him to bed. As a baby he was placid, dozing in her arms while she rocked him to sleep, and as he got older he required even less trouble. But when he was three years old he developed a severe case of croup and had a terrible time of it, sometimes needing to be rocked for over an hour before the coughing subsided enough to let him sleep. Helen finally eased him into the crib after one such session, checking the water level in the vaporizer and longing for sleep herself.

She staggered into the parlor, where she had left the copy of *Gone with the Wind* she had taken out of the library last week. This was her second reading, and she had seen the movie too, so she was in the company of an old friend. She tucked her feet under her on the couch and found her place. Her eyelids were heavy, her concentration dim. She would read to the end of the chapter about the burning of Atlanta and then go to bed.

There was a noise that might have been Johnny whimpering in his sleep; it was not, and Helen relaxed. She was incredibly attuned to the boy's needs, as if he were her son and not her brother. Drowsy, she went back to the book. The burning of Atlanta, Scarlett's escape to Tara with Rhett and Prissy and Melanie and the baby. . . .

She felt hot, hot and closed in, trapped, helpless. Great walls of flame engulfed her, and there was no escape. Helen threw her hands in front of her face and screamed. Rhett Butler could not get through to save them from the flames and the Union soldiers; Helen would have to drive the wagon alone, get back to Tara with Loretta and Kat and Johnny. They were depending on her, and she must save them. Her

Woman of the Year award, her successful career as a journalist, were behind her now. All that mattered was that she save her family from the fire, the terrible fire.

She could smell the smoke, the acrid smell of stale wood and crumbling plaster, like the time the building next door had been gutted by an electrical fire that blackened the walls in the buildings on either side and left them too hot to touch for hours. They had to be evacuated in the middle of a November night, Helen and Danny in their nightclothes and all the women on the block making a fuss and wrapping them in blankets. Helen had been ten at the time, and all she remembered was the water freezing around the hydrants and hanging in great stalactites from the windowsills, and the fireman, sooty-faced and sweating, leaning down from the pumper truck to tell her it would be all right, and the horrible smell of the house the next morning when they were allowed to move back in.

And the smell she remembered became mixed in with the burning of Atlanta, and a fireman came out of the wall of flame and put his arm around her shoulder to steady her and tell her it would be all right, and take the reins from her hands to lead the horses so she could stay in the back of the wagon to comfort Loretta and Kat and Johnny. And Helen looked up at the fireman to thank him, and saw that his face was not the face she remembered from that night in her childhood, but had become the face of Rhett Butler/Clark Gable. Or was it Spencer Tracy? Or—it was suddenly the face of the Union soldier who tries to rape Scarlett when they get back to Tara, and he seized Helen by the throat and she tried to resist, but knew if she didn't surrender something terrible would happen to Johnny. "No!" she cried once, feebly, as he started to tear her clothes off; then she surrendered. "Do what you want with me," she sobbed, "but spare Johnny!"

Someone was pounding on the door, pounding on the door at Tara, coming to save her. Johnny! Helen sobbed once more, hearing his crying in the next room, hoping the Union soldier would be too distracted by his lust to hear it too, and nearly falling off the couch in her turmoil.

Quite awake now, she stumbled into her shoes and went to the door. Her parents were back from bingo, and Red had forgotten his keys. Neither of them noticed the ordeal Helen had just suffered through, nor thought it unusual of her to dash into the room to stop Johnny from crying and put more water and Vicks VapoRub in the vaporizer. After all, she did have him spoiled rotten.

Helen had been working for a little less than a year when she first encountered Francis Xavier O'Dell.

"Frank," he corrected her, though not rudely. "My name's Frank."

"It says Francis Xavier in your personnel file," Helen said primly. She was replacing a girl in Employee Benefits who had the flu. "I never met a Francis Xavier who was under fifty, that's all. I like the sound of it."

She was not looking at him, but at the form he'd handed her. He was filing for compensation for jamming his hand in the freight-elevator door. Helen had read the form over six times, simply because she could not look him in the eye. She had never seen such a handsome man.

"It's an ugly mick name," he said with startling violence. "I can't stand it. I've punched out guys in bars for starting in on my name. You call me Frank, and leave it alone."

No, not handsome, Helen corrected herself, wondering if he expected her to answer him. Certainly not Clark Gable handsome, or Cary Grant handsome. Not even Spencer Tracy ugly-handsome, but downright ordinary. His neck was too thick for his body, and his hands—even the one he hadn't mashed in the elevator door—were blunt and ugly and looked like the knuckles had been broken. If she thought about it rationally, he was extraordinarily average-looking. He was average height, average weight, had an average pug-nosed, freckled, blue-eyed Black Irish face. Within the limited orb of her experience, Helen could think of half a dozen men who were better-looking. Then why couldn't she look him in the eye?

"Okay," she said, penciling something on his disability sheet. "Tell me exactly what happened, slowly, so I can write it down. They'll have to inspect the elevator and prove it was defective or you won't get compensation for it. They'll say it was your own clumsiness."

He had his hands on the corners of the desk and was leaning toward her. Helen resisted the urge to jump up and run out of the room. She would show him she couldn't be intimidated. She put the pencil down and stared at him. It had never failed when she was a kid.

"Listen," he said in a low voice, refusing to back down. "If you were a man I would've slugged you the minute you started in with my name. Now don't go telling me I'm clumsy, sister. Not me. You're looking at a former Golden Gloves contender. I had a five-win, no-loss record before I was sixteen. And a couple of years ago I managed to pick my way out of a minefield all by myself in the dead of night and lived to tell about it. So don't tell me I'm clumsy."

"I will tell you you've got some colossal chip on your shoulder!" Helen retorted, unblinking. "And *I've* ridden in the freight elevator without getting *my* hand caught."

He laughed wryly. "Okay," he said. "Suppose I had my mind on other things? Call it daydreaming. But that shitty door still snaps back too goddamn fast."

He saw her blush at the language, and that plus her steady stare made him back off at last. He took a few steps away from the desk and folded his arms, awkward, forcing bravado.

"So what about it?" he demanded, looking at the carpet. "Is this cheapo corporation gonna compensate me for three broken bones in my hand or not? I mean, if I ever get back in training, this is just the kind of injury that could screw up my boxing career."

"That's too bad," Helen said without inflection. "But it's not my problem. I'm just here for this week. It's up to the regular girl to decide."

"That's right, you work in the back—in Traffic—don't-cha?" he asked, trying suddenly to be friendly, putting Helen off. "I see you once in a while when I have to bring the mail up that way. What're you, executive secretary or something?"

"More like 'or something,' " Helen replied, finding a wit she never knew she had. "What's an ex-boxer doing in the mailroom?"

He shrugged, embarrassed by the question, less aggressive than before. "Never got around to going pro. I got drafted."

"Into the marines?" Helen looked at him skeptically. She had all the information on her desk.

"Yeah, well. I figured they were gonna get me anyway. So I jumped the gun and enlisted. How'd you know?"

"It's all in your file," Helen said drily, tapping the closed manila folder with her pencil. "I know all there is to know about you: name, address, date of birth, height, weight, marital status—"

He shook his head, pretending amazement. "I guess you got my number, all right. And I don't even know your name."

"Helen," she said involuntarily.

"No kidding?" he said. "Helen. Would you believe it if I told you my mother's name is Helen?"

"No," Helen said flatly, tapping the envelope with the pencil. "In here it says Victoria."

"All right, all right!" he said, throwing up his hands. "What it doesn't say in there is that I can't stand smart-ass women!"

The phone rang then, sparing Helen the confusion that would have accompanied a second blush. By the time she finished the conversation she had regained her composure.

"I've got work to do," she snapped, stuffing his file into a drawer and slamming it shut. She trained her eyes on his face, trying to burn holes in him. "If you've got nothing else to do, why don't you go slam your other hand in the elevator?"

Stuck-up marine! she thought later. Even a boy from the neighborhood would have more manners.

"What's the matter with 'the Blister' anyway?" Loretta remarked out of the clear blue. "God, I said hello to him on the subway platform the other morning and he damn near bit my head off!"

Loretta's pet name for Alistair was "the Blister." Not only did it rhyme, she argued, but it suited his personality. Helen had to agree. Her adopted cousin was exceptionally intelligent—in the same grade as Danny at St. Augustine's even though he was a year younger—and sly. Too small to defend himself against his peers, constantly tormented because of his name and the Limey accent that still clung to him, he got by on wit and subterfuge and sometimes pure nerve. He survived, but at the expense of trusting no one. Friend and foe were one to him. As Loretta put it, he was a blister on everybody's big toe.

Helen thought about Loretta's remark and shrugged. "I don't know," she said. "Can't be any worse than usual. He's always been antisocial."

They were in the kitchen of Helen's house, leafing through the kind of women's magazines that specialized in wedding gowns and exotic recipes. They could thumb their way through this fantasy land and gossip at the same time. It was their way of unwinding after work.

"I wonder about him," Loretta mused, forming her phrases carefully. "Does he—go out with girls much?"

"He might," Helen replied vaguely, a recipe for home-made napoleons catching her eye. She had a weakness for desserts. "Aunt Ag lets him come and go as he pleases. She's not nearly as strict as Mom. Anyway, I think he just walks around most nights. He's too young for girls."

"He's sixteen," Loretta pointed out. "My brothers used

to hang around with girls when they were sixteen. 'Course, I wasn't allowed out with boys until I was seventeen. I never understood that."

Helen just looked at her. For all Loretta's sophistication, she could be pretty thick sometimes.

"What do you think about a—a younger boy getting interested in—in an older woman?" Loretta blurted out suddenly, blushing until her freckles disappeared and sending Helen into hysterics.

"You've *got* to be kidding!" she gasped, when she could breathe again. "*You* and *Alistair*? Are you out of your mind?"

"I'd be willing to wait!" Loretta snapped, offended and embarrassed. "Until he's old enough to notice me, I mean. I'm not talking about anything *per*manent. I think he's cute, that's all."

Helen shook her head. "It would never work."

"You don't think so? But why?" There was a note of anguish in Loretta's voice.

Helen looked at her incredulously. "Can't you figure it out?" Loretta shook her head. "It's obvious. You're a head taller than him. How could you ever go out dancing?"

Loretta was crestfallen, but she could see the logic of it. "And if I wore heels to the wedding I'd make him look like a dwarf," she sighed. "Well, maybe he'll grow another inch or so and it won't be so bad. I still think he's kind of cute."

"But he's still got a rotten personality," Helen pointed out, not disloyal but simply accurate. "The only person in the whole world he cares about is Aunt Ag."

"That's only because he lost his family in the war," Loretta said, undaunted. "I could change that."

"No, you couldn't," Helen said.

Danny and Alistair graduated that June, and Helen took a day off from work—her first—to go to commencement exercises. There was was no bitterness in her heart that day. She felt almost magnanimous, knowing that Danny had barely squeaked through the college entrance exams and that if she had not stepped aside a year ago he would not be able to go. And she was proud of Alistair, had learned to look past the toughness and cynicism and accept him. They had talked at length the night before.

Kat had been attending novenas for Danny for over a year; the current cycle was in gratitude for his passing all his Regents exams. This was the last night, and she had succeeded in dragging Danny and Red along. Red went along because he feared for her safety walking home alone at night, and Danny because it was in his best interests to appear grateful. Only Divine Intervention could have gotten the likes of him into St. John's University. Helen was home alone, listening to a radio drama and taking care of Johnny.

The doorbell rang—two long, one short—Alistair's signal. He often dropped in on his nocturnal prowls, especially when he knew Helen's parents weren't home. Helen hoisted Johnny up in her arms and rang the buzzer. She stuck her head out into the long hall to watch the slightly bowlegged figure, truly glad to see him. When he came close enough to give her the familial peck on the cheek, she had to stop herself from laughing. He was barely three inches taller than she, who was just a little over five feet, and she kept thinking of Loretta— poor, tall, gawky Loretta with her missing front teeth and her romantic soul. If it weren't so funny it might have been sad.

"Whatcha doing out tonight?" Helen demanded of her cousin when they settled into the parlor and he scooped Johnny up into his lap. "You're graduating tomorrow."

Alistair shrugged. "Nothin' else to do. Nerves as well, I guess. Cripes, just think—I'm off to the big world out there. Scares me to death, I tell you." Then, as if he weren't safe making such an admission even to her, he turned his attention to Johnny, tickling him and roughhousing until the baby got hiccups. "Say, shouldn't this little squirt be in bed?"

"I always keep him up late Sunday nights," Helen explained. "He'll sleep later in the morning and give Mom a break."

"How's she lately—your mum, I mean? Don't see much of her, and she's always so weepy."

Helen shrugged. "She's a little better the past few months. All wound up about Danny getting into St. John's. It's like it's the only important thing that's ever happened to her. Leave it to the Pig to flunk out or something. I think it'd kill her."

"Mmm," Alistair said, listening but not listening. He couldn't wait for tomorrow, couldn't wait to get as far away from Danny as possible.

"So you are excited about tomorrow, then?" Helen asked him, taking Johnny and patting his back to get rid of the hiccups.

"Dunno," Alistair said. "Glad to be finished high school, able to get out and earn a living. Ag's in an awful twit about that. About me turning down college."

He never called his guardian anything but "Ag," by mutual agreement. He had felt too old at eleven, after what he had left behind in London, to give her any maternal title, and Ag always felt that the "Aunt" aged her. Alistair used it sometimes to get under her skin; at all other times she was simply Ag.

"How come you did that?" Helen asked. It was something that bothered her the minute she heard it. "You could have gotten a scholarship—your marks were much better than Danny's. And Aunt Ag wanted you to go to college. She was really mad when you said no."

Alistair tried to take Johnny from her, to avoid answering her. Helen wouldn't let him.

"Uh-uh. You'll get him all excited again, and he's got to go to bed soon."

"Okay," Alistair acquiesced, leaning back on the sofa and turning the radio up, as if the drama unfolding over the airwaves were of vital importance to him. Helen gave him a piercing look, got up to put Johnny in his crib, and came back just as the program was ending.

"Well?" she demanded, snapping the radio off before Alistair could get to it. "You didn't answer me."

"Suppose it's none of your beeswax?" he shot back, getting defensive. He let down the shield with few people, and even they could cause him to snap it back up without any warning. "Ag and me had it out and it's all settled. I'm starting work at the Y beginning of August. In the fall I do a few courses at night at City College. The only thing I'll back down on is getting me own apartment. Ag says I'm too young and she won't sign for me, so I'm staying with her for the time being. Other than that, I'm on me own."

"But Aunt Ag offered to pay your way straight through college," Helen objected. "And she can certainly afford it. If you were like Danny I could see, but you're smart, and you'd have a better chance—"

"Listen," Alistair interrupted. "Will you quit being thick long enough to understand that I don't want to take any more from that woman than I already have? If it wasn't for her, you know where I'd be now? Dead in the bombing, most like, or starved to death on one of them damn pittance farms they sent orphans to. I don't know why she took me in, and I'll never know why she didn't ship me back once she got me— I'm such an ugly-minded runt in case you haven't noticed— but I can't—can't owe her any more than—"

His voice broke; Helen could swear he was starting to cry. She sat frozen on the tired old sofa, staring at the faded flowered carpet, wishing she had kept her mouth shut. There was a great flood of devotion beneath his cynicism, and she had loosed it at the wrong time. He might never trust her again.

"Excuse me for living!" she snapped, handling the situation the only way she knew how, trying to goad him into being the person she knew. "If you want to complicate your life, I guess it's none of my business!"

"I'll pay me own way from now on," Alistair said, lighting

one of the cigarettes he no longer bothered to hide from Ag or anybody. "One of the blokes at the Y's gonna train me to be a masseur. If I get licensed I won't hafta spend the next five, six years picking up towels after people."

"What're you taking at City College?" Helen asked, a little envious of how easy it was for a boy to have his life mapped out, while she. . . .

Alistair shrugged. "Dunno. Place'll be jammed with GIs. Hafta see what's left over for a foreigner like me."

He said it without bitterness, but there was no disguising the way his alienness—the refusal of the microcosm he inhabited to accept him—ate at him. In a way, Helen decided, it was better for him to go to work, to expand his horizons, to meet people who could appreciate him. She thought of her conversation with Loretta and began to giggle.

"What's funny?" Alistair said warily, as if even she would ridicule him.

"Nothing!" Helen gasped, shaking her head. "I just thought of something."

"What?"

"Nothing, really! It was nothing to do with you, honest!"

He was eyeing her suspiciously, taking the situation too seriously, not believing her. She would have to do some pretty fancy explaining.

"It's just that someone—a girl I know—told me she liked you a whole lot. I don't mean that it's funny; it's just that she's such a tough cookie I was kind of amazed she'd admit something like that in front of me. It was funny, that's all."

Alistair watched her intently through the cigarette smoke, his irises so pale they seemed almost white. Menacing.

"Who?" he asked, attempting to be casual.

"I can't!" Helen objected. "I mean, you know her, and if she found out I told you she'd kill me, and she's bigger than me and—"

"Loretta!" Alistair exploded in disgust. "It figures! Boy, does it figure! Of all the girls in the neighborhood, that dizzy dame. . . . Still . . . she's a good Joe, Loretta. Sure, she calls me names behind my back, but I never heard her insult me to my face. I guess that means something. I never had anything against her."

"Can I tell her that?" Helen asked hopefully, relieved that she had extricated herself, somehow, from this conversation. "Can I tell her you like her, too—a little?"

"And how're you gonna tell her that without letting on that you told me about her, dimwit? Besides, what's it gonna accomplish? There's no future in it. I ain't got time for girls."

There was a sound of keys and footsteps in the long hall. The novena was over. They were back. Alistair stubbed out his cigarette and tried to wave the smoke away. Helen switched the radio on again and grabbed the newspaper, becoming engrossed in the funnies. Everyone knew kids their age never talked about anything serious; if they were caught doing any such thing they would be called upon to explain themselves. Alistair gave Helen one final look as Kat burst into the parlor, complaining she smelled something burning.

And the next morning Helen sat between Aunt Ag and her mother in the sweltering high school auditorium, taking her turn at holding Johnny, who was becoming increasingly cranky with the heat. She would not allow herself to think of her own graduation day only a year ago; would not complain, even in her own mind, about all the chances the boys had that she had never been offered.

"Missed you yesterday," Frank O'Dell said at the office on Tuesday.

"Did you?" Helen's voice was sharper than it had to be. "Good!"

Undaunted, he lingered at her desk for longer than dropping off the mail required. He was always in trouble with his supervisor; it no longer bothered him.

"What I mean is, you never missed a day since you been here. I notice things like that. Were you sick, or what?"

"None of your business!" Helen said, too loud. The girl at the next desk down the hall looked up to see what the noise was all about, which was exactly what Helen had in mind.

She was depressed today, could not say why. She did not usually take her moods out on other people, but he was asking for it. He managed to make a nuisance of himself at least once a day, and if she didn't straighten him out once and for all this could go on forever. It was so bad that she had taken to hiding in a vacant office every time she heard the squeak of the mail-cart wheels. It made her feel immature and ridiculous. Enough was enough.

"What's the matter—female troubles?" he asked confidentially, deriving secret delight from seeing her blush. "Listen, I got two older sisters. I know all about that stuff."

"You know all about exactly nothing!" Helen seethed, her voice barely above a whisper but her eyes flashing. "If you don't get off my back I'm calling your supervisor!"

He backed off a little, but made no effort to leave. Helen tried to stare him down; it didn't work and she reached for the phone. She started to dial the mailroom, but he swooped down on her and put his finger on the button.

"Before you do anything crazy, give me a minute, will you?" he demanded, talking rapidly. "I been trying to ask you something for weeks but I didn't have the guts—"

"Didn't have the guts?" Helen repeated, sarcastic. "An ex-marine with no guts? A Golden Glover—"

"Will you just *listen?*" And it was the plea in his voice, the first sign of vulnerability, that silenced her. "I hafta ask you something important. On the level, no shit. Something I hafta make a big decision on, and I gotta get an opinion from a whatta-you-callit—disinterested observer. It's something that means a lot to me, and I'm willing to spring for dinner if you'll just listen."

"Oh," Helen said, not sure what she meant by that. It was the childhood pattern repeating itself. She could stop a fight between total strangers, keep her father from killing Danny, even get through to Alistair. Now she had gotten through to this—whatever he was: part stranger, part acquaintance, part coworker. There was something he wanted to talk to her about. Or was this just a way to wrangle a date? She decided to take a chance.

"Are you busy this weekend?" Frank was asking her, and Helen shook her head without realizing she was doing it. "Say Saturday night? You live in Brooklyn, don'tcha? I know this place in Brooklyn. Someplace real special. Where we can talk without nobody bothering us. We could even go dancing later if you wanted."

"Okay," Helen said vaguely, hearing her own voice as if it were a stranger's. "Only you've got to pick me up, and meet my parents. They're very strict about that."

"I figured that," he nodded. "You tell your old man, though, that I'm as upstanding a mick as he is, and I won't do no harm to his daughter. You tell him that beforehand."

Helen hated that kind of talk; wanted to tell him so, but didn't.

"See you around." He grinned at her, pushing the mail cart down the hall.

Frank survived the meeting with Helen's parents unscathed, and they left the apartment and headed for Fourth Avenue. Helen assumed they would take the subway, and was dazzled and horrified to see Frank hail a cab. Cabs were for emergencies like going to the hospital, or for times when there were enough people crowded into the back of a big Checker to make it cheaper than taking the bus. Only rich people rode in cabs just to get someplace. Helen was about to say as much, but thought it wouldn't be tactful. It was his money, and he was trying to impress her. She did keep one eye on the meter, and winced a little every time it clicked, and when she saw where they had ended up she couldn't keep her mouth shut.

"Gage and Tollner's!" she half-shouted, rocking on her high heels on the sidewalk and staring up at the fancy white facade while Frank paid the cab driver. It was the most expensive restaurant in Brooklyn, a nineteenth-century landmark: the kind of place Helen could walk past in a kind of awe, gazing wistfully at the menu in the window, but certainly not a place where anyone she knew could afford to eat.

Frank took her by the elbow and propelled her inside; she seemed glued to the spot, paralyzed. He had even taken the trouble to make reservations. Helen was speechless, until she saw the menu.

"Oh, Frank!" she gasped, thrilling a little at the sound of her own voice saying his name. "This place is much too expensive!"

"Let me worry about that, will you? Or did I ask you to go Dutch?" he demanded, mock-belligerent. "Quit bellyaching and pick what you want. Or do I hafta order for you?"

"No," Helen said meekly, searching quickly for the cheapest item on the menu. It was considered good breeding, she'd been taught in high school, to choose the second least expensive meal, so as not to offend one's escort.

Frank had sisters who had gone to Catholic schools. He caught on immediately to what she was trying to do.

"Oh, no you don't!" he said, taking the menu out of her hands and signaling the waiter. "You like lamb chops?"

Helen nodded, helpless. If he had said rattlesnake she would have acquiesced as easily. She listened in a kind of wonder as he ordered for both of them: melon, French onion soup, salad, braised lamb chops with mushroom caps, and sautéed potatoes. Would the young lady care for a drink before dinner? "A Manhattan, please," Helen heard herself say in the smallest of voices, determined to have just a sip. She was surprised to see the waiter nod deferentially, never questioning whether she was old enough to drink. She had had trouble with that before. She remembered the name "Manhattan" from some movie she'd seen recently, knew it had a cherry in it, and nothing more. She looked at Frank in amazement, seeing him grinning at her as he ordered a Jack Daniels over ice. She'd taken him for just another blue-collar brat, a boy from the neighborhood, like all the boys she had ever known. When had he learned to order a meal with such finesse?

Frank sat fiddling with the silver and his water glass, while Helen sat in abject silence, the full significance of this evening beginning to dawn on her. What was this absolutely urgent problem he needed her advice on? Was this only a ruse to get her to go out with him? Couldn't he figure out from the way she treated him in the office that she wasn't the least bit interested in him? Or was she? Why could she still not look him in the eye? An eerie feeling—bred out of all the romantic postwar movies she'd been taking in lately—crept over her, giving her a minor case of the shudders. Had he cooked up this entire evening just to—God forbid—propose to her?

Their drinks came, and he gulped half of his as if he were inhaling it, then put the glass down and pushed it away toward the middle of the table. Helen tasted her Manhattan and gagged in disbelief, contenting herself with eating the cherry. Then she looked across at him, gathering courage.

"I've never been here before," she said. "Or anyplace like it. It's wonderful!"

"Class is for class," Frank quipped, but he obviously wasn't up to being clever. "I'm glad you like it," he said in a lower tone. "Only quit worrying about the price tag. I got money."

"I guess you must have, if you come to a place like this regular," Helen said, ingenuous, but needing to get to the bottom of this thing that worried her. "If you set out to impress me, you're doing a swell job."

He gave her a sharp look, offended, and became belligerent. "You hafta read into everything, don't you? Cripes, can't a guy spend a little money on a girl without her jumping to conclusions? I give up!"

"I just wonder why," Helen said.

"You look hungry, okay? Skinny. Thought I'd fatten you up a little."

"Fatten me up for what?"

"Cripes!"

He reached for his drink, brought it to his lips, but stopped without tasting it. He held it level with his chin and pointed his finger at her past the glass. "I mean, what'd you think, I was gonna propose to you?" he demanded. "You're too damn skinny, for one thing; you got no imagination, for another; and if I ever do get married it's gonna be a blonde. I don't like dark-haired women."

Another girl might have burst into tears, might at least have started to whimper under his criticism. Helen just looked at him. "I'm very glad you're not going to marry me," she said sincerely. "And I'm glad we got it straight now so I can eat with a clear conscience. I'd hate to think you were buttering me up for a proposal, because I'd have to say no."

"Ain't it terrific we got it all out in the open so early in the game?" He put the drink back on the table and pushed it away again; it was the second time he'd done it, and Helen wondered what it meant.

"Okay," she said. "Then you really *do* have a problem you want to talk about."

"Good for you!" he said drily, slapping the table lightly for emphasis. "The lady has decided to trust me! You get an A-plus on that one!"

"Men like to play games sometimes," Helen said, reciting a piece of wisdom she had acquired she knew not where. Too many movies; that was it, she thought. She was using the Lauren Bacall approach—cynical, suspicious—when the Ingrid Bergman method—all starry-eyed innocence—was more suited to her. "I wanted to be sure you were on the level."

"Well, am I?"

"Yes," she nodded, satisfied. Ingrid Bergman again.

He picked up his drink for the third time without drinking from it. Again he held it at chin level, looking at her over the glass. "Now that we've settled that, would you like to listen to why I took you out in the first place? I said I had something to discuss with you. Did you think I was kidding?"

"I'll listen," Helen said, a little too sharply. Back to Lauren Bacall.

"Terrific!" he said, putting the drink down and pushing

it away again. "And after we eat I'll take you dancing. You ever been to Roseland?"

She shook her head.

"I didn't think so," Frank said, sarcastic.

Who was he playing? Helen wondered. Bogart to her Bacall? Something he had said moments before was beginning to rankle her. What did he mean when he said she had no imagination? She had imagination and to spare; her problem was what to do with it within the confines of the life her upbringing had assigned to her. If she was somber and deadly serious on first acquaintance, what else did he expect of her? She would show him!

"I'm listening," she said, copying his dryness of tone. Best to stay with Lauren Bacall for the rest of the evening. Even a touch of Hepburn, if she could bring it off.

"Well, it's like this," he began, picking up the drink for the fourth time, but putting it down almost immediately. "I'm an only son of a widowed mother with no other means of support. What I mean is, she's never gone out to work and she wouldn't know where to begin. My sisters are both married, and they send her a little now and then, but she depends on me. My father, thank God, croaked while I was overseas, which is a damn good thing because I swore when I joined up I was never going to look at his sodden mug for the rest of my life. His liver was going, so it was just a question of time. Are you with me?"

"What?" Helen asked vaguely, Bacall and all the rest of them rapidly deserting her. The waiter had brought their dinner, and she was transfixed by the lamb chop on her plate.

In her experience, lamb chops were dry, paper-thin, and riddled with fat; something splurged on for Sunday dinner when somebody special was coming. They were usually fried or broiled to a leather-like consistency with Kat's vengeful culinary artistry, and their taste was something not to be described. When Frank had asked her if she liked lamb chops, she had said yes only to hasten the end of an uncomfortable conversation. As she had come to know them, they were awful.

But the thing on her plate looked like something out of a magazine. One surely couldn't be meant to eat it. It was over an inch and a half thick, oozing juice, and the end of the chop bone was dressed in a little fluted white paper bootie, like the kind they put on turkeys in Norman Rockwell's *Saturday Evening Post* covers. There was beside it a minuscule paper cup filled with something kelly green and wiggly—mint jelly, Helen was to learn—something she had never known existed. The mushroom caps glistened, fat and brown and flawless. How could she possibly eat anything that looked so lovely?

"Hey, are you there?" Frank demanded, a little annoyed. He was already slicing through his chop—the little paper bootie crumpled and left to float aimlessly in the gravy on the side of his plate.

Helen looked at her chop one last time, knife and fork poised in her hands, trying to etch it in her memory for all time. With a sigh, she put the flatware down and plucked the white paper bootie delicately off the end of the chop, tucking it into her purse.

"You're a real slum kid, you are!" Frank shook his head. "Another Depression mick. How do I pick 'em? I gotta find me a girl with class!"

"Don't you dare use that word in front of me!" She had been pushed too far this time. She plunked the knife and fork against the edge of her plate for emphasis. "And I'm not a mick anyway! I'm a Newfoundlander, and I've got other things in me besides Irish. If you don't like what you are, that's tough. Maybe I oughta feel sorry for you, but I don't. If you want a girl with class, what you need is some class yourself!"

He seemed to be amazed by this sudden display of fire, amazed and embarrassed.

"I'm sorry," he said, dropping the bravado for the first time that evening. "Maybe in my mind micks and drunks come out to the same thing. Like my old man. He was a mick, and a drunk, in that order. His father was a pretty rich man for an immigrant. Lace-curtain Irish, I'll have you know. Big brownstone off Parade Place in the Slope and everything. But my stupid old man was his only son, and he inherited too young, and he drank. I used to send my mother my service pay at a post-office box so she could get her hands on it before he did, the bastard!"

Helen let him finish, eating as he talked. She was trying very hard to listen, to be sympathetic, but she was distracted from his tale of woe by the exquisite things happening to her palate. She forced herself to swallow, about to murmur something compassionate, when he burst out again.

"Say," he began. "If you were me would you join the Fire Department?"

Helen nearly choked. "Is that what you brought me here to ask me?"

"Well, yeah," he said, looking hurt. "It's important to *me*!"

She laughed so loudly she drew attention from the surrounding tables. When she realized other people were staring she covered her mouth with the linen napkin and rocked silently in the chair until she could control herself.

"Big joke, huh?" He grimaced. "You figured right—I do have rocks in my head."

"I didn't mean to hurt your feelings," Helen gasped, putting her hand on his wrist in a maternal gesture. "You just hit me with it so sudden, I—"

"Well, I figure it this way," he explained. "I'm twenty-four years old and I'm nothing but a mailroom clerk. I got brains enough to figure I'm not gonna make it as a boxer. That was a kid dream, and I don't have time for kid dreams. Besides, is it worth messing up this beautiful mug of mine?"

Helen giggled.

"So before I end up wasting my life like my old man, I gotta make a choice. I could go to night school. I'm eligible for the GI Bill, and I got a little inheritance from my grandfather— left it to me when I was a baby; I guess he could figure how my old man was gonna end up. But I'm no genius, and I don't know what I'd take up in college, and it'd probably take me five-six years to get a degree. That's five-six years I'm still stuck in the mailroom, and I'd be nearly thirty by the time I got out. So I got it figured. I ought to go for some kind of municipal employee job. I'm not keen on getting my head blown off, so the cops are out. And garbage isn't exactly my field. But I figure any man with good reflexes has a crack at surviving as a fireman. So why not?"

"So why not?" Helen echoed him. "You sound like you've made up your mind already. Why do you need to talk to me?"

Frank shrugged, at a loss to explain himself. "I don't know. Maybe I just need somebody to bounce the idea off of. Somebody to convince me it isn't just another dumb mick job, like bartending, which was what my old man ended up doing, when he did work. Funny, I think the only people who drink more than bartenders are cops and firemen."

"Do you think being a fireman means you *have* to drink?" Helen asked quietly. At last she understood the half-finished Jack Daniels on the table between them.

"I don't know." He shrugged again. "Scares the crap outta me, though."

Helen thought a moment before she spoke. "I like you a lot better when you're not being—tough," she offered, hoping he wouldn't be insulted. "Like now. Every time at the office I kept thinking, 'That stuck-up marine! If he thinks I'm going to bother with him, he's got another think coming!' I guess I only went out with you because you sounded so desperate about asking my advice. But when you're not trying to impress people with what a tough guy you are. . . ."

It had come out all in a rush, and she stopped herself, embarrassed. Frank laughed.

"Women! I can't figure 'em. So whatta you say? You think I oughta take the exam? It's coming up in a week. That's why I gave you such a rush job. Could you see yourself—or any girl you knew—married to a fireman?"

Helen frowned. "I don't see what that's got to do with it."

"Well, okay, strike that," he said, a little too hurriedly. "Do you think I oughta take the exam is all I'm asking."

Helen took a deep breath. "Is that what you want to do with your life?" she asked, all Ingrid Bergman starry-eyed innocence once more. "What do *you* think?"

"I think maybe I'll give it a whirl," he said.

"What d'yer think of him, then?" Red asked Kat out of the clear blue.

"Think of who?" Kat did not look up from her knitting.

Red drew on his pipe for a moment. "Helen Mary's young man."

Kat dropped a stitch, murmured "Mother of God!" under her breath, and raveled out to the beginning of the row. "She's only just brought him round," she said, more irritably than necessary. "Sure, seein' him the one time don't make him her 'young man.'"

Red nodded, acknowledging her point. "Right enough. But what d'yer think of him, anyways?"

Kat lowered the knitting needles to her lap, as if it were a different, and more absorbing, matter to diagnose the young man apart from his relationship to her daughter. "I'd say he's a bit of a brass in him," she observed. "Bit of a cock-o-the-walk for him just bein' a mail clerk."

"And what would yer have in mind, then?" Red teased. "Some little mousy type that yer don't hear a peep out of him? Or was it him not being president of the corporation yer objectin' to?"

Kat scowled at him. "Yer a terror, you are. That's not what I meant at all."

She went back to her knitting with a vengeance, as if the subject were closed as far as she was concerned. But Red put his newspaper aside and continued to watch her, puffing on his pipe, eyes twinkling.

"I'm thinkin' it might do Helen Mary good to find a man as has some spirit. She's too quiet herself."

"Maybe," Kat acknowledged, still knitting. "Only it might mean him getting louder and her getting quieter as the years went by. It's not likely he'd bring her out of herself."

"I wouldn't know," Red mused. "But now, just lookin' at the two of them tonight—d'yer think they're after likin' each other?"

Kat was counting stitches. She had made the same mistake all over again. She gave Red a sharp look and started tearing her work out again. "Sure, he'd have to be after likin' her to take her out!" she reasoned. "As for herself, I couldn't say. We don't talk much now she's out to work."

Red thought about that. He wanted to suggest that Kat and her daughter had stopped talking to each other sometime earlier than that, but that would be placing blame, and he could not do that. He might be driven to say that it had something to do with the gloom that had settled over Kat after Johnny was born, but that might only serve to drive her back into that same gloom, which she was only now, and very gradually, emerging from.

"She's a young lady now is all," he offered by way of explanation for the rift. "She's a mind of her own. And I'm thinkin' I rather like her taste in young men. So what if he's got a bit of brass to him? He's a go-getter, and he's after havin' a sense of humor. That's not a bad mix, then."

Kat looked at the shambles of her knitting, and abandoned it with a sigh. "It's near ten," she said, putting it back in her knitting basket and getting up from the chair. "Will yer be after waitin' up for her, then? I'm wantin' to go to the early mass tomorrow."

"Aye, go on then!" Red said. "I'm not tired, and I'll mind Johnny for yer and go to the late mass meself."

Kat was halfway down the hall when he called after her. "Serious now, what d'yer really think of the lad?"

Kat stuck her head back into the parlor. "Sure, if she marries a dark-haired lad I'll no more have redheads for grandchildren than I did for children!"

Red threw back his head and roared.

Helen and Frank did not speak in the cab on the way to Roseland, but he took her hand in his and she did not pull away. She did edge as far away as she could on the seat, so that the door handle nudged her in the ribs sometimes, and stared out the window at the lights along the river as they crossed the Brooklyn Bridge. The driver smoked a cigar, which brought tears to Helen's eyes and made her cough sporadically; otherwise there was no sound other than the hum of the tires over the metal roadway of the bridge, and the squawk of the wipers where a light summer shower splashed the grimy windshield.

Helen had never been to Roseland, legendary pinnacle of big-band-era dance halls, or any other dance hall for that matter, but listened enviously to the girls in the office, some of whom went there regularly. It turned out to be exactly as she expected, bigger than life, a glittering fairyland where one could glide across the largest polished-wood dance floor in New York until the sun came up. Helen, of course, had to be home by twelve, but the thought that the place would go on glittering and humming long after she left enchanted her.

Frank was a good dancer, she discovered, though she was not surprised since he *had* been a boxer. She usually had trouble dancing with men who were much taller than she—in heels she barely reached his shoulder—but he adapted to her easily, and they danced, still unspeaking, for over an hour. It was during a lights-low dance that he broke the silence.

"Did you check your guardian angel at the door?"

"What?" Helen frowned up at him vaguely—the heat and cigarette smoke and something else she couldn't define making her dreamy.

"Aren't you supposed to leave room for your guardian angel

when you dance?" His voice was serious, but his eyes were laughing.

Helen realized what he was talking about and unconsciously drew away from him. They *were* dancing close; closer than she'd ever danced with anyone. Too close.

"How'd you know about that?" She was flustered, annoyed, whether at him or herself she couldn't tell.

"My sisters went to Catholic school, remember?" He winked at her, conspiratorial, trying to tease her into a less serious mood.

But Helen grew more serious. It had been a lovely evening until he'd spoiled it.

"Can we sit down?" she frowned. "My feet are killing me."

"Sure," Frank said, still smiling, but inwardly cursing himself for starting the whole thing. He should have known that she would freeze up on him, that it would take more than one evening to wean her away from this somberness, if it could be done at all.

They walked away from the dance floor, and he went to get her an ice. Helen took off her white gloves—constant adjunct of a lady, she'd been taught—and dabbed at the perspiration on her forehead with a small embroidered handkerchief.

"When I was in eighth grade," she said for no particular reason, absently taking the ice from Frank, "I was the best speller in the school. I went on to the Knights of Columbus diocesan semifinal spelling bee. There were just twenty of us from the whole Diocese of Brooklyn, and the winner would go on to the finals, and the winner of the finals got a full scholarship to any Catholic high school in the city. And I lasted till the third-from-final round, and I will never forget the word that got me. I couldn't spell 'handkerchief'!"

"No kidding!" Frank was impressed, not with the facts of her narrative, which did not interest him—overachievers, particularly girls, were usually drips—but with the sudden sparkle she had taken on in the telling.

"Uh-huh," Helen said. "'Cause in my family we always said 'hankerchiff.' It never occurred to me it had a 'd' in it."

"Isn't that something?" Frank remarked, fighting with a number of sarcastic responses that came to him.

"Yeah," Helen sighed, unaware of his struggle. "For as long as I live I'll never misspell 'handkerchief' again."

A silence ensued. Helen sipped at her ice, which was starting to melt.

"I've had a good time tonight," Frank said quietly, embarrassed a little by his own sincerity and a strange kind of tenderness he'd never expressed before. "Have you?"

Helen nodded, unable to speak, realizing with a pang that she had to be home soon and not knowing what the outcome of this evening would be. Would he ask her out again? Did she want him to? What would she say if he did ask her? What would she do if he didn't?

"Why don't we have one more dance?" he suggested, seeing the downcast look. "Then I better get you home before you turn into a pumpkin or something."

When the number started he pulled her toward him gently, the lightest pressure of his hand against her spine preventing her from edging away from him. Helen stiffened slightly and tried to hold herself away, but he shook his head.

"Uh-uh!" he whispered into her hair. "This ain't the school dance. No chaperones, no guardian angels. Relax!"

She did relax a little, but the fun had gone out of it. She had not remembered to put her gloves on; her right hand felt sweaty in his, her left would leave damp spots on his seersucker jacket. She was in a panic about this for a while, then decided it was futile, began to grow dreamy from the heat, and found she had something else to worry about.

He was just that much taller than she so that his knee as he moved tended to brush against the insides of her thighs, and though she was amply protected by nylons and a pantygirdle and two taffeta slips and her dress, this began to have the strangest effect on her. On one hand, she felt hot and uncomfortable and scared; on the other, she suddenly had a cold, clear remembrance of her first-grade class and Sister Misericordia and the sufferings of the martyrs and virgins and—

She uttered a little cry and stood stock-still on the dance floor. Frank looked at her in alarm.

"What's wrong?"

"Nothing. I—have to go to the ladies' room," she gasped frantically, and bolted.

"It must have been the Manhattan," she excused herself lamely as they stood on the stoop of the row house to say good-night. "I'm not used to alcohol, I guess."

"Sure. That's okay," Frank said, understanding the problem, or so he thought. "Say, am I going to see you again?"

"I—I can't say." Helen frowned, completely enervated, unable to make decisions. "We'll—talk about it Monday—at the office."

Frank was puzzled. She had been remote all the way home, as if his patient efforts to relax her had failed, suddenly and for some reason he could not understand. Was it his fault? What had gone wrong?

"If that's what you want," he said with a shrug, and they shook hands—his firm and hopeful, hers gloved and unpromising—and she disappeared into the long hallway.

Red was waiting up for her, snoring in his chair, the newspaper fallen from his lap into a shambles on the floor. Helen shook his shoulder gently. She could not let him sleep in the chair all night on her account, regardless of how awful she felt, and how apparent her feelings must be on her face.

"Did yez have a good time, then?" Red mumbled, stretching and orienting himself to his surroundings.

"Yes," Helen said vaguely; it was partially true. "He took me to Gage and Tollner's and to Roseland. In a *cab*."

"Big spender," her father remarked. "He must be mad about yer!"

"Don't joke, Pop. It's not funny." She was close to tears.

"I wasn't tryin' to be funny, sure." Red was offended. "I was askin' yer how yer felt about him is all."

Helen sighed. "When I figure it out myself, Pop, I promise you'll be the first to know."

With that cryptic remark, she kissed the top of his bald head and went to bed.

Helen went to the late mass with her father the next morning, but to Red's surprise, she did not accompany him to the communion rail. She seemed lost in thought as they walked home, barely murmuring to the neighbors when Red stopped on the corner to chat. Those who lived on the block had seen the strange young man escort Helen down the stoop and into a cab the night before ("A cab! Sure, and he must be well-heeled to ride about in cabs, for a fact!") and had not seen them come home. Helen declined as politely as she could to answer their oblique inquiries, and at one point tugged at Red's elbow as if she were a child, anxious to get home.

It was nearly a week, the following Saturday afternoon, before she could get to confession. During all that time she avoided Frank at work, returning to her old habit of dodging into an empty office when she heard the squeak of the mail-cart wheels. She was a nervous wreck.

The little sliding door in the confessional swished open the minute Helen sank to her knees inside the curtain, and it made her jump violently. But she caught her breath and plunged right in.

"Bless me, Father, for I have sinned. . . ."

It would have been impossible to disguise her voice. This very same priest, ancient now, had married her parents, baptized her, given her First Communion, officiated at her confirmation. He was nearly deaf, which made him very popular among school kids and nervous adolescents; he let a great deal slip by because he couldn't be bothered asking anyone to repeat, and he notoriously gave the lightest penances in the parish. But his deafness had not impaired his sense of humor.

Helen rattled off the half-dozen minor offenses she remembered from the past three weeks, and then got down to cases.

"Father, I—there's a young man I've been—seeing recently—someone I met at my place of business—and we—last week he took me out to dinner—and then dancing. I—well, we had a drink with the dinner, and it was very hot where we were dancing and—"

She hesitated. How to put it into words exactly? Suppose she just used the stock phrase about having impure thoughts? Suppose he told her to clarify that?

"And?" the old priest half-shouted, getting the whole picture and giggling a little at how many times he had heard this tale of woe from young girls. "Got you excited, did he? Well, what of it?"

Though he couldn't see her blushing in the dark, he no doubt felt the heat waves. Before Helen could open her mouth, the priest had more to say.

"So what'd you do—send the young man packing, huh? Now, was that a nice thing to do after he spent all that money on you? Tsk, tsk, you ought to be ashamed!"

"But, Father," Helen piped up, anxious to justify herself. The priest's assumptions annoyed her. "How'd you know it isn't worse than that? Maybe I—encouraged him."

"If you'd gone any farther with it you wouldn't be telling it in confession," he said with absolute conviction. "Three Our Fathers, three Hail Marys, and stop giving the young man a hard time. If you go no farther than dancing before you're married, you're the exception and not the rule. Act of Contrition, now, and out with you. I'm a busy man!"

"But, Father—"

"Can't hear you, young lady. Deaf as a post, remember? Come along, now: 'O my God, I am heartily sorry. . . .'"

Helen recited the Act of Contrition obediently, and left the confessional. She knelt at the altar rail and said her penance, and left the church with the curious sense of having had a burden lifted from her shoulders.

When she got to the office on Monday there was a hand-written note on top of her typewriter. "Taking F.D. exam Wednesday," it began without introduction. "Be out the rest of the week. Thanks for advice. Sorry the rest didn't work out."

It was unsigned. He must have left it Friday after she went home, Helen thought, feeling numb and a little sick inside. She would not see him for an entire week, could not apologize or explain. What if he did pass the exam and quit his job without speaking to her and she never saw him again?

Calmer, she realized he would have to give two weeks' notice, and she could always get his address from personnel. Now, if she only could find the courage to write to him. . . .

Helen's Aunt Ag started going through her changes about a year after Kat had Johnny and her hysterectomy. Now, at forty-five, she had quietly slipped across the hinterland of menopause without a ripple, and without bothering to mention it to anyone. If she was saddened by the finality of it, by its making definite her never marrying or bearing children, Ag showed no sign. As far as she was concerned, her spinsterhood had been finalized by the bullet in Freddie's brain that day in Belfast, and the rest of her life was an uninterrupted continuum.

This was why her feelings toward her younger sister, and the profound, self-induced gloom Kat had assumed since Johnny's birth, vacillated between pity and plain exasperation. True, Kat had neither the strength of personality nor the shock of events in her early life that had made Ag endure, but on the opposite side of the coin, she did have the faithful husband and fine, healthy children she had always wanted. Just how long did Kat expect people to feel sorry for her?

Ag was more than a little surprised when Red began to confide in her. He was concerned about Kat and her moods, he said; they had gone on long enough. Ordinarily, Ag thought, Red was the sort to keep his troubles to himself. Not only that, but he had never quite forgiven Ag for letting Kat take on the burden of their mother by herself. But the old woman was dead nearly three years, and Kat was still walking around with the air of a martyr. Red talked about it to Ag one Sunday while Kat was busy in the kitchen.

"Yer sister is after talkin' of buyin' a cemetery plot," he began in a low voice.

"So?" Ag had her stockinged feet up on the coffee table as usual. Menopause had made her gain weight, and her feet hurt that much more. "I was planning the same for myself once I turn fifty. It's a natural concern at our age, I'm thinking. But don't yez have space where you put the old woman?"

Red nodded. "Aye, there's that. Only it's Harmony Bay she's after talkin' about."

Ag looked at him blankly. "Come again?"

Red sighed, knowing it was going to sound foolish no matter how he phrased it. "It started when the old one died," he began. "Kat got it into her head as how we should have her dug up and shipped back to Harmony Bay."

"Now, isn't that foolish!" Ag clucked, in a tone she had used to flatten Kat's romantic notions since they were girls. "Sure, the expense!"

"That's what I was after tryin' to tell her." Red got up to get an ashtray, opened his clasp knife, and began to work on his pipe. "I says, not only is it gone ter cost an arm and a leg, but it don't make sense. Sure, I says, yer dad was lost at sea, and herself was an orphan. She had no people that she knew of down to home, so she's better off here where she has got people. Besides, I says—and here's where I should of kept me mouth shut—besides, once yer dead, what do yer care where they put yer?"

"And what'd she have to say to that?" Ag leaned forward, fascinated, but Danny came in just then, bringing conversation to a halt.

At five feet ten and two hundred pounds, Danny was the

biggest Manning in history, recorded or otherwise. Self-interested, overweight, seventeen years old and on the verge of starting college, he was no more mature than he had been at ten or twelve. Red cringed every time he came into the room. More than anything else, Danny was the end product of the meddling of his cracked and usurping late grandmother, and Red was torn between cursing the old woman for pushing Kat aside in the mothering of this child and cursing himself for not stepping in years ago. It was too late now. College or the service might make a man of Danny, but if they failed there was no further hope.

"Dinner ready yet?" he demanded, sticking his head through the door while the rest of his pale and flabby body remained out in the hall. He had his Sunday suit on, shirt open at the neck, tie stuffed raggedly into his jacket pocket. He had come from the twelve-thirty mass, where he stood rocking on his heels in the back so he could be the first one out when it was over. He had also—God knew where, because the bars were closed on Sundays—been drinking. Red winced. The beer on Danny's breath was evident even from this distance.

"Not yet," Red growled at his son. "And clean yer teeth, would yer? Yer mother don't like yer drinkin' on a Sunday."

Danny made a face and would have headed for the bathroom, but he caught sight of Ag and stuck his head in again. "Say, is Alice-stare coming?" he asked, his voice laced with more than a touch of malice.

"As a matter of fact, no he's not," Ag snapped a little too quickly. She and Danny were less than friendly, but it wasn't that as much as her sensitivity to criticism about Alistair. Ag felt, at sixteen, that he was old enough to come and go as he pleased, regardless of the unsought opinions of family and neighbors. In Danny's case it was simple envy, because he did not have as much freedom. "He said he had other plans."

Danny snorted at that. "I'll just bet he does," he said cryptically, and disappeared.

Red looked after him. "And what's that supposed ter mean?"

"Your guess is as good as mine," Ag said with a shrug, anxious to change the subject. "Where were we, then? Aye, Kat and her cemetery plot. So what did she say when you made that remark about not caring once you're dead?"

Red had finally gotten his pipe filled and ready. He lit it, and puffed deliberately. "Well, as I was after sayin', that's where I should of kept me mouth shut, because it really set her off. 'Yer can say what yer like!' she says. 'Because I'm after goin' down to the country to die.'"

Ag was silent for a moment. "She said that?"

"Aye."

"Well, does she mean to have her body sent back after she's gone, or is she for moving back while she's living?"

Red's hand came down on the arm of the chair. "Jesus and Mary, how do I know? God save us from you women! If it ain't sickness or death it's sickness *and* death! Are yez never satisfied until ye've something eatin' yer guts out? I'll not talk about death or cemeteries or goin' down to Newfoundland! It's all one to me! When they put me in the ground I don't give a gull's ass whether it's Brooklyn or Harmony Bay or the Canarsie dump! All I ask is that yer see can yer talk some sense into herself, because it's beyond me!"

Ag waited until she was certain he was through. "It's like she's got a case of what the old woman had," she observed thoughtfully. "Planning her death a way before the fact. The thing is, herself was near twenty years older than Kat when she started this nonsense."

Red gave her a guarded look. "Can yer talk some sense into her?" There was a tinge of anguish in his voice. "Sure, I'm at me wit's end!"

Kat's voice came to them from the dining room. "It's on the table!" she called.

"Aye!" Ag shouted back, exchanging glances with Red as she slipped into her shoes.

They were barely finished saying grace when Ag jumped into the fray with both feet.

"So it's real estate you're interested in now?" she said airily to Kat, passing the potatoes to Danny without so much as looking at him.

"Real estate? I don't know what yer mean." Kat was cutting meat for Johnny; the knife hesitated for a second, perilously close to her thumb.

"Looking for a plot with a view back home, I mean," Ag remarked drily. "I'm hoping you'll wait till you get there to die and save us the expense of shipping you!"

There was a silence around the big table. Even Danny stopped wolfing and stared at his mother. Helen, preoccupied with thoughts of Frank, put down the platter she was holding and stared from Ag to Kat to Red. Red put down his knife and fork and leaned back in his chair, uncomfortable. Only Johnny, nearly three and oblivious of the problems of adults, went on eating, babbling softly to himself.

Kat directed her anger at Red. "Where do yer get the brass?" she hissed at him.

Red cleared his throat, plainly embarrassed, but not about to be told off in public by a woman. "I was after hopin' she could put some sense in yer head, then. God knows it's beyond me!"

With that he picked up his cutlery and started eating, as if the matter were settled. Helen sat and waited, wishing Alistair had come this week so she'd have someone to trade signals with across the table.

Thwarted in her attempt to bring her husband out in the open, Kat turned on her sister. "And it's none of yer concern!" she railed, in a rare moment when she could permit her anger to show. "My plans for my life are my business!"

"Aye," Ag said, unperturbed, reaching for the big china teapot and pouring with a steady hand. "And you having a husband and three children—one of 'em just a baby—that don't matter, I suppose. You can start planning your own death any time now, and not think of it as selfish. Sure, and who needs you, then?"

"Yer don't understand it," Kat said more quietly, picking up Johnny's spoon where he had thrown it on the floor.

"I've no need to," Ag said. "All I have to do is hear it. And what I'm hearin' sounds like the same load of blather we heard from Mom for how many years?" She was getting so worked up she forgot her carefully nurtured Americanisms and lapsed back into the dialect of her youth. "Is that what yer wish on yer children, then? And I'm after thinkin' not so much of the big ones, who'll marry and be out someday soon, but of His Nibs there, who'll have to stomach it all his life or all yours!"

"But listen to me, then!" Kat's voice was shrill, rising above Ag's. "It's not that I'm plannin' for to die, only bein' prepared! I'm only thinkin' on the future!"

"A cemetery plot!" Ag sneered. "Sure, that's a lovely future!"

They were at fever pitch now, so loud that only Helen heard the doorbell. She tugged at her father's elbow. "It's the bell."

"Aye." Red waved her aside, his attention fixed on what could become a hair-pulling match any time now. "Go tell whoever it is we don't want any. This is better than the fights at the Garden, then! And sure, who in his right mind would bother a family of a Sunday?"

Helen dabbed at her mouth with her napkin and hurried down the long hallway. Whoever it was—no doubt a nosy neighbor to see what the harangue was about—she would not buzz them in, but would deal with them on the stoop. She opened the glass-paned inside door, ready for a confrontation. Jehovah's Witnesses had been around the neighborhood lately; Helen was expert at dispatching them. She pulled the outside door open and found Frank.

There was a long moment when Helen did not know what to say. "What are *you* doing here?" she finally managed.

"Just thought I'd let you know your advice paid off. I made the F.D." His voice was low, partly because he didn't want to brag, partly because he had grown up in a similar neighborhood where all the venetian blinds had ears. "They released the top grades right away, and I was one of them. I was gonna call you to let you know, but I forgot you cheap micks don't have a phone. So here I am!"

"That's wonderful!" Helen said, ignoring the ethnic slur, the whole week's fear that she would never see him again evaporating. "But, Good Lord, did you come all the way from Greenpoint? Listen, I'm very glad for you, and I'd invite you in, but we're right in the middle of dinner. . . ."

"Oh," he said, hands in pockets, nonchalant, as if knowing she couldn't send him all the way back to Greenpoint on an empty stomach. "That's okay."

"I mean, I'd ask you in, but—well, they're having this terrible fight," Helen explained lamely, as if he couldn't hear the voices from the apartment behind her. Family matters belonged in the family, her father always said, but she could not risk another misunderstanding, not now, not for anything. He had come all the way from Greenpoint just to see her and share his good news, and she couldn't. . . . "See, my mother and my aunt are in this big battle over a cemetery plot, and I don't think they'd shut up even if they saw I had a guest, so I just can't let you come in and have to sit through all that. . . ."

He was laughing. "Hey, don't I know it? When I left the house this morning my mother and my oldest sister were at it already. It don't matter!"

"I'm sorry." Helen looked down, away from him, too many things rushing to be said. Nothing she tried to say would come out right. She could not risk it, could not.

"Hey," he said. Helen felt the back of his hand touch her cheek, tenderly, in spite of the venetian blinds, sending chills down her spine. "Are you all right? I get the impression somehow that you're mad at me, like I did something wrong. Maybe I was crazy coming all the way over here without telling you, but I had to see you."

Helen gave him an anxious look. "Of course I'm not mad at you! I just feel funny leaving you standing out here."

"I told you I don't care about that." An edge of exasperation came into his voice; he was running one hand through the hair that hung down on his forehead, frustrated with circumstances, with the fact that there didn't seem to be anyplace they could relax and talk. "Christ, I didn't think, I guess. I just jumped on the subway and rushed over, because I wanted to tell you about me, about the future. Does that matter to you? Do you care about what happens to me?"

"Yes, I do," Helen said simply.

"Okay then, I gotta go." Again he brushed his hand against her cheek, and Helen began to be uneasy. The venetian blinds. "I'll see you tomorrow, at the office. I'm giving my two weeks' notice. And you take your lunch hour at twelve-thirty, you hear me?"

"Okay." Helen smiled for the first time.

He was halfway down the stoop, but the smile stopped him. He turned to look at her. "I like that face. I like it a lot. Do that more often, would you?"

She could not stay to watch him saunter down the block toward the subway—she was too aware of the eyes and ears behind the lace curtains. So she slipped inside, back into the fray. Her mother's voice, then Aunt Ag's, point-counterpoint, went on. Helen slid unnoticed into her seat and began picking at her lukewarm dinner, oblivious. Her father, who had been following the battle with growing amusement, shot an inquiring glance in her direction. One look at his daughter's face, and he did not have to ask her who was at the door.

"Aw, come on! You know I can't sew worth a damn!" Loretta moaned. "I'm all thumbs!"

Helen sighed. "Well, you can't afford to buy a gown, can you? And you can't be maid of honor in a street-length dress. I want this done right. I guess I'll have to make it for you."

"I'm sorry, but I'd botch it. You know I would."

"It's all right!" Helen said with the air of a martyr. She was irritated to the point of explosion, but was restraining herself with great effort. "I'll just add that to the four million other things I've got to worry about!"

"Well, I don't see what all the fuss is about," Loretta said, lolling on Helen's bed. "You got the priest, you got the two witnesses, you'll make yourself a wedding dress. What else is there?"

Helen gave her a poisoned look. Loretta's lack of a sense of protocol drove her insane. "What else is there? Oh, nothing much! Just scrounging up enough money for a little reception for the families; it'll probably just be breakfast, because that's all we can manage. Then there's finding an apartment, getting furniture and dishes and all that, figuring where we're going for our honeymoon and planning that out, dragging Frank to a pre-Cana conference, etcetera, etcetera. This is not to mention my mother. Or Danny."

Loretta sprawled out on her stomach and looked up at Helen, who was beginning to pace. "Your mother I expect to be a pain. But what's up the Pig's ass?"

"Loretta!"

Loretta shrugged. "We're friends. If I can't talk frankly around you, who can I trust? Besides, even you call him 'the Pig.' "

"And don't use that word," Helen mumbled, rummaging through her bureau drawers, folding underwear, pairing socks, engaged in the endless Saturday morning busywork.

"What—'ass'? Nothing wrong with it. Perfectly useful word. Besides, it's in the Gospels."

"I don't mean that." Helen slammed a drawer shut. "I mean 'frankly.' It sounds funny."

"Oh, yeah. Because of Frank." Loretta had caught on. "Frank, frankly. Yeah, I guess that would sound funny. I guess that's what it means to be in love."

Helen sat on the edge of the bed and thought about it. She smiled. "I guess so."

"*Are* you in love—really?" Loretta asked wistfully. "What's it like?"

"I'm not sure," Helen said, pushing the hair up off her forehead, groping for the right words. "Sometimes it's like—like birds singing, and everything going right all day. Sometimes it's like wanting to throw up and getting your period all at the same time. Sometimes I can't wait for the day to come, and other times I think I'm crazy. Sometimes I'm scared. I can't say it any better than that."

"What're you scared of?" Loretta wanted to know. "Is it about—you know—about S-E-X?"

Helen looked down at her hands. She had trouble talking about those things. "I guess so. Wondering what it'll be like, what *he'll* be like. Whether it'll hurt a lot."

"Yeah." Loretta rolled over on her back and kicked her loafers off. "It's too bad neither of us has an older sister we can ask. I mean, my sisters are dumber than I am. And I can't exactly ask my *brothers!*"

"No." Helen sighed.

"What's wrong with Danny?" Loretta asked, thinking of brothers in general. "Why wouldn't he want you to get married?"

"It's a long story." Helen didn't want to talk about it, wished she'd never brought it up.

"I've got all day," Loretta said complacently, settling in on the bed.

"Danny thinks I'm getting married so he can't go to college."

Loretta sat up suddenly. "That doesn't make any sense."

"It does to Danny."

"But why?"

"I don't want to talk about it." Helen got Loretta's loafers from the floor and held them out to her. "Are we going downtown or not?"

"I don't know, are we?" Loretta did not look inclined to move.

"I'm going to look at silver patterns," Helen said firmly. "You can come or not." She threw the shoes at Loretta and started out the door.

Helen's confrontation with Danny had been especially ugly because it was so unexpected. Helen had never consciously wished evil on anyone, though if she had cause to curse someone it certainly was Danny. But to have him accuse her of plotting to wreck his life, and threaten her the way he had. . . .

Danny's timing was flawless. He waited until the very night Frank and Helen announced their engagement. It was as if he had no inkling that any such thing could happen, although as Red put it when they told him, even a blind man could have seen it.

Frank had done all the planning when it came to how they would tell Helen's parents they were engaged. He had a flair for the dramatic. Helen had known for a week that he was going to show up at the house with a ring, but she had no idea what he would do.

They had had a serious talk the weekend before, walking along Broadway on an early fall night, holding hands, coming out of the movies. He proposed to her in the middle of Times Square, being perverse, knowing Helen was too introverted to show any emotion in such a public place. They walked all the way down to Thirty-fourth Street, not talking, holding hands, until they ended up in one of those Irish bars on the West Side where it was so noisy—Guinness and darts and a great deal of open-mouthed, thigh-slapping laughter—that no one paid any attention to them. No one noticed, as they slipped into a booth in the back near the dart board, that Helen's cheeks were wet and the powder was worn off her reddened nose. Frank was grinning smugly.

"You dirty mick!" she hissed at him for the first and last time, blowing her nose, her eyes sparkling. "What a lousy trick to pull on me!"

He held out his hands, palms up, what-do-you-expect-from-a-dumb-Irishman, still grinning.

"Whatta you say?" he asked her. "Will you or won't you?"

Helen tucked her handkerchief back into her purse. "Now

that you bring it up, I'm not so sure," she said slyly, uncharacteristically toying with him. He brought out, had been bringing out, the little bit of mischief she possessed. "I'm not sure if I want to spend the rest of my life with a man who has no eyebrows."

It was meant as a joke, but he looked hurt. His first day out as a rookie, he had been putting out a grease fire in a restaurant kitchen. A sudden flare-up singed off his eyelashes and eyebrows, leaving his face naked and defenseless, and his sensibilities on the subject very tender indeed.

"They'll grow back before the wedding!" he growled. "Come on, quit fooling around. Will you or won't you?"

"Do I get an engagement ring?" Helen teased. "Because if I don't, then you're not much of a bargain. No ring, no eyebrows—"

"Any kind you want," he cut her off. "We'll go down around Canal Street tomorrow after mass. The Jews stay open Sundays. You pick out any ring you want, as long as it's not a thousand bucks or something, because that I can't handle."

"No." Helen shook her head primly. "That's not the way it's done. You're supposed to pick it out for me."

"Well, Jeez, what do I know about engagement rings? I never been married before!"

"I want a one-carat diamond solitaire in a yellow-gold setting," Helen rattled off unselfconsciously. She, after all, read all the bride magazines and knew about such things.

"Now, what in hell is that?" Frank scratched his head, bereft of his false bravado as often happened when he was with her, pared down to the simple, true self Helen liked better. "A diamond solitaire—what?"

"You just ask when you go to the jeweler's. They'll know."

"Let me get this straight: a one-carat diamond solitaire—"

"In a yellow-gold setting," Helen repeated. "Anyone who can pass the Fire Department exam should be able to remember that much."

He squinted at her to see if she were making fun of him. "If you were a guy I'd belt you in the mouth for that," he said without real anger. "You're getting to be as much of a wise-ass as I am."

"Takes one to know one," Helen quipped.

"You still haven't given me a straight answer."

"To what?"

"Will you or won't you?"

Helen hesitated for the tiniest fraction of a second, then reached her small hand across the scarred tabletop toward his. "I guess I may as well," she said with mock weariness. "But only if your eyebrows grow back."

She had managed to suppress this great bubble of happiness for an entire week, afraid to share her news with anybody lest she put the jinx on it. Everyone knew talking about good news always spoiled it. It wasn't hard to keep her secret from her parents; it would have been harder to try to find the words to tell them. But keeping it from Loretta was next to impossible. Only the thought that she was the youngest person she knew to be engaged, and the suspicion that Loretta feigned indifference to men because she was mooning over Alistair, kept Helen from opening her mouth.

So when Frank came to call for her the following Saturday, his hand noticeably protecting something nestled in his suit-jacket pocket, Helen found it difficult to keep a straight face. And when he said hello to her parents and exchanged a little polite small-talk the way he did every week, then threw himself on one knee before her with a great deal of dramatics, Helen could not hold back any longer. She burst into giggles.

"Is that any way to treat a man while he's proposing to a girl?" He turned toward Kat and Red, who comprised a very startled audience. He had stopped on the way for a drop of Irish courage; Helen could smell it on him. "I ask you! The girl's got no sense of romance!"

With some difficulty, he fished the little velvet box out of his pocket, fumbled it open, and slipped the ring awkwardly onto Helen's slightly trembling hand. With that, he too began to laugh.

Kat was not surprised that her daughter had chosen to marry this man, but she made very little effort to mask her disapproval. Still, she was not one to make scenes in public, so she would keep whatever she had to say for another time. She accepted Frank's kiss on her unresponsive cheek, and made excuses about needing to get the supper dishes done.

Red, on the other hand, was delighted, and said as much. He broke out the blackberry brandy, which was the only strong liquor Kat would let him keep in the house, and they all drank a toast. He was feeling warm inside when they left, and it was not from the brandy. He had known all along that his daughter would choose well.

Helen and Frank went to Roseland again, a favorite haunt of theirs now, and it was well past midnight when he took her home this time. Assuming that even at this hour the faces behind the venetian blinds would still be watching, they stepped into the hallway to kiss good-night.

Helen crept through the apartment to her room, shoes in hand. Red had not waited up for her this time; it was his tacit blessing on her and her young man. Helen slipped into her nightgown and started to brush her hair—a hundred strokes a night no matter how tired she was—when she realized she was being watched.

Danny was standing in the doorway to her room. How long he had been there was anyone's guess. He did not bother waiting for an invitation, but strode into the room the minute Helen caught sight of him and stood over her as she sat on the edge of the bed.

The big room seemed suddenly smaller, and Helen's mind skipped back to the time when this was her grandmother's room and she hated to come in because of the stink of Sloan's Liniment and the old woman's endless tirades. She remembered how she and Aunt Ag had scrubbed every inch of the floor and walls and ceiling with Lysol after the old woman died, and how sometimes on damp nights when the wind rattled the window sashes she could swear the stink was still there, in spite

of the scrubbing and two coats of paint and a time lapse of
nearly four years. She had that feeling now. She stopped
brushing her hair and looked up at her brother.

"Hello," she said uncertainly. Even standing up she had to
tilt her head to look at his face; from this perspective he loomed
uncomfortably large. "Did I wake you up? I'm sorry."

"No," he said, unsmiling. "I didn't go to sleep."

He was in his pajamas, a light summer robe tied carelessly
around his large stomach, but neither the pajamas nor his
usually unruly hair showed any evidence of having been slept
in. He had undoubtedly been waiting up for her. Why didn't
she see a light on in the room he shared with Johnny? Had he
been waiting in the dark? What did that mean?

At a loss for words, Helen sat looking up at him, wishing he
would sit down or at least back off. She had never noticed
before how strange-looking he was, how asymmetrical his
features were, how unhealthy he looked with his pallor and
his fat. Small wonder his peers ridiculed him. Even the nuns
in grammar school had called him a lump of lard. Why did he
have to eat all the time, make himself deliberately ugly? Red
blamed it all on their grandmother's spoiling. Was there more
to it than that? And what, Helen wondered, shuddering a little,
did he mean by coming into her room at this hour of the
morning? How long had he been standing in the doorway,
hidden in shadow, watching her? He had tormented her
throughout childhood and adolescence, barging into the bathroom when she was in the tub, peeking through keyholes
while she dressed. Red had beaten him raw for it a dozen times.
Had he been doing that again tonight? Had he watched her
undress, leering silently in the dark hall? Helen stared up at
him, unblinking, masking her growing terror with that piercing look that had been her only defense against him all her life.

"What do you want?" she asked, trying to sound calm.

Danny laughed mirthlessly. "What do I want? You pick a
helluva time to ask that. Now that it's too late."

Helen frowned at him. "Speak English. What're you talking
about?"

"You know damn well what I'm talking about!" His tone was surly, his voice deeper than Helen remembered it. "You couldn't wait, could you? You know what Monday is?"

"Sure." Helen nodded. Kat had spent every day since Labor Day dragging Danny to men's shops for suits and shirts and a decent topcoat. "You start St. John's Monday. Orientation Week."

"Yeah, that's right." Danny took a step closer to her. "And you two had to go and announce your engagement this very weekend. You just couldn't wait!"

Helen was at a loss. "What does one thing have to do with the other? We were going to ask you to be best man, but that's not for months—"

"When're you getting married?" he demanded, increasingly belligerent. "Gimme the exact date."

"We don't know yet." Helen shrugged. "Sometime in the spring. Probably April. Say, what's eating you anyway?"

He backed off a little then, as if building to the punch line. "You're so damn innocent, aren't you? You don't know what I'm talking about, do you?"

Helen just looked at him. She was tired; she wanted to sleep. She ought to tell him to get lost, if she could find the nerve. She glared at him. He leaned toward her, as if what he had to say were incomprehensible beyond spitting distance.

"When you get married you'll move out of here. You'll quit work. You'll quit paying Mom the ten bucks a week she's been putting aside for me. And there goes my college education. Now figure that!"

Helen sat there, positively dumbfounded.

"She never told me," she said with great sincerity. "I thought she had money put aside for you."

"Yeah, well . . . she does. Some," Danny acknowledged, growing suddenly diffident. He had expected remorse, not a questioning of his facts. "But most of it was coming from what you gave her. She wasn't counting on books and fees and that. And the price of clothes."

Especially when all you can fit into is Husky, Helen thought with a flicker of malice, but didn't say it. It was still possible that he could hit her.

"Well, you'll have my income till the spring," she pointed out, gathering her courage. "After that maybe you'll have to get a part-time job. I mean, look at Alistair."

"Fuck Alistair!" Danny said, as loud as he dared be in the sleeping house. "I'm not getting any job. They want me to go to college, so I'll go to college. But I ain't sweating out some lousy job to pay for it."

Helen's anger flared up then. "Don't use dirty language around me!" she hissed. "What do you want, anyway? Am I supposed to wait until you're out of college to get married? What kind of crazy thinking is that? I don't owe you anything!"

"Why can't you wait? Mom and Pop waited years and years."

Helen gave him a piercing look. "That was different."

"Why?" He was leaning over her again, his rancid breath hitting her in the face, spittle flying. "Why can't you wait? Are you so hot for him you can't wait? Or did he already get in your pants, and that's why? Is that why?"

Helen had seen a lot of movies, and knew that the proper response to this sort of behavior was to strike him hard across the face with her open palm. Repentance and a change of heart would follow. But his ugliness disgusted her, and this was not the movies, and she hit him with her fist, belted his flaccid jaw with her small clenched hand, so that her knuckles split against his teeth. She was on him then, pounding at his chest until he grabbed her wrists and squeezed, until the pain brought her to her senses. She glared at him, fearless.

"Hit me, you gutless creep!" she railed at him, not caring if anyone heard or not. "But don't you ever talk filth to me again!"

Danny snorted and threw her effortlessly onto the bed. He stood over her, rubbing his jaw. "You just better think about it," he said, his voice neutral. "If I drop outta school it'll be all your fault. You just think about it!"

When he was gone, Helen rolled over on the bed and turned out the light so she could cry in privacy.

"That's a nasty scrape on yer hand, Helen Mary," her father observed at breakfast. "How'd yer manage that?"

Helen looked directly at Danny, who did not look up from his plate. "Caught it in the door last night," she said.

"After all this time yer still can't handle that door?" Red shook his head, not catching her tone. "Or was it love was in yer eyes?"

Helen blushed and said nothing. Red interpreted this simply as shyness, having no way of guessing at the real reason.

Loretta was the only one to smell a rat, and when her repeated questions got her nowhere with Helen, she took more direct action. She knew there was no point in confronting Danny, so when she and Helen got back from their shopping trip that Saturday, Loretta went directly to Red.

"Go in your room and wait for me," she ordered Helen, pushing her past the parlor door. "I want to talk to your father a minute."

"What for?" Helen wanted to know, suddenly suspicious.

"None of your damn business!" Loretta snapped, shoving her again. "Someone who's getting married in six months shouldn't be so nosy."

Helen still refused to move.

"You want me to just tell you what I'm getting for a wedding present, or you want to be surprised?" Loretta demanded, her hands on her hips, tall enough to be bossy. "I'm asking your old man's advice on something I saw in the store this afternoon, that's all. Now beat it!"

Helen was still suspicious. Loretta always got the giggles in Red's presence, and Red was of the opinion that she didn't have a serious thought in her head. In Helen's memory, they had never had a private conversation. Something was fishy here. Halfway to her room she doubled back toward the parlor. She could eavesdrop through the closed door.

But Red had the radio on when Loretta came in, and he turned it down only halfway while they talked. Helen heard voices, but could decipher nothing. There was a seriousness to Loretta's tone that was totally out of character, and Helen thought she heard Danny's name mentioned more than once. Then Red slammed the arm of the chair and began to curse, and Helen needed to hear no more.

Frank had to work that weekend, so Helen stayed home Saturday night. She wondered if the apartment was always this silent. She and Johnny had a rollicking game of hide-and-seek after supper, but Kat lost her temper at the noise and carted Johnny off to bed. Danny slammed out of the house without even waiting for dessert, so there were just the three of them. Helen had started *Gone with the Wind* on the subway to work—for the third time since high school—and curled up on the couch with it. Kat occupied the other end of the couch, knitting furiously, her eyebrows pinched together as if she had a headache. Red was in his chair with his pipe and his newspaper, but the pipe had gone out without his noticing, and the newspaper had been open to the same page for nearly half an hour. There was no clock in the room, and the radio was silent. The silence seemed to tick, and whenever Helen finished a chapter she glanced at her wristwatch, amazed at how little time had actually passed. Was it only that she was used to going out on a Saturday night, or was there something ominous about this silence?

As if on cue, Red discovered that his pipe was out the instant Kat stuck the knitting needles through the ball of yarn and stuffed her knitting back into the basket.

"I'm for bed," she announced, giving Red a look that puzzled Helen. Red appeared not to notice, and nodded in her direction without looking at her.

"I'll be along in a while, then," he said, unconvincing.

Kat leaned over to Helen to receive her requisite peck on the cheek, the only show of affection either would permit. Helen saw that her mother's face was more sullen than usual, but did not know what to attribute it to. When Kat was out of earshot, Red broke the silence.

"Has yer brother been after sayin' anything about yer gettin' married?" he asked so directly that Helen jumped, even though she'd been expecting the question all evening.

She found herself faced with a dilemma that had confronted her often in this room; her need to tell the truth was threatened by her desire to spare her father's feelings. Confronted with this directly, she had no way out, and no one to ask for advice. Loretta had already done more than enough; it was easy for her to spill the beans and run. Frank could not be consulted. This was a family matter, and he was not part of the family, yet. Besides, he would solve the problem by beating Danny to a pulp, and Helen did not want that. All she wanted was to be left alone to pursue her own life, and Danny was trying to interfere. Overburdened, Helen spilled her troubles to her father, leaving out Danny's physically threatening her, sketching in as few details as she could get away with.

Red sat in thoughtful silence long after she had finished, leaving Helen in an agony of guilty feelings. He puffed on his pipe.

"And how d'yer feel about all this, then?"

Helen took a deep breath before she spoke. "Like I shouldn't have to feel guilty. Like I don't owe him anything. Like he's got a helluva nerve!"

"Good for yer!" Red slammed the arm of his chair for emphasis. "And stick by it, then. Don't let him or anybody else change yer mind. Yez love each other, and yez are after wantin' ter marry. That's the way it should be. Yer leave Danny boy to me."

"Don't be hard on him, Pop," Helen pleaded, wondering who else might want to change her mind. "To him it makes perfect sense, what he's saying."

"I'd call him a son of a bitch," Red remarked, "if it wasn't for what that'd make yer mother—or me. But there's words I could use for him, and for yer miserable old grandmother that spoiled him rotten! Ah, but it's all spilled milk now. But I'll fix him. Don't you worry about it!"

"All right," Helen said, trying to sound grateful, but there was a tinge of fear in her voice. Red would set Danny straight; she had no doubt of that. But what form of reprisal would Danny employ? She looked up from where she was twisting her hands in her lap to see that her father was scrutinizing her closely.

"What is it, Pop?"

"I'm after wonderin' when it was Danny and yer had yer little talk," he said, his eyes peering closely at her face.

"Oh—uh—last weekend. Saturday, after I came home from Roseland."

"Aye." Red nodded, digesting it. "In the middle of the night, then. When the house was asleep. He came into yer room, did he?"

"Well, yes." Helen felt trapped suddenly, as if he had caught her in a lie, as if she, and not Danny, had been the instigator of their little rendezvous.

"Look me straight in the eye when yer answer this," Red said ponderously. "Did he harm yer? Did he lay a hand on yer?"

"Pop—"

"Straight in the eye, miss!"

Helen broke his stare, looked away. "Yes, he did."

"Did he hurt yer?" Red's voice was the voice of doom.

"N-no, Pop. Honest!"

"Aye." Red leaned back in his chair, puffing the pipe. "Oh, I'll take care of Danny boy, all right!"

It was Helen's turn this Saturday night to lie awake waiting for Danny to come home. The luminescent dial on her small alarm clock had passed two A.M. when she heard the front-door latch.

From the heaviness of his tread he had probably been drinking. For a panic-stricken moment Helen wondered if he would come to her room for a repeat performance of last week's scene, made worse by the alcohol. Then she heard

Red's voice, low but authoritative, and heard them go into the kitchen.

As always in the labyrinthine apartment, voices carried but not words. At first it was mostly Red's voice, starting low but rising on a gradual plane, phrases growing shorter. Then Danny's voice, surly at first, then whining.

When she heard the first blow fall, Helen leaped out of bed. But modesty prevailed. The nights were still warm; she was wearing a thin summer nightgown. She could not appear in Danny's presence without a robe. By the time she struggled into it and got to the kitchen, the scene had frozen into tableau.

Danny crouched on the floor in the corner, the same corner where he used to sit smug and fat on the high stool while his grandmother slipped him tidbits of food from her cooking. He crouched there, one arm raised over his head, defensive, blubbering. Red stood over him, his small fists, hardened by over four decades of work, clenched at his sides. At the sound of Helen's footsteps he turned.

"There'll be no more bullshit about who owes what in this house!" he said, then turned back to Danny. "On yer feet, yer lummox! I'm thinkin' yer'll not raise a hand to a woman again."

There was no graceful way to escape this scene, Helen thought, as her father stalked past her, loosening his belt, on the way to the bathroom. She watched as Danny pulled himself awkwardly to his feet, not crying now, but crawling back into his usual surliness. He glared at her; she could not look away. Finally his nose began to run, and he had to fumble for a handkerchief. This was Helen's chance and she took it, fleeing wraith-like in the direction of her room. She did not cry tonight, but lay awake for a while longer, praying for Danny. It was the only thing she could think of to do for him.

"I'll need to borrow a suit, mate," Alistair said softly, picking the damp towels off the locker-room floor and dumping them into the wheeled canvas hamper that was his constant companion. "Dark one. Maybe the navy, if you can spare it."

"That a fact?" The older man, a paid-up member of long standing at the Y, was tying his tie, squinting into the cracked shaving mirror hanging crookedly on the damp green wall. "What makes you think I'd loan you one of mine?"

Alistair shrugged, grinning the sort of lopsided grin he used to charm people. "Figured you owed me a favor. Figured we were close to the same size. Figured I'd soften you up by telling you it's for my cousin's wedding and I'm best man."

"Figured all that, did you?" The older man reached into his locker for his suit jacket and looked at his wet hair a final time in the mirror, smoothing one gray wing with a manicured hand. "Well, figure this: I don't owe you nothing. And you told me you was an orphan."

"I am," Alistair said, the grin fading, his face becoming more purposeful. He didn't own a suit, couldn't afford to rent a tux, and wasn't going to let this one slip by. "She's my guardian's niece, which makes her my adopted cousin. We're real close."

The older man gave him a peculiar look. "Real close, huh? Only she don't know you like I know you. Or you wouldn't be so close."

Alistair blinked, the suggestion of a nervous tic, but did not otherwise react. He waited.

"I don't owe you," the older man said. "Anything."

Alistair shrugged. "Maybe not. Unless you count the cost of silence."

The older man started slightly. "What in hell's that supposed to mean? You can't threaten me! You're in just as deep as me!"

Alistair lit a cigarette; his hands were steady. "Me? I can pick up a job anywheres, if they fire me. But you—I understand you're a somebody. If they found out about you at your job. . . ."

The older man's face went white; he seemed to be sweating. "Now, look here, you—" He shook his fist in Alistair's face. "I don't do that kind of thing regular. I mean, I've got a wife.

Three kids. It's just every so often I—well, shit, you weren't any good anyway!"

Alistair shrugged again. "Maybe I just lack experience." His grin was lopsided, charming. "By the by, when I told you I was overage? I lied."

"Jesus Christ!" The older man was definitely sweating now. He ran one hand through his fresh-from-the-shower hair, messing it badly. "All right, all right. You want a suit—I'll loan you a suit. I'll *give* it to you, for Chrissake! But you gotta swear to me you'll keep your mouth shut about—about that time. Swear to me!"

Alistair took a final drag on his cigarette and stubbed it out against the "No Smoking" sign on the wall. "Navy blue, mate. The one with the pinstripes you wore last Tuesday. I like the cut of that one." He started to push the laundry hamper down the row of lockers, picking the damp towels off the floor.

"Swear to me on your mother's grave!" the older man shouted after him, his voice bouncing off the metal lockers.

Alistair stopped, looked at him whimsically. "Me mother's got no grave," he said without feeling. "Neither has me dad. They never found 'em in the rubble of the house that fell on 'em."

Tomorrow night at this time I'll be married, Helen thought, her stomach doing a little flip each time she thought about it. Tomorrow night I'll be Mrs. Frank O'Dell, and we'll drive away from the reception (if he can get that sad old used car he bought two weeks ago to start) and we'll check into the motel together and—

"More, Lelen, more!" Johnny hollered at her, lying on the rug, shirttail hanging, out of breath, where she'd been turning him head over heels in somersaults. "Do it again!"

"No, no more," Helen said gently, sobered at the thought of what the next twenty-four hours would bring. She gave Johnny's belly button a final, playful poke, and got up from the couch. "That's enough, Squirt! My arms are tired. You're getting heavy!"

"Pullease!" he whined, crawling into her lap and patting her cheeks with his palms in a way that usually melted her. "Do it again."

"I said no!" Helen was edgy, knew it wasn't fair to him to let it show. After tonight she wouldn't be able to see him every day, would visit this house like a stranger or a distant relative. She could no longer roam through the railroad rooms freely, would have to be reserved and sit in the parlor like a Sunday visitor. She would sit at the dinner table like Aunt Ag did every week, although unlike Aunt Ag she would have to stay and help with the dishes. She looked down at Johnny, her little brother/surrogate son, the model of what she would want her own children to be, and she felt lost, abandoned, thrown out among strangers. "Go get your pajamas now, and scoot!"

"You going away," the boy said solemnly, looking down and then suddenly up into her eyes. "Gettin' married and going away."

"Only for a little while," Helen assured him, sensing that it was a lie. "I'll come back every Sunday. Promise. And I'll bring Frank with me. You like Frank, don't you?"

"Yup. Him's a fireman!" Johnny announced, proud of his knowledge. "But you won't be *here*. In your room. You'll be all gone."

"I know. But then Danny's going to move into my room and you can have the other room all to yourself. Won't that be fun?"

"Yup," the boy said, and his eyes twinkled. "Danny farts!"

"Johnny! Don't say that word!" Helen pretended horror, though she had to suppress a smile. "Come on now, it's getting late. You've got to be in bed before Mom gets home."

"I got a idea," Johnny said, stalling for time, but also wondering if she would reject what he had to say. "Whyn't you bring Frank here? He could live in your room!"

Helen blushed, amazed at the insight of the child. "I just
can't, that's all. Now come on, stop wasting time! I'll be here
every Sunday, and that's all I have to say about it!"

She watched him amble reluctantly down the long hall to
the bathroom, his body too small for his big head, the marks
of the forceps still engraved on his temples. She felt depressed
and frightened all over again.

It was Friday night, the first Friday of the month, and her
parents had gone to evening church services. They would
come home smelling of incense and refreshed by the early
spring evening. In a way, Helen was relieved that they weren't
here. There was no way she could bring herself to talk to
them now, on the last night she would spend in this house, her
house, the only home she had ever known. Oh, she and Frank
had found an apartment—three rooms in a six-family house on
the downtown side of Prospect Park—it wasn't that. It was
that she knew every crack in the plaster, every ripple in the
floorboards, every sound and smell of this place, and she was
being cut off, by her own choice, from everything she had
ever known, thrown into the arms of—yes, she had to think
it if she couldn't say it—a total stranger.

She had not gone to work today, but had finished some
last-minute shopping and then met Frank for lunch. She had
not seen him since the weekend before, when he dumped her
at Loretta's house without a word, and half a dozen girls
she'd gone to high school with surprised her with a bridal
shower. Frank had gone off somewhere, picking her up when
it was all over and depositing her at home, with barely a word
spoken. Disturbed, Helen violated one of the principles of
her upbringing, asked the landlord if she could borrow his
phone, and called to ask Frank to take her out to lunch. There
were things they had to discuss. Once again, as they had so
many times in previous weeks, they ended up arguing.

". . . but then you can't receive communion!" Helen said
with an insistence bordering on nagging. "I've talked to the
priest, and he says if you quit being stubborn he'll hear your

confession right there in the rectory this afternoon. Why can't you give in just this once?"

"It's a little late for this, don't you think?" He was irritable; had been hearing variations on this theme for weeks. "I sat through their goddamn pre-Cana conference—bored to the gills, in case you're interested—but I will not go to confession. I haven't been to confession since I was in high school and there's no reason . . . no, wait a minute. I did go once when I was overseas. One of those nights I figured I wasn't going to make it back, so it wouldn't hurt. And since all the chaplains kept telling us it was our God-given duty to kill Japs, and since I ain't killed anybody since, I don't need to go to confession."

"But you don't go to mass on Sundays," Helen half-whispered. It was an ominous accusation. "That means you're living in a state of mortal sin. Do you realize if you were out on a call and the roof fell in on you, you'd go straight to Hell? Frank, that's a horrible thought, and I can't see why you won't *do* something about it!"

She had long since stopped eating, and sat with her fork suspended over her salad, leaning tautly at him across the table. Frank put down his coffee cup none too gently and gave her a disgusted look.

"Does it bother you that much? We've been around this mulberry bush a dozen times. As far as you're concerned, if I die, my life insurance is paid up and I got no outstanding bills. What happens to me after I die is my own business, and if it bothers you to marry a sinner then maybe we better call the whole thing off."

Helen saw that he was serious, as serious as she, and as adamant. She would have to tread carefully. "It's just that I wanted you to go to communion with me at the wedding, Frank," she said, barely audible. "Is that too much to ask?"

"Hey, look," he said, leaning toward her. "You want me to receive with you, I will. The priest don't have to know whether I went to confession or not. He gets nosy, I'll tell him I went in my own parish, okay?"

Helen was so horrified she could barely speak. "Frank! That's adding another mortal sin to your soul! My God, you shouldn't offer to do that for anybody!"

He looked at her, absolutely miserable. "Jeez, I wanted you to be happy! I can't do anything right, can I?"

Helen gathered herself together with a great show of dignity, sliding her chair out and groping for her purse. "My mother got mad when I told her where I was going today," she said shakily. "She said it was bad luck to see the bridegroom so close to the wedding. I guess for once in her life she was right!"

She should have turned on her heel and walked away, Katharine Hepburn this time. Had he been Spencer Tracy or Cary Grant he would have jumped up from the table and gone after her, acquiescing, offering her a compromise. But she was not Hepburn, he was not Tracy or Grant, and this was not a movie. She would either have to walk out of the restaurant without knowing if he would even show up at the wedding tomorrow or she would have to turn around, give in, and find out what he would say. She stood by the table struggling into her new Easter coat, waiting for him to speak.

Frank looked at her for such a long moment that Helen wondered if he would say anything at all. She could not interpret the expression on his face, and that frightened her.

"Are we going to go through with this thing or not?" he asked finally, as if it didn't matter to him at all.

Helen managed a weak smile. "I guess we have to."

"Okay," he said, picking up his coffee cup. "Can you get home all right? Good. See you tomorrow, kid."

And without even kissing him she walked out of the restaurant, brushing nervously against tables in her haste to get away.

A total stranger, Helen thought again, tucking Johnny under the covers and kissing his forehead absently. I'm going off to spend the rest of my life—until death do us part—with a total stranger. Drifting into the kitchen to make herself a cup of tea and calm her nerves, she heard the front door slam.

It was Danny. He strode past the kitchen without so much as acknowledging her existence and went into his room. Good, Helen thought. I've got the place to myself and I can think. But for how long? She looked at the clock and put the tea kettle back on the stove. Her parents would be home in half an hour, unless they met somebody outside of church and stopped to chat. She couldn't face them, couldn't cope with the awkwardness she had experienced with her father all week, couldn't handle the explosion she and her mother had been building toward for months. Why did it have to be so difficult? All her life she had been told—even by the nuns, who had foregone it themselves—that it was her duty, her sacred vocation, to marry and to bear children. Why was her rite of passage so resented by the very people who were supposed to offer her support?

Baffled and miserable, Helen went to her room for a nightgown and shuddered at the sight of her brand-new leather suitcase (she had never gone anyplace before, to need one) lying beside her bureau, stuffed with new dresses and lingerie and nylons and—the thought made her want to sink into the ground—desperately new and filmy nightgowns, almost transparent, which she had never so much as dreamed of wearing before. She hadn't bought them; would have been embarrassed even to pick them up to look at them in a store. They were shower gifts, bought by her blushing girl friends, or worse, their smug mothers. Even Aunt Ag had given her one, a white one with a lace peignoir and a neckline that plunged forever; held against Helen's birdlike chest it was a bad joke. And all of the people who for years had cautioned her against impure thoughts and words and actions had suddenly thrown open the gates to this forbidden world, smirking a little, as if they would be watching from some unseen vantage point on that night in the motel room when she put on one of those nightgowns and emerged from the bathroom to face *him*. It all seemed so evil.

Helen shook the thought from her mind and locked the

bathroom door, rinsing out the bathtub and searching for the
scented bath salts she had been hoarding for tonight. Sinking
into the steaming water, she studied the body that was so
familiar she seldom looked at it. Was it possible that now
another person would come to know this body almost as well
as she? It did not seem likely. Would he think she was beautiful, or at least pretty? Helen doubted it: She was so small,
so thin, so pale. Why had he chosen her, when he must certainly know any number of girls with stunning figures? He
had told her once about a woman he'd rescued from a very
smoky fire—how she'd thrown her arms around him and
kissed him passionately to thank him for saving her life. When
Helen showed no sign of jealousy, he seemed almost disappointed. How could she explain that she didn't feel entitled
to be jealous, because she didn't feel deserving of his fidelity?

Drying herself carefully—this bath would have to carry her
through an awful lot tomorrow—dutifully getting the scour-
ing powder and the scrub brush to clean the ring out of the
tub, Helen studied herself in the door of the medicine chest.
She couldn't see much, because she was so short, only the
upper half of her torso. Her face wasn't bad, she decided,
even without makeup. Except for the too-sharp nose, unwanted legacy of her probably Portuguese grandmother. But
she had the body of a twelve-year-old. How could any man
desire her?

I'll find that out tomorrow night, Helen thought wryly,
getting frightened all over again. She heard the front door
again and fled to the safety of her room. She switched off the
light and feigned sleep, knowing it was only nine-thirty and
the whole sham was idiotic, but she just couldn't—

Besides, she thought, or rather hoped, maybe Mom will
come in and sit on the side of the bed and brush the hair out
of my eyes with one hand and talk to me the way she did when
I was little. And in the safety of darkness I will have the
courage to ask her why she doesn't like Frank and why she
is angry with me for wanting to marry him. And we can talk

about it, just the way we used to talk when I was little. All she has to do is open the door a crack and call me by my name and find out that I'm not asleep. . . .

She lay still, listening, hearing her parents' muffled voices as they passed her door, waiting breathlessly as her father's footsteps faded off in the direction of the parlor and her mother's paused, faltered.

Helen thought she heard the door open a crack, saw the light from the next room spill onto the wall beside her bed.

"Helen Mary?"

She rolled over to see her mother's silhouette framed in the doorway. "Yes, Mom?"

"Were yer sleeping? I wanted to talk to yer before I went to bed."

Without waiting for an answer, Kat came into the room and sat on the side of Helen's bed. She studied the girl's pale face in the light from the doorway, brushing the thick brown hair up off her forehead with a work-roughened hand.

"So yer after gettin' married in the morning," Kat said, giving voice to the obvious. "I'm thinkin' yer must have wondered why I've said nothing about it all this time."

"I did wonder why you seemed so—upset." Helen propped herself up on one elbow. "I didn't know if it was because of Frank, or me being too young, or what it was. I thought you were mad at me for some reason."

"Not at you, sure, but at the way things happened," her mother said with a sigh. "There was the age of yer. Nineteen is not a grown woman; sure yer must see that. And as for himself—well! It was his attitude put me off at first. So sure of himself: stuck-up, like. I was after thinkin' he'd walk all over yer. But then I had a serious think about it (and a lot of prayers went into it, too), and I says, maybe it's just that she's picked him for herself without asking yer advice, and that's what's got yer in such a snit about it."

She paused, whether groping for words or simply run out of them, Helen couldn't tell.

"I wanted to tell you about it, Mom," Helen said, taking the opportunity of her mother's silence. "Only, it seemed like it happened all at once. One minute I wasn't in love with him, the next minute I was. I didn't know how to explain it."

"Aye," her mother sighed. "And there was more to it, then. There was me bein' not of this world for all them months after Johnny was born. And you takin' care of him; I'm not forgettin' that. I'll never know what come over me then, but I've not been myself for the longest time. There was that, wasn't it? That yer couldn't talk to me?"

"I guess I was afraid to sound too happy around you," Helen admitted, unable to look her mother in the eye. "Because you were always so unhappy."

"Aye." Her mother nodded, also looking away. "I'm sorry, then. For makin' yer feel that way."

"Mom—" Helen groped; it was the first time her mother had ever apologized, ever admitted to fallibility.

"I want yer to be happy," Kat interrupted, looking at Helen meaningfully. "I want you and yer young man to have a good marriage, and not to fear that I'd be a burden on yer. Sure, I've been through that myself, and I'd not wish it on anybody." There was a long pause. Helen waited. "It's not easy for me to say this, then."

"I know that, Mom!" Helen said with feeling, squeezing her mother's hand suddenly, impulsively. "And I really appreciate it."

"Right, then!" Kat said perfunctorily, getting up quickly. The air was too rarefied for either of them here. "Get to sleep now, or ye'll be after havin' circles under yer eyes on yer wedding day."

When she had gone, she left the door open a crack. Rolling over to face the wall, Helen stared at the warm glow of light on the wall until sleep crept over her. She was no longer afraid.

Helen thought she heard the door open a crack, saw the light from the next room spill onto the wall beside her bed. She rolled over to see that a draft had pushed the door open. There was no one there. Rolling over to face the wall, Helen stared at the stabbing strip of light on it until she could no longer fight sleep. Tomorrow she would marry a total stranger. Until death did them part.

Kat was the first one up the next morning, and she was in her daughter's room before the sun was up. Helen, surprisingly groggy for someone facing the most important day of her life, blinked up at her mother from the pillow.

"There's work to be done," Kat said perfunctorily. "Yer'll want to be up and dressed before everyone gets here."

"Okay, Mom." Helen yawned. "Just give me five more minutes."

"Now," Kat said, in a voice that brooked no opposition.

Helen threw off the covers and fumbled for her robe, alarmed at this hostility. She gave her mother a puzzled look, but said nothing. It would come out in the open if she waited long enough.

"I only hope yer have it as easy with yer stuck-up husband as ye've had it here with us," Kat began. Helen waited. "Sure, yer know what I'm talkin' about."

"No, Mom, I don't," she said calmly, taking the bait.

Kat sighed, as if she had expected ingratitude but not denseness on top of it. "I heard what yer was after sayin' to Loretta and them when they came over after the rehearsal. How it's only to be a small breakfast after the wedding 'cause that's all yez could afford."

"So?" Helen frowned, beginning to get annoyed, more at her mother's nit-picking than her eavesdropping. "It's true. Frank and I have to save a lot for furniture, and since we're paying for it and the wedding ourselves—"

"I oughta slap yer face!" Kat hissed. "Don't yer think that made yer father and me look cheap? Like we didn't give yez anything towards it?"

Helen said nothing, her passion for truth making her want to choke. Neither of her parents *had* offered to pay for the reception. Why shouldn't her friends know that?

"Who gave yez the sterling silver?" Kat demanded. "Who let yez have all the furniture we didn't need?"

Helen looked her mother in the eye, biding her time.

"Who gave yez the crucifix that's been hangin' over me own bed more than twenty years and has the holy water from Lourdes in the back of it?"

Helen was silent.

"Who gave yez the dresser cloths I crocheted me own self when I was yer age? Who lent yer the veil from me own wedding?"

Helen was silent.

"Did yer have to make us look cheap?" her mother demanded. "After all we're after givin' yez, did yer have to make us look cheap?"

"Who used my money to send Danny to college when he didn't want to go in the first place?" Helen's voice was barely audible.

Her mother slapped her very hard across the face. "So that's it, then!" she hissed. "Oh, yer a fine one!"

When she stormed out of the room, Helen was breathing hard. I will not cry on my wedding day! she thought fiercely, clenching her fists, her vision blurring. I will not!

And I will never do that to any daughter of mine, she promised herself.

Loretta arrived before breakfast, an hour earlier than she was supposed to, ready ahead of schedule for the first time in her life.

"Well, for God's sake, say something!" she said to Helen, grinning from ear to ear. As usual, she was lounging on Helen's bed while Helen rummaged about distractedly.

Helen stared at her for a long time before she realized what it was. "You've got new teeth!" she shrieked in delight. "How did you—?"

"It's a bridge," Loretta explained. "They hook over the ones on either side." She pulled her upper lip up to demonstrate. "See the little gold hooks? They cost me nearly a month's goddamn salary and I can't get used to them. They hurt." She began to cry. "I got them for you—for your goddamn wedding!"

Helen put an arm around her shoulder to comfort her, and Loretta subsided gradually.

"My nose is red," she lamented, staring at her face in Helen's mirror. "But Jeez, I can't help it! You're getting *married*! You're going away from the neighborhood and you're going to have babies and I'm so happy for you and— oh, Jesus!"

She continued to burst into tears at the slightest provocation all morning.

Helen didn't eat any breakfast. Neither did Red. Loretta gobbled up everything in sight, outdoing even Danny, who usually ate more when he was sulking. Helen smiled across the table at her friend, grateful for her chattering, giggling, crying, breaking up the tension as tangible as the dust motes whirling in the April sunlight through the kitchen window. Loretta was also the only one to succeed at stuffing Johnny into his ring bearer's suit—blue serge blazer and shorts, long white socks, and real bow tie—which he had balked at violently before.

"And don't get dirty!" she warned him, trying to brush his wild black hair into place. "'Cause even if your sister's going away, I'll still be here, and if you spoil her wedding I'm going to *get* you!"

She said it with such ferocity that he almost fell for it, but nothing could scare Johnny for long. He raced into the parlor, laughing.

"Stay on that couch and don't move a muscle!" Loretta warned, then broke into another crying spell because she realized even as she said it that Helen would no longer be just down the block from her. There would be no one to sympathize with her, give her advice, keep her out of trouble. Helen was really getting married, really going away, and Loretta would be all alone.

Helen listened to this lament for as long as she could stand it, then went to her room to start fussing with her clothes.

Alistair stopped by for a few minutes, looking spiffy in what might be a new suit. He kissed Helen good luck, antagonized Loretta by calling her "Stilts," and was on his way. A procession of neighbors and well-wishers began that threatened to make the wedding party late at the church.

The last time Helen had ridden in a limousine was for her grandmother's funeral. There was something funereal about this ride too, she thought, wedged between her silent parents in the back. The car smelled like the inside of a movie theater; they must have used some kind of spray on the upholstery. Helen's bridal bouquet—she had wanted lily of the valley, but it was too early in the season and she'd had to settle for stephanotis—smelled for some reason like carnations, funeral flowers. The trip was not only funereal but idiotic, since she lived half a block from the church and had to be driven around two entire blocks to get to the front entrance. Helen sighed, wishing the whole travesty were over.

Indeed, "travesty" might have been the best word to describe the wedding ceremony. There were the obvious things, like Danny's sulking, and Kat's being led down the aisle looking exceptionally dowdy in a dress the wrong shade of lavender for her complexion and a hat that didn't match, her tight-lipped expression pulling the whole look together into what could only be called Silent Disapproval. There was the fact that Loretta, even in flats, was still taller than Alistair, and when they met in the nave as maid of honor and best man the hostility emanating from them was almost electric. There was Helen's trying to hurry down the aisle, to swim through that sea of—it seemed to her—leering faces and be with Frank, where she felt safe, but Red, reveling in the role of Father of the Bride, and hopelessly uncomfortable in the suit he saved for wakes and weddings, shiny with age, was determined to be dignified and keep a slow and measured pace.

But there were other things, too, things even Helen could not have foreseen. There was the pastor, who had been fighting with Frank for months over his refusal to go to confession, and who sought his own revenge. Stern and intractable, he stood in the sacristy the entire time, his rheumy blue eyes riveted on Frank throughout the ceremony, as if he could somehow frighten this young man into submission even at this late date. Frank ignored him, but Helen was a nervous wreck.

Johnny dropped first one, then the other ring. The priest saying the ceremony was young and inexperienced, newly ordained, nervous. He droned on and on about the duties of married life, ignoring the joys, promising a dreary future indeed for those foolish enough to make such a decision. The organist played the wrong music for the communion service, got halfway through, realized her error, and started from the beginning. Helen's voice was so low when she said "I do" that only Frank heard her. The priest had to ask her to say it again.

Danny slipped out of the crowd around the outside of the church, still clutching the rice someone had poured into his hand to throw at the newlyweds, and beat it for home. He tossed the rice into the gutter just in front of the house, when he stopped long enough to rip off his tie, stuffing it into his pocket and slipping out of his jacket in a single motion. He took the front steps two at a time, then pelted down the long, dark hall as fast as his heavy legs could carry him. He stopped in the doorway of his room, a little winded, but not nearly as much as he might have been six months ago. He laughed a dry, silent laugh in the empty apartment. Nobody had noticed. They'd all been so fucking wrapped up in Helen Mary and her wedding they hadn't seen that he had dropped over twenty pounds since October. It was all part of his plan.

He hurried, even though he knew he had ages. They would miss him at the wedding breakfast, but it was unlikely anyone would come here to look for him. Nobody cared about him since his grandmother had died, except his mother, a little, and she was so wrapped up in being Disapproving she would never notice his absence. And then they were going to Aunt Ag's apartment so Helen could change to her travel clothes, and there would be endless cups of tea and gabbing after the new couple had left for their honeymoon. It would be the middle of the afternoon before anyone wondered where he was.

And by then he would be long gone, Danny thought, laughing silently again. All the same, there was little time to waste. He would not be comfortable until he was out of here.

He tore open the closet and the bureau drawers, piling clothes on the bed, taking out from the space in the closet behind Johnny's H & O trains the regulation seabag he had stashed there three weeks ago. The sight of it sobered him. What the hell, he thought. If his father could survive the merchant marine, Danny could go him one better. Once Uncle Sam found out he'd dropped out of college they'd come looking to draft him anyway. Better to enlist in the navy beforehand. Danny thought of the looks on their faces—especially Red's—when they found out what he had done. Oh, he'd fix them! They'd be sorry for the way they treated him, all right!

On his way out of the room, he banged against his desk with the heavy seabag, sending the pile of textbooks with the St. John's University book covers flying. Good! Danny thought. Fuck St. John's. Fuck everybody.

Helen stood barefoot on the bathroom floor, wondering why she felt so peculiar. Obviously there was something peculiar about her situation. She was standing in front of the mirror in a motel bathroom, door securely locked, outside of Saratoga

Springs, New York, wearing the sheer white nightgown with
the lace peignoir that her Aunt Ag had given her, brushing her
hair to keep from going to pieces, while beyond that door—
doing what, anticipating what, she didn't know—was her husband. This was the scene they never showed you in the movies.
What was really going to happen once she unlocked that
door? Would she find the same wry, shyly affectionate man
she thought she knew, or some strange ravening monster,
heady with the thought of what she would have to do, as a
dutiful Catholic wife, to satisfy him? No wonder she felt
peculiar. She had felt, ever since they emerged stiff-legged
from the car, as if she had to go to the bathroom, and she
kept going, squeezing out a few drops each time, but never
relieving the feeling. If that wasn't enough to drive a girl
crazy, what was wrong with her feet?

"Helen?" His voice, inches away from the bathroom door,
was only a whisper, but it boomed inside her head like thunder. "You okay in there?"

"Of course!" she snapped, unable to trust her voice. "I—
my feet feel funny, that's all."

"Your feet?" he repeated. "What's wrong with them?"

"I don't know," she said, realizing how stupid it sounded.
"But they're usually freezing—they were in the car all
afternoon—but now they feel hot, like it's July instead of
April."

She heard him laugh, holding it back as if knowing any loud
noise would frighten her. "Feel the floor," he said.

"What?"

"Reach down and touch the floor," he instructed her
through the door. "Feels warm, doesn't it?"

"Yes," she said, puzzled. Tile floors always felt cool, even
in summer.

"It's heated from underneath," he explained patiently.
"They put electric coils in before they lay the tile. It's supposed to be a luxury."

"Oh," she said, feeling foolish.

"Shanty Irish!" she heard him mutter, and wanted to throw the door open and sock him one until she remembered the way she was dressed. Well, she couldn't stay in here all night, could she?

"Frank?" she said softly, hoping he had at least moved away from the door.

"What?" He was still there.

Might as well get it over with, Helen thought. "Frank, I'm scared!"

There was a pause. When he spoke again, she imagined that he had his forehead pressed against the bathroom door.

"There's nothing to be scared of. It's just me. I'm not gonna bite you. Listen, I turned off all the lights, I'm in my pajamas. Everything's all right." He waited for her to answer. "Helen?"

"I'm listening."

"Why don't you turn off the light and come out? Just get into bed. We don't have to—you know—do it tonight. If you don't want to."

Helen sighed. "I'll be out in a minute."

She heard him move away from the door, counted to ten, shut off the light, and fumbled with the lock.

"Where are you?" she asked the darkness, steadying herself against a piece of furniture.

"In the bed already," he said. "Follow my voice."

He began to sing, softly, an uneven baritone rendition of "I'll Take You Home Again, Kathleen," most of the words to which he had forgotten. Finding the bed at last, Helen sat on the very edge.

"I thought every Irishman was a tenor," she quipped, disguising her terror.

"Some of us have bigger balls than others," she heard him say, then stop himself. "Hey, that was a lousy thing to say. I'm sorry!"

"S'okay."

She felt him move toward her in the bed, touch her shoulder in a way that made her flinch.

"Please don't be afraid of me," he pleaded. "I wouldn't hurt you. Not for anything in the world!"

He held the covers aside for her to crawl in next to him. Helen curled away from him, realizing as he put his arm around her from the back that he had lied. He was not wearing pajamas. She popped her head up from the pillow, but he shushed her.

"Only if you want," he said.

She lay in the dark, her senses so sharp now that she could pick out the shapes of the lamps and the ugly watercolors on the walls. I don't want! she thought, although she had to admit there was something lovely and tender about lying together like this. She allowed him to massage her shoulder and kiss her hair, feeling drowsy and comfortable.

It all happened at once then, that feeling of having to urinate combined with the warm drowsiness and the realization that he was unbuttoning the peignoir and she was not preventing him. For some reason she heard Sister Misericordia's voice again as in her childhood, going on about the missionaries, saw the faces peering through the barbed wire at Auschwitz. Then that scene faded somehow into the famous scene from *Gone with the Wind,* which she had seen three times by now, where Clark Gable sweeps Vivien Leigh off her feet and carries her up the red velvet staircase. Helen had always wondered what happened at the top of that staircase. Now she was about to find out.

She rolled over toward him, not knowing whether she ought to lie still or respond in some way, so she simply lay quite still. He seemed content for a moment to slip the peignoir off her shoulders, not touching the nightgown, not touching her except to kiss her face. When he got to her mouth, Helen kissed back, as she had all the times they'd kissed in the hallway of her house, or in the movies, or on a park bench—innocently, tentatively, feeling all tingly inside.

In retrospect, she supposed she should have kept every moment of that first encounter etched in her memory, but she was so dazed with exhaustion and suppressed fear and romantic imaginings that it was no clearer when it was over than while it was happening. All she could remember was a great deal of fumbling and caressing, a quick burst of pain and a strangeness in his movements and his breathing, and the next thing she knew he was lying beside her all warm and sleepy, alternately dozing and nuzzling her hair.

"It'll be better next time," she heard someone say, and tried to focus the voice on the man beside her in the bed.

"Mmm?" she asked sleepily.

"It wasn't any good for you," he said, a little impatiently. "It takes a while for me to figure out what you like, and anyway, it's always strange for the woman the first time. It'll get better."

"Oh," Helen said, and her head cleared suddenly, as if she were abruptly emerging from a fog. "How do you know all that?"

"What?" He was drowsing again.

She propped herself up on one elbow. It was over, after all; she had lived through it. If it was really no worse than this. . . . "I said, how do you know all that about women?"

He pulled his head up a little from the pillow before he answered her. "Never mind. I just know, that's all!"

She stared at him in the dark, feeling his body tense beside her.

"Well, cripes!" he exploded, half-laughing. "I was in the marines, remember? And I'm damn near twenty-five. Did you think I was a virgin, too?"

Helen blushed in the darkness. Could a man be a virgin? How could a person tell? Had she said something stupid?

"It just—occurs to me," she said, swallowing hard to make the words come out slowly. "Occurs to me that if you did— that—to other girls—decent girls—they would've expected you to marry them."

"And if they didn't then they weren't decent, is that it?" he finished the train of thought for her. "Is that how it goes?

Well, it's none of your beeswax, young lady. You and me can talk about any subject under the sun except that. You must've gone out with other fellows before you met me."

"Yes, but I didn't—" Helen couldn't finish.

"Well, I didn't think you did," he said knowingly. "Say, are you all right, by the way? I didn't hurt you too much, did I? Are you bleeding much?"

His solicitude escaped her; the mention of blood was enough to make her leap out of bed and switch on the light, not caring if either of them was dressed, concerned that she might have left some evidence of their activity on the motel sheets. She imagined the expression on the chambermaid's face: the same look she had seen on the neighbors' faces when her mother had had Johnny so late in life, the same look she had seen in church this morning. Those leering, dirty minds!

But there was no blood on the sheets, and Helen sat on the edge of the bed to contemplate the rest of what he had said to her.

"It didn't hurt that much," she said, trying to look him in the eye but finding her gaze drifting over his body instead, at least what she could see of him from where the sheet cut him off at chest-level. It was a boxer's body; she could see that. A middleweight, even a light-heavyweight body—flat, conditioned muscles standing out along his arms and chest. She would have that body to feast her eyes on for the rest of her life. Until death do us part. But how many other women had seen that body and thought the same?

"I don't mind you having—other girls," she said, finding his eyes at last and seeing that they were laughing at her. "I just—maybe I wonder what made you settle for me. Why you got tired of them and didn't marry them and if maybe someday you'll get tired of me even if you did marry me."

It was all out, and she was panting slightly. Frank watched her intently. He supposed he should have been annoyed at the way she was carrying on—on their *wedding* night, for crying out loud—but she looked like a little girl in the bad light from the motel lamp, a little girl playing dress-up in that vampish nightgown, and he felt he owed her some kind of explanation.

"It wasn't anything like what you're imagining at all," he said gently. "Try to understand something about men, will you? Men need love, just like women do. But sometimes a man just needs sex, and he can usually find someone—a woman— to give it to him, sometimes for a price, sometimes just because she's that kind of woman. None of those women—and there weren't that many, so don't go making lists—none of them loved me, and I didn't love them. We got that out in the open right away. But I do love you, though it embarrasses my Irish ass to say it out loud too often, so don't get in the habit of expecting it. I don't have to say it to mean it, you get me?"

"I get you," Helen said, but he could tell she was not satisfied.

"And listen, you don't have to worry that maybe I left a trail of little slant-eyed micks halfway across the Pacific, because I was very careful about that. You understand what I mean?"

"Of course I know what you mean!" Helen flared up, remembering Loretta's brothers. "And I didn't ask you! You better not pull anything like that on me!"

"Oh-ho, so that got your Irish up!" He grinned at her, then grew serious. He lifted her chin a little with his fingertips. "But I wouldn't do that to you, not without your say-so. I'll give you as much joy as I can and as many babies as you can stand. How many you want?"

"Lots!" Helen said, like a little girl imagining ice cream. "Oh, Frank, I'm so glad you want babies! I was afraid you didn't."

He looked chagrined. "All you had to do was ask. Say"— he leaned closer to her—"whatta you say we practice some more tonight?"

If Helen had craved sleep before, it was now the farthest thing from her mind. She thought about *Gone with the Wind* again. In the scene after the staircase scene, Scarlett was seen lying in bed the next morning with the most delicious smile on her face. Helen was going to learn the secret of Scarlett O'Hara's smile if it took her all night.

No one mentioned Danny once the shock of his disappearance had worn off. Once he had gotten clear of the house and settled in at the downtown Y (he was not due to report in until Monday) his first stop was the Western Union office. His telegram, telling his parents of his intentions but not his whereabouts, immediately sent Kat into a fit of hysterics. Everyone knew telegrams only brought bad news, and Danny's only confirmed her superstition. Red had to rush upstairs to the landlord's and call Ag to come over to straighten Kat out; there wasn't a thing he could do for her. While the two women railed at each other in the master bedroom, Red took a near-exhausted Johnny, still in his ring bearer's suit, out of the apartment, onto a bus and then to the ferry, where they rode back and forth until nearly midnight, the boy sound asleep in his father's lap while the engines thrummed rhythmically beneath them. When Red finally got home and tucked the boy in bed with his clothes on, Ag had gone, and Kat was alone in the big bed, sobbing intermittently.

There were confrontations over Danny in the ensuing weeks—Kat's eyes were usually red-rimmed, her face grim— but there was never a word spoken when Helen and Frank returned from their honeymoon and began showing up for Sunday dinner every week. They knew, of course. Aunt Ag had somehow gotten the number of the hotel at Niagara Falls where they were staying and called them. Frank nearly fell off the bed from laughing; Helen grew very quiet. Now, on Sundays, even Ag dared not broach the topic. Conversation went on at a great rate—Frank was a talker once he got started—and only Kat stayed silent most of the time. Red noticed that Helen picked at her food worse than ever, but she looked healthier than he'd ever seen her. He took it as a good sign; the marriage was going well.

"You've got Rh incompatibility," the doctor told her. "Didn't they tell you that when you took the blood tests for the marriage license?"

Helen nodded, shyer after her second examination by this stranger than she had been after the first. "Yes," she said slowly. "But I never asked what it meant. I was afraid they'd think I was stupid."

All her life, Helen had gone to the family doctor, a general practitioner. But this man was a specialist—an obstetrician/gynecologist, Loretta had said when she gave Helen the phone number. Helen had looked up both words in the dictionary before she called him, wondering how or why Loretta came to know about such things. But prying into Loretta's private life left her open to the same, so Helen didn't ask.

Helen liked the doctor, or thought she did. It was difficult to tell; she always felt like a child in the presence of medical people. But she enjoyed chatting with him in his warm little paneled office; it was that other business she disliked; that horrible little green room and the ominous leather table with the stirrups, which she found medieval and frightening. She would never get used to it, and wondered why all of this was necessary just to have babies.

But they were finished with that part of it for today, sitting in the little paneled office, and Helen was beginning to relax after the examination when the doctor told her of this complication in her pregnancy she had never even known existed.

"Mrs. O'Dell, do you know your blood type?" he asked patiently.

Helen startled slightly, still getting used to the name that had been hers a mere two months. "Yes. O-negative. They told me that at the hospital when I went for all those tests."

The doctor nodded. "And your husband's is B-positive?

That's going to be a problem. I wish we'd known that before you went and got pregnant."

Helen frowned at him. Did it mean there was something wrong with her baby? Her pulse began to race.

Her baby. The phrase itself made her pulse race. Women had babies, grown-up women who were sure of themselves and loud in their pride in their husbands, who knew what they would name their children and where they would go to school and what they would be when they grew up. Women had babies, not skinny little girls of nineteen who had only been married for two months. Helen was elated, but also frightened.

And what did he mean it was "going to be a problem"? What horrible threat hung over her teeming womb? Helen stared at the doctor, wide-eyed. He swung a little in his swivel chair; it squeaked and Helen winced. Everything made her jumpy lately.

"Is there any history of miscarriage in your family?" he asked her. "Your mother especially?"

Miscarriage. So that was it, the worst possibility. "I don't know," Helen said vaguely, thinking of her grandmother's ravings about her lost children but attributing it to the hard life in Newfoundland. "We never talked about—things like that."

"No, I suppose not." The doctor sighed. Many of his patients were Catholic. "Well, that aspect of it isn't as important as your blood type. O-negative is very rare, and that causes complications. Your baby will ninety-nine times out of a hundred have B-positive, because that's a dominant type. Now, this means very little when the first baby is developing, because the uterus is pretty much isolated from the rest of your body—are you with me so far?"

Helen nodded, and he continued.

"Well, toward the end of the pregnancy, and during labor and delivery, your blood and the baby's blood interchange to a degree, and in your case that may be harmful to the baby."

He stopped, uneasy under the intent gaze of those somber brown eyes. It was an oversimplified and inaccurate explanation he was giving her, but he didn't know any other way. He was accustomed to being a kind of god to his patients, and the unspoken accusation in those eyes bothered him. When she first walked into the office he thought she must have lied about her age, thought surely she couldn't be more than fourteen or fifteen. He still had trouble addressing her as an adult. And those eyes! They burned into him, accusing, as if it were somehow his fault she had been born with an incompatible blood type. Probably his fault that she was pregnant, too, he thought wryly, almost expecting her to say as much.

"What you mean is, I could be poisoning my baby," she said slowly, unblinking. "Killing it."

He thought hard before he spoke. "No, there's very little danger to this baby. You'll have a slightly higher than normal tendency to miscarry in the first three months, but if you carry to term you should have a perfectly normal baby. But you should think very carefully about future pregnancies. Because each additional pregnancy adds further—immunities—to your blood—that would endanger a baby with—incompatible blood."

"More poison, you mean. I shouldn't have any more babies is what you're saying," she said flatly, cutting across his paternalism.

"It's not a *poison* exactly," he corrected her, annoyed that after twenty years of practice he should be put in his place by an adolescent.

"But it does the same thing," she said, picking at a loose thread on the hem of her skirt, eyes downcast. "Is there any cure for it?"

The doctor found a glimmer of light in her question, a way to save face for himself and the medical profession. "Researchers are working on it all the time," he said brightly, offering her more hope than he should. "Who knows, by the time you've got this one toilet-trained, they may come up with something."

Helen looked up at him, wanting to believe, skeptical.

"Look," he breathed, leaning across the desk, avuncular.

"There shouldn't be any trouble with this pregnancy. I just want to warn you about the risks in the future."

Helen nodded, smiled faintly, and got up to leave.

Poison, she thought—only once—on the bus going home.

"Well, I wouldn't be after askin' yer in yer present condition," Red was saying. "Only, it's yer mother."

Helen was cooking supper, the sweat beading on her forehead and upper lip as she stood over the stove. It had reached ninety that afternoon, but she could not turn on the kitchen fan for fear of blowing out the gas pilots.

"How long do you want me to take him?"

Red shrugged, knowing he was asking a lot. He was embarrassed to admit to his daughter that he couldn't handle Kat, and that Kat couldn't manage her own problems.

"For the couple weeks we'll be up to Connecticut anyways," he said, hoping she wouldn't refuse; knowing she had every right to. "I got me vacation all to once this year, and I'm after rentin' a little cottage on a lakefront. It's to get herself out of the city, and her mind off of Harmony Bay."

Helen gave him a despairing look. "Good Lord, Pop, is she still on that kick? Can't she realize she's got Johnny to take care of? What's wrong with her?"

"It's why I was thinkin' yer might take the boy for the two weeks," Red avoided the question. He and Helen both knew what was wrong with Kat, knew that rich people went to psychiatrists for it, knew that poor people talked to their parish priests and if that failed, rented a cottage in Connecticut to try to stave the thing off for a while. "Sure, I'd love to take him with us—poor wight's never seen an honest-to-God lake— but yer mother's gone back to her crying spells, and it's pitiful to see him tryin' to cheer her up. So I thought if it was just her and me I could maybe talk some sense into her. Would it be too much trouble for yer, then?"

"Of course not, Pop!" Helen stopped fussing over the pots on the stove and turned to face him, her thin arms folded over her chest. Red realized how mature she seemed suddenly: married, expecting a baby, running her own household. "Johnny's no trouble. I'd keep him a million years if he'd stay. It's just I've got to ask Frank first."

Red nodded, looking tired. He had stopped in on his way home from work. Helen realized with a jolt that he must have walked it, knew how he hated the heat, saw how old he looked. Her father would be fifty soon, but it wasn't that. All her life she had thought of her father as ageless, suspended somewhere in his mid-thirties, the age he was when she first became cognizant of such things as age when she was a child. Was this the price of her own maturity, to watch her father age so rapidly?

"That's how it should be," her father agreed. "Sure, he's head of the household."

"He'll say yes, Pop, I'm sure of it." Helen placed a reassuring hand on his arm. "He loves Johnny, you know that. Have you said anything to Johnny?"

"I wanted to get yer go-ahead before I told him," Red explained. "Supposin' I give yez a call from the landlord's after dinner, then?"

Helen thought about it. "Call me after nine," she said. "Frank's on four-to-twelve tonight, but he'll call me around nine. I can ask him then."

"Good enough," Red assented, shifting the *Journal American* under his arm and getting ready to leave. "How're yer feelin', then? Baby settin' well with yer?"

"Fine," Helen assured him, though she had another three weeks before the danger of miscarriage was officially past. There was no point in alarming him. "I'm getting used to the idea now."

"And are yer happy, then?"

"Well, sure, Pop," Helen said, taken aback slightly. "Why shouldn't I be?"

Her father looked uncomfortable. "I wanted to be sure, is all," he said with something approaching tenderness, and then he was on his way.

Johnny came to stay with Helen and Frank for two weeks and ended up staying the entire summer. Red had come back to Brooklyn and his job, leaving Kat to sit in the sun by the side of the lake, chatting with the other women who rented every summer and brooding when she was alone. He would stretch the budget every weekend, taking the train up to be with his wife, coming home exhausted Sunday night. He would not let her go back to Newfoundland, but he would not drag her back to Brooklyn until she was ready.

Johnny loved staying with Helen, who took him to the playground every afternoon and told him stories before she tucked him into his makeshift bed on the couch nightly. She gave him a childhood, as Kat had never found time to do. People stared at them in the street, especially toward the end of August when Helen's pregnancy became apparent. Johnny looked so much like her that strangers thought he must be her son, until they saw how young she was. Helen ignored their pointed questions, because answering them would embarrass Johnny and bring disgrace on her mother. She walked the streets with her head up, grateful for her little brother's company during the hot, empty days when Frank worked his ever-changing shifts.

Even when the summer was over and Kat finally home, there were weekends when Red would appear at Helen's door on a Friday evening, holding the boy by one hand, a small overnight bag in the other. Helen never refused. Someone had to see to it that Johnny had something close to a normal childhood.

And every summer until he turned eighteen, Johnny Manning spent at his sister's. Somewhere in his early teens he could have insisted on staying home alone while his father worked and his mother sat by her lake in Connecticut, but he always went to Helen's.

"Victoria Mary," Kat said for at least the tenth time, rolling it on her tongue and trying—but not too hard—not to sound hurt. "And that's after Frank's mother, is it? Are yer sure that's Irish, then? Victoria?"

"Yes, Mom," Helen said in answer to all three questions.

The object of all this discussion lay on her stomach with her small pink feet curled under her diapered behind in the white wicker bassinette trimmed with pink rosettes, calmly sucking her fat pink thumb, unaware that she gave her mother the shudders every time she was picked up, because she had not so much as one hair on her head, and the beating of her pulse in the soft place where the skull had not yet fused frightened Helen half to death.

"Sure, how can a name like that be Irish, then?" Kat demanded, but since no one was about to answer her, busy as they were fussing over the baby, she tried a different tack. "And what would yer be after callin' her? Sure, yer can't exactly stand on the stoop of an evening and yell 'Victoria Mary, come in to supper!'"

Why not? Helen wondered, when I nearly died of embarrassment for years listening to you bellowing "Helen Mary, Helen Mary!" up and down the street.

"We'll call her Vicki," Helen said, and as far as she was concerned, the subject was closed. She was going to have more babies no matter what the doctor said, so she could always name the next girl after her mother. She had come to the conclusion, after a very short labor and no complications, that the doctor was being an alarmist as far as this blood-type business was concerned. It was a simple case of prejudice. The doctor knew Helen was Catholic and would want a lot of babies; the doctor wasn't Catholic, wasn't any religion that Helen could see, so naturally he would be against big families. Helen didn't know why—he should be grateful for all the business—but she was certain he was prejudiced. She would have as many babies as she wanted, in spite of him.

Kat looked at the baby in the bassinette, engaged in the Irish grandmother's perpetual need to find a dominant resemblance to her family in the infant features.

"Well, at least," she sniffed, making sure everyone knew

she was offended about the name, "at least she's fair-skinned. She's a chance for having red hair, anyways."

Kat did not have long to be offended. Vicki was only a few months old when Red appeared on Helen's doorstep with Johnny, still in his school uniform, in the middle of a weekday afternoon.

"What happened?" Helen demanded immediately, pulling them both inside. Her father's face, under the weathered ruddy color, looked ashen.

"It's Danny," Red gasped, as if he had been running. "The damn fool's home for good. Got a medical discharge and showed up at the door, scared yer mother half out of her life. The landlady had to call me home from work. Himself is after losin' three of his fingers!"

It took a shot of strong whisky to get the whole story out of him, though his initial announcement covered most of the facts. Helen sent Johnny outside and told him to rock the baby carriage. He didn't need to hear the gory details.

To make a long story short, as Red put it, Danny had gone into machinist's training in the navy. An accident during a routine work-up—Danny was vague on details; it was thought he might have been less than sober when the event happened— had so badly crushed the first two fingers of his left hand that they had to be amputated at the second joint. The tip of the middle finger of his right hand was missing as well. He was granted a medical discharge, to which he raised little objection. The navy was a prison, Danny said. The officers picked on him, nobody really understood him. He got a small disability pension as well. Through a typical military foul-up, the letter informing his parents of his accident arrived the day after he did. Danny, of course, had not written to anybody since the day he enlisted.

If he expected a hero's welcome, all he got was Kat's hysteria. She kept kissing his mutilated hands, or at least the bandages, wailing about what "they" had done to her "baby." Red's first instinct, when he managed to comprehend what she was saying between sobs on the landlord's phone, was to rush home to comfort her. But as he sat on the bus—it was getting harder every year to walk the seven blocks uphill to the apartment—staring at his own scarred hands, thinking of the number of men he and Kat had known back in Newfoundland who had lost fingers, hands, eyes, legs, or even their lives in the war against the sea, not to mention his own missing fingertip, he couldn't see what the hysteria was about. If Danny had grown up in Harmony Bay, he would already be an old man. Disgusted, Red got off the bus and went straight to the grammar school to pick up Johnny, then brought him to Helen's without stopping home.

"Just overnight, then," he asked without asking. "He can miss the day's school tomorrow and sleep in his underwear for one night. I'll come get him when things is normal again."

"I've got his pajamas from last time," Helen said, resigned. It wasn't keeping the boy that bothered her, but the way he represented her having to cope when no one else in her family could. "What's Danny going to do now?"

"Damned if I know," her father said wearily, eyeing the bottle of Paddy's thoughtfully. "Though I'm after thinkin' we'll have to take him back now. It's not up to me, but yer mother'll see it that way."

"I suppose," Helen nodded, pouring him two fingers and no more.

Helen read Dr. Spock, who was all the rage among the other young mothers she met when she pushed Vicki's stroller to the playground. She was pleased that her daughter seemed so much brighter than the very average baby depicted in the thirty-five-cent paperback copy of *Baby and Child Care* that she carried with her until the pages started to fall out, but the chapters on behavior and discipline bewildered her. Vicki never had any of those problems. She had never had three-month colic, never cried all night. When she was old enough to sit up and eat solids, she gobbled up whatever she was given, was never finicky, never threw food on the floor or smeared it in her hair or spat it in Helen's face. She never cried when Helen walked out of the room. When she learned how to crawl she did so eagerly, chugging from room to room like a miniature locomotive, but she never tipped over waste-baskets or stuck bobby pins in the wall outlets. Even now, at sixteen months and beginning to walk, she never climbed out of the stroller or threw fits when it was time to go home. She had never had a tantrum. Helen read about such things in Spock's handbook and marveled. The other mothers in the neighborhood smiled enviously, and called Vicki a Model Child.

Helen got pregnant again. If it was this easy to raise a child, she didn't see what all the fuss was about.

The doctor gave her a stern lecture on the risks she was taking. Helen faced him with the kind of fortitude she imagined St. Agnes must have had when the evil Roman governor demanded her virginity in exchange for her life. Perhaps Daniel in the Lion's Den might have been more appropriate, but Helen identified more closely with St. Agnes. The issue was slightly different, but her religion was being challenged just the same. When she was well into the fourth month of pregnancy, without having had a miscarriage, Helen felt a little smug.

Everything was fine until the end of her seventh month, when Frank had his accident.

It was a big fire, a four-alarmer that ripped through a block of stores. Frank was on the roof of a supermarket toward the end, hosing down the tar to keep it cool, spreading piles of smoldering debris so they wouldn't reignite, his boots imbedded in the tar as it began to harden again, when with a single deafening crash the roof caved in. Frank plunged through feet first to the ground floor, where the flames were out but everything was still white-hot—display cases and cash registers melted into grotesque shapes, the metal still glowing orangely. He was pulled out almost immediately: dazed, one

ankle sprained, several ribs bruised, his price for his visit to
the inferno a pair of seared lungs, and second- and third-degree
burns of the hands and face. He was rushed to the hospital.

Helen dumped Vicki in Kat's lap without waiting for an
argument and took a cab to the hospital. She sat clutching the
rail of the bed where this stranger lay, his face swathed in
bandages, his hands like raw meat soaking in some strange
liquid, an intravenous stuck in his arm and a tube for oxygen
taped to his nose. She clung to the rail staring at her own
white knuckles, because if she looked at his hands she would
vomit. All sorts of people in white coats kept patting her
shoulder and talking about skin grafts and how strong he was
and how rapid his recovery would be, when all Helen kept
thinking of was how much he must hurt, yet he never made
a sound. And she sat by the bed all night even though everyone
tried to make her go home and the fire chief himself came in
and held her in his arms in a fatherly way and told her that
getting herself exhausted wasn't going to help her husband
any. And it wasn't until Frank roused a little from the drugs
they had him on and began to cough and retch, then hemor-
rhaged and heaved up bits of charred lung tissue, that two
orderlies came and physically removed Helen from the room.

She didn't scream, didn't fight them, didn't go into hysterics
the way her mother might have done. She allowed them to
half-carry her from the room, and sat on a bench in the hall
while someone called a cab, and simply whispered Frank's
name once before she recognized that she had had a stitch in
her side since early evening, and that by now it was so bad
she could barely walk.

And the nurse who had called the cab had to call again to
cancel it, after she contacted obstetrics and told them to bring
a wheelchair.

"She's a little over four pounds, eight weeks premature, and
severely jaundiced," the doctor told Helen when she was
fully awake. "I think I told you this might happen."

"What's going to happen to her?" Helen was utterly calm; she had no tension left.

"If she gets through the next forty-eight hours she should be fine, but just barely," the doctor said. "We're transfusing her now, and she'll be in an incubator until she tops five pounds."

Helen frowned, absorbing it but not unduly alarmed. "How long?"

'Probably about six weeks. Also, I want her to have breast milk. We didn't give you any medication to dry up your milk this time. Preemies don't do well on formula, and there's no point in giving her a harder time than she's had already. I'll send a nurse in later to show you how to use a breast pump."

Helen tried to pull herself up in bed. The stitches from the episiotomy made her wince, and she lay back again. "You mean I can't feed her myself? Can't I even hold her?"

The doctor's face was grim. This is what you get for being so stubborn, he seemed to be saying. "She's a high-risk baby. Her lungs aren't fully developed yet. A slight upper-respiratory infection and we'll lose her. She's to stay in that incubator until she's over five pounds."

Helen stayed in the hospital a full week on Frank's medical coverage, riding the elevator between the obstetric wing and the burn ward. It was against hospital rules—she might be carrying germs—but nobody wanted to argue with the determined little girl with the big brown eyes. She spent her mornings hovering by the nursery window staring at the scrawny, blotchy baby with the egg-yolk-colored eyeballs that they'd told her was hers. The bracelet that said "Girl O'Dell" on a wrist no thicker than a pencil was the only thing that convinced her.

"Hey, Girl O'Dell," she would whisper at the glass, trying to cheer herself up. "That's not your name, you know. How's Kathleen Mary O'Dell sound to you? Name's bigger than you are!"

Was this really her baby? It would be different when she could bring her home and cuddle her and dress her and be close to her. Then she would feel the same warmth and love she felt with Vicki. And Helen would think about her older daughter with a pang. Once they all got out of the hospital. . . .

After lunch, a lot of people managed to look the other way when she went downstairs to the burn ward to see Frank.

His hands were healing. They were no longer soaking like chunks of corned beef in brine, but the new skin on them was shiny and hairless and very tender, and all his fingernails had fallen out. Once they grew in and the skin got tougher he would be able to hold things, to do more than let the tips of his fingers graze Helen's cheek while he held back the pain.

As for his lungs, they would take the longest to recover. The day Helen went home from the hospital, he no longer needed the oxygen tank, but he could not be released for two more weeks. The sprained ankle was taped, and he was hopping around a little with the use of a cane. And the skin grafts on one side of his face had taken successfully; there would be only minimal scarring.

"I'll have to grow a beard," he wisecracked out of the side of his mouth where there was no bandage. "So I don't scare the crap outta my kids."

"You do and I'll leave you!" Helen snapped, eternally grateful that he was better but in no mood for jokes.

"Hey," he said, stroking her cheek again. "Fireman's wife's gotta have a sense of humor. Otherwise you go nuts."

"I'll manage," she said dryly, and kissed the tips of his fingers as gently as she could. She wondered, now that they were sending her home, how she was supposed to get down here every day to be with Frank and feed the new baby.

It was Alistair who solved the problem. He came to the hospital to bring Helen home, driving what looked like a brand-new car.

"Is this *yours?*" Helen asked, running her fingers down the upholstery. Any car impressed her; until Frank bought his ten-year-old Chevy she'd never ridden in a car regularly. "It's an Olds, isn't it? They're *expensive!*"

"Not mine. Belongs to a—friend," Alistair said, avoiding her eyes and turning the key in the ignition. "He's on vacation for a few weeks and asked me to keep it humming for him. Got me license last year when I turned eighteen. Have to practice on something till I can afford me own."

"It was very thoughtful of you to pick me up," Helen said, putting her hand on his arm the way she used to when they were children. Was it her imagination, or did he flinch ever so slightly? "How'd you get the day off?"

"Oh, didn't I tell you? I quit the Y," he said airily. "Looking for something better. Staying with Ag awhile. She's kept me room up, y'know. Lets me come and go, don't ask any questions. So I'm free for the time being, except for school, and that's nights. I can pick you up and drive you down to the hospital every day if you like."

"You don't have to do that," Helen said softly, hoping he wouldn't refuse all the same.

"I don't do things because I have to," Alistair said softly, taking a curve with the big car as if he'd been driving all his life.

Helen didn't know what to say. She was accustomed to having favors doled out grudgingly by Kat and other members of her family, with constant reminders of how generous they were being. She had a hard time dealing with open generosity.

"Thank you, Alistair," she said, adding the only thing she could think of. "I'm going to pray for you to find a new job. I'll pray for you every night."

He swerved to avoid a dog loping across the intersection, its back to the traffic, and looked at her, distressed. "Cripes!" he said. "You don't have to do that!"

"I will anyway."

He drove in silence for a while. "How long you staying with your parents?"

"Just until Frank gets out of the hospital. Another two weeks."

"Good thing it's no more'n that," Alistair said. "I'd almost offer you to come stay with Ag and me, except neither of us is home all day."

Helen frowned. "What's wrong with going home? It's only temporary."

Alistair studied her face while he waited for a traffic light to change. "You haven't been over there much since Fatso's been back, have you?"

"I think we can call him by name," Helen said sternly, though she had to push the hair up off her forehead to keep from smiling. Why was it so easy to make fun of Danny, even now? "We're not kids anymore. Only Sundays, for dinner. Why?"

Alistair shrugged, driving again. "Only that he ain't found a job yet, and your old man threatens to kill him at least once a week. Then your mother starts crying, and little Johnny just sits there watching 'em all. It ain't pretty."

"I should think they'd keep it down since I left Vicki with them," Helen said grimly. She had forgotten all this, pushed it out of her mind because she was wrapped up in Frank and the new baby. "It's only till Frank gets out."

Helen hadn't planned to get pregnant for the third time so soon, but using rhythm—there was nothing else a decent Catholic girl could do—was chancy, and there was so much else going on when it happened. . . .

It all started with Loretta. She and Helen kept in touch as much as they could, which meant that Loretta called Helen once a week from work—she was an executive secretary now—and once a month or so, when Frank was on night duty and could mind the kids for her during the day, Helen went into Manhattan to meet Loretta for lunch. They talked a great deal, talked for hours on the phone when they could, but both began to realize that the more they talked the less they were saying. They talked about clothes, movies they had seen, Helen's kids, and that was about all. That was why Helen was so shocked when Loretta decided to bare her soul one afternoon over lunch.

They were in the tearoom at Lord & Taylor having salads. Helen had been talking about Kathleen's new teeth. "I'm just so glad it's over," she groaned. "The poor thing started teething so early—five months—and she's got such a miserable, whiny disposition as it is. . . ."

She stopped. Loretta had started to cry, soundlessly, big splashy tears dropping into her salad. When she realized Helen was staring at her, she groped for a tissue and started to sob.

"What's the matter with you?" Helen said, coldly perhaps, but then Loretta could cry over anything.

"It must have been the way you said 'I'm just so glad it's over,' " Loretta sniffed, getting control of herself. "I feel the same way. About something I've been—involved in. I've been having an affair with my boss."

She said it with no emotion whatsoever. Over twenty years of indoctrination boiled in Helen's throat; she wanted to rage about the evils of adultery, get up from the table full of righteous indignation. But she held off on the sermon. This was her very best friend. If they had grown so far apart in the past few years that she hadn't even seen this coming. . . .

"Tell me about it," she managed to say, keeping her voice level.

"It was stupid," Loretta began, blowing her nose. Women at the other tables were staring at them, but she didn't seem to notice. "I mean, he was married and everything. And I didn't even love him. I just thought he was—attractive. Sort of a Henry Fonda type. But it wasn't even that. Nothing romantic. Just stupid. I mean, I don't know how many boys I've dated, but it's never been more than once or twice and they start kidding around calling me 'Stretch' or something.

Can I help it if there're so many short men in this world? I'm only five-nine! Why do they have to pick on me? And I saw myself still being—you know—a virgin when I was twenty-five, and I said to myself, every girl oughta have some kind of memory before she's that old, and my boss took me out to lunch—just business—and I started to cry like just now, and he got very sympathetic and I figured, we'll just do it once so I'll know what it feels like, and then I'll go to confession and everything'll be fine. But it didn't work out that way. He kept taking me out again and again, and I couldn't say no because I figured I owed him something, and we must've— you know—done it about a dozen times before he found out how miserable I was. And I said we'd have to stop or I'd have to quit my job. And you know what he said to me?"

Helen had been absolutely silent through all of this. Now she shook her head.

"He said"—Loretta imitated a deep, masculine voice—"he said, 'In that case we'll stop, because I can't afford to lose you. You're a damn fine secretary.' And it's been like that for over a month. And now I've got to go back to that office in fifteen minutes and sit there listening to his voice all day, and I don't even have the guts to look for another job."

She was crying again, more quietly this time. Helen put down her fork in despair. She was still hungry, had barely started to eat before Loretta broke into her sob story, but it didn't seem polite to go on eating under the circumstances.

"I went to confession," Loretta went on, drying her eyes, her makeup a shambles. "When it was all over, I went to confession and I told the priest everything I just told you. You know what he said to me?"

Helen shook her head again.

"He called me a fallen woman. He started yelling so you could've heard him through the whole church. He said Christ could've forgiven Mary Magdalen because she did it out of love, but even He couldn't forgive me. He threw me out of the confessional. Helen, what am I going to do?"

"Go to another priest," Helen said abruptly, annoyed that

they were still being stared at, annoyed that she could be friendly with anyone so brainless. "There's a Franciscan mission down around Thirty-fourth Street. They hear confessions for murderers. They'll give you an easier time."

Loretta gave her a dirty look and her crying stopped abruptly. "That was lousy of you!" she sniveled. "It's easy for you to be smug. You've got a decent husband, two kids. I've got nothing. If I got hit by a truck on my way back to work, all my mother would say is 'Thank God, now we've got an extra bedroom.' Nobody cares about me. I thought I'd get some understanding from you, but I guess I was wrong."

Helen sighed. She supposed she was being harsh, but then Loretta could be counted on to be a sloppy, romantic fool, and someone had to keep a clear head. When the waitress had brought their checks and gone, she leaned across the table.

"What did you expect me to say?" she asked. "If you'd asked my advice before you did anything this stupid, what would I have told you?"

"You're right," Loretta admitted, then laughed. "It's crazy. I don't know what I've accomplished by talking to you. Maybe I thought I'd get something different than what I got from that priest, that's all. Maybe I thought you had some solution."

Helen picked up her check and gave Loretta a piercing look. "I can't solve this for you. You've got to solve it yourself. Don't you think you should be getting back to the office?"

There was one thing Helen could do to help her friend, and when she was assured that the boss was out of Loretta's life forever—she had given her two weeks' notice and was hunting through the classifieds—she talked Frank into bringing one of the single men from the firehouse to the apartment one evening a week. She invited Loretta, and the four of them would have a quiet dinner after the kids were in bed, and then they played bridge. All of them were beginners, and the play was very serious. No one had time to talk. Frank's friend would bring Loretta home afterwards, and Helen kept her fingers crossed. But then Frank's shift was changed again, and while he worked nights Helen was stuck keeping the conversation going between the other two. After a week or two of this, Frank's friend stopped by less often, and Helen was stuck with Loretta alone.

It was on one of those evenings that Loretta announced she was going to relocate in Europe, had gotten a job with a travel agency there, and could travel whenever she got bored. She dug out a lot of brochures and travel folders, and Helen was green with envy by the time she left.

She probably got pregnant that very night, because Frank woke her up when he came in and she told him about Loretta and started to cry. It wasn't fair, and she was plainly jealous. Frank cheered her up the only way he knew how. Of course, with the ensuing uproar over Danny, she didn't have time to worry about it for several weeks.

Danny, it seems, had at last found a field in which he needed neither academic nor manual skills, but had to rely solely on his personality, or at least an artificial personality he manufactured for himself out of a Dale Carnegie course, a crash diet, and some expensive suits bought out of his disability pay. Danny became an appliance salesman, dealing between wholesaler and retailer, an on-the-road man, a back-slapping, artificially hearty sales representative, whom his customers regarded as a Good Joe because they saw him two or three times a year, and then usually over a three-drink lunch.

He continued to live at home whenever he wasn't on the road, and Kat did his laundry and kept his room neat without dreaming of asking him to pay rent. She did not get insulted when he told her not to empty his pockets or go through his bureau drawers when he wasn't home; she was more than a little apprehensive about what she might find if she looked too closely, and was grateful when he clarified the issue. Still, she couldn't help noticing the number of matchbooks accumulating on the top of his bureau, all from the same cocktail lounge somewhere in Queens. She wondered if it was business that made it necessary for her son to drive that far in the company car nearly every night he was in town. She mentioned none of this to Red, who was always dead to the world by the time Danny came rolling in.

So when Danny brought home an overly made-up young woman named Paula, who just happened to be a cocktail waitress, Kat was shocked but not surprised. Red, on the other hand, was dumbfounded. There were arguments between them whenever Danny was on the road.

"He's a grown man, sure, and entitled to do what he pleases!" Kat shrilled at her husband, only half-believing it herself. "And under all that paint she's probably a decent girl. She goes to mass every Sunday; she's very religious. She was after tellin' me herself."

"And yer gullible enough to believe it," Red simmered, beyond anger. What did he care what the ugly lout did with his life? "But if he's that much of a man it's time he cleared out and went on his own. Let him do his own dirty laundry, then. Or at least pay his way."

"A young man's got to save his money," Kat said firmly, unwilling to admit she had no idea how much her son made per week. "He'll need it to spend when he's after gettin' married."

That was an event which was to transpire sooner than anyone, except perhaps Paula, expected. Less than a month after he brought her around to introduce her to the family, Danny announced that they were getting married very soon.

"I've kept me mouth shut around yer mother," Red said; he had come to Helen's alone for a change, and sat bouncing flame-haired Kathleen on his knee while four-year-old Vicki stood behind him in the kitchen chair brushing his sparse hair with a doll's brush. "But I'm wonderin' if I'm the only one has noticed anything about that girl."

Helen had met Paula the weekend before at Sunday dinner, and she and Frank had exchanged looks across the table more than once.

"That girl's expecting, Pop," she said. "Even Frank saw it, and he can be so thick sometimes."

"Yer mother won't hear it," Red sighed, relieved that he had some allies. "If I even hint at it she blows up. Sure, I don't know why I'm after gettin' excited about it. Only, I'm thinkin' she's trapped the great jackass and it burns me. We're still family, for all I can't stand the sight of him!"

Helen reached past him to pluck Vicki out of the chair, then dumped Kathleen on the floor, patting both of them on their small round behinds to hurry them out of the room. "If he's stupid enough to get involved with someone like her, they probably deserve each other," Helen said, then stopped herself. Even she was beginning to notice how much she sounded like her mother. "Besides, the only way to prove you're right is to see how long it takes after the wedding. It's my opinion that's going to be a very premature baby."

Red squinted at her. She was getting cold lately, almost bitter. He supposed it was necessary to a mature woman, which she was now, and in a way he was glad she wasn't as vulnerable as she once was. Still, there was a hardness to her face, a set of the jaw he found disquieting. She was only twenty-four, but she might have been forty.

"And yerself?" he asked, trying to sound casual. "How's life been treatin' yer, then?"

Helen looked flustered for a moment before she could answer. Since the beginning of the week she thought she might be pregnant again. "I'm fine, Pop. Busy with the kids, and Frank's on crazy hours again. A little frazzled, that's all."

"Aye," her father said, not satisfied with the answer.

Danny married his painted bride, who wore an out-of-style gown with an Empire waist to the big expensive wedding her parents provided for her. They seemed relieved to have her off their hands—she was nearly thirty—though they didn't think much of the groom or his family. There was considerable silence on either side of the table on the dais in the big catering hall. Both sets of parents sat glaring stonily across an almost-tangible barrier of hostility. All the fun seemed to be at the table where the rest of the groom's relatives sat. Aunt

Ag had had a bit too much champagne, and was holding court between Alistair—who arrived alone, and dressed to the hilt as usual—and Frank. Helen sat next to Frank, feeling queasy with early pregnancy and the smell of all that food, wondering if the girls were all right with her upstairs neighbor. She had never left them with anybody but her mother before. Only once did she give the new bride a glance, saw her dancing with one of her uncles, with the same greenish look around her eyes that Helen had worn for weeks. Poor girl! Helen thought in a rush. Sin might be sin, but a baby was a baby, and she felt sorry for poor, pregnant Paula. She thought of the grief Kat would give her, once the truth became too apparent to ignore.

Helen talked Frank into leaving early, and when they got home she went straight to the bathroom while he went upstairs to pick up the kids. When she heard their footsteps in the hall, she called out to him. "Frank?"

"Just me and the Munchkins!" he yelled through the bathroom door. "Jack the Ripper took the day off."

"Don't kid around, will you?" she gasped, and he knew something was wrong. She had only told him she was pregnant this past week.

"I'm here," he said, leaning his forehead against the door as he seemed to remember doing somewhere, sometime else. "What's wrong? What can I do?"

"Bring the—bring the girls back upstairs." There was panic in her voice. "There's blood."

She was less than ten weeks pregnant, and the miscarriage was not that severe. She was released from the hospital the next morning. Her doctor did not lecture this time. Kat came to the apartment to mind the kids and tidy up for a few days, but she made no effort to spend the night. She never offered her daughter a word of sympathy either.

"I'll not be comin' tomorrow, then," she announced on the fourth day.

Helen looked surprised. She had barely lifted a finger in

four days, except to rearrange the dishes and flatware and
laundry after her mother left each evening, putting things
back where *she* was used to keeping them. She hadn't expected this much pampering, and was startled that her mother
found the need to apologize—in her own way—for stopping
now.

"That's okay, Mom," she said, with what she hoped was the
right amount of tact. "You've done enough already."

"It's that I've me own work to do as well, and Johnny home
after school by himself. He's eight, sure, and old enough to
manage, but I don't feel right about it."

"Mom?" Helen had been told to stay off her feet for a week;
to her mother than meant staying in bed. "I said it was okay. I
feel strong. You've been a big help to me in the past few
days."

"And don't sulk because yer got no sympathy from me!"
Kat lashed out, striking at an opponent who had no desire to
fight. "Ye've only lost the one, but I was after losin' three,
and no one to feel sorry for me!"

"Mom—" Helen was speechless. Things suddenly fell into
place. All those blank spaces in her childhood ("Yer mother's
got a bit of a stomachache: she's after needin' a rest in the hospital, then.") suddenly filled in, the colors stark and primary.
Kat's gloom after Johnny was born, her chronic sliding in and
out of depression—were they symptoms of delayed mourning
for the babies she couldn't have?

"I didn't know," Helen said, thinking she should resent it,
annoyed that she had to be this old before her mother could
confide in her. If she hadn't lost her own baby, Kat might
never have said a word.

"Of course yer didn't know!" Kat was exasperated, bundling
her possessions into a shopping bag, ready to go home. "Was
I supposed to scare yer to death? Yer morbid enough as it is.
If I'd told yer, yer mightn't have had any babies yerself."

Helen sat down, defeated, the guilty party yet again.

"I'll never understand it, sure," her mother muttered, fishing change out of her purse for the bus, fumbling with the buttons on her sweater. "Down to home yer expected to lose babies. It was the way of things, the hard life. But all the doctors and medicine in this country and they still couldn't help me none."

"Even doctors can't always—" Helen began. Whatever she said would have to come from her own experience, and her mother didn't want to hear advice from her. She said nothing.

"So don't be after feelin' sorry for yerself because yer lost the one. Yer life ain't over, then," Kat finished, snapping her purse shut for emphasis and grasping the handles of the much-used paper shopping bag. "I'll be gone, then."

Helen gave her a pallid kiss on the cheek and brought the girls in from the next room to say good-bye. By the time her mother left, Helen was more depressed than she'd been even on the way to the hospital when she knew she was losing the baby.

Helen remembered her twenties, in later years, as being a vague sort of blur. She remembered events not by the day or year they happened, but by how old the kids were when such-and-such happened, whether it was before or after her miscarriage, before or after Frank's promotion to lieutenant. It was as if for an entire decade she stopped being herself at all— if she had ever really been herself and not Somebody's Daughter—and became Somebody's Wife and Somebody's Mother. She was also Somebody's Sister, Cousin, Sister-in-Law, Aunt, and Friend. But who was she?

Other things happened in those years besides Helen's having babies. There were important things, happy things, sad things, but they happened to the people around her. Her sister-in-law Paula had her baby five months after the wedding. Helen and Red chuckled a great deal between themselves, while Kat went into a snit and ignored them. Danny started to gain weight again, and Helen suspected he drank more than anyone cared to admit. When he wasn't wearing his salesman personality, he was short-tempered and surly. Paula seemed happy to see him leave for the road.

Alistair finished college, got a summer job as a basketball coach in the public school system, and was hired as a gym teacher the following fall. He bought a car and wore impeccable clothes. His social life was a deep, dark secret, except possibly to Ag, who said nothing to anybody.

Ag had been playing the stock market for years, and by the time she was fifty she could afford to work part-time and live off her dividends. She traveled a lot, mostly to Florida and California, and spent the rest of her time at home watching the soaps, her delicate feet up on an ottoman to rest her varicose veins.

Red was sent home from work one afternoon by the company doctor, looking gray in the face and suddenly exhausted. His family doctor said it was a mild heart attack and told him to give up smoking. He came home from the hospital after a few days, gathered up all of his pipes—some of which he'd had for twenty years or more—and the humidor filled with his special blend of tobacco, and carted everything out to the garbage can.

Kat developed mild arthritis in her hands, which she used as an opener for most conversations, unless she was in one of her moods and not talking at all. She spent several afternoons a week in the church basement while Johnny was in school, sorting old clothes for the missions and comparing diseases with other menopausal women.

Johnny, at ten, was considered the brightest boy in his class. He came home with his ears burning one day to report that a girl in the schoolyard had kissed him, right in front of everybody. Kat marched up to the school the next day and lectured the young nun on keeping an eye out for such things.

Loretta stayed in Europe for a year, working for a travel service in Switzerland. When she came back, she found another job, got an apartment in Manhattan to be nearer work, and she and Helen gradually lost contact.

The week after his thirtieth birthday, Frank was presented with an award by the mayor for pulling three kids out of a tenement fire. There were articles about the awards ceremony in all the newspapers, and Helen cut them out and pasted them in a scrapbook, underlining Frank's name in red. The *Daily News* ran a picture of Frank in uniform, with Vicki and Kathleen on his lap and his eyebrows scorched away again. She was especially fond of that.

Helen got pregnant again.

"I suppose you think this is an intelligent thing to do so soon?" her doctor demanded. "It's less than a year since you aborted."

"That makes it sort of like falling off a horse, doesn't it?" Helen asked primly. She was developing a rudimentary sense of humor, mostly in self-defense.

"More like falling off a log," the doctor said, not amused. He gave her a wry look and wrote out two prescription slips. Helen looked at them, then at him, and frowned.

"I recognize the vitamins," she said. "But what's the other one?"

"Something new," he said. "Experimental drug—combination of hormones, really—that's been found to prevent miscarriage in susceptible women."

"Experimental?" Helen repeated. "Is it safe?"

"It's been on the market about seven years," the doctor said. "No noticeable side effects. And it works to prevent miscarriage in nine out of ten cases."

"I've got nothing to lose, then," Helen smiled, tucking the prescriptions into her purse.

Family interest in Helen's pregnancies had begun to wane by the fourth time around, especially since Kat predicted none too quietly that, drug or no drug, Helen would probably lose this one as well. When "this one" not only survived the three-month mark but turned out to be twins, interest picked up at once. Everyone from Kat to Ag to Frank's mother to the neighbors wanted to be on record as saying they *thought*

Helen carried big this time, and they *knew* it would be twins.

Helen was annoyed at the circus atmosphere that engulfed her as soon as she brought Maureen and Mary Frances home from the hospital—both miraculously over five pounds, so there was no concern about incubators—but she was too busy and too exhausted to fight it. She ordered another bassinette, bought more diapers and baby clothes, and got a double Coachman perambulator to replace the old single one that had survived Vicki and Kathleen. She got her name, and a terrible photograph of herself and Frank and all four girls, in the *Home Reporter/Sunset News*, a neighborhood weekly paper, as well as in the Fire Department's newsletter. There was an endless stream of visitors, mostly obscure relatives she hadn't seen since her grandmother's wake, and there was always a dirty teapot and a stack of cups and saucers in the sink. The twins were nearly six months old before Helen had a chance to sit down with a cup of coffee and watch the leaves on the maple tree in front of their apartment redden in the fall. Then Frank decided to buy a new house.

They had to buy it now, because of the twins, he argued. Helen agreed in principle, but the idea of having to pack and juggle four kids did not appeal to her. They had been squirreling away every spare dime since the day they got married, because neither of them had ever lived in a real house and both wanted it for their kids. Helen thought they ought to wait until the twins were a little older, even if it meant overcrowding and the inevitable winter mornings when there was no heat. But Frank had a lead from a fellow fireman, and it sounded like exactly what they needed.

They bought the huge old colonial in Bay Ridge, and Helen spent the next six months with plaster dust in her hair and the smell of paint in her nostrils, while Frank hammered and sanded and put up wallpaper and she tried to keep the girls out of the mess. By the time Vicki started first grade and the twins were nearly one, she had managed to unpack all their possessions—which for months had been piled into boxes and crates

and shifted from room to room as the renovating went on—
and return to something resembling normalcy. It was only then
that she realized how depressed she was.

Helen's alienation began slowly, subtly, had perhaps started
even before the twins were born, but her awareness of it began
only when Vicki started school. It startled Helen more than a
little to realize that she was old enough to have a school-age
child, and it saddened her that she could account for so little
of that time, apart from the endless sorting of laundry and
changing of diapers. She brooded about it for a few days, then
shrugged it off as self-pity, and went on walking her eldest
daughter to school every morning, watching with pride the
little figure in the parochial-school uniform striding ahead of
her with a look of fierce determination. Helen followed behind
Vicki, pushing the double stroller with the twins and tugging
at the small hand of a heel-dragging Kathleen, who made plain
her resentment at being left home with "those babies" while
her big sister got to go to school. Kathleen was probably the
first cause of Helen's alienation, or certainly its catalyst.

It wasn't so much that Kathleen was balky, that she was still
tantrum-prone at four, that she seemed of all Helen's kids the
most susceptible to cantagious diseases and the most likely to
pass them on to her siblings. The underlying problem was that
Helen didn't, had never, didn't think she could ever, love this
little carrot-topped monster. She blamed herself for it, of
course—how could a child possibly be responsible for a parent's dislike?—and while she never came out and said it to
anyone in her family, her monthly confessions were filled with
repetitions of her "impatience" with her children, although
she seldom raised her voice to the other three. It had almost
been bearable as long as Vicki was around; polite, docile Vicki
had been a buffer between her younger sister and their mother.
But now that Vicki was in school all day. . . .

"Kathleen Mary O'Dell! What *are* you doing?" Helen
heard herself say it a dozen times a day, but here it was again.

"Shitting," the girl replied matter-of-factly (God knew

where she'd picked up *that* word), squatting in a corner of her bedroom, fully dressed, her face bright red with the strain.

"You're *what?* How can you make in your pants—a big girl like you? You should be ashamed! March into that bathroom this minute!"

She wanted to kill this child, not drag her into the bathroom, take off her soiled clothes, and wash her in the tub. She wanted to kill her. All right, it was true she had had a bout with colitis as an infant and she still alternated a week of constipation with a day or two of the runs, but she was too old for this kind of behavior. When she had hoisted the child out of the tub and dried her off, Helen gave her two sharp smacks on her bare behind.

"That's bad!" she heard her own voice, high-pitched and grating. "That's ugly and filthy and disgusting! Why did you do a thing like that?"

She saw the marks her hand had made—red fingers outlined against the white skin—but Kathleen had not cried when she was struck, and had no tears to offer now.

"Because I want to," she pouted, her lower lip trembling but her jaw set in a way that defied remorse. "*Them* does it and you says it's cute!"

She pointed a stubby, accusing finger at the twins, who had assembled in the doorway like two small owls when they heard all the commotion. Helen turned to look at them and had to keep from laughing.

"They're just babies." She frowned, remembering the seriousness of the issue at hand, pulling a clean polo shirt over Kathleen's head. "You're four and a half years old!"

"If I can't go to school then I be a baby," Kathleen announced, and that was that.

"But you gotta admit she's logical," Frank argued when Helen told him about it that night. He always stuck up for his second daughter, sensing the animosity between her and her mother.

"I know, I can't really blame her," Helen sighed, ready for

bed though it was only nine o'clock. "But it's a dozen times a day, and it wears me out! And that's all I get from her—never a hug or a kiss or a cuddle; she won't even stay still so *I* can cuddle *her!* She's so damn prickly I wonder if there's something wrong with her."

"It's a phase," Frank said vaguely, not very sure of it himself. "They all go through phases. Once she starts school. . . ."

The twins were the next to turn away from her, or so Helen saw it. If she had been reacting in a manner that was less than paranoid, she would have had to admit they had never turned *toward* her. Except for the necessities—feeding, washing, dressing, trips in the stroller—they required nothing from anyone. They formed a completely self-sufficient microcosm; mirror-images, one of the other, they had such compatible dispositions that they seemed like two halves of one person. Maureen was placid, easily amused, shy; Mary Fran was inquisitive, impatient, extroverted. When Mary Fran discovered something new in her endless creeping from room to room, she brought it to her sister's attention; Maureen examined it thoroughly and they discussed it. They developed their own exclusive language, comprised mostly of gestures and facial expressions, and found it unnecessary to learn English until they were nearly three. If one twin was cranky on a given day, the other was sanguine enough to compensate. Though their mother refused to follow the trend of dressing them alike and treating them like dolls to be displayed around the neighborhood, but tried rather to give them separate chances to develop as individuals, they thwarted her whenever possible. They pooled their carefully separate toys in the middle of the floor and shared them; they were never more than a few feet away from each other at any time. When they were put in their separate cribs at night, they twisted their small bodies around so that each could see the other, so that the last thing each girl saw before dropping off to sleep was her sister's face. Any effort to rearrange the cribs into a new pattern brought tantrums and head banging. Helen surrendered and moved the cribs together again. One night when she went to tuck them in, she found that they had reached across the expanse of a few inches between the cribs to grasp each other's hands; they slept that way the entire night. Helen swore they even rolled over in unison.

All right, Helen thought. Kathleen hates me, and the twins don't need me. But there's always Vicki. Vicki the Model Child. Vicki still needs me. She is out there facing school and new friendships and sudden growing up. She will need my advice. *She* will need *me*.

". . . and he stuck it in my face and tried to scare me with it but I said 'Peter, that's just an old spider and my daddy says spiders in Brooklyn don't bite people only in places like Mexico where they've got scorpions and things' and he said—well, he said a dirty word—and Sister heard him and pulled him out of his seat by the ear and washed his mouth out with soap and then she took his spider and threw it out the window and then Linda who sits behind me whispered 'I think he's the most dis-*gust*ing boy in the whole world' and I nodded my head because Sister was looking at me and anyway Linda's a real snob and when we go to the bathroom they don't have any locks on the doors so we have to take turns holding the doors closed and she always opens the door on her partner and laughs but if somebody does it to her she cries and screams and tells Sister and we all get in trouble. . . ."

Helen nodded her head as was required during this endless narrative. It went on every afternoon when she picked Vicki up from school. Vicki talked, whether anyone listened or not, but it was necessary to pretend absolute attentiveness. Helen kept a fixed smile on her face as she checked to see that the drizzle was not leaking through the side flaps of the stroller onto the twins, who slept shoulder to shoulder like bookends. Every so often she looked back to be sure she hadn't lost Kathleen, who was systematically mucking through every puddle on the block, her rain hat lost three blocks ago and her hair plastered to her skull as she obstinately dragged her open

umbrella behind her on the sidewalk. Vicki walked beside her
mother with her rain hat tied precisely under her chin and her
umbrella pointed at just the proper angle above her small, dark
head. She was still talking.

Helen stopped pushing the stroller and stood stock-still, the
rain making little ticking noises on the shoulders of her raincoat. She was clutching the stroller handle so ferociously her
knuckles had gone white. If she were anywhere but her own
street, if she were anyone other than the person she was, she
might have screamed. Screamed for the frustration of being
the mother of four absolutely autonomous children, all of
whom were completely alien to her.

"Mother?" It was Vicki, who always pounced on any aber-
ration. She had abandoned the affectionate use of "Mommy"
the first day she went to school. "Mother? Why on earth are
you standing here in the rain? What on earth is the matter?"

Helen shook her head, breaking the trance. "Nothing,
honey," she replied. "I was resting for a minute, that's all."

It's a phase, she thought. Frank is right. They're all going
through some sort of phase. But how much longer can I stand
it?

It was probably at that moment that a small, rebellious opinion flickered for a moment at the back of her brain; a small
voice made a suggestion that she had been trained to reject
from the day she was born.

Maybe there was more to life than marriage and babies.

Helen rejected the thought by instinct the first time it happened, but it returned periodically, depressing her, making her
restless for something she could hardly articulate. What good
would it do? She had opted for marriage, and she had to cope
with the babies. There was nothing else, for the moment.

The symptoms, the small indications that all was not well,
continued to accumulate. She started to sleep more than usual,
napping when the twins napped instead of using the time to
sew curtains or clean closets, going to bed as soon as the girls
did in the evening. Trained to neatness from the day she could

walk, she became a sloppy housekeeper. She sometimes had to iron Vicki's school blouses while she made breakfast and kept one eye on Frank's last pair of socks, hand-washed and drying in the oven while he shaved. Dust gathered and newspapers accumulated, bills went unpaid, library books were lost or stayed overdue for months, food spoiled in the refrigerator.

Helen put up a good facade. Mostly to get away from the mess in the house, she took the girls—hair combed, shoes polished, little faces scrubbed—out for a walk every afternoon that the weather was bearable. She became the Ideal Young Mother, earning the beaming approval of every old lady on the block.

If they only knew, she thought, nodding and smiling and exchanging inanities about the raising of children; every old lady had her own bit of advice. If they only knew!

To make matters worse, she began having trouble with Frank.

Frank, too, had a reputation in the neighborhood. It was actually several reputations rolled into one complete aura just slightly less awesome than canonization. Frank was, everyone in the neighborhood agreed, a go-getter. He had been promoted to captain by now, had earned nearly every honor and award a fireman could earn and still be alive to tell about it. And he was, after all, a Model Father and an Ideal Husband.

And we have nothing in common anymore, Helen thought. We talk about the kids, which is to say that I complain and he listens, or we talk about the Fire Department, which is to say that he gripes about paperwork and wants to get back into the action again and I listen. We are bored with each other. And the fact that I collapse into bed at eight-thirty every night and can't wake up in the morning doesn't help much either.

She and Frank agreed on one thing. Four kids were enough, for now at least. But Helen's periods were regular, and she'd been lucky with rhythm since the twins were born, so it wasn't that.

"Look, let me ask you something." Frank broached the subject, trying to be considerate, but the constant state of chaos was beginning to get to him. "If you get your—your friend—pretty regular every month—I mean, it's thirty days, right on schedule, right?"

"I guess so," Helen sighed, too wrung out to even open her eyes. It was eight o'clock and the girls were in their respective rooms, if not asleep. She lay on top of the bedspread in her clothes, too tired to grope for her pajamas.

Frank sat on the bed beside her, wanting to rub her shoulder, wondering if she'd even feel it. "What I mean is, if you knew what days you might get pregnant, all we'd have to do is skip those days, right?"

"Yeah," Helen murmured, dozing.

"So what about the rest of the month?" he demanded, an edge of exasperation in his voice. "I mean, I know you got a lot to do during the day and sometimes you're too tired, but I think we must've—you know—maybe twice in the past three months."

"Three times," Helen corrected him, opening her eyes and rallying a little.

He ignored her. "Look, what I'm saying is, just because we're not having any more kids for a while, are you gonna lay down and die on me or what?"

She didn't answer. He realized she was asleep and jogged her shoulder slightly. She muttered, made a face, and tried to settle in more comfortably.

"Say, what is it with you anyway?" he said, loudly enough to make sure she was awake. Her eyes started open, and he softened his tone. "Maybe you oughta see a doctor or something. Have him give you some vitamins. You're really a mess."

She was dozing again.

"I'm worried about you," he said tenderly, saying what was really on his mind.

Helen did not respond. Frank looked down at her, rubbing the side of his face where he'd had the skin grafts; it tingled sometimes when he was tense. He went to touch her again, realized it made no difference in the state she was in, wanted to shake her violently, and did not.

"Jesus!" he exhaled, getting up. He would go down to the kitchen, where he had been hanging Sanitas all week. Maybe he could finish tonight. Or he could sit in the living room flipping the selector dial on the new television until he found something boring enough to put him to sleep in the chair, so he would be numb enough to stagger upstairs later without thinking of anything but sleep. He hated to sleep beside her when she dozed off this way, hogging the bed-clothes, too dopey to move until somewhere near dawn when she would fumble her way into the bathroom to put on her pajamas, without even bothering to wash the day's dirt off her scummy face before she fell back into bed again. It happened almost nightly, and it made Frank heartsick. *Was* there something wrong with her?

There was no one breaking point; there were several. Helen's approaching thirty had a great deal to do with it. Her parents' installing a phone pushed her closer to the edge. The problem of Sunday mass had been escalating for years. And then there was Kathleen and the library book. . . .

Thirty is a frightening age for a woman—not quite as frightening as forty, with its portents of menopause, wrinkles, and gray hair—but frightening in its insistence that youth is over. If twenty was the verge of maturity, thirty was its depth and height and breadth. Between twenty-one and twenty-nine, one could afford to be playful and serious by turns; at thirty the party was over. It had to be seriousness now, or nothing. The rules, of course, applied only to women. Men could still play football on weekends and make fools of themselves at parties, but women. . . .

Helen was only twenty-eight, but with that innate craving for precision that Vicki had perhaps inherited from her, she insisted that from the day of her twenty-ninth birthday forward she would in fact be living her thirtieth year. In short, her youth was coming to a close, though she'd only recently recognized its existence. Helen had never been playful, only serious. She had been a mother at twenty, at twenty-two, at twenty-five. She had never had time to be anything but serious, had never had time for youth. How could she lament the passing of something that had never existed?

But this was an abstraction, and she had more concrete things to drive her mad. No sooner had she started Kathleen in school, confident that now that her hellion was in the nuns' capable hands she might have some time to herself, than her phone started to ring at eight-thirty every morning. Her father had relented after all these years and gotten a telephone. This gave Kat an excuse to call her daughter daily with a catalogue of ailments and sorrows that no one else had the patience to listen to.

"Mother of God, I'm after callin' yer three times!" Kat began one typical call. "What's happened?"

"Nothing, Mom," Helen gasped, winded from running the length of the house to grab the phone in the kitchen. She propped the receiver between her ear and shoulder so she could unbutton Maureen's coat. "I had to walk the girls to school. There's three inches of snow on the ground, and since Kathleen refuses to walk close to Vicki I have to walk them both in or—ohmygod, Mary *Fran*ces!"

"What is it, sure?" Kat demanded, certain the child had been eaten by a dragon at the very least.

"Nothing, Mom. She was walking on the rug with her wet boots, that's all. You sit *right there* and take them off, young lady! Anyway, here I am and everything's fine. How're you?"

"Oh, Jesus and Mary, me hands is killin' me!" her mother began. It was a predictable litany. "It's this terrible damp, sure. I never remember it's bein' this damp down to Newfoundland. Cold, yes. Sure, it went to thirty below and yer never gave it a thought, but this terrible damp. . . ."

"Um-hm," Helen agreed, stretching the phone cord so she

could stack the dirty breakfast dishes on the table and transport them to the sink. It was important not to let them rattle; Kat got annoyed if she felt she wasn't getting her daughter's undivided attention. "Are you taking anything for the arthritis, though?"

"No, sure the doctor says aspirin, only I took the one aspirin one day last week when I thought I'd die from the pain, and it gave me the sweats so bad I swore I'd never take another. Sure, Mary Donohoe passed away, Lord have mercy on her!"

It was said without pause, neatly segued into the lament over her arthritis, as if both bulletins were of equal significance. Helen nearly dropped the stack of cups she was balancing halfway to the sink, wracking her brains to remember who Mary Donohoe might be. Someone from the neighborhood or from Harmony Bay? Friend or distant relative? Old or young? Sick for a long time or taken suddenly? Helen was at a loss. Her mother always knew someone who was dying.

"Oh, my God, that's a shame, Mom!" Helen clucked with the right degree of somberness. "Thanks for letting me know. I'll have to send a mass card. How's the rest of the family— Maureen! Find out what your sister just dropped! What was that noise?"

Neither twin was in sight; both had ambled upstairs to play moments ago and there had been no noise. It was one of the many ploys Helen used to get off the phone.

"Mom, I have to go," she said urgently.

"Sure, I don't understand why yer can't manage them two," Kat began, but Helen hung the receiver back on the wall. There were limits.

I shouldn't answer it, she thought, sitting at last on a kitchen chair and pulling off her galoshes. The floor was covered with muddy tracks where she'd been pacing back and forth. Someday I should let it ring and ring and ring, except that within the hour she'd have the U.S. marines on my front doorstep. She threw her galoshes down the cellar steps and went to get the mop.

It was not uncommon for the mother of young children to ask her confessor for a dispensation from attending mass on Sunday. Helen knew this. She also knew that she and Frank could go to mass in shifts, taking turns staying home with the kids. Helen prided herself on never having done that, except for the month after each girl was born, when she stayed home and tried to say the rosary while Frank went to church and she took care of the kids alone. But every Sunday since, they had gone to mass as a family, mother and father and four little darlings, taking up an entire pew and causing smiles among the parishioners. Frank was at one end with Vicki beside him, her back like a ramrod, her hands folded like a cathedral roof, small white fingers pointed toward Heaven the way the nuns had taught her, eyes transfixed with the agony of the badly carved Christ writhing on his cold bronze cross above the altar. Kathleen sat in the middle, pouting and restless, swinging her legs endlessly, endlessly under the seat. Then came Helen, near the aisle with a twin on either side of her, ready to spring out of the pew and escort to the door any of her brood who proved unmanageable. Between mittens and scarves and hats and galoshes in the winter, the breathless humidity of summer, and the fidgeting and sneezing and whispered sibling controversies, it was a wonder Helen had the vaguest idea what was going on at the altar.

She came home week after week feeling despondent, wrung out—knowing that the day was only half over and they'd all have to file into the car and go to her mother's for dinner; that she'd somehow have to keep four frilly dresses, four pairs of white knee socks, four pairs of black patent leather shoes, and their four occupants clean, quiet, and ready to perform their songs, nursery rhymes, alphabets, and poems by Robert Louis Stevenson at a moment's notice. An insidious headache developed somewhere during the Creed, and mushroomed until by the time they got home from her mother's and got all the kids to bed, Helen wasn't sure whether her head was in one piece or two.

"Why don't we skip your mother's once in a while?" Frank would plead with her, knowing from the pain on her face exactly how she felt. "Or let me take the kids to church and you go by yourself. Or get them some clothes that don't have to be ironed and scrubbed and polished all the time. Or something. For God's sake, nobody enjoys this routine. Why can't we call it off?"

Helen propped herself up on the bed and counted her answers on her fingers. "Because my mother'll be insulted, because every other mother in the neighborhood dresses her kids well and I won't have mine in rags, and because I don't want us to go to church separately. We're a family, and we'll go to mass as a family."

"Because you're jealous of me and the kids," Frank added, to see how she would react.

"Yes, I am!" she snapped. "Because you—you monopolize them. They're always stepping all over each other to get your attention, and I can sit there for an hour while you all wrestle and tickle each other and horse around, and the only time anyone comes near me is when they have hiccups or can't find something or need their shoelaces tied. They adore you, but they treat me like a—like a housekeeper or something. You're damn right I'm jealous!"

It was more spirit than she'd shown in a long time, and it gave him hope. She had been steadily fading away from him over the past few years. Any contact, even hostility, was welcome.

"Maybe if for once you'd put down your needles and thread and pincushions or that goddamn iron and play with them, get into the spirit of fun—hell, roll around on the floor with us a little. Loosen up, for God's sake, Helen! Every time one of us comes near you, you tense up and growl at us. No wonder the kids don't pay attention to you!"

"And I suppose you'll take the hems down on their clothes and iron the school uniforms? I get enough gripes about the housework as it is! I don't have time to play!"

She rolled over on the bed with her back to him, making herself as small as possible.

"Christ!" Frank exploded. "We shouldn't've had so many kids so soon!"

"Don't you dare say that!" Helen shouted at him, then started to cry because it was true. God help her for thinking it, but it was true!

When they're all in school it will get better, she told herself, knowing it wasn't true. When I can have some time to myself during the day. . . .

What? What will I do when I have some time to myself during the day? Sew more curtains? Repaper the walls? Finish the gardening that never gets halfway started? Iron more uniforms and take down more hems? Listen to my mother on the phone all day? Sleep? And then what?

Of course not, she would reason—I will not waste my time on those things at all. I will go to museums and art galleries, and take walks in the park. I will improve my mind, educate myself so that I can educate my children as well. But for what? So that they can all grow up and get married and have babies and go through what I'm going through? No, because I promised myself that they would go to college. All four of them will go to college, if I have to scrub floors to put them through. I will not let them be shortchanged.

The way I was, she thought, finishing her sentence. I will not let them be shortchanged the way I was, cheated out of a chance to be somebody simply because I was born a girl.

All I have to do is wait until the twins start kindergarten, Helen thought. A few more years, and I'll be able to go to the library and stay all day because I don't have to jump up every three minutes to see who's knocking books off the shelves and who's crying. A few more years. . . .

She had always been an avid, a desperate reader. It was her only form of escape. Everyone knew daydreams were evil thoughts in disguise, and she was too old to daydream. So Helen read, sometimes as many as six books a week. She read while she cooked or ran the vacuum cleaner or waited for the washing machine to change cycles. She read in the playground, on line in the supermarket, even when she was on the phone with her mother. It didn't matter what she read—newspapers, magazines, Harlequin novels, travel books, film-star memoirs, mysteries—anything would do, as long as she could lose herself in it and forget the insignificance of her life.

It was her thirst for new things to read, and Kathleen's peculiar sense of morality, that tipped Helen's world on its ear and forced her to reach a decision. All it took was a rainy day, a fever of one hundred and two, and a pair of scissors. . . .

Red rang Helen's doorbell just as the uproar reached its climax. As usual he had Johnny in tow, Johnny who was thirteen and embarrassed that his parents had to push him off on Helen every time they needed to argue. Both of them could hear Helen's voice, high-pitched and raging, from inside the house, but before either of them could make a move in any direction the door was nearly wrenched off its hinges.

"Oh, swell!" Helen exploded. "Just what I need!"

She stood blocking the doorway, unwilling to let them in. Red had never seen her in such a state. He blinked at her and waited, not certain what to do. Johnny had started to shrink down the steps, reluctant to be here under any circumstances, but especially unwilling now. Helen saw that it was raining hard, and pulled them inside.

The living room was cluttered with old magazines and pieces of paper cut into all shapes and sizes. In the middle of the mess sat Kathleen, face red from crying, clutching a bundle of papers to her chest, sobbing for breath.

"Is Frank home, then?" Red began, clearing his throat, uneasy at having stumbled into a scene between mother and daughter.

"No!" Helen snapped, bunching the mess together in a heap on the coffee table. Johnny tried to help, but she pushed him abruptly in the direction of a chair and he sat down. "He doesn't get home till five, Pop, if he doesn't get off until four."

"Aye," her father wheezed, settling in on the couch. "Sure, I was after forgettin' everybody ain't a gentleman of leisure."

Helen gave him a sharp look. He had been reduced to part-time this past year, because of his heart. He joked about it only because he could not afford to express his anger.

"If you were planning on leaving Johnny with me tonight, you can't," Helen said flatly. "I can't take it today, I really can't!"

She did not look at Johnny, who was making himself invisible.

"Yer'd make it that much easier on me," her father pointed out.

"What's wrong this time?" Helen demanded. There was a bossiness about her, an aggressiveness Red had never dreamed her capable of. And all this time she continued to ignore the huddled, sniveling figure of her daughter in the middle of the room. "Well? What now? Danny got drunk and slapped Paula around again. Or Mom and Aunt Ag had another go-round over Alistair. Or what Frank says about Alistair is true, and he really is a fa—"

"Mother of God!" Red shouted, looking from Helen to Johnny, who was soaking up every word. "The boy's too young to hear such things!"

"The boy's thirteen, and old enough to realize something's terribly wrong with his family if they have to ship him out every time there's an argument!" Helen shouted. "Well, it stops right now! No more! I've had it up to here!"

With that she lifted Kathleen bodily off the floor and sent her out of the room with a sharp smack on the backside. "Go wash your face!" she ordered. "And tell your sisters to come down and say hello to Grandpa. And you can keep your lousy scrapbook! I'm not going to take it away from you!"

Red watched this scene without a word until Kathleen was safely upstairs. "And what's between the two of yez?" he asked.

"Nothing I can't handle myself, thank you!" Helen snapped,

collapsing into a chair at last. When she saw the look on her father's face she relented a little. "She had a temperature this morning, so I let her stay home from school. She was quiet, she stayed in bed and didn't bother me. After lunch I gave her some old magazines to cut up for a scrapbook. And she took a big, fat, brand-new, expensive library book and cut the pictures out of that! I went crazy, that's all! It's a brand-new book. And the damn thing costs ten dollars, which I have to pay for, and how the hell am I going to look the librarian in the eye when I tell her? I've never been so embarrassed in my life!"

"Was she after tellin' yer why she did it?" Red asked calmly. He was stunned by his daughter's overreaction to what he saw as a simple problem.

"She told me she just wanted to," Helen said, exasperated. "There were some pictures from Easter Island—those big statues they have there?—and she wanted them. She saw nothing wrong with cutting up a ten-dollar library book to get them."

"Maybe she didn't know the difference—you giving her the magazines and all," Red offered. He loved all of his grand-children, even Danny's two, but he, like his son-in-law, favored Kathleen.

"Pop, she's nearly seven years old! She knows the difference! But she's never satisfied with anything. She always has to poke her nose where it doesn't belong, badger me with questions all day long. She wants to know everything, and she's never satisfied with the answers I give her. She's impossible!"

"Aye," Red said. "Or she's simply curious. Like her mother. Or like yer used to be at her age. When yer grew up yer seemed to stop wantin' to know. Like yer curled up inside yer-self and stopped carin'."

There it was. Helen wanted to scream, but she thought of his bad heart. Whose fault is it I stopped caring? she wondered. Why did I accept it when you told me I couldn't go to college? Why have I always done what people said I should do, and never done anything for myself?

She left the twins with her next-door neighbor the following day and went to face the librarian. The experience was less harrowing than she expected. Children always did this sort of thing, the librarian assured her. On her way out the door, Helen stopped at the shelf full of brochures labeled "Careers." She also got a catalogue of all the Catholic colleges in the city, took it home, and made little penciled check marks next to the ones that interested her. She got the bank book, and the check book, and promptly lost heart.

Then she remembered that both the Fire Department and the Knights of Columbus had scholarship programs for families of members. She talked Frank into joining the K. of C.—not difficult, since they had regulation billiard tables in the local hall—and then she told him why. If she expected any resistance from him, she was surprised to find him enthusiastic.

"You're sure you wouldn't mind?" she asked him cautiously.

"Mind what? You going to college? Why should I?"

She looked at him but could not answer. He answered for her.

"If you're worried you might end up smarter than me, don't worry about it," he said. "I married you 'cause I knew you already were smarter than me. College won't make any difference in that. I figure I was smart enough to pass the exam for fire chief, and that's all I need. I'm just a dumb Irishman, and like you said years ago, you got other things in you besides Irish."

He was laughing at her.

"Don't kid around, Frank." Helen frowned. "I'm serious!"

He took her face between his hands. "You always are," he said. "Hey, you think maybe college'll teach you a sense of humor?"

She looked down, shamed by the question. He gave her a playful sock on the jaw and kissed her forehead.

"I'm only kidding," he whispered. "I think you need a change, that's all. A crack at something new and better. You want to go to college, go. You want to start a career, go.

Whatever's best for you can only make things better for me and the kids. Get you back to being yourself again."

Helen looked into his eyes, grateful, speechless. He had solved her problem.

"Hey," he said. "You safe tonight?"

"What?" She frowned, not understanding him.

"I said, are you safe tonight? You know, Russian roulette. The old rhythm-and-blues game. Safe or sorry tonight?"

"Oh, that!" Helen said, and actually had to find a calendar to remind herself of where she was in her menstrual cycle. If she was going to spend the next few years in college, she'd have to do something about contraception, she thought. "Safe tonight!" she announced.

To her surprise, Frank scooped her up and started to carry her up the stairs. "Doing my part for higher education!" he teased, kissing the tip of her nose.

Scarlett O'Hara, Helen thought, eat your heart out!

She tried to tell her mother she was going to go to college. It was an awesome course she was about to pursue, attempting to become the first female child, the first person in the entire family, ever, to earn a degree. How would Kat react if her daughter succeeded where her son had failed? Best to get her used to it gradually.

Helen had been doing much soul-searching once she made the decision about college, examining particularly the relationship between her mother and herself. Having children of her own made her understand how a mother could favor one child over another, how circumstances could affect the raising of children. Seeing the way the girls flocked to Frank, often excluding her, she thought she could see herself interacting with Red, shutting Kat out. Was it that simple? Was that why she and Kat could not talk to each other now?

Kat was to blame as well, Helen decided, Kat and her own mother and all the generations of women who had taught their daughters that the only way to get attention from people was to whine and sulk and go off on a mood. It was a difficult problem to solve within a single lifetime, but Helen intended to try.

I will break free of it, she thought. I will study psychology, so I will begin to understand why it is that families need to squash the individuals that comprise them. I will take courses in childhood education so that I can teach my own children, and other people's children, how to be themselves, how not to be submerged by the will of the family.

And I will confront my mother with the decision I have made in my life, so that she will stop complaining about her ailments long enough to hear what I have to say. I will make her sit up and take notice. And she will be proud of me.

". . . and the doctor says my blood pressure's up and I got ter lose some weight, but I says, 'I've borne three children and lost three, and isn't a woman after puttin' on five pounds for every baby?' and he says, 'Mrs. Manning,' he says, 'it's no excuse. Ye've got ter lose some weight or it's gone ter affect yer heart,' and I says—"

"Mom," Helen tried to interrupt, without success. She had washed the breakfast dishes during the early part of this monologue, and rehearsed what she had to say. "Mom, listen a minute, I—"

"Oh, but sure, yer'll not want ter listen ter my troubles, then. How're the children?"

"Fine, Mom, all of them. Listen, I've got something to tell you—"

"How's Kathleen's leg, then? When she was to our house last she said it was after hurtin' her, and all I could think was—"

"She's fine, Mom. She bruised it running up the stairs the day before. I want to tell you something."

"All I could think of was the polio, but then she's had her shots, has she? When you and Danny was small we was after worryin' so much for fear the polio would take yez—"

"Mom," Helen gritted out between clenched teeth. "Mom,

I'm starting college in the fall. I'm going to make something of myself. Did you hear me?"

There was a pause, a dead silence, for about five seconds.

"Sure, I'm not deaf, yer know! And how's Frank, then? Sure, I'm after worryin' meself sick every time I hear on the radio there's a fire in the city. I keep thinkin' it's himself'll get killed goin' in after one of them little colored babies and leaving yer with the four of yer own and no money comin' in. . . ."

Blinking back tears, Helen hung up the phone without slamming it.

And my mother will be proud of me, she thought one last time, wishing it could be true.

BOOK IV
The Pitcher Plant, 1963–1979

It was hot. It was hot when they left Brooklyn early in the morning, but Helen had hoped it would be cooler in New Jersey. It wasn't. The metal folding chairs spread in a semi-circle on the big expanse of grass burned the backs and legs of the visitors even through their clothing, and there wasn't a suggestion of a breeze. The chairs faced away from the lake, so it was impossible to steal a glimpse of its cool, blue-brown surface throughout the long and tedious ceremony. Midges, breeding by the millions in the mud at the edge of the lake, enlivened the air and caused small red welts on the exposed arms and necks of the visitors trapped and hypnotized by the voice of the Brother General.

He was an old man, so white of skin and hair he seemed bloodless, which might have been why neither the heat nor the midges disturbed him. Seated below the dais, looking up at him from the first two rows of chairs, their black habits crackling new under the late August sun, were the thirty-seven postulants being inducted into the Order of Christian Brothers of Ireland by this afternoon's ceremony. Most were

boys in their late teens, tight-lipped and ashen in their determination, and with the exception of the several applicants
from the missions in the West Indies, all had last names of
Celtic origin. There were Canadians as well as Americans. Of
the latter, most, like Johnny Manning, had attended high
schools like Power Memorial, where the Christian Brothers
taught.

Behind the two rows of postulants in the semicircle of
folding chairs under the August sun, fanning themselves lan-
guidly with their folded white programs, sat the relatives and
friends of the inductees. Most, except for the very small children, sat quietly, brought to silence by the heat and solemnity
of the moment.

But Kat Manning was crying. She had not stopped crying,
it seemed, since Johnny told her what he planned to do as
soon as he graduated from high school. That had been in early
June. When she was not crying for joy that her baby should
be among God's chosen ones, she was crying because he was
the best of her children and she was losing him forever.

"Will you talk some sense into her, please?" Johnny pleaded
with Helen in June. He was spending the summer with her
as usual, though it was his choice this particular summer, since
his mother would give him no rest. He mowed the lawn, took
his nieces to the beach, and was helping Frank paint the outside of the house in the evenings when it was cooler.

"No, I won't either, Gutless," was Helen's answer. "Because
I think you're out of your mind."

"Cripes, not you too!" Johnny wailed, but Helen gave him
a look that silenced him. "Okay, spit it out! Instruct me in the
error of my ways."

"You're eighteen years old," Helen began, trying to disguise her shock at the realization that this black-haired lady
killer had once been an infant she'd held in her arms. "You're
just a baby. You have no experience in life, but you're all set
to lock yourself away from it. Christian Brothers are a teaching
order, aren't they? How are you going to teach anybody
anything when you don't know anything about anything?"

"How old were you when you got married?" Johnny asked complacently, helping her sort the clean laundry to be folded. He had a way of standing by watching her do a thing, then slipping into the momentum and working with her before she knew what had happened.

"Nineteen. But that was different."

"How different?" Johnny demanded. "You did all the things you just accused me of: locking yourself away from a career or travel or anything, tying yourself down with four kids—"

"But I found an escape clause. It took me years and a lot of breast beating, but I finally got the nerve to set myself a goal," Helen pointed out, sorting the socks by color. To save her sanity at laundry time, she bought socks of only one color for each girl. Vicki wore white; Kathleen, various shades of scarlet; Maureen and Mary Fran, pink and pale blue respectively. "I've finally got my B.A. I start grad school right away in September."

"So what?" Johnny shrugged. "I'll have my master's by the time I'm twenty-five. I can be sent to a mission anywhere in the world, and all expenses paid. I'll never be tied down with a family, never have to worry about bills or where my next meal's coming from. I'm not depriving myself of life. I'm taking advantage of a golden opportunity."

"There are other things," Helen said meaningfully, uncertain how to broach the topic with her baby brother.

"You mean sex?" Johnny came right to the point. "No problem. I don't need it."

Helen had to laugh. "What do you mean, you don't need it? How the hell do you know? You're a baby!"

"I'm eighteen," he said evenly. He was seldom perturbable, never angry. "And I've never been aroused by anyone, male or female. I never even got a rise out of those pictures we used to pass around the locker room. Nothing. Not a quiver. Eighteen is supposed to be a man's sexual peak. If I don't need it now, I'm not going to miss it later."

Helen gave him a narrow look. "You read too much," she

said. "And you draw the wrong conclusions from what you read."

"Maybe," he acknowledged, digging into the bottom of the laundry basket and separating Helen's brassieres from Vicki's training bras, as calmly as if he were sorting apples and oranges.

Helen watched him, annoyed that he showed no sign of embarrassment, ready to pull her trump card. "Would you like to know what Frank thinks?" she asked, knowing how much Johnny respected his brother-in-law's opinion on anything. "You know he nearly choked when I told him?"

"The way you probably sprang it on him, I don't doubt it," Johnny remarked. "What'd he say?"

Helen went on pairing socks, not looking at him. "He's a pretty good amateur psychologist, you know. I've taken a lot of courses in child psych, and half the stuff I read I've heard him—"

"What'd he say?" Johnny interrupted, but not urgently.

Helen took a deep breath. "Frank says you're unable to relate to women—to anybody, really—because of the way you were neglected as a child: bounced back and forth from Mom to me and back again, ignored whenever Mom was in one of her moods. He says you're afraid to become emotionally involved because you're afraid of being ignored or neglected again."

"That's garbage!" Johnny said evenly, but his voice was tight. Criticism of Kat was one of the few things that could make him lose his temper. "She didn't neglect or ignore me. And if I didn't like people I'd become a hermit, not a teaching brother. You tell your husband to stick to the fireman business and stay out of amateur psychology. And don't change the subject. I want you to talk to Mom for me. Otherwise I can't go home all summer, because she's driving me crazy. All she does is cry all the time. She makes me feel like some kind of criminal. Why can't you give me a break—smooth things over for me?"

"Uh-uh." Helen shook her head, hoisting the laundry

basket off the work table and heading for the basement stairs. "It's your ulcer. And I'm going to do my damnedest to talk you out of this insanity before the summer's over."

"Don't waste your time!" Johnny called up after her, savoring the coolness of the cellar, unwilling to move.

And now, three months later, Helen shifted uncomfortably in the scorching metal chair, eloquent proof that she hadn't been able to talk Johnny out of anything. She could see the back of his head in the second row, the black hair cropped close and the back of his neck covered with freckles. He had not moved throughout the Brother General's discourse. He might have been petrified, or asleep, if it were possible to sleep in so upright a position, and under this sun. Helen allowed her head to pivot slightly to the right, so that she could see the entire clan of Mannings and O'Dells curved around a half-row of folding chairs. Everyone was here, except Alistair, and if one had the gift of mind reading, Helen mused, groggy from the heat, what a wealth of thought could be discovered here.

Victoria Mary O'Dell, age thirteen years, wearing despite the heat the real nylon stockings she had been permitted since making her Confirmation the year before, riveted her eyes upon the withered face of the Brother General, lest they stray and seek out the familiar and adored figure of her Uncle Johnny.

O my God, I am heartily sorry for having offended Thee, she prayed, but if Uncle Johnny becomes a Christian Brother I think I'm going to die!

Only five years older than she, Johnny had been Vicki's brother, friend, confidant, the first person she had recognized after her parents when she was an infant, because he spent so much time at her house. He had taught her how to read by reading the comics to her from the Sunday paper, had taught her to swim by conquering her basically timid, hesitant nature with patience, holding the back of her head in the surf off Manhattan Beach and coaxing her until she could float. He had helped her with her homework, fixed her bicycle, put calamine lotion on her mosquito bites, comforted her when she did not get the part of the Virgin Mary in the third-grade Christmas pageant. And he was the only male person beside her father whom she felt safe with, after that dreadful experience when she was nine. . . .

It was clearly her own fault, Vicki admitted even now, because if she had come straight home from school when her mother told her, she would never have encountered *him*. She had been as filled with guilt as with horror and disgust, had even gone to confession the very next day, only to find herself tongue-tied and unable to tell the priest what had happened, so that in the end she received his absolution under false pretenses, worsening her sin. Only Johnny had been able to understand.

It had been a day in early spring, a day in the middle of Lent, when a good Catholic child was under obligation to feel somber and devout—despite the glorious surge of vitality in the weather—in honor of Christ's impending passion and death on Good Friday. Vicki was on her way home from Lenten services on a Friday, having followed in Christ's footsteps up Calvary, dragging with Him the heavy wooden cross laden with the sins of humanity. The Stations of the Cross were a must every Friday afternoon, dripping with gore and sentimentality, piercing to the soul the more serious of the large-eyed schoolchildren marched out of the classroom an hour early to attend the service. Heavy-eyed and headachy from the dreary hymns and the incense, Vickie lingered on Third Avenue on her way home, looking at the premature Easter displays in the store windows, trying to shake the intense melancholy brought on by the church service. Why, in just a few short weeks, the nuns had promised her, Christ would again rise symbolically from his borrowed grave, trailing glory and freeing mankind from the burden of Eve's sin! Today's shuddering gloom was only temporary.

The sun was warm on Vicki's face, and a soft breeze blew

up from the Narrows, but these had no effect on her. When she finally started down the side street, she saw that there were crocuses in the front yards, a suggestion of tulips and hyacinths pushing up from the ground, and even Vicki was moved. Abandoning her usual businesslike stride, which she kept up purposely to hurry Kathleen along when they walked home together, she strolled from house to house, running her fingers along fence rails and privet hedges, looking at the flowers, entranced.

He was probably waiting behind a tree, one of the ancient sycamores or big, shaggy locusts that shaded the best blocks in Bay Ridge—lurking near the intersecting paths of the parochial and public schools in the neighborhood, seeking an audience. He was essentially harmless, a flasher, a slightly brain-damaged drifter of indeterminate years who slept on benches and roamed the streets with his pants open, his engorged organ cradled ponderously in his dirty hand, needing only to show it to someone in order to fulfill himself. Today's someone happened to be Vicki.

She did not scream. Nice girls didn't scream, and even if she had willed it she would not have been able to, for her throat was constricted, paralyzed. She could not run away, could not even avert her eyes, but stood stock-still, clenching her schoolbag, staring at the grotesque protuberance he offered her, moist-eyed and grinning. It wasn't until he spoke—rather, growled at her—that she could lift her eyes at least as far as his face, and this only because she'd been taught that a well-mannered child always looked an adult in the eye when spoken to.

"Like it?" he slobbered at her. "Nice, ain't it? Like it?"

Vicki's mouth opened. She gasped for air, claustrophobic and suffocating. Something—the courage of purity or only a shot of adrenalin—gave her the strength to run, to put as much concrete as possible between herself and this horror. When she was half a block from home she stopped, a stitch in her side, and tried to restore herself to normalcy. The neighbors were always watching from behind their curtains, and she didn't want to arouse their suspicions.

Kathleen was home already, excused from Stations because the incense always made her vomit. She was sitting on the front stoop when Vicki hurried past, and stopped struggling with the strap on her roller skate when she saw the look on her older sister's face.

"What's wrong with you?" Kathleen demanded, but Vicki breezed past, ignoring her. Determined, Kathleen kicked her skates aside and ran after her.

Helen was in the kitchen with the twins, finger painting. She looked up as this short parade hurried past her. "What's going on?" she demanded, blocking Kathleen's path.

"Vicki's acting funny," Kathleen announced. "She won't talk to me."

"Did you have a fight?" Helen asked, expecting it. Vicki was already up the stairs. Helen called after her. "Vicki?" She waited. "Victoria Mary O'Dell, I'm talking to you!"

Vicki never sulked. Something must be seriously wrong. Absently wiping the paint off the twins' hands and sending everybody outside, Helen went upstairs.

She felt Vicki's forehead and found it clammy with sweat, but not feverish. She questioned Vicki closely. Had there been trouble in school? Did she get hurt? Was there anything else she wanted to talk about?

Receiving vehement negatives to all these questions, Helen surrendered, unconvinced. Downstairs someone was crying already, and she ought to see what the trouble was. Stopping by the bathroom by reflex to get the Band-Aids, Helen forgot all about Vicki's problem.

Left alone for about an hour, Vicki recovered, at least superficially, from her experience. It made her think. Maybe all men, and even little boys, had those—those *things* that could be made to stick out of their pants like that. Maybe that was what made the boys she knew so silly and hostile and secretive. She had no brothers with whom to study comparative anatomy, and had only seen male infants when they were fully dressed. Was it possible that even her own father—?

The thought gave Vicki a case of the shudders as she perched on the side of her bed in her big, sunny bedroom—where everything around her was still pink and precious and feminine, although the sunlight was colder now, the sounds of birds in the sycamore tree in front of the house less promising than before. Surely her own father couldn't have anything as horrible, as grotesque. . . .

That would mean that even Johnny, her beloved Uncle Johnny—more brother than uncle, all of fourteen, his voice still reedy, bearing no trace of the changes that would come to him over the next few years—even Johnny could be like that.

Then all men were to be feared, Vicki decided at the age of nine, and any contact with them could be deadly, could cause them to swell up and free that awful weapon from its hiding place to wreak some unspecified destruction upon little girls who didn't come straight home from school when they were told.

If Kathleen noticed that Vicki avoided a certain block on their way home from school over the next few months, she said nothing. Girlhood was predicated on a number of carefully prescribed superstitions, all of which had to be kept from the ears of adults. Step on a crack, break your mother's back. Drop a piece of candy or other edible on the ground, and if you kissed it and offered it up to God, it was immediately rendered germ-free and safe for consumption. Say a Hail Mary when you heard a fire engine pass—this one was dearest to Kathleen's heart—and nobody would die in the fire. There were many more, known only to the initiate, who learned them from friends or older siblings. If Vicki was not going to tell her why they couldn't walk down Eightieth Street for the rest of the school term, Kathleen would not be so gauche as to inquire.

If Frank noticed that Vicki began to shy away from him, he

did not make an issue of it. Vicki was the quietest of his four daughters; if she was more subdued than usual, the other three would surely compensate for it.

But Johnny noticed, possibly because he was only at the house on weekends and he was able to sense a change, and because Vicki usually threw herself at him the minute he came through the door. When he had to go looking for her, he knew something was wrong.

"Boys are stupid!" he was told as soon as he made inquiry. He had found her jumping rope by herself on the concrete in front of the garage, breathless from one of those unending counting rhymes.

"No kidding?" He had heard this one before; no doubt some squabble with a fellow third-grader had set her off. "So what?"

"And men are—are ugly. They've got whiskers and smelly old cigars and—yech!"

"I'll go along with that. But so what?"

"So go away. I don't want to talk to you." She started to jump again.

"Why not?" Johnny stuck his foot in the rope to trip her, and caught her before she fell. Vicki nearly jumped out of her skin, and he released her.

"Because you're a boy!" She was pouting, on the verge of tears, wanting it to be untrue.

"No, I'm not," Johnny said airily, confusing her. "I'm too old."

"Then you must be a man, 'cause you're almost big enough," Vicki reasoned, trying to jump rope again.

"Nope," Johnny answered, holding on to the rope.

Vicki snatched it away from him and wound it in loops between her elbow and shoulder. She was completely confused by now. "Then what are you?"

"I'm an adolescent," he explained importantly. "I'm halfway between a boy and a man. So if you think boys are stupid and men are ugly, you can still like me, 'cause I'm not either one."

"Oh." Vicki sat on the rustic wooden bench by the wall of the garage, nonplussed.

"Hey," Johnny said, sitting beside her. "Wanta ride my bike? I'll ride you down along Shore Road on the handlebars. We can see the big ships come in."

Vicki's eyes sparkled. Johnny rode his bike, the bike he'd saved to buy himself, over from his house to theirs every weekend, a distance of two and a half miles. Sometimes he let her sit on the handlebars while he steered. None of her sisters would be allowed on his bike until they were eight; Johnny had said so himself.

"Down on the bike path, right by the water?" she begged, remembering the time there had been whitecaps and the spray hit them as they sped along. She was smiling for the first time since. . . .

"I don't see why not," Johnny said, and they were off.

No, Johnny wasn't like other men, Vicki decided, closing her eyes to keep from screaming as they flew down the big hill on Narrows Avenue. Johnny would never frighten her. And he couldn't possibly have one of those *things*.

Vicki sat immobile on the hot metal folding chair, as impervious to the heat as the Brother General. She was four years older now, and so was Johnny, and she knew by now that the ugly man who had accosted her on Eightieth Street was sad and sick and couldn't help himself. She knew by now that every man, even Johnny, had a penis, and she knew what it was for. But if Johnny joined the Christian Brothers he would take a vow of chastity, and that meant he must never. . . .

Offering a silent prayer to keep impure thoughts from her mind, Vicki clenched her fists in her lap. Unseen, her perfectly manicured nails with the pale pink polish that matched the pale pink lipstick she was allowed to wear for special occasions dug deeply into her palms as a form of penance, as mortification of the flesh for what she was thinking, what she dared desire. For while most girls she knew had a crush on

Elvis or Michael Landon or the cute young photographer who had taken their eighth-grade graduation pictures, Vicki had a crush on her Uncle Johnny, and while she had never heard the word "incest," she knew that what she desired was wrong and evil and sinful, and that if she did not put it out of her mind it would probably send her to Hell.

Her sister Kathleen, meanwhile, was already living her own special Purgatory. Sitting between her father and her grandfather—the only two members of the family she could be with for more than five minutes without picking a fight—she was sweating. Her sleeveless cotton dress was limp, and stuck to her back and her flat pre-pubertal chest. Her bare freckled legs squeaked damply against the metal chair every time she moved. She wore a big, ungainly straw hat to keep the sun off her already peeling face and shoulders, and she yawned incessantly. Religion bored her, and the heat destroyed her. The combination of the two made her feel more dead than alive.

She jabbed her grandfather with her elbow. "When's it gonna be over?" she demanded in a loud whisper.

Red gave her a sideways glance from under the knotted handkerchief that protected his bald head from the sun. The question had occurred to him as well. "Mind now, he's almost through. It can't be much longer!"

"I hope not!" Kathleen whined, loud enough to merit piercing looks from her mother and her grandmother. "Why can't they let us sit in the shade?"

"Don't raise a yap about it or yer'll have us both into trouble," her grandfather warned, winking at her, a fellow conspirator. Kat, on the far side of him, gave him a poke to silence him.

Kathleen yawned again, and began to scratch at the dead skin peeling off her shoulders from last week's sunburn. She went at it industriously until her father could stand it no more.

"Knock it off, Toots! That drives me nuts!" Frank growled, slapping her knee playfully with the back of his hand. Watching her reminded him too graphically of the week she was born, the time he'd needed skin grafts, when he watched from a safely drugged distance while an intern picked the charred skin off his jaw with tweezers. Every time he watched Kathleen pulling nonchalantly at her own dead skin it made him wince.

She was his favorite, though Frank tried to deny it. Was it because she had been born so soon after his brush with death, and because she, too, was in danger of dying at the very same time? Was it because even now she was the thinnest and sickliest of his kids, but also the one with the biggest mouth and the most fight? Was it the red hair and freckles, stolen straight from her mother's father, that made her look so different from the others, who were all dark-haired and clear-skinned? Was it because none of the women in the family could penetrate that prickly exterior, and only he and Red were allowed to get close to her?

Whatever it was, Kathleen was Frank's favorite, though he covered himself by sometimes being arbitrarily stern with her. It was a game they had to play before the others, and Kathleen learned to accept it as such.

Frank's participation in parenting did not include changing diapers, reading bedtime stories, or making breakfast on Saturday mornings. It did not include correcting homework or going to the dentist or combing bubble gum out of hair. It only occasionally included tying shoelaces, playing Tooth Fairy, or settling sisterly brawls. This was not to say that he was a negligent father, only that his working hours were irregular and that he was typical of the men of his generation.

He did, however, take the girls to the zoo and museums and movies and whatever cultural events they were old enough to sit through. There were picnics and nature hikes and Yankee games. And there was always a great deal of boisterous affection and roughhousing.

Kathleen remembered these tickling sessions most especially, because she was the one who would never give in, the one

reduced to hysterics and hiccups because she wouldn't say
"uncle." Her sisters participated in the wrestling, too, but the
twins were too little to get rough and Vicki was prissy and
gave up too easily. Kathleen was also the aggressor, attacking
her father when he was watching television, turning the hose
on him in the garden, springing out from behind the couch
when he tried to take a nap. Vengeance was swift and merci-
less.

"Give up?" he'd demand when he had her gasping and weak
on the rug or in the grass.

"Nope!" she'd wheeze. "Never in a million years!"

He'd tickle her until she got hiccups, or started to cough and
couldn't stop; once she peed all over herself. Helen had a fit
that time.

"Stop it, you two! It's disgusting the way you carry on!
Frank, one of these days you're going to hurt her!" Frank always said it was because she was jealous of them, but Helen
had other fears. She was learning about child psychology in
school; she did not think it was healthy for a girl Kathleen's
age to be too attached to her father.

Kathleen was also the only one of the girls who was allowed
to go with Frank to the firehouse. He made excuses about that.

"Vicki's too chicken," he reasoned. "If an alarm rings in
she'll get scared and start to cry. And the twins are too little.
I'll take them when they're older."

By the time she was ten, Kathleen knew the firehouse inside
out. She could read the dispatcher's cards and interpret the
alarms, and swung off the ladder truck like a monkey. On
practice runs she sometimes sat with the tiller man and helped
him pull the big steering wheel in the opposite direction on
the turns. As she got older, she spent as many days of the
summer as she could at the firehouse—her mother usually
threw a fit and told her to stay home and act like a girl midway
into July—listening to the men curse and tell dirty stories
when they thought she wasn't there. She was an able surrogate
for the son her father didn't have.

At eleven, her concept of life was vague. She knew what she *didn't* want to be, but not what she wanted to be. She certainly didn't want to be like Vicki, all self-righteousness and piety. She didn't want to be like the girls in her class, who played with dolls and gossiped and giggled about boys. And since she knew girls couldn't be firemen, she took a dim view of the future.

The present, she had found, consisted mostly of enduring certain situations until a way could be found to weasel out of them. Today's ceremony was a classic example: Kathleen and religion had never mixed well.

It all began in first grade. It was bad enough to be the younger sister of a straight-A, butter-wouldn't-melt-in-her-mouth model student, bad enough to be the class butt because she had red hair and the mulish disposition to go with it. But it was the Missions that soured her on religion for good.

The nuns called it "buying Chinese babies." For every five dollars the first-graders contributed to the Missions, they were told, a baby somewhere in China could be baptized and saved from the clutches of Satan and the Communists to become one of God's shining stars forever. The children were urged to give up candy at recess and contribute their pennies for the souls of the Chinese babies. There was considerable competition between the different grades to see who could contribute the most. At the end of the week, the winning class was usually rewarded with no homework.

Hopeful that this might be one way to compensate for being Victoria Mary O'Dell's less-than-perfect younger sister, Kathleen became caught up in the fervor. That Saturday morning she got up early, ahead of anyone else, to lie in wait for her father.

"You finish your homework last night?" he asked her, buttoning the shirt of his uniform. "I don't like taking you during school, you know. The deal was, only in the summer or Christmas vacation."

"Homework's finished," Kathleen replied, swinging her

skinny legs over the sides of the toilet seat. She had watched him shave before she asked him to take her with him. "Can't I come just this once?"

"It's quarter to seven," he pointed out. "Aren't you tired?"

"Nope." She hoped he hadn't seen her yawning.

Frank watched her in the mirror, pinning on his insignia, seeing her yawn again. "What's so important about this once?"

Kathleen shrugged. "Nothin'. Gonna rain today. Said so on the news last night. Got nothing else to do."

When they got to the firehouse, he was too busy to keep an eye on her. She helped two of the men scrub down the pumper truck, then put her plan into motion.

"Hey, Mike, you got a quarter?" she asked one of them, her favorite, a veteran one year short of retirement. He had six boys and no daughters. If she asked him for the moon, he would start climbing ladders. Kathleen knew this.

"Whatta you want—a Coke? Machine's busted. Gotta go down to the candy store. Hang on a minute, I'll walk you. Don't want you out alone in this nutsy neighborhood."

"No, that's okay," Kathleen said, her eyes widening as she heard the jingle of coins in his pocket. "It's not for me. It's for school."

"What is it—chance books? Lemme see. I'll buy some off you."

"No. It's for—for the Missions," Kathleen blurted out. She had better not tell him about the Chinese babies, having heard enough about Chinks and Spics and niggers to know better. Her face must have been expressive of some great tragedy, for her auditor immediately reached for his wallet.

"Here you go," he said, handing her a crisp dollar bill. "If you'da said it was for the Church I wouldn't've tried to give you change. Lemme see can I get the other guys to cough up a little."

Within minutes he had collected over nine dollars, even from some of the men who weren't Catholic. He sold them with his plea for "the boss's kid who's got such a big heart," and sent one of the rookies to the candy store to get her a Coke.

"Take this now," he said, handing her the Coke and putting the money in the little brown bag it had come in. "Get it home safe. Don't lose it!"

When she got home that evening, Kathleen ravaged her piggy bank and rounded the money off to ten dollars exactly. On Monday she got to school early and went straight to Sister Aethelred's desk.

"I want to buy two Chinese babies," she announced, dumping the contents of the brown paper bag on the big green blotter.

Sister Aethelred counted the money in stupefied silence.

"Kathleen Mary O'Dell," she said at last, gaping like a fish. "Wherever did you get so much money?"

"Is it enough for two babies?" Kathleen demanded, unintimidated by the nun's reaction.

"Why—why, yes it is. Ten dollars and one cent," the nun answered, counting it again. "Quite enough for two babies."

"I'll keep the penny then," Kathleen said, snatching and pocketing it before the nun could protest.

"Well, all right. If you feel you ought to do that," the nun said weightily, trying to impose some measure of guilt on the child, but Kathleen was impervious. Something was nagging at Sister Aethelred's brain, and she had to have it answered. "Kathleen, where *did* you get all this money?"

Kathleen looked her straight in the eye. "Someone gave it to me."

The nun's face clouded over. "Are you certain?"

"Yes," Kathleen said calmly. "And I want to know something. These'll be my very own babies, won't they? I don't have to share them with the rest of the class?"

Sister Aethelred was momentarily confused. "Why . . . yes, I suppose you could say that they were 'your' babies, but why wouldn't you—"

"Okay," Kathleen said, folding her arms, pleased with the information. "When do I get them?"

The nun frowned at her. "Get what?"

"The babies. When can I take them home with me?"

Sister Aethelred did something no one in the class had ever seen her do before. She laughed. Actually, she roared until there were tears in her eyes. And to make matters worse, she repeated what Kathleen had said to the entire class.

"Kathleen is of the opinion that she ought to be allowed to take two Chinese babies home with her!" she said, with such obvious enjoyment that the class began to titter as well. Red-faced, hurt, and confused, Kathleen stumped back to her seat in a blind rage. She had been robbed. She would fix them, all of them!

She did not understand. It had all seemed so simple. She had hoped that, having collected enough for two babies, they might give her twins: two beautiful honey-colored babies with shiny black eyes to keep for her very own, to replace her two twerpy younger sisters. She hadn't worked out what should be done with Maureen and Mary Fran; maybe they could be sent to China as a trade-off. What could be simpler? And why were they all laughing at her?

That week, thanks to her contribution, Kathleen's class won the Mission drive, but at the cost of her disillusionment.

And a few Saturdays later she was in the firehouse when a five-alarmer rang in, and in spite of her anger at the Church and religion, she stayed behind with the dispatcher and said Hail Marys for over an hour so no one would get hurt in the fire. And on the way back to the firehouse after a three-hour battle her friend Mike, a year short of retirement and with six kids to feed, suffered a fatal heart attack in the cab of the pumper truck. Kathleen never said another Hail Mary again.

The two folding chairs on either side of Helen were vacant, and had been vacant long enough for the metal to become so hot from the sun that no one could possibly sit on them. Helen was not overly concerned. She knew the occupants of the chairs would not be back until the ceremony was officially over.

The twins had taken themselves off in great haste to the main building of the priory, where a temporary ladies' room was set aside for visitors on special days such as today. They would be there for as long as the formalities endured, appearing like elves when it was all over and time to eat. They had managed, whether through actual telepathy or some pre-arranged signal, to develop bladder trouble simultaneously, and given permission by their mother, fled hand in hand across the lawn in silent glee.

The lavatory was cool, at least cooler than outside, and Mary Fran was running cold water over her wrists to refresh herself. Maureen was in one of the booths, teetering on the toilet seat to reach the window and see what was going on out on the lawn.

"We should—" she began.

"No!" Mary Fran interrupted, sloshing water up her bare arms and not having to look at her sister to read her thoughts. "We won't go back until it's over."

"Okay." Maureen jumped down and came out of the booth, hopping on one foot to scratch a mosquito bite on her leg.

Unaware that she was doing it, Mary Fran scratched the same spot on her own leg, though there was no bite. "We could go down by the lake," she said, looking at Maureen knowingly. "On the other side, where they can't see us."

"She'll *kill* us!" Maureen said, meaning their mother.

"Not if we—"

"Not even where we went exploring before," Maureen insisted. "Mud on our shoes. She'd know."

"Mud on our shoes," Mary Fran echoed, ruminating. "So we'll stay here."

"It's almost over," Maureen soothed her, and they took turns combing each other's hair and rubbing wet paper towels on their necks until they heard a stirring in the crowd outside as they stood for the final Benediction. The twins looked at each other and without a word dashed for the picnic tables, so they could be there ahead of everybody.

Helen, standing with the others, saw them out of the corner of her eye. There was no point in disciplining them; their mischief was harmless and ingratiating. And their interlocking personalities frightened her just a little. Even her psychology professors said there was no telling with twins. They might lose interest in each other and expand their world of friends as they grew older or they might not; at any rate, it was best to leave them alone. Helen pretended she had not seen them; her mind was on other things. Her mother and Aunt Ag were feuding, and Helen was literally caught in the middle.

She sat in the exact middle of the half-row of chairs that her family occupied. Her mother sat at one end, Aunt Ag on the aisle at the other. They had not spoken in over a year. Between spells of quiet sobbing and long-drawn-out sighs, Kat mopped at her eyes and glared past everyone else at her older sister. Aunt Ag sat complacently fanning herself, ignoring the venomous looks aimed at her. The seat between her and Danny's wife was empty at her request; it was where Alistair would sit, she said, had he been invited.

A few years ago a similar feud might have gotten Helen upset; nowadays she was less affected by the childish behavior of her relatives. If her mother and her aunt wished to act foolish, what difference should it make to her? And they were fighting over something that was none of their business.

The object of the dispute was Alistair. Kat had banished him from all family gatherings when she discovered what Ag had kept secret for years—that Alistair was a homosexual. Kat seemed to think Ag was directly responsible for his life-style; Ag told her sister to mind her own business. They had quarreled, and now neither spoke to the other, though they could sit in the same room for hours, each pretending the other wasn't there. It drove Helen mad.

She remembered the first time Alistair told her, and realized that she had suspected for years but had always sought other explanations for his behavior.

"When did this happen?" she asked when she could find her voice.

"When did what happen—me being a fag, y'mean?" He grinned when he said the word, using it lightly, as if it had no power to hurt him. "I always have been, luv. Just didn't advertise is all."

He'd been coaching a baseball game, and Helen brought the girls down to Shore Road to watch. They were rained out in the fourth inning and the girls ran home. Helen invited Alistair to come over and visit for a while after he dismissed the team. He declined in a tone that made her realize something serious was afoot.

"You mightn't want me at your house once we talk," he said, and Helen sat on the bleachers in the gym while he locked the baseball equipment in the phys-ed office and then told her what he had to say.

"But why are you telling me?" was the next thing she asked.

"Because I wanted you to hear it from me before your mother got to you," he explained, lighting a cigarette. "You talked to her recently?"

"Not since yesterday," Helen said. "She might've called this morning, but I have an early class. I was out before the girls this morning."

"Good," Alistair said, exhaling. "Then she hasn't had time to tell you about the row she and Ag had last night. She's probably still in shock, I wouldn't wonder. Ag told me about it when she came home. God, was she ripping!"

Helen repositioned herself on the bleachers, pushing the rain-wet hair out of her eyes and trying to sort out her emotions. This was Alistair who was talking. Her cousin Alistair—by adoption, true, but that had never made a difference to her, regardless of what anyone else in the family had to say—and he was telling her quite calmly that he was in league with all of those sordid, swishy stereotypes who lisped and wore eye makeup and preyed on little boys. Helen's world picture had expanded somewhat in recent years, and she had gradually outgrown the racial and ethnic prejudices that were her birthright. She believed, in theory at least, that consenting adults could do whatever they liked. She knew from adolescent psych courses that any number of things could have made Alistair what he was, and the more she thought about his growing up—the aversion to girls, the nocturnal ramblings— the more she realized that this was not a sudden change; he had always been this way and she had simply not seen it. Did he look any different, act any different because she now knew something about his private life that she had merely guessed at until five minutes ago? Did he swish or lisp or wear eye makeup? Did he pick up little boys? She could answer the first three for a certainty, but when she thought about the last. . . .

"Tell me about it," she said, clenching her teeth, which were chattering, either from her soaking in the rain or from contained hysteria, she couldn't tell.

"What, the row? Oh, it was a big blowup, let me tell you. Ag's known about me for some time—since high school, I guess—only she kept the confidence. But leave it to Danny to spill it to your mum. He's known about me for a while, only he never let on because he . . . well, he might have been implicated in a very ugly scene. No, don't ask me, because I won't tell you. Old Fat Ass isn't queer, if that's your concern. He's got more mundane problems. But he must've let it out when he was boozing (he's doing more and more of that lately, in case you haven't noticed), and your mum called Ag in for tea last evening (not a word to her beforehand, mind you; your mum's good for that) and sailed into her, all full of righteous indignation. Naturally, Ag gave back as good as she got, and at one point even your dad got into it—on Ag's side, which really set your mother off. So now they're not talking, and I'm never to go near Kat or any of her kin for all eternity. That's why I had to talk to you now. She'll be after you to take some kind of moral stand, and I want you to know I won't be offended if you decide, on the grounds of my being a dangerous influence on the kids or anything. . . ."

He did not finish. Helen let out a sigh as he stubbed out the cigarette in a little aluminum-foil ashtray he'd swiped from the teacher's lounge. She took a deep breath.

"Now, listen," she said. "I'm trying to—to understand what you're saying—trying to respond to you without—hurting your feelings, but—"

"Spit it out," he said, but not unkindly. "You and I go back a long way. You couldn't hurt my feelings if you tried."

"I'm trying to figure out—I mean, I know that kids go through a latency period before puberty, and that it sometimes can carry over to adolescent preferences for . . . for the same sex. What I'm trying to say is, how could you be so sure in high school? Isn't that kind of young?"

"You mean, how could I make up my mind what I was going to be as an adult? Well, I didn't decide all at once. I tried going out with girls—nice girls, easy girls. I tried doing without sex. That didn't work. I'd end up cruising, then running to my confessor for advice, not getting it, and going out on the street again—Hey, I don't mean to shock you," he said warily, seeing the alarm on her face. "That was a while back. I'm much more settled nowadays. And I'm no galloping pervert. I don't hang around playgrounds or make overtures to minors. I'm not out to convert anybody. I just want to be left in peace."

Helen's mind was a jumble of images, confused. "But what about your job? Suppose they found out?"

Alistair put one sneakered foot up on the lowest riser of the bleachers, his hands dangling, relaxed. "You'd never see anybody get fired faster. That's why I don't exactly advertise. And I leave the kids alone. I'm very strict with myself on that. I keep a low profile most of the time, tell a lot of jock jokes so nobody gets suspicious. That's why it's been rough taking you into my confidence: I counted on your being understanding, but I've no doubt you could blow the whistle on me if you felt strongly about it. Do you think I'm a monster?"

"No!" Helen jumped up from the bleachers and started to pace. "And I wouldn't—how could I possibly tell on you? But

I don't know what to think. You're surrounded by young boys all day . . . locker rooms, showers. It's an awful lot of temptation."

"Never lay a hand on 'em," he said sincerely, raising his calloused hands as if in evidence. "Honest to God (and I still go to church, by the way, for all their fire and brimstone and Sodom and Gomorrah—me and Ag, like mother and son, every Sunday), but I made a kind of private vow (private because no priest wants to hear my troubles) that if I ever started getting yearnings for any of the boys, I'd go into another line of work. So far, so good."

Helen stopped pacing and walked to the far end of the gym, head down, hands in her cardigan pockets, thinking. Why couldn't she take his word for it? If he were a male teacher in an all-girls' school, would she be as uneasy? She looked up at him, far away from her across that expanse of polished wood floor, small and defenseless-looking, slightly bowlegged, boyish and impeccable in his coaching uniform.

"Well?" he questioned her from that distance, not daring to say anything until she came closer, for fear of eavesdroppers. Helen walked over to where he was. "I'm waiting for the why-don't-you-see-a-head-shrinker-and-get-yourself-straightened-out lecture. What happened to that?"

"You won't get it from me, Alistair," Helen said softly. "I may not be able to accept—all of what you've told me—for a while yet; but I don't reject you, and I don't think you're . . . sick or anything. It takes me a while to get used to it, that's all."

"Would you tell Frank?" he said.

Helen thought about it. "Maybe not yet. He's kind of strong in his opinions. I think you know that. I don't think he'd go to the School Board or anything, but every so often he thinks it's necessary to Stand Up for What's Right."

Alistair laughed at that. "He's an all-right guy, your husband. And I couldn't fault him for feeling that way. I know I'm asking a lot of you to keep it from him."

"Oh, I don't tell Frank everything." Helen smiled a little,

mischievously. "That's probably why we've been married so long."

Alistair laughed with her, then grew serious. "Are we still friends?" he asked. " 'Cause if your mother wants you to ostracize me—"

"My mother doesn't pay my mortgage!" Helen snapped, more vehement than she needed to be.

"Bless you!" Alistair said, and kissed her tenderly on the forehead.

Helen smiled at him, a little uncertainly. The rain was letting up at last. She buttoned her cardigan and decided to make a run for it.

That had been over a year ago, Helen thought wryly, watching as her mother and Aunt Ag managed to keep a distance between them even when the crowd broke up and started moving away from the folding chairs to where the picnic tables were.

Danny was drunk before he came to Johnny's investiture, and to make matters worse he had brought a small pocket flask with him, which he dipped into frequently during the picnic.

Helen was the one who had to find Johnny in the sea of cassocks that surrounded the visitors once the Benediction was over. She waded through the crowd and found him with his back to her, talking to his classmates. Whirling him around and tugging him by the hand, she led him, sheepish and grinning in his new uniform, to where the twins had staked out two of the best picnic tables.

The entire family could not fit at the tables, so a blanket was spread on the grass nearby for the children—Helen's four and Paula's two girls. There were adjustments to be made and some squabbling; the cousins rarely saw each other since Danny had decided to buy the big house in Jersey. Among the adults, feelings ran even higher, with Kat and Ag not speaking, Danny and Paula doing little to mask their growing hostility toward each other, Danny drunk as well, and Kat bursting into tears every time she looked at Johnny. Red and Frank bolted their food and got up to walk around the lake, leaving Helen to juggle personalities and keep the afternoon from exploding.

It had taken her thirty-three years and most of a college education to accept the fact that there was something wrong with her family, that there might in fact be something wrong with *all* families, though what it was or what could cure it was anybody's guess. It pained her that the more she learned about life and philosophy and human behavior, the less she could reintegrate herself into the role of docile and obedient daughter that Kat expected. On the other hand, there was no reason for her to assume this role anymore. All her life she had been made to feel ungrateful, abnormal, guilty. She did not have to feel that way now.

She understood this crazy family of hers, understood the longings and weaknesses of its individuals, she thought, so it was her place to play the diplomat and keep people from flying at each other. She juggled, dividing her attention equally between Aunt Ag and her mother, keeping conversations going with Paula and Johnny, supervising all six children because Paula never paid much attention to hers. No one needed to pay attention to Danny, who was carrying on an extended monologue with himself.

"Eight goddamn days outta work, six goddamn days in the hospital for tests because the boss says I was rude to a customer and maybe I oughta watch my liquor intake. 'Oughta take a look at your waistline while you're at it!' he says. 'You sure been puttin' it on this past year!' Like the sonabitch is streamlined himself. But okay, so I don't wanta leave this job like I had to—like I left the other one, so I do like he says. Goes on the company medical plan, so what the hell I care? 'Diabetes,' they says. 'Diabetes?' I says. 'How the hell'd I catch that?' And they tell me I gotta watch my diet and lose forty pounds and no booze or I gotta take insulin shots. Give myself shots every day like some goddamn junkie. Or else I'll have blackouts, they say. Bullshit, I says. So I sign outta the hospital, and I been fine ever since. 'Cause I got wise, and I don't drink ona job anymore. Got it set up with the bartender before time, so every time I say Scotch and soda he gives me ginger ale. Looks like the real thing. Then I save the real thing for when I ain't working. I don't need no goddamn insulin shots. I'm no goddamn junkie. They're all fulla crap!"

He drained the pocket flask and got up with a grunt to find the men's room. Helen looked at Johnny, who looked at Kat, who was pretending nothing out of the ordinary had happened.

"If what the doctor told him is right, he ought to be more careful," Helen said, addressing her mother directly. "Diabetes is a very dangerous disease."

"What's that?" Kat said, as if coming out of a trance. "What're yer after sayin', Helen Mary?"

"I said, Mom, that Danny should listen to the doctor," Helen said with infinite patience, knowing both Aunt Ag and Johnny were trying not to smile. "Diabetes can kill you. Or it can make you blind, or a whole lot of other things."

"Diabetes?" Kat frowned, as if she'd never heard the word before. "Sure, and where would he get diabetes, then? Only dirty people gets diabetes. People that leads evil lives and don't take care of theirselves."

"Mom. . . ." Helen gritted her teeth. It was senseless. Her mother would rationalize Danny's actions up to and including murder. Why was she exerting herself? "He'd better quit drinking at least. Too much of that could kill him all by itself."

"A little liquor never hurt any man," Kat insisted querulously. "He's a lot of pressures to his job, sure. Yer shouldn't be after criticizin' him for doin' the best he can after his terrible accident and losin' them fingers. It's all he could do to find any work at all, and him after earnin' enough to buy that big house over to New Jersey. . . ."

Another monologue, Helen thought, and one that would go on longer than Danny's. She looked across the table at Johnny, who was trying manfully to pretend he didn't mind the family's spoiling his special day. They spoil everything, Helen thought bitterly, watching the sun begin its downward slide into the lake. They could go home soon.

"It's me heart, then," Red was explaining to Frank as they walked—heads bowed, hands clasped behind their backs—beside the turgid lake. It was the privilege of the men in the family to find some time for themselves. "They're after lettin' me out for retirement the two years early on account my heart is so bad. But don't ask me what I'll be doin' with meself once I quit workin'. I haven't the faintest idear."

"You'll still get full pension, won't you?" Frank asked, always a union man.

"Aye, I'll have that." Red nodded. "It's not money I'm cryin' over, only what in hell ter do with the rest of the time that's left ter me. Sure, I've been out to work since I was a lad. I wouldn't know what ter do with meself."

Frank slapped at a mosquito that was drilling into his neck; they grew more aggressive as the day waned. "Jeez, I can't wait till I retire! I've got the whole thing mapped out."

"Do yer, then?" Red was interested. "And what've yer got in mind?"

"Well, for starters I'm getting season tickets for the Yankees. I've been reading up on trout fishing. Sounds like something might be up my alley. And once the kids are old enough to stay on their own for a few weeks, maybe Helen and me'll take a cruise. See Europe, then I don't know what. Boy, I can't wait!"

"Aye," Red mused, "I might take in a few ballgames at that. But I done my share of fishing when I was younger. Traveling, too, for that matter. And herself don't want ter go anywheres but up ter that lake. Or 'home.' Jesus and Mary, but she's still talkin' about Harmony Bay as if it's not changed in the thirty-odd years since she's seen it! I'm half-tempted ter send her back ter see for herself, only I'm thinkin' it'd kill her."

"How bad is it up there?" Frank stopped walking, and began skipping stones over the surface of the lake like a boy. "You'd think it wouldn't change much."

"It has, though," Red sighed, a wave of homesickness forty years overdue all but bringing tears to his faded blue eyes. The scars on his hands from the fishing lines, long calloused over by thicker skin, still ached a little when it was due to rain. "I've a sister went for a nun; she writes me once or twice a year. More out of duty, I expect; we was never close. Says the young kids're movin' out ten times as fast as we did in our time. Says in the summer there's twenty tourists for every home-grown man, all tearin' up the inlands for campgrounds and killin' off the wild things. The west coast's gone for industry—coal and paper mills and what have you—but the east where we was is fadin' away. Sure, fishing's a dyin' art. It's all machines now."

"It's a crying shame!" Frank stopped in mid-throw and looked at the old man, his father-in-law, dearer to him than his own father had ever been. "What's this about your heart, though? On the level—are they telling you the truth? How bad is it?"

"Well," Red hesitated, embarrassed. Bewailing ill-health was a woman's pastime. "I was after havin' the one attack. I had it out with the doctor that time—Jewish fella, but a good sort—and I made him give me the whole of it. Says the heart is after growin' weak, but if I takes things slow and plays by the rules I could live ter be a hundred."

"Well, you can't beat that," Frank reasoned, searching for the bright side.

"Aye," Red sighed. "Only, sometimes I gets so disgusted!"

Red had used his bad heart, at least indirectly, to keep from going to Helen's graduation back in June.

"Yer mother says ter tell yer she'll not be goin' ter the graduation" was how he put it over the phone. Never comfortable with this alien device, he had a tendency to shout. His own hearing was no longer strong, owing to hardening of the arteries, and conversations with him were grueling. Helen held the phone a good three inches from her ear when her father spoke, and had to shout when it was her turn.

"Why not?" she shouted this time. "Why can't she come? Pop, I'm getting a bachelor of arts degree. I'll be the first woman—the first *anybody*—in the family to get through college. I think I have a right to expect—"

"What?" Red said, and there was no telling how much he hadn't heard.

"I said WHY CAN'T SHE COME?" Helen roared.

"Oh," her father answered, and Helen could hear him groping for the words. She knew Kat had put him up to this because she didn't have the courage to say it herself. It's pitiful, she thought, what a weak woman can make a strong man do. "Well, yer mother says ter tell yer it's on account of Johnny. On account of his goin' into the Brothers, and her havin' to go to that. It's got her all broke up, then. And yer graduatin' comin' so close to that—"

"Is that all?" Helen asked, her voice brittle. I must not take it out on him! she thought, trying to control her temper.

"What?"

"I said IS THAT ALL? IS THAT THE ONLY REASON?"

"Oh." Again there was a pause while Red worked it out; Helen could hear his labored breathing against the mouthpiece. "Well, she give me some blather about not knowin' how to dress in front of them college perfessors, and I says 'Who's gone ter look at yer anyways?' and she blew up at me. And the upshot was that Danny called her this afternoon—"

"Oh?" Helen had known there was more to this story than met the eye. "What did *he* want?"

"What? Oh, Danny. Aye. Him and Paula was for askin' yer mother to stay with the kids that week so's they could get away someplace. A kind of vacation. They been after havin' troubles with their marriage, and they were thinkin'—"

"I see," Helen said. "That's what I'd call perfect timing."

"What?"

"I said HE'S DOING THAT ON PURPOSE! Doesn't Mom realize what he's up to? He's jealous because he never finished college, so he's trying to spoil it for me."

"Sure, I know that!" her father said irritably. "Am I such a gommil as yer mother thinks I am? Between you, me, and the wall, she's glad of havin' an excuse to get out of it. She don't want to face the God's honest truth that you can do something Danny boy can't!"

He was out of breath now, gasping into the phone until Helen grew alarmed.

"Pop? Take it easy now. It's not worth getting excited. To tell you the truth, I don't need either of them. He'd show up drunk, and she'd cry all afternoon. As long as you and Johnny and Frank and the girls are there. . . ."

She did not finish, because it was beginning to dawn on her that he had been building up to something else.

"Pop?"

"Aye, I'm still here. I'm after tryin' out ways ter tell yer what I've got ter say. I've not talked ter Johnny, but I'm sure he's no reason for not goin'. Yer mother's never had any hold on him and she knows it—"

"But you won't be coming," Helen said, sparing him the need to say it.

"What?"

"I said YOU AREN'T COMING, ARE YOU?"

"No," Red said.

Helen left him in silence, wanting to punish him for caving in to Kat's influence so easily. But she was concerned about his heart, and couldn't keep him waiting for long.

"It's okay, Pop," she said.

"But ye've got to see the point of it," he was arguing. "If it wasn't I had a bad heart, I could stand up to her. But if I tell her I've made up my mind to go, she'll rag me day and night till the minute I walk out the door. It's give in or end up in the hospital again, Helen Mary. I can't go up against her anymore!"

"It's all right, Pop, for God's sake!" Helen shouted, hating him for being old and weak, hating herself for reminding him. "IT'S ALL RIGHT!"

"Create no regrets," Sarah Morrow had said. "Only way I know of to get along with your family. Don't let them hand you down any guilt, and don't will any of it to your own kids."

"Explain, please." Helen frowned, tilting her head to one side as if it would help her think better. "I don't follow you."

Dr. Morrow was Helen's favorite teacher. In her four years of struggling to win her precious degree, she had not felt this comfortable with any other professor. Her awe of nuns and priests still clung to her from high school, and no matter how friendly and helpful the other students were, she always felt awkward and inferior among them. She was a full decade older than the eldest of them, suddenly matronly after all that childbearing, and neither as agile intellectually nor as easy-going morally as they were. Among the professors she also felt inferior: a housewife, a blue-collar drudge with dishpan hands and outmoded clothes, a nonintellectual who took voluminous notes in every class and memorized *everything* because she did not trust herself to have an original thought. She was doing well, had a straight B average, but college was hard, harder than she had dreamed possible, and she couldn't count the number of evenings she had cried from sheer mental fatigue on the subway going home. But she was going to see this through. She was going to break the cycle of childrearer reverting to childishness that she had seen in her grandmother, recognized in her mother, and knew herself susceptible to as well. She had heard Sarah Morrow's words and jumped at them. There was a meaning here that might save her from herself and her heritage.

Sarah Morrow—fiftyish, widow, medieval scholar—had taken a shine to Helen almost immediately. She admired her for the courage to try college at her age, encouraged her in original thinking, pounced on her when she lapsed into despair. They talked often.

"I suppose what I mean is, none of us can choose our parents," Sarah was saying, putting her feet up on a cafeteria chair and trying to get comfortable. "So it shouldn't be necessary for us to cater to their every whim solely on the basis of biology. I gather you don't get along with your mother."

"No, I don't," Helen said, fingering a corner of her child psychology book absently, avoiding Sarah's eyes, which were gray and piercing. Family matters belong in the family, she could hear her father saying, but she had admitted to a virtual stranger that her family wasn't perfect.

"Why?"

"Because she's impossible!" Helen blurted out. A few years ago she could not have done this; accused of not getting along with her mother, with any member of her family, she would have lied, denied it vehemently. But if her family could not stand behind her, what loyalty did she owe? "She's reverting into a spoiled child again, just like my grandmother did. I guess she figures she can retire now, let other people do her thinking, and let me fetch for her and do the shopping for her and make decisions for her. I wouldn't ask my own kids to do that for me, so I'm not going to do it for her!"

"Brava!" Sarah applauded her. "Good for you! You're putting my theory into practice right there."

"But you said 'Create no regrets,'" Helen pointed out. "I do have regrets, all the time. The older I get, the more guilty I feel, because I can see what the trouble is with my mother, but she can't, and in that sense I owe it to her to help her because she can't help herself."

"Oh, honest to God, will you listen to yourself!" Sarah took a sip of tea and twirled the teaspoon absently. "Is your mother ever going to change? Whether you wait on her or not?"

"No," Helen said.

"Then what are you going to accomplish by giving in except to wear yourself to a frazzle?"

Helen had no answer.

"All right, then!" Sarah sat back in her chair, pleased with herself. "You see what I mean? You cannot regret what you cannot change. All you can do is shape your own life out of the ashes they've given you, and be careful as hell that you don't mess up your own children."

"That's simple in theory," Helen said dryly. She was developing a wit, however primal. "You don't have any kids, do you?"

"No," Sarah said, her face clouding over for a moment.

"I don't mean to pry," Helen said quickly. She did not like to know too much about people's private lives, unless they insisted on telling her. "I'm just saying: I've got four, and each one is different, and each in her own way drives me stark, raving mad. And I know I've made a lot of mistakes in raising them, but if I could start all over again with each of them I'd probably just make different mistakes."

"Okay." Sarah nodded. "Perfectly legitimate. But have you done the best you can?"

"Most of the time."

"Then you mustn't have any regrets," Sarah said. "As you say, each of your daughters is an individual, and there will come a time when each will go out on her own and lead her own life, with respect for, or in spite of, what you have tried to teach her. If, God forbid, one of them should take it upon herself to turn ax-murderer, is that your fault?"

"That's ridiculous!" Helen protested. "And I honestly couldn't answer it."

"Well, I can. Unless it was implied in your nurturing of this child that it was imperative to go out and chop people up, then it is her character flaw, her moral problem, not yours."

Helen was silent, picking at the corners of her textbooks. It was this sort of thing that made her want to give up, to go home and sew curtains again. Her face said as much.

"What'll you do when you get your degree?" Sarah asked, sensing the trouble she was visiting upon this earnest young woman, wanting to alleviate some of it.

"There might be an opening in my daughters' grammar school next year," Helen said, brightening a little. "One of the nuns is going to retire. Or I might apply to the Head Start program and work with disadvantaged preschoolers. I was thinking of taking some graduate courses at the same time."

"Got it all planned, hmm? Are you excited?" Sarah asked, knowing that she must be, though she was always so quiet.

"It's more than I ever dreamed I could do!" Helen said, her eyes sparkling. "I never thought about it when I was younger. I thought I'd be happy just having kids of my own. But now I can work with other kids too, teaching them, compensating for what their own mothers can't teach them—"

"Aha!" Sarah pounced. "Don't you think that's a tiny bit arrogant? How dare you tinker with other people's kids when you're not even sure you can handle your own?"

The bell rang for the next class. Helen would not have time to defend herself, though all the time in the world would not have given her the right words.

"Look at it this way." Sarah had gotten up from the table, briefcase in one hand, teacup in the other. She put the teacup down for a moment and let her right hand rest on Helen's shoulder. "The institution of the family was created to protect its members from starvation, hostile gods, other tribes, and saber-tooth tigers. Trouble was, after the first million years it began turning in on its own members, eating them alive. Watch out for that. Keep your own identity! Don't let them eat you!"

She turned on her heel and was gone. Helen scrambled for her books and tried to blend in with the crowd, hurrying to her next class.

It had been grueling, an uphill battle, but it was the only thing Helen had ever done on her own. She wanted her family to be proud of her. But her mother wouldn't even come to her commencement.

Frank blew up when Helen told him, and threatened to

march over to his mother-in-law's and give her a piece of his mind. To calm him, Helen tried to explain how complex the situation was, to reassure him that she didn't really care. She had never lied to him before, and he believed her. Two nights before commencement he learned the truth.

He came in from work around one A.M. Helen was already sound asleep. Frank stood over the bed, shading the reading lamp with his hand so he could study her face. She looked so very calm. Forgotten were the nights a few years ago when he'd fallen asleep in front of the television because he could not bear to be beside her in this bed. Taking all those college courses had paradoxically made her less harried than she had been before. He had worried when she first went to school, thinking she would make college the cure-all for everything that had gone wrong in her life. But she proved more sensible than that. College was a means to an end, not magic.

And the immediate goal of the college degree had given her the impetus to see her gynecologist and start taking the Pill. Rhythm no more, Frank thought with a secret grin. Yes, things were much better now.

God, he was proud of her! Frank thought, resisting the urge to stroke the dark-brown hair with its suggestion of gray at the temples. He did not want to wake her yet. Stepping out of his clothes until he wore nothing but his shorts, making sure the bedroom door was locked, he caught sight of himself in the vanity mirror in the dim overspill of light from the reading lamp.

There was no doubt about it, he was developing a gut. He had gained some twenty or thirty pounds in the two decades since his last Golden Gloves bout. He didn't know exactly how much; there was a point where his pride no longer permitted him to step on a scale. It was enough to merit a warning at his last department physical, and that was a bad sign.

It was a strange body he contemplated in profile in the half-shaded mirror. From the neck up and the wrists down he was ruddy and weathered. The rest of him was as white as a chunk of wartime oleomargarine and about as appetizing. Jesus, men were ugly-looking things! he thought. How the hell could women stand them? He was going to have to lose some weight.

He dropped his shorts on the floor—an incurable habit and a wasteful one, since he'd put them on right out of the shower before he left the firehouse—and got under the sheets beside his wife. The curtains were moving a little; it was cool for a June night, and there were crickets. Flicking off the reading lamp, nuzzling the hair behind Helen's ear, and cupping one hand around her breast, he woke her. She giggled, and rolled over toward him.

"Good morning!" he whispered, and they made love.

Helen didn't have an orgasm. Instead, she burst into tears. By the time Frank finished coming and realized something was wrong, she was sobbing mightily.

"Jesus, I know I'm good, but I'm not *that* good!" he said, rolling over on his side, trying to tease her out of it. She went on crying. "What's *wrong*, for Chrissake?"

"It's this business with my mother," Helen sobbed, groping for the tissues on the night table. "What would it cost her to come to commencement? I mean, I'd expect her to carry on— she always does—and I'd put up with that, but to refuse to come at all . . . and then to twist my father around her finger and spoil it for him—that hurts worst of all. Why does she have to do this to me?"

"I don't know, honey, I really don't," Frank said soothingly, brushing the hair up off her forehead and kissing her between each word. "I told you I should've set her straight the minute she started this baloney. I can't stand to see it eating at you like this!"

"Maybe I'm puffing it up all out of proportion," Helen said, blowing her nose. "I mean, what the hell do I care? I've got you and the girls—that's more family than a lot of people have. I shouldn't make such a big deal out of it."

"But it is a big deal for you!" Frank said, propping himself up on one elbow and punching his pillow in lieu of his mother-in-law. "It's a very important day for you, and who the hell is she to spoil it for you? I should've told her off! And I will the next time she starts any bullshit with you. That's a promise!"

"It wouldn't make any difference," Helen said. "No one can convince my mother of anything." She sat up and straightened her nightgown, then remembered what they'd been doing when she started to cry. First she giggled, then she grew serious. She reached over and stroked Frank's shoulder. "Hey, I'm sorry!"

He shrugged. "That's okay. Some comment on my skills as a lover, let me tell you!"

Helen made a face.

"I'm only kidding!" he said. "Jesus, all the stuff they taught you in college, you still don't have a sense of humor!"

If the twins expected any special treatment from their mother now that she was also their fourth-grade teacher, they were disappointed. Mrs. O'Dell's reputation as a strict but eminently fair teacher spread quickly throughout the school. The children saw through the stern face she put on in the early weeks and grew to love her. The nuns and the other lay teachers admired—a little enviously—her ability to bring out the shy ones and tone down the boisterous ones. She made each of her charges feel important. She was a good teacher.

When the nun who taught fourth grade in her daughters' grammar school had retired, Helen had gone through a great deal of soul-searching. Caught up in Kennedy-era fervor, she had wanted very much to work with minority children. But Frank didn't want her traveling in unsafe neighborhoods, and kept at her about it until she gave in. Rethinking it, she was ultimately satisfied with her decision.

"Middle-class white kids need good teachers, too," she would answer anyone who criticized her.

Somehow she managed to teach, take graduate courses, raise her own kids, and occasionally get the dishes done. The girls were old enough to help, and each had her particular chores assigned to her. There was surprisingly little grumbling. They realized that helping their mother was their only defense against the encroaching chaos of dirty windows, piled-up laundry, and an empty refrigerator. And they were proud of their mother, and knew that if she was busy with her teaching it left her less time to nag and fuss over them.

Things rattled along at breakneck speed, with only an occasional crisis to disrupt a steady progression of days and months and years. There was the time Kathleen ran into a brick wall with her roller skates, shattering her glasses and driving a piece of one lens into her eyebrow; the cut required eight stitches. There was the time a news bulletin on the radio announced that three men from Frank's unit were trapped inside a collapsed building, and it took four hours for Helen to get through the switchboard to find out that Frank was safe. It was not until the twins were in high school that Helen realized she had been teaching for five years. It hardly seemed possible.

I am getting old, she thought. My babies are in high school, my eldest will be starting college in the fall, I've got scads of gray hair and I'm getting wide in the backside, and when I stop laughing the laugh-lines around my eyes don't go away anymore. How can I be this close to forty without feeling it?

There were other musings on mortality, most of them frivolous, until one stifling July night, or rather early morning, when the phone rang. One short, sharp sound against the crickets and the sleeping silence, and Frank lumbered up out of uneasy sleep to grab it.

Groggy, squinting against the light to see the clock, Helen could not comprehend what he was saying—mostly a series of grunts and affirmatives—nor determine whom he was talking to.

"Right," he said finally. "Appreciate your getting to me first. So long."

He pressed the button down, but sat with the receiver

cradled loosely in his hand, struggling with something. Helen
sat up in bed and rubbed his back inquiringly.

"It's your father," he said, his voice shaky. "One of the cops
from your folks' precinct—"

"Oh, my God!" Helen breathed. "Another heart attack.
How bad?"

"Bad," Frank said, avoiding her eyes.

Helen swallowed hard. "He's dead, then," she stated, knowing it, sparing him from saying it.

"It was fast," Frank said, trying to be comforting. "Went
in his sleep. No pain."

Helen contemplated it, mechanically getting out of bed and
gathering her clothes. A thought reached her out of the buzzing
turmoil in her head (I've expected it for years, since he had
the first attack. Every time I've looked at him in the past few
years I've known it might be the last. Then why am I so
stunned?), and she stopped, her stockings in her hand.

"How's Mom? Is anybody with her?" she asked.

Frank was feeling under the bed for his shoes, cursing because he could only find one of them. "Cops. Parish priest.
And the doctor. And how else would she be? She's hysterical.
Cop had to call the priest and the doctor for her. Doctor gave
her a sedative, but I could hear her screeching in the background."

"It figures," Helen sighed, sitting on the side of the bed
and easing the hot nylons onto her tired legs. "We'd better
get over there fast. You want to wake the girls, or should I?"

"No sense in that," Frank reasoned. "I'll wake Kath and
tell her. She can break it to the rest of them when they get
up. Otherwise you'll have them weeping all over the place
all night."

Helen shot him a look. "Why not tell Vicki? She's the
oldest. It's more her responsibility."

"Your dad and Kath were very close," Frank said, avoiding
her eyes again.

And not the only ones, Helen thought, but didn't say it. She
needed her strength for what lay ahead.

Red had been feeling the heat all week. For all the traveling he had done as a young man, for all the years he had lived in the States, his metabolism still belonged to the east coast of Newfoundland. The coldest day of winter never bothered him. But every day of the summer did.

This past week's heat wave had been the worst he could remember. It was all he could do to heave himself out of the armchair, switch off the ballgame, and stand leaning against the wall unable to move, the sweat pouring off his bald head and his heart banging fearfully.

"I wisht I was dead!" he groaned, shuffling into the kitchen where Kat was peeling potatoes. "Sure God, I wisht I was dead! I'm fed up livin' like this."

"Hush with yer or yer'll end up gettin' yer wish," Kat said sternly, not looking up from her work. Red noticed something about her he had never seen before. Her lips had all but disappeared from the constant tight severity of her mouth, a mouth that had once been able to laugh as well as remonstrate, and blather with the best of them instead of always preaching. It was now reduced to a straight line, a mere slit of an opening to allow sustenance and the Eucharist to enter, and prayers and sharp-edged platitudes to come out. He understood now why she had to paint on an artificial mouth with lipstick whenever they were going someplace, exaggerating the shape of the frightened little one that was her own. Red shivered despite the heat.

Kat was beginning to look just like her mother.

"D'yer have to cook them potatoes on a day like this?" he asked, bracing for her temper. "Sure, if it's not hot enough, with them after boilin' and heatin' up the whole kitchen—"

"And what would yer want, then?" Kat demanded, dumping them into the colander and rinsing them under the cold water with a vengeance. "With the doctor after tellin' me to see yer ate good, wholesome meals. I'd like to know how I'm to please the both of yez."

"I can eat wholesome without yer havin' to cook, I'm sayin'," Red argued, exhausted and wishing he'd never brought the subject up. "Sure, when yer went out for the paper this morning yer could've stopped to the delicatessen and got some of that potato salad. Yer know I'm fond of it, then."

"They're after puttin' salt in it when they make that stuff, and yer don't know what else. It's not clean, buyin' stuff someone else is after makin' up, and yer don't know did they wash their hands or what," Kat stated irrevocably, dumping the potatoes into the pot of water on the stove and salting the water liberally while she spoke. "The doctor says yer not to have salt."

"And what'd yer just—ah, never mind it, then." Red waved his hand at her irritably. If he mentioned the salt she'd put in the water, she would explain quite rationally that it always got lost in the cooking and then go off about how he thought she was trying to kill him. He couldn't go over that bit of ground again. He changed the subject instead. "And what else're we having for supper, then?"

"Butter beans," Kat said, facing the stove, the tone of her voice indicating she was mollified somewhat. "And cold corned beef."

Red opened his mouth and something like a squawk came out, muffled a little by the renewed banging of his heart. It was impossible to explain to her that corned beef, cured in brine, was one of the worst things he could eat. As far as Kat was concerned, only salt that she could see, poured directly from the shaker onto one's food, was the enemy. Besides, Red thought, he had given up smoking and beer for the sake of his heart, and sex for the sake of his wife's scruples. Corned beef was a small vice.

He did feel a little better after supper, taking a good hour to digest while he reread the *Daily News* for the third time. It was a morning paper; Kat had brought it home after eight o'clock mass, and he'd had all day to look it over. But he had memory lapses whenever his blood pressure went up; there were things in this newspaper to intrigue him afresh every time he turned a page.

Thanks be to God, Kat thought, at least the television was silent for a change. She hated the damned thing, except for the game shows she watched sometimes, and treated it like an uninvited guest caught snooping through the drawers. She was convinced the people inside the little gray box could see and hear her as well as she could them, and more than once had been caught talking back to it when she disagreed with something they had to say. She had never minded baseball on the radio, but sitting in the same room all afternoon with a boxful of little gray men chasing a little white ball on a big stretch of gray grass only proved how childish the game really was.

"Yer quiet," Red observed as she sat with her endless knitting. She was making mittens for all six grandchildren, though Helen Mary's girls were too old to wear them, and Danny's wife always thanked her sweetly and gave them away to the next Goodwill drive. Kat knew none of this. Had anyone had the gall to suggest she was wasting her time, she would have pretended not to hear.

"I usually am," she snapped, needles flashing. "It's only yer don't notice with that television goin' all the time."

"Aye, that's it, maybe," Red agreed, watching her, fascinated. How she could stand the feel of wool in her hands on a night this hot was beyond him. "And why is it, then? There was a time yer couldn't keep still only to catch yer breath and go on talkin'."

"And then yer was after complainin' I talked too much!" Kat snapped again, hauling more yarn out of the basket with a vengeance. "Sure, there's no pleasin' yer!"

"Oh, I'm not so certain of that," Red mused, a suggestion of a twinkle somewhere in the back of his blue eyes. He tossed the newspaper toward the coffee table—half of it missing and sliding to the floor—and pulled himself up by the arms of the chair. "I'm for bed, then."

"I'll be along," Kat said without looking up. "Sure, leave that!" she ordered as he struggled with the fallen paper.

"Aye," Red sighed, defeated, and shambled down the hall toward the bathroom.

Kat deliberated over her knitting when he was out of the room, counting stitches, stretching the thumbs on a finished pair of mittens so they would be the same length. She wanted to wait until he was already in bed, well drifted into sleep, before she joined him. He had a tendency in recent years to groan and talk aloud in the early stages of sleep which frightened her; she did not know what it signified, and she did not want to be in the room with him when it happened. It reminded her too graphically of the moment in the not-too-distant future when she would lose him.

But what was she thinking? Kat reprimanded herself, crossing herself lest the Devil read her thoughts and snatch Red away from her as punishment. Sure, he came from good stock, and even the doctor said he could live to be a hundred. If only he wouldn't take retirement so hard! It was a killing thing, retirement. It was the blue-collar worker's dream, the union man's Heaven on earth, but it tolled slow death for a man who had worked since he could walk and knew no other way.

Well, and what of it? Kat wondered in an impulsive and selfish moment. If he was as sick of living as he claimed he was, then let him go to his reward and have done with it. He would find peace, and so would she. She would mourn him for the proper number of years, gathering overdue sympathy from family and neighbors, and then she would go and live with Danny in Jersey, or, wildest of dreams, return to Harmony Bay. She would buy up one of the old houses—there were so many for sale dirt-cheap what with all the young folk emigrating—and live out the rest of her years as a kind of local royalty. For she had a son who had gone for a Christian Brother of Ireland, and wasn't he after being sent to teach in a boys' school in St. John's as soon as he took his final vows? And she was the daughter of Petey Blake, who owned one boat more than any other man in Harmony Bay, and whose name was surely still spoken there though he'd been dead for more than half a century. And, too, she would be the widow of James Daniel Manning, who, for all his red hair and Indian blood had a fair report in Torbay and its environs, as well as a sister who went for a nun. It would be enough to set her up for the rest of her days, with people coming to call daily, and perhaps one of Red's grandnieces staying at the house to do the heavy work and serve tea. This had been Kat's unvoiced ambition all these years, alluded to vaguely as "goin' down to Harmony Bay for a visit." But once she went back, she never meant to return. In Harmony Bay she would be somebody, as she could never be in Brooklyn, where only the neighbors on the block knew who she was. Why, she had been getting her fruit and vegetables at the same "Eye-talian" fruit stand for thirty-five years, and no one had ever thought to ask her name.

And Kat crossed herself again for wishing her husband dead, for wishing harm on the only man she had ever loved, at a time so long ago she could scarcely remember it. Was it a dream, this love, or could it possibly be something that had really happened? There were photographs of the two of them together, to be certain, but that didn't prove anything. They had shared the same bed for over three decades, and had three living children to show for it, but was that proof of love or only lust? If there was a time when love had filled Kat's heart instead of melancholy, she could no longer remember it clearly. Stuffing her knitting back into the big wicker basket—an old picnic basket without handles, reminiscent of weeks at the lake in Connecticut, with him coming up on weekends and sitting in the woods beside her, waiting for her to break the self-imposed vow of silence she had kept all week—and straightening the wrinkled skirt that, like all her clothes, never quite fit the small flabby shape of her (though she still had good legs; anybody could see that), Kat turned off the lights, made sure the front door was locked, and went toward the bedroom.

She was surprised—actually startled enough to break out in goosebumps—to find Red sitting up in bed and watching her.

"Jesus and Mary, yer gave me a fright!" she exploded. "I thought yer was—"

Thought yer was dead and sitting there staring at me with yer eyes glazed over, she thought. Thought me evil thoughts had come ter pass.

"I wasn't tired, then," he said evenly, his eyes venturing to say that he knew what she was thinking. "Thought we might sit up a bit and have a talk."

"Aye, maybe *you're* not tired, but I've been on my feet all day," Kat scolded, taking a nightgown out of the bureau and marching off to the bathroom to get undressed.

There had been a time, Red thought with a sigh, when she would undress in the same room with him—shyly, of course, and half-hidden behind the open closet door, but that had only made it more exciting. They had always made love with their nightclothes on (Kat insisted on that), but somehow that brief glimpse of her slipping into the long nightgown, her hair down around her face, cheeks burning, sustained him, and he hadn't really minded. All that was before she lost all the babies and began to develop the notion that it was God's punishment for taking too much pleasure in the act of love itself. Where she got the idea was anybody's guess; no priest in his right mind could suggest it, assuming Kat had ever found the nerve to broach the subject with a priest. But it was her pet notion, and she clung to it like dogma, and after Johnny was born and she had her hysterectomy she decided it wasn't necessary to engage in all that dirty business at all anymore. She gave in to Red's quiet yearnings once or twice a month, but with such a sense of duty that most of the joy was lost for him, and he swore she couldn't wait to pack herself off to confession when it was over.

Red couldn't remember the last time they'd made love, though since he'd had the scare with his heart the need seemed to have left him altogether. He could not understand why he felt so good tonight.

He watched Kat march determinedly back into the room, sitting at the dressing table to attack her iron-gray hair with the hairbrush. A hundred strokes a night, no matter what. When she turned off the light and got into bed without so much as wishing him good-night—a kiss would be more than he could hope for—when he heard the familiar tinkle of the rosary she kept under her pillow, heard her whispered breathing in the darkness as she recited the beads, he decided to do something impetuous.

"Beggin' yer pardon, Mrs. Manning," he said playfully, in a voice that was loud in the close, dark room.

"Mother of God!" Kat exploded. "Don't do that to me! Sure what's eatin' at yer tonight?"

He could make out her small arthritic hand in the darkness, groping for the lamp.

"Sure, there's no need," he said, quieter. "I only wanted to ask yer something."

"What is it, then?" And he heard the rosary rattle as she searched for where she'd left off.

"I was after thinkin'. It's not as hot as it was," he began, searching for a way to phrase what was on his mind without setting her off. "I was wonderin' could we have a talk. Just lie here in the dark and gab a bit—d'yer remember the way we used to? When the kids was small and the house was quiet, and we'd be here all to ourselves (yer old mother snorin' in the next room, too; I'm not forgettin' that—but just us, alone). And I'd have my arm around yer. . . ."

"Aye." Kat nodded in the darkness, and seemed almost to relax. Red sensed that she had moved closer to him across a valley of bedclothes that separated them. Tentatively, he did the same, trying to put his arm around her shoulder the way he had all those years ago. He felt her stiffen suddenly and move away from him. "Oh, aye, I remember," she said, scolding again, groping for the light in earnest. "I remember we'd start off talking and end with a lot of—a lot of dirty business. Stuff that's better off in the past, then. We're too old for that nonsense now!"

"There's no need for that!" Red cried, and it was almost a plea. "Sure, I'm not even sure I can anymore. I only wanted to hold yer."

"Jesus and Mary, man! Can't yer leave me in peace?" Kat hissed, flashing the light on and sitting up in bed, her rosary clasped in her hands like a weapon. "What's the point of it, now?"

"Oh, nothing! Never mind about it! I'm sorry I asked!" he exploded, his anger out of proportion, Kat thought, to her refusal. "It was a little human comfort I was lookin' for, that's all. Mother of God, yer'd think I was a stranger yer found in yer bed!"

"Sure, if that's what yer think . . ." Kat answered, trailing off, not knowing what to say to him. It was almost as if he *were* a stranger to her, as if all the years of marriage had made them so different from each other that there was no point at which they touched anymore. And why was he so angry? "It's just I'm concerned about what it might lead to. We're too old for that stuff, and I'm after worryin' about yer heart."

"Never mind about my heart!" Red roared, rising up out of the bed like a volcano. "We're never too old for anything as long as we still want it! Are we too old to love each other?"

His face had turned the color of his few remaining strands of red hair, and Kat grew frightened. His heart—

Even as she thought it she could see his color changing, see his skin go leaden while his eyes popped and the blue veins stood out in his forehead. He cried out once and toppled over, his temple striking the headboard of the bed. His mouth opened and he twitched convulsively, while Kat sat paralyzed within inches of him, unable to think what to do, unable even to think that there was something she could do. It was over before she could wrench her eyes away from Red's face. He stopped twitching suddenly and lay perfectly still, eyes glazing over but his face calmer, the blue veins receding. Madly, Kat thrust the rosary she still held into his cold hands. His dying fingers clutched at it in a final convulsion, catching at her hand and making her shriek.

She sat staring at him for an indeterminate amount of time, unable to move. She would have to do something, could hardly go screaming out into the street in her nightgown, though the thought had a mad, dramatic appeal. One spark of logic penetrated her brain. She must call the police. Her son-in-law had written down the number of the local precinct, and she was to call the police if anything happened to Red. Frank had taped the number on the phone so she would not forget. Kat had lost her temper with him that day, accusing him of planning Red's death beforehand, but later, when Helen and Frank had gone, she had added the number of the family doctor and the parish house, so a priest could come and give Red the last rites.

Kat dragged herself off the bed now, tearing her eyes away from the body of her husband, and sidled over to the bureau where the phone was. She picked up the receiver, then thought of something else, and put it down. She moved back toward the bed as if she were sleepwalking, and covered Red up to the shoulders with the sheet. When the police came she would tell them she woke to find him dead beside her. She did not feel up to explaining what had really happened. Satisfied with her decision, Kat recrossed the room, and, trance-like, picked up the phone.

Helen sat toward the front of the funeral chapel, fingers aching from shaking hands with dozens of well-wishers, face sticky from their rheumy kisses, ears humming from the drone of the ill-concealed air conditioners and the buzz of voices broken by an occasional ill-timed laugh from someone recounting a story thirty years old or more, the sound reducing the room to reproachful silence before conversation surged back again. She was not called upon to receive anyone's condolences at the moment, did not need to respond with any of the required numb platitudes, and so was free to listen for the hundredth time as her mother repeated her great fiction.

"Sure, it was meant to be, I'm thinkin', that I happened to

wake at that moment and realized he was after stoppin' breathing, and I got up quick as I could and put on the light and
there he was, just goin'. I was after havin' me rosary in me
hand as I always say the beads to help me sleep, so I give it
to him, put it right in his hand, cold as it was, and wasn't he
holdin' it tight even as he was dyin'. Sure, the look in his
eyes—was as if he knew I was there to comfort him in his
passin'. And he was after goin' so peaceful! Sure, it was
God's mercy!"

Helen sighed. She had not been there, of course, and didn't
know what really happened on the night her father died, but
something about her mother's narrative was too polished to
be true. It might be the way she kept telling it again and again,
using the same words over and over, as if she'd rehearsed it
beforehand so no one would question her. It was either pure
fiction, or at least half the truth had been eliminated. Whatever
it was, Helen would never know. Perhaps she didn't want
to know. But if she had to hear her mother tell it this way
one more time. . . .

The wake was not as monstrous as she'd expected. There
was the usual drunken wrangling among her father's cronies
from the Terminal, the usual carrying on by the Rosary Society ladies. But Danny had managed to show up sober for
two nights running, and was conducting himself like a civilized
person for the first time Helen could remember. Even so, she
thought, he looked like hell.

He had ignored the doctor's advice about his diet and his
drinking, until several blackouts—including one when he was
on the road that nearly killed him, and totaled the company
car—frightened him enough to make him abruptly change
his life-style. He was taking some sort of oral medication for
his diabetes, which made him feel good enough to chance a
few drinks now and then. The results were predictable. He
would black out again, go through a spell of remorse, then
start sneaking drinks again, in an unending cycle. His weight
fluctuated over a range of twenty pounds either way, and

he looked older than his thirty-seven years. None of his health problems had improved his disposition

But Helen's advice to both Paula and Kat had gone unheeded to the extent that she no longer bothered giving it. If her brother chose to destroy himself, it was beyond her concern.

Johnny was at the wake too, grown into a man in the five years since he had joined the Christian Brothers. He had come down by train from Iona College, where he was taking summer courses toward his master's. Frank had picked him up at Grand Central the afternoon of Red's death, without any sleep, though Frank was used to that. Johnny had permission to stay with his mother—he would lose the summer-school credits, but that didn't seem to bother him—for the rest of the summer. It was ironic, Helen thought, watching every female relative from her thirteen-year-olds to the most ancient great-grandmother fawn over him and his rugged, Black Irish looks (pale face against the black habit, very ascetic for a soccer player), that his father's death had given him, sum total, more time than he had probably spent with his mother in his entire life.

Aside from his polite banter with the women of the family, Johnny hardly spoke at all. He had been virtually silent, Frank said, as they plowed through rush-hour traffic from the train station back to Brooklyn. How his father's death—certainly no surprise—had affected him was impossible to say; while there were no visible signs of mourning, there was about him a kind of strangeness, a withdrawal. Possibly he was already pondering the weeks he would spend caged up with Kat and her lamenting; perhaps he had become so otherworldly since he took his vows that this sad little human drama did not reach him. Watching out of the corner of her eye as he said something to Vicki, seeing Vicki turn precipitously and leave the chapel, Helen wondered. But she had too many other things on her mind to wonder long.

"Oh, Jesus, look what the cat dragged in!" Danny half-whispered beside her, resting his pudgy hand on her forearm. Helen turned toward the entrance foyer as the entire room suddenly dropped into silence. The air conditioners droned imperturbably, but there was no other sound. Resplendent in her best black dress and veil, crossing herself with the rosary clasped daintily in one white-gloved small hand, the mink furpiece with the melancholy little bead eyes thrown about her shoulders in defiance of the heat, Aunt Ag was walking the length of the funeral chapel, ramrod-straight despite her sixty-five years, most of them spent on her feet. Behind her, dapper as always, knowing the silence was for him and embarrassed despite his best efforts, stood Alistair.

Helen's eyes sought her mother's face, saw that Kat had stiffened in her chair and sat staring straight ahead, as if her older sister, Medusa-like, had by her very presence turned her to stone. Some great conflagration was about to take place.

"Ke-rist, what's the matter with her?" Danny whispered again, loud enough to be heard by those in proximity, strangely confidential, still grasping Helen's arm. "She coulda come by herself if she had to, without dragging the little fag along too!"

"Shut up!" Helen hissed at him as the eldest member of the family with any sanity, and as Aunt Ag strode grandly past Kat to kneel before the casket—Alistair squiring her, standing behind her as she knelt, blocking the whispers that assailed them from all sides—Helen made a decision. As Aunt Ag rose slowly from the kneeler, Helen shook free of Danny and bolted toward her.

"Aunt Ag!" she greeted her, stumbling a little on the thick carpet with her high heels, her voice a little louder than necessary, as if everyone in the room weren't already staring at them. She took her aunt by the shoulders and kissed her cheek, withered and dry under the shakily applied rouge. "How good of you to come when we needed you!"

And as if that weren't bad enough, she turned toward Alistair, threw her arms around him, her mother's thunderstruck face somewhere in the background—bad enough to let him come to the house on the sly, but to acknowledge his right to exist in public—and kissed him. After a moment's hesitation, he kissed her in return.

"It was so good of you both to come," Helen babbled on, linking her arms through theirs, and, in a tour de force of dramatic talent she never knew she had, she led them out of the chapel—the crowd at the door parting like the Red Sea—and into the adjacent lounge, where Frank had been ensconced with Kathleen and the twins most of the night. The implication was clear. Not only did Helen welcome her cousin's presence, she thought him worthy to sit with her family. She had upstaged her mother for the first time in Kat's illustrious career. No one would ever hear the end of this.

And the next morning, when the carnival aspect of the wake was over; when the Rosary Society ladies and the drunks had been packed off to attend the funeral at the church; when the ashtrays had been emptied and the chapel was about to be readied for the body of some stranger—worked over in the mortuary, lying blue and naked on the cooling slab, ready to be dressed in its best clothes and painted the right colors to make it look human again—Helen persuaded the funeral director, a ten-dollar bill folded damply in her hand, to let her in before anyone else from the funeral party got there. She knelt by the still-open casket in the silent, stifling room—no air-conditioning until the new customers arrived this afternoon—and tried to say good-bye to this mass of viscera that had once been her father.

She crossed herself and her mind went blank. No easy rote prayers would bail her out now. This was her *father* who lay dead here, and forever after the words "Our Father, Who art in Heaven . . ." would have an alien ring to them, reminding her of this moment in this room, and the smell of decaying carnations, and the sound of the funeral director clearing his throat in the next room.

Helen stared at the face of the corpse for the longest time, trying to recognize in it someone she had once known. Could it be only that she had never seen her father with his eyes closed—and his mouth, for God's sake, the man who loved to blather as much as he loved to breathe—his face so composed, so devoid of bemusement or anger or exasperation or "Mother of God, and what am I goin' to do with yer mother, then?"

No, Helen thought, the message of her lifetime of Catholicism suddenly coming clear. This *thing* was not her father, was not even a reasonable facsimile, but was some gaudy, painted replica, some false god to be worshiped before it was sunk into the ground to fertilize the cemetery dandelions. This was a joke in poor taste, a mockery of the man who had never in the thirty-eight years she had known him held a rosary in those ugly, scarred, powerful hands, yet who now had one twined artfully about his composed, waxen fingers, and, if anyone took her mother seriously, had sought for these superstitious beads at the moment of his death. Sick and frightened, utterly alone, Helen sprang up from the kneeler, unable to pray for her father, fighting down the thought submerged since grammar school that if he was in Heaven he had no need of her prayers, and that those in Hell could not profit from anyone's prayers. Helen bolted from the chapel, grateful she had come alone so that not even Frank could see her behaving this way.

How small he looks! she thought, staring back at the casket from the doorway, her crisis of faith passing like a wave of nausea. She had never realized that her father was less than five and a half feet tall; he had always seemed like a giant to her. A good giant, a saint in the rough, who, if he hadn't suffered enough on earth to deserve Heaven—she would not pray for him; no man she knew deserved Heaven more. There were those still living who needed her prayers far more than James Daniel Manning. Red. Her father. Helen sat in the lounge to wait for the rest of the family. They could close the casket without her; she had already said her good-byes.

Helen had never dreamed about her father before. Now that he was dead she dreamed about him almost nightly. Dreamed not of the tired old man with the quaver in his voice who could no longer stand up to her mother, but of the man in his prime—the man who took her to the park and let her play on the grass, the man who taught her to read a newspaper backwards. There was an ugly twist to these dreams, which always ended with her reaching out to touch his face, only to have it blow away like charred newspaper, or slip out of her fingers like the skin on a piece of rotten fruit. No matter how often she dreamed the same dream, no matter how often her conscious mind tried to force its way into the dream and prevent her from reaching out to him, Helen was helpless. After a few months Frank began appearing in the dreams, sometimes standing behind her father as if he were the next one to decay in her hands, or, more graphically, trapped inside a burning building that disintegrated as she watched. This last one made her wake up screaming.

She became morbidly concerned about Frank, which was unnecessary now that he was a chief and no longer saw that much direct action, no longer needed to be the hero. Frank put up with her hysteria, knowing it was the result of losing her father, and breathed a sigh of relief when the new school term started in September and she had lesson plans and homework assignments to take her mind off her worries.

Still, Helen did not look well. There were dark smudges under her eyes, and she was beginning to gain weight, to look puffy and bloated. When she broke the zipper of her favorite skirt one morning, she decided it was time to go on a diet.

She tried to skip lunch in school, but felt light-headed and had to eat something. Sitting at the lunch table, feeling ravenous and nauseous by turns, she realized that strange things had been happening to her body for several months, but she had been so caught up with the wake and the funeral, and dragging her mother to banks and lawyers and the Social Security office to settle her father's affairs. . . .

There was the acne to begin with. Even as an adolescent she had never had more than a handful of pimples at a given time. Suddenly and for no apparent reason she had started breaking out, not a lot but enough to be embarrassing to a woman her age. Then she had started to gain weight—over ten pounds so far—and she felt tired all the time. Nerves, Helen had decreed with each new symptom. A reaction to her father's death. It would pass in time.

But she was in the lavatory, washing her hands before she went back to her fourth grade, when the Kotex machine on the wall caught her eye.

Good Lord! Helen thought, the water running over her hands unnoticed as she calculated frantically. I haven't had my period in over two months!

The ten-to-one bell rang just then, and she had to dash upstairs before the nuns brought her class up from the school-yard. Helen tried to appear to be her normal self as she set up the slide projector for a social studies lesson—Land of the Free: America Against Communism—but her mind was in a whirl. What could possibly be the matter with her?

She automatically ruled out pregnancy. She had been on the Pill for eight years, and the Pill was supposed to be ninety-nine percent effective. It was out of the question. But hadn't she read in one of her women's magazines that the Pill was suddenly suspected of causing cancer? If she had cancer of the uterus, would that make her periods disappear?

Watching the slides on the screen with a fraction of her consciousness, narrating from the script the film company enclosed with the slides, reprimanding the wise guy shooting spitballs from the sixth row, Helen let her mind race. Uterine cancer. Surgery, chemotherapy, possible death. That was the worst possibility. What was on the other end of the scale?

Could she be going through some sort of early menopause? She had heard of women going through their changes as early as thirty-five. Couldn't she, at thirty-eight? It was improbable, since Kat had been forty when Johnny was born, but Helen was grasping at straws and willing to believe anything.

She switched off the slide projector and raised the window shades, wishing more than anything that it was quarter to three so she could bolt for home and call her gynecologist.

If I had cancer I'd be losing weight, not gaining, Helen

reasoned, dumping her books on the hall table as she let herself into the house and rummaging in the drawer for her address book.

When she picked up the phone in the kitchen, she heard Kathleen's voice. She was on the bedroom extension, talking to one of her girl friends from school. Ordinarily, Helen never eavesdropped on her daughter, but she was not quite herself at the moment, and the bit of conversation she broke in on fascinated her so much she forgot her scruples.

". . . or some such bullshit," Kathleen said.

"You don't think she'd actually *do* it?" said the voice on the other end, probably a girl named Rita, who was Kathleen's closest friend, at least for this week. "I mean, like, my God! That's outrageous!"

"Isn't it? Nah, not Vicki. Vicki wouldn't have the balls." Kathleen again, her language at sixteen a constant source of friction between her and her mother. "It's a flaky idea, though. Saccharin tablets. Did you ever hear anything so *weird?*"

"Yeah," the other girl reflected, "I mean, they do look the same. Could you just imagine?"

Helen's head was spinning by now, but she was not so confused that she couldn't remember to replace the receiver without making a sound. What did it mean? Drugs? If she had overheard a similar conversation from Vicki, minus the dirty words, of course, she would find it plausible. Kathleen would try drugs, would try anything. She'd been caught with a cigarette in the bathroom when she was ten. The signs were all there. But Vicki? Vicki would never experiment with drugs. Vicki was always the predictable one, the safe one. Saccharin tablets? What did it mean?

But she couldn't very well confront Kathleen with what she had just heard without admitting she had been eavesdropping. Besides, to ask Kathleen anything directly was to produce instant catatonia. Whatever this was all about, Helen would have to try another approach. And there was something more urgent at hand.

She marched upstairs to the bathroom, making as much noise

as she could to let Kathleen know she was home, to encourage her to get off the phone. By the time she came out of the bathroom, the door to Kathleen's room was closed, a Dylan record wailing, and the phone in the master bedroom was unemployed but still smoking slightly. Helen started to dial, then decided the hell with it. If she just went to the office and waited until after nine, when all his other patients were gone. . . .

"I don't know how to break this to you, babe," he said, removing the disposable glove and peering at her over the sheet that covered her legs. "But you're two months pregnant."

Helen's regular gynecologist had decided he would rather play golf than practice medicine; he had retired within the year since she had had her last Pap test. This was a new man, less cynical and condescending, but perhaps less experienced. He had to be mistaken!

"That's impossible!" Helen pulled her feet out of the stir- the hall.

"Let me ask you something," he said before she could open her mouth. "You've got how many daughters?"

"Four," Helen answered, dutiful as always in the presence rups and sat up so fast the room spun momentarily. "I've been on the Pill for—"

"For too long without a layoff," he interrupted her, steadying her on the examining table. "Your doctor should have taken you off them for six months every two to three years. Eight years straight? That's dangerous!"

"But I can't—" Helen began, but he tapped her on one sheet-covered knee with his index finger, then put it to his lips.

"Get dressed," he said. "We'll talk inside."

She sat in his private office while he took care of the last patient and said good-night to his receptionist. It was nearly ten o'clock. Helen was grateful for his taking the extra time with her. But how could she possibly be pregnant? She sat twisting a tissue in her hands until she heard his footsteps in of a man of medicine, though it was difficult this time because he was so young and easy to like.

"How old?" he asked, lolling back in his chair and clasping his hands behind his head.

"Eighteen, sixteen, and thirteen," Helen said, ticking off four fingers. "Twins on the last set," she explained when he looked puzzled.

"Okay." He nodded. "I don't think we need to consider them. But the older two—they have boyfriends?"

"My oldest, no. My middle one, yes. But nobody serious."

"You mean nobody serious that you know about," he said, leaning forward and looking at her intently.

A light was beginning to dawn somewhere in the recesses of Helen's brain. She had always tried to be open with her daughters on matters of sex, had tried to make them understand that while she didn't approve of their getting too seriously involved with boys at an early age, she was always willing to talk about it. Would either of them dare to sneak around behind her back, stealing her contraceptives—?

"Saccharin tablets," she said aloud, startling herself and making the doctor roar.

"I hate to laugh," he said finally, wiping his eyes. "I mean, it's a helluva predicament for you. Although you're lucky now, with all the advances in Rh pregnancies. But I've had patients with this problem before. You can't imagine what these kids will try! You've probably been taking saccharin for months. That's why your face broke out and you developed all those other symptoms; when you try to get back to normal after eight years on estrogen. . . . Listen." He was suddenly very serious, very concerned. "Do you *mind* being pregnant again?"

Helen shrugged. Something more than relief that she didn't have cancer had been stealing over her since he'd told her. "It's not as if I planned it," she said, whimsical. "But what the hell can I do about it? Besides, maybe I'll finally get the boy I wanted."

She got up from her chair. He looked fatigued; she shouldn't keep him. And she had to get home while the anger was still on her, and find the thief who had stolen her pills. There would be bloodshed at the O'Dell house tonight.

She took a cab home, but it was nearly eleven when she walked in the door. Frank would be on until twelve tonight, and the twins were already in bed. It was a perfect time for a confrontation. Her target was Kathleen, but she wanted to talk to Vicki as well.

Vicki's door was open. She was already in her pajamas and robe, reading Thomas Aquinas for a test tomorrow. Her radio was on at the lowest possible volume, playing Mantovani or something equally innocuous.

Kathleen's door was shut. The same Dylan record she'd been playing this afternoon droned on, loudly. She was not doing her homework, but was sketching something on a piece of loose-leaf paper, which she crumpled as soon as her mother knocked.

"I'd like to see you downstairs," Helen said calmly to each girl in turn, then went into her own room to the big double dresser and opened the top drawer. She took out the little cardboard case with the little circle of twenty-eight pills and studied the pills closely. Sure enough, they were the same size and shape as birth-control pills, complete with the little dividing line down the middle, but it was obvious from the condition of the cardboard that each pill had been carefully poked out of position and replaced by—Helen touched her tongue to one and winced at the intense tinny sweetness—saccharin. Why hadn't she seen the evidence before? How could she have been so stupid?

All right, it was a dirty trick, she thought, and she was shocked and unprepared and a nervous wreck at the idea that she could be two entire months pregnant and not know it. But the moment she started taking the Pill she'd promised herself she wouldn't get upset if she got pregnant anyway. And the older the girls became, the more she wished she could have had

a boy as well, the more she missed holding a baby in her arms
again. She loved children, was hopelessly hooked on them;
there was no getting around it. And she wasn't really that old,
and she'd been thinking of taking a break from teaching, and
the girls were old enough to practically raise this one for
her. . . .

No, it wasn't that she minded being pregnant again, even if
she had been tricked into it. What was eating Helen's insides
out at the moment was that Kathleen was only sixteen, and
she was fooling around with—please God, let it be just one
boy instead of half a dozen, or someone's husband—and she
had not had the slightest inkling.

Bringing the evidence with her, Helen marched down the
stairs to the living room.

"Tell me what you know about this!" she demanded, slapping the cardboard case onto the coffee table in front of
Kathleen and glaring at her.

Kathleen stared right back at her. Blue eyes. Her grandfather's eyes. Never-tell-a-lie eyes. "They're birth-control
pills," she said calmly.

"Are they?" Helen shrieked, losing her temper in the face
of such lack of conscience. "Are you sure? Or are they saccharin tablets?"

Kathleen jumped slightly then, or twitched nervously, and
shot a glance at Vicki, who had not said a word.

Helen exploded. "I picked up the phone by accident this
afternoon—I'm two months pregnant on account of you—
my whole metabolism's a mess—because you snuck up to my
room and—stole my pills and—for God's sake, who are you
sleeping with and why didn't you tell me? I would've taken
you to my doctor for something—even if I didn't approve—
but to have you sneak around and steal and—"

She stopped then, out of breath, amazed at the turmoil of
emotions on her daughter's face. Had she expected remorse,
breakdown, tearful confession? Or, more likely, defiance and
sarcasm? She saw neither. She saw Kathleen's expression turn

from wounded pride to momentary amusement and then to vicious anger, directed at Vicki, who was a veritable sphinx, picking trancelike at the upholstery on the arm of her chair.

"You really did it, didn't you, tight-ass?" Kathleen spat at her sister. "Jesus Christmas, I didn't think you had the guts! So tell her, then. Go ahead and tell her!"

"I took your pills, Mother," Vicki said, barely audible.

"*You?*" Helen couldn't say another word. She looked helplessly toward Kathleen, wanting to apologize, totally at sea with this new development, but Kathleen ignored her.

"Tell her why, tight-ass!" Kathleen hissed at her sister. "*Tell* her!"

"Kathleen!" Helen said, unable to stop herself from correcting the girl's language even under these circumstances. Vicki? This afternoon's overheard conversation suddenly made sense. Vicki had done this thing, by her own admission. It must have been premeditated, if Kathleen knew about it. But Vicki, on the Pill? If Helen had any fear for Vicki it was that she would die a virgin. Her fear was apparently ungrounded, replaced by a new fear. "Vicki?" she ventured. "Would you mind explaining to me—?"

Vicki's face, when she finally looked up at her mother, wore a familiar expression. It was her self-righteousness-in-the-face-of-adversity expression, and Helen braced herself for yet another shock.

"The Pope has decreed that birth control is a sin," Vicki announced, as if no one in this household had ever heard it before. "After reading *Humanae Vitae*, I have come to a moral decision. I flushed your pills down the toilet and replaced them with saccharin to prevent you from continuing to commit a grievous sin."

"And you never—it never occurred to you—" Helen spluttered. This was all really too much. "You never thought to discuss it with me instead of doing something as underhanded— What *you* were doing was a sin. Didn't that occur to you?"

"I know that!" Vicki said grandly, an aura of martyrdom

enfolding her. "But I took it upon myself to try to open your eyes. I knew I couldn't convince you that you were doing wrong until you suffered the consequences of your wrong-doing. Once you got pregnant, I could—"

Helen slapped her as hard as she could. She had never hit Vicki before. "You're an absolute monster!" she snarled, hating herself for her part in creating this bundle of moral superiority. "A vindictive, cold-blooded monster!"

Vicki winced slightly at the slap, but rose from her chair with great dignity. "I was merely following the dictates of my conscience. Good-night, Mother. I'll pray for you."

She sailed grandly up the stairs to her room, and it took several minutes before Helen could look Kathleen in the eye.

"I'm—I'm sorry," she said finally, sitting beside Kathleen and resting her hand on the girl's arm. "I'm sorry I accused you, and I'm sorry for all the rotten things I've been thinking about you all evening, and everything I said."

Kathleen shrugged it off. "Doesn't matter. I mean, I can see why you'd think it was me. If I found the right guy I probably would start screwing around. But I'd never steal your pills."

"That's a comforting thought," Helen remarked drily. "Did you know what Vicki was up to?"

"No, I didn't, Ma. Honest to God! She mentioned it to me once—you know—theoretically, like. If I'd known she was serious I'd've told you immediately. God, what a shitty thing to do!" She grew very serious for a moment. "Hey, Ma? I'm awful sorry you're pregnant."

Helen exhaled, calming down. She had underestimated this one among her daughters. That, at least, would change. "I'm not. Sorry."

"Oh." Kathleen was surprised. "I'm glad to hear that."

Her face was working again; Helen couldn't tell if she was going to laugh or cry until she burst out laughing. "Jesus, what a way to get pregnant!" she roared, and Helen for once didn't mention her language. "Nobody'd believe it if you told them!"

"You *would* think it was funny!" Helen snorted, starting to laugh herself. She threw her arms around her daughter and they laughed until they cried.

"You wouldn't!" Frank said. "Tell me you're kidding. You wouldn't!"

"Francis Xavier O'Dell, Junior," Helen murmured contentedly, looking at her son through the nursery window. "I already have. The lady with the birth certificates came around this morning."

Frank tore his eyes away from the little dark head in the nursery and gave her a sideways look. "You son of a gun!" he said in admiration. "But I can give the priest a different name when he's baptized."

Helen shrugged. "We'll call him Frankie. If he wants to change it when he grows up, that's his business."

"But why?" Frank wanted to know. "You know that name drives me nuts. Why the hell burden my kid with it too?"

"Because maybe he won't be as embarrassed by his origins as his father is," Helen said mildly. "And maybe he'll remind me of you after you've played the hero once too often and I don't have you around anymore." That last was covering dangerous territory, and she knew it, and changed the subject. "Look at the way his hair sticks up in the middle! And he's got the same cleft in his chin that you have. Did you see that?"

"You son of a gun!" was all Frank said, patting her robed backside and smiling in spite of himself.

They walked down the hospital corridor, arms around each other, peaceful. Helen had gotten over her initial embarrassment at being one of the oldest women in the maternity ward, and was feeling quite pleased with herself.

"Frank? How much money do we have?"

He was surprised by the question. "Enough. Why?"

"I mean, how much, really? Dollars and cents?"

"Enough so you don't have to worry about going back to

work for a good long while, if that's what's on your mind," he said.

"That's not what I mean," Helen said, pushing the hair up off her forehead with her free hand. "What I want to know is, after we pay off everybody's tuition and the car insurance and everything else, how much will we have in the bank?"

She was in charge of their finances, and had been since they were first married. She knew how much was in the joint savings account, the checking account, and the kids' trust accounts better than he did. What was she driving at?

"I guess if you don't count the kids' accounts, we got about five grand put aside," Frank said cautiously. "Why?"

"And if you had to, how much could you borrow from the pension fund?" Helen persisted.

"Offhand I don't know," he said, vaguely annoyed at this line of questioning and wondering where it was leading. "Maybe another five grand. Why? What are you driving at?"

Helen shrugged. "It's just an idea I've been rattling around in my head for a while."

"Well, spit it out! If you're gonna blow all our money on something, I think I'm entitled to know what. What've you been up to—playing the horses, running up debts? Come on, spill it!"

Helen giggled, even though it made her stitches hurt, even though she was trying to be serious. She had been plotting something during all the months of relative idleness before her son's birth. She had had to stop teaching in the middle of the term, partly on doctor's orders because she was high-risk, partly because the nuns in the grammar school where she taught were not prepared to field questions about why Mrs. O'Dell was suddenly getting fat. She had been home twiddling her thumbs from February until June, and the hiatus reminded her too vividly of the years and years she had stayed home when the girls were small. She was not going to go through *that* again.

"I had an idea," she told her husband. They were back in

her room now, and they sat side by side on the bed looking out the hospital window at the laundry hanging from fire escapes across the street, at the half-naked kids running through the water spewing from an open hydrant.

"Jesus, will you look at that!" Frank exploded. "Don't those kids realize what that does to the water pressure? Open one of them things on every block and God forbid there's a fire. Turn on a faucet on the top floor of any of those buildings and you might as well spit on the fire for all the water you're going to find!"

"It's the only recreation they've got," Helen pointed out. "You can't blame them."

"Nah, but they can go down to the precinct and pick up one of those spray caps. You can still run the water and it won't affect the pressure. They just can't be bothered. We spend half the summer putting caps on the hydrants—the minute we're gone some dumb Spic gets a crowbar and pries the thing off and you're back to Square One. Then they're the first ones to holler when their apartment goes up. And the first ones to throw bottles off the roof while you're trying to put it out. Dumb Spics!"

Helen sighed. "Why do you have to talk like that?" she demanded. "Are you listening to me at all?"

"Just a minute!" he said abruptly, cutting her off. "Just a goddamn minute! Before I do anything else, I'm gonna call this in to the precinct. All that water they're wasting down there is supposed to safeguard this hospital. Somebody's gotta get things shaking around here!"

He was off down the hall to use the phone at the nurses' station. Helen sighed again, resigned. Firemen, like cops, were never really off duty. She had to admit he was right about the water pressure, but she didn't share his prejudices.

She waited. He was back in five minutes, pleased with himself. He would not sit and listen to what she had to say, but stood at the window with his arms folded, a self-appointed sentinel until the squad car arrived to remedy the situation.

"They'll throw you out in ten minutes," Helen said patiently, glancing at her watch. He frowned at her. "Visiting hours."

"Oh, yeah!" he said, tearing his eyes away from the window, but standing near it just in case. "Jeez, I'm sorry. You were telling me something, weren't you?"

"I want to start a daycare center," Helen said all at once. Frank looked at her blankly. "Come again?"

Helen took a deep breath, knowing she'd have to speak fast so he couldn't interrupt. "You know Mrs. Malloy, the kindergarten teacher? The twins had her—the one with the gray hair and the warm smile? Well, she's retiring this year, and the school has no pension, so she was looking for something to supplement her income. She has a little put aside from investments and her husband's estate, but it's not enough. She's also got thirty years' experience. We got to talking, and we decided that if we pool our resources and our talents, we could start a little day nursery—preschool, maybe even infant care for working mothers—and if it really works out, in a few years we could expand to a summer camp and—"

"Whoa!" Frank shouted, so loud his voice echoed off the walls. He had been distracted by the scene in the street, which looked like it might escalate at any moment. Two cops had arrived in a patrol car, turned off the hydrant, and started to install a sprinkler cap. A small crowd was beginning to gather, and the children who had been playing in the water from the hydrant were complaining loudly. Only half of Frank's attention had been given over to his wife's narrative, but what he had been hearing had suddenly penetrated, and he didn't like the sound of it. "Slow down a little, and then back up. How long've you had this one on the back burner?"

"Since I quit in February," Helen said diffidently.

"Holy Jesus H.! You sure can keep a secret!" he said, quieter. "And you're talking about investing *our* money in this project?"

"I wouldn't need more than a few thousand for starters,"

Helen said, being eminently reasonable. "There's a storefront on Third Avenue in the Seventies that's been vacant for months. I checked with the real estate agent. The landlord wants eight hundred a month, but he'll renovate and put in some extra toilets if we'll sign a two-year lease. Mrs. Malloy's got a list of potential customers. And the kindergarten teacher at P.S. 102 says they're throwing out some old tables and chairs. She'll let us have them for nothing, and with a little paint. . . ."

The two cops in the street were still struggling with the sprinkler cap, trying to talk to the kids at the same time. People were appearing in tenement windows, shouting opinions and advice. Frank's attention was riveted by the scene. He could not make out what was being shouted from the windows in rapid-fire Spanish, but it looked as if people were taking sides. Some shouted for the cops to leave the kids alone, others seemed to be complaining about the lack of water pressure and siding with the cops. A big Puerto Rican in a torn tee shirt emerged from the bodega on the corner, arms folded across his stomach, confronting the sweating cops in front of the hydrant. The kids gathered around him, and a heated exchange ensued. Frank cursed softly from the window, itching to get in on the action.

". . . and we can get arts-and-crafts stuff and coloring books at a terrific discount. And Mrs. Malloy's sister can run off copies of our brochure at her office and—Frank?"

She was staring at the back of his head. A voice on the PA announced that visiting hours were over. Helen grimaced. He hadn't heard any of it. It was probably just as well.

The two cops and the big Hispanic were still arguing, gesturing. One cop gave the final turn to the bolt that held the sprinkler cap in place, while the other gesticulated in the direction of the hospital. The first cop turned the water on again. Some of the kids were delighted; the bigger ones complained. The big man in the torn tee shirt said something that silenced them, then called up to an old woman with her head out the fourth-floor window of one of the tenements whose shrill voice had carried above the others during the worst of the confrontation. She stuck her head back into the apartment and was gone for some minutes. The people on the sidewalk were reduced to near-silence as they awaited her verdict.

"Frank?" Helen repeated, determined to get some response from him, whether it was in her favor or not. "If we can make this work, then I can bring little Frankie along with me. It won't start till September, so we'll have the whole summer to fix things up. Otherwise I'm going to have to sit home and do nothing until he's old enough to go to kindergarten. I don't have the patience for that anymore. Please tell me I can use what we have in savings, and we can borrow from your pension fund for emergencies? Please? I won't ever ask you for anything like this again."

The old woman emerged finally from her apartment, holding up a cup from which the water slopped visibly, indicating with toothless glee that the pressure had been restored. The man by the hydrant was satisfied. He shook hands with each of the cops in turn and went back to the bodega. Within minutes the squad car was gone and there was no one in the street but the half-naked kids frolicking in the sprinkler.

"It's a needed service in the neighborhood, Frank, and I'd rather see working mothers leave their kids with someone who'll play with them and teach them instead of sticking them in front of the boob tube all day. I know I can make it work, and it could turn out to be a nifty little investment. . . ."

"Mr. O'Dell?" It was the floor nurse, hovering in the doorway. "I'm sorry, but it's after five."

"Okay, sure." He nodded from the window. The scene below pleased him, though he was not about to retract any of his opinions about Hispanics. He turned to find Helen looking at him expectantly.

"Well, what do you think?" she demanded.

Frank exhaled profoundly. The nurse was still standing in the doorway, as if she fully intended to escort him to the elevators. "Honey, honest to God, I can't make heads or tails out of what you've been saying, but you sound so damn excited about it that I know I'm gonna come across as some kind of Scrooge if I try to put a damper on you. How much do you think you'll need?"

"Just five thousand," she said complacently.

"Ke-rist!" he breathed, looking at the nurse, getting agitated. He started toward the door, then came halfway back to where Helen was. "Hey, listen, we'll go over it again when I come tonight, but I have a hunch you've already talked me into it. Okay? See you later!"

Embarrassed by the nurse's presence, he gave Helen a quick peck on the forehead and was gone. Helen sat on the edge of the bed, hugging herself in silent glee.

The nursery school began to pay for itself in its second year. In addition to Helen and Mrs. Malloy—who did all of the administrative work as well as teaching—there was one other full-time teacher, and two mothers' helpers who came in the late afternoons to entertain the kids who stayed until their mothers got off the subway from work. The original storefront was expanded to the two stores on either side, providing three versatile play areas and office space. By the end of the third year, with the help of a small-business loan, Helen had parlayed a vacant lot on a nearby side street into a play area for a summer day camp. Frank and some of the men from the firehouse erected swing sets and constructed an in-ground wading pool, and neighborhood teenagers, including Helen's twins, were hired as camp counselors. Little Frankie scrambled around with the other kids, apparently content at being part of such a large extended family.

And on Labor Day, reluctantly and after an entire summer of wrangling, Helen and Frank and all five of their children, riding in the Volkswagen minibus that was the only thing large enough to accommodate them all comfortably, picked Kat up in the morning and drove to New Jersey because Danny and Paula had decided to have a barbecue.

Helen had not wanted to go, had suggested to Kat as far back as June that they should all be sensible and go to some nice air-conditioned restaurant for Labor Day, instead of sweltering in Danny's backyard all afternoon and fighting traffic back to the city that night. Kat wouldn't hear of it.

"Sure, what's left of the family, what with yer father gone and Johnny so far away and the rest of us all tore apart, ought to stick together on the holidays!" went the lament, and she was not to be moved.

"I'll drive her over that morning and come back," Frank had offered, as far back as June. "Then we can go out and have some peace. Or Vicki can take her car and stay over there with your mother. It'll be her good deed for the day. But why the hell do we all have to—"

"We'll see," was all Helen said, busy writing names in on the diplomas for her four-year-old graduates. "It's too early to get mixed up in that yet."

They had been to Danny and Paula's house only twice in all these years; their impression of the place had been dismal. The house was a converted bungalow built into the side of a cliff. For the first two years after they bought the place, Danny and Paula had no central heating, nothing but the fireplace in the living room to protect them from the ravages of North Jersey winters. Even now, after some renovations and an attempt at landscaping the front lawn, the house was still depressing. The cliff loomed ominously, shutting out the sun for most of the day, its badly eroded red clay face threatening to mud-slide straight through the kitchen after a spell of rain. The principal flora and fauna of the area were scrub pines and mosquitoes. No one relished the thought of spending the day huddled under that cliff, plagued by insects and the smoke from the barbecue grill, but Kat had her way.

"We'll humor her just this once," Helen reasoned, after turning it over in her mind all summer. "Then we'll have peace until Thanksgiving. It's worth it. What else does she have to look forward to?"

"Nothing!" Frank acknowledged, throwing up his hands, disgusted. "I'll give you that. She's got nothing at all to look forward to because that's the way she wants it. She'd rather accept a lot of phony buttering up from Danny and his wife than recognize that you've done your share and more for her all your life. I'll make you a fifty-dollar bet she's got him down for more than you in that will she keeps having changed every six months."

"Oh, for God's sake, Frank!" Helen grimaced at him. "That's not the point! Do you think I care about the few dollars she has to leave to me? I'd just once in my life like to hear a word of praise, or a real inquiry about what I'm doing with my life. If she'd ask me how the nursery school was doing, instead of pretending it doesn't exist because I should be home with my kids. If she cared about whether I'm happy with my life. Anything but 'And how are the children?' Period. One of these days she's going to have to recognize me for what I am."

"And you're going to get this by going to your brother's for Labor Day?" Frank was skeptical.

"No, of course not!" Helen said, though she was at a loss to explain her motivation. "It's a question of giving in once in a while to keep her pacified. It won't kill me."

Frank gave her a look. "I should've told her off years ago, when she wouldn't come to your graduation. I still should tell her off."

"It's a waste of time," Helen responded.

"And going to your brother's on Labor Day isn't, I suppose?"

"It'll keep her quiet until Thanksgiving," Helen said.

"Jesus!" he said.

". . . and you start any of this political garbage and I'm gonna give you a rap!" was Frank's advice, uncharacteristically harsh, to Kathleen before they got to her grandmother's house.

In her second year of college Kathleen had suddenly become a student radical. It was the first time she and her father became direct adversaries on any issue. He tolerated her funny clothes and her peace signs and her spending every waking hour signing petitions and handing out leaflets, but there was a limit. He would not allow any further disruption of a family gathering that promised nothing but turmoil from the outset.

Kathleen was riding shotgun in the minibus, jouncing along in the suicide seat across the stick shift from her father, map in hand, navigating. "I'm not going to start anything," she said grandly. "But I'm not going to sit still and listen to a lot of fascist bullshit all af—"

"And you watch your language in front of your grandmother!" her father said.

"Right, Chief!" she shot back, and they rode along in silence.

Helen sat behind Frank, the seat next to her—the one closest to the door—vacant and waiting for her mother. Kat always complained about the minibus, but she'd have to put up with it. It was her idea to bring all of the "children," even though all of them could have been left home.

Vicki sat by herself in the row behind Helen, a box of floral stationery in her lap, trying to jot down a few words between potholes to one of her legion of pen pals. She was writing, Helen knew, to two boys in the service, brothers of high school friends, who were in Vietnam. She also kept up a voluminous correspondence with her Uncle Johnny in Newfoundland. Helen did not know how or when that one had started. But, just as she had long ago forgiven her the incident with the contraceptives, Helen had also abandoned hope of ever deciphering Vicki.

In the back of the minibus, bouncing wildly on the almost springless seat, Frankie sat between the twins, alternately waving to trucks from the back window and climbing over the seats to sit first with his mother, then with Vicki, then back with the twins again. Maureen and Mary Fran giggled and gossiped for the entire trip, finishing each other's sentences and wearing out the pages of the newest issues of *Glamour* and *Seventeen*.

Everyone grew properly serious, of course, the minute Kat got into the minibus, helped up the steps by Frank. She adjusted her seat belt three times, complained about the bumps in the street, and fussily arranged on the floor at her feet the two tattered shopping bags she had brought, full of home-baked bread, back issues of the Brooklyn diocese's religious newspaper, *The Tablet*, and copies of the parish bulletin: inspirational reading for those in the family suspected of irreligious tendencies; she brought with her, too, the perpetual cloud of gloom she wore like a badge of distinction. Helen automatically tensed up, readying some strong ammunition in case her mother felt like picking a fight.

It didn't take long. They were not yet out of New York, barreling along the West Side Highway on the way to the George Washington Bridge, when Kat started.

"Sure, yer poor father, Lord have mercy on him, is only in his grave three years, and already ye've forgotten him!" she sighed. "I can't understand why yer couldn't find the time to take me to the cemetery on the anniversary of his passing!"

Helen gritted her teeth. Kathleen and Frank, in the front of the 'bus where Kat could not see their faces, stifled grins. Even politics couldn't divide them when it came to their opinion of Kat. Vicki, behind her, was pretending not to hear. Helen met the challenge head-on.

"It was the middle of the week, Mom," she pointed out. "I was working at the day camp. I explained it to you well ahead of time. And we went to the cemetery the following Sunday."

"It's not the same, then!" her mother wailed. She had had a month and a half to brood over it, undistracted by anything else, since her life, by her own choice, was so exceedingly dull. "Sure, it's not the same as bein' there on the very day of his passing! I'd like to know which is more important: whatever it is yer doin' all week instead of bein' home to look after yer children—"

"Why didn't you go to see Aunt Ag when she was in the hospital?" Helen countered, cutting right across her mother's monologue.

Frank and Kathleen looked at each other. Uh-oh! Frank took the approach ramp for the bridge and braced for battle.

"Ag and me is not speakin' one to the other," Kat declared. "And it's none of yer concern!"

"But she's your only sister," Helen said. "And it was a very serious stroke. Alistair says she could have died."

"Yer'll not mention that—person's—name in my hearing!" Kat retorted.

"He's staying with her now, since she's home from the hospital," Helen continued, relentless. "He says she's like a child. He has to feed her and help her dress and—"

"Then it's no less than he deserves, with the sinful life he's after livin'!" Kat said smugly, justified.

Helen had saved the cruelest blow for last. "He says Aunt Ag's been asking for you. He says when she's lucid and she can talk a little, she cries because you won't come to see her. He says she talks about the times when you were younger and she took care of you when you first came to the States. . . ."

Helen let her voice drift off, for she could see the effect her words were having on her mother. For the briefest of moments Kat's pinched face showed signs of some inner wrestling with conscience. Then she adjusted herself in her seat with a sigh.

"Sure, it's good to know Ag's after developin' a conscience," she announced to the Hudson River beyond the window of the 'bus and the girders of the bridge. "She never had when she was a girl, then."

At least Danny no longer tried to hide his drinking. The bottle of Johnny Walker and the Styrofoam ice bucket were sitting plunk in the middle of the picnic table when Frank pulled the minibus up onto the gravel of the driveway. A rancid odor of charcoal with too much starter fluid greeted the O'Dell clan as they clambered stiff-legged out onto the damp grass. Kathleen of the weak bladder bolted for the bathroom, while everyone else stood around awkwardly, playing at family reunion. Kat gushed over the rosebushes fighting for survival in the red, clayey soil along the rustic fence. After a while everyone broke up into little artificial clumps: Frank and Danny laboring over the charcoal, Helen and Paula puttering aimlessly in the cluttered and dirty kitchen, the younger generation sprawling on the grass making conversation. Kat sat in a lawn chair, isolated, a dowager empress bereft of empire. She would not help in the kitchen, would not participate in conversations that did not concern religion, sickness, or death; and if she expected homage from her progeny, no one was about to make the first move. Eventually, Vicki got her a glass of lemonade and tried to talk to her.

"What's this I hear about you going to graduate school?" Paula wanted to know, carrying macaroni salad to the picnic table, licking mayonnaise off her thumb. Her voice was more strident than it needed to be. "You're gonna be a what—a librarian?"

"I'll be taking courses in library science, yes," Vicki said, dutiful as always. "It's a field where there are always opportunities."

"Yeah, but you're not going to work or anything?" Paula's tone was accusatory. Imperceptibly over the past decade, her figure had begun to spoil; she was now a solid mass from shoulders to hips, with no indication that she had ever had a waist. She wore too much makeup. "I mean, four years of college and then graduate school? Who's paying for all this?"

Vicki looked embarrassed. Money, like sex, was one of those topics polite people didn't discuss in public. Her father bailed her out.

"I am!" Frank said loudly from his place by the grill. "As far as I'm concerned, my kids get the best education I can afford to give them."

"Oh, but those colleges are such a money-grubbing racket, though, aren't they?" Paula objected, loudly enough to be heard three houses down. "Daniel and I have decided to take out National Defense loans for our girls. Then when they're graduated and out working they can pay them back themselves."

"Or their husbands can," Frank said sarcastically, understanding now why Danny and Paula's elder daughter, who was starting college the following week, looked so sullen all the time. Frank would have said more about his brother-in-law's stinginess, but a look from Helen silenced him.

"Well, we don't all have money coming out our ass!" Danny remarked, pouring himself another scotch.

It was the first of many such comments from him in the course of the afternoon. His style as a drunk had changed. Gone was the holiday atmosphere that spiraled down into the endless monologue on what was wrong with the world. It had been replaced by a moody silence punctuated by what Danny thought were pithy statements. Frank let most of them go by, for his wife's sake, but his patience was wearing thin.

After they had eaten their half-raw, half-charred hamburgers and lukewarm salad, Danny started on politics.

"I hear your carrot-top's turned into a hippie," he said, addressing Frank. He had abandoned scotch for beer, but was no less obnoxious.

Kathleen and the other girls were playing a halfhearted game of croquet against the face of the cliff, trying to make the hours pass less slowly. She heard her uncle's remark—it wasn't difficult, considering his volume—and unbent from where she was about to take a shot at Maureen's ball, mouth open. Her father gave her a look.

"Last I heard, this was a free country," Frank said evenly, wanting to defuse this one before he was called upon to defend his daughter's views, which were not his own.

"Either of mine started that bullshit I'd take 'em over my knee, big as they are!" Danny roared. Whether or not he did hit his daughters was a moot point; the tone of his voice was enough to cow them. "Popping drugs and screwing around. Long-haired freaks! Commie weirdos! No sir, not my kids!"

Helen was in the kitchen when this one began. Even Kat had roused herself enough to pick up a dishtowel. With no women in his immediate vicinity, Danny felt free to express himself. Helen dried her hands and stood with the screen door half-open, ready to interfere. Frank leaned back and spoke to her over his shoulder.

"You're letting the bugs in!" he said, which was his way of telling her to butt out. Helen slammed the door and went back to the dishes. Frank turned his attention back to his brother-in-law. "The way I see it, a kid's got strong convictions and you try to beat 'em out of her, she's gonna develop a martyr complex. Get her back up and come on stronger than ever. I figure if I leave her alone maybe she'll grow out of it."

"My ass!" Danny pulled himself to his feet, swaying a little, pounding the hand with the two missing fingers on the picnic table. "That's why this whole generation's a waste. Parents're too goddamn soft on 'em. You know how many drug addicts there are in this country today?"

No one had seen Kathleen come closer, her croquet mallet over her shoulder, casual. Both men were startled when she spoke.

"About one million," she said quietly, her chin stuck out in a way she'd had since she was a child. "One for every ten drunks."

She had turned on her heel and gone back to the game, cracking Maureen's ball into the underbrush near the cliff, before Danny reacted.

"You little snot-nose!" he roared, all the blood rushing to his face. He started toward her, but Frank stood suddenly and restrained him.

"Ease off!" he said, sotto voce but ominously. "Ease off or you'll have another blackout."

"I don't have no fucking blackouts!" Danny bellowed, trying to bull his way past. "That little shit of yours insulted me, and I'm gonna straighten her out!"

Paula and Helen were both at the screen door now, helpless to interfere. The croquet game had stopped abruptly. Everyone was motionless. Only Kat, who had gone to the bathroom some minutes before, had no idea that anything was going on.

If Frank's self-control had been extraordinary before, it was superhuman now. He ignored the insults against his daughter and himself. He was a professional—the Chief, the smoke eater, rescuer of babies and calmer of hysterics. He held Danny's arm.

"Listen, it's hot. You been breaking your balls over that barbecue all day. What say you and me go drive around a little—"

"Fuck off!" Danny snarled, shaking him off and slamming into the house, pushing the two women out of his way.

The bedroom windows were open, and he could be heard throwing things and cursing. When his mother at last emerged from the bathroom, he pushed her aside, slammed the door, and locked himself in. Little Frankie, who had been playing around the side of the house, came running.

"Daddy! Daddy!" he shrieked. "Is a monster in the baf-room!"

Frank got to the bathroom door first, heard Danny's desperate gasping, and waved everyone else back into the living room with his arm. He braced himself against the wall and kicked the bathroom door in.

"Kath!" he bellowed, seeing Danny's distended, purple face pressed against the medicine chest, distorted further by the mirror. "Everybody else out! And stay!"

"You heard him!" Kathleen shrieked, pushing past them as they huddled in the hallway. She all but threw her grand-mother into Vicki's arms. "Outside! He's prob'ly having a heart attack!"

Kat began to wail, and it took Helen and Vicki to half-carry her out to the yard. They stood around aimlessly, wait-ing for some clue from inside the house.

Frank half-dragged Danny into the hall; there wasn't enough space in the bathroom to stretch him out. By now Danny's heart had stopped, his face turned grayish-blue.

"CPR!" Frank ordered Kathleen—he'd trained her in

coronary resuscitation himself—and he began mouth-to-mouth breathing while she started chest pressure, kneeling over her uncle and pressing rhythmically on his sternum with both hands.

"Switch!" Frank gasped after a full minute, and put his ear to Danny's chest. There was a heartbeat, faint and erratic. When Kathleen was fully engaged in mouth-to-mouth breathing, Frank took up the chest pressure while giving her rapid instructions. "Okay. When I call 'Switch' again, let me take over. You go out and tell your aunt to get a neighbor—some big guy who can help me carry him. Better yet, let your cousins go. There's two of 'em and they can run faster. Tell Paula to call the hospital, let 'em know we're coming. Then you start the 'bus and fold down the seats in the back. Got it?" She looked up at him, acknowledging. "Good. Ready? Switch!"

Kathleen drove, the minibus careening wildly down the hilly North Jersey roads, her tearful cousin in the suicide seat giving directions. Frank continued cardiopulmonary resuscitation until they got to the hospital.

But ten minutes into the emergency room, Danny was dead.

"What is it with us lately? Seems like we only meet at wakes." Alistair sat beside Helen, massaging her free hand where it rested on the arm of her chair.

Helen's other hand shielded her eyes from the funeral parlor lights, dimmed to a subterranean quality but painful to her all the same, for she had been crying nonstop since they'd gotten home from Danny's that horrible night. Not crying for Danny, surely, because he was and had always been not just a stranger but a hostile stranger. Helen was crying for the incredible waste of it, of a human being who could not find his place in the scheme of things drinking himself to death at an early age. Danny had been inconsiderate enough to leave no will, disregarding the needs of his wife, his daughters, and his poor half-crazy mother. Rage, not sorrow, had made Helen cry until her eyes felt gritty and inflamed, and any sound over a whisper made her jump out of her skin.

"Forty years old," Alistair mused. "Je-*sus*, it's enough to make a man stop and think. Hell, I'm only a year younger'n him myself!"

"And I'm nearly two older," Helen reminded him, her voice hoarse from exhaustion. "Only neither of us is hell-bent on self-destruction."

"Quite right," Alistair acknowledged. "God, if I was that anxious to cash in, I'd do it clean. All my affairs in order, then Zap! Pills'd be my thing. I'm a total coward."

Helen gave him a dull look.

"Sorry," he said, looking sheepish. "Occupational hazard among us queers, didn't you know that?"

Helen continued to look at him. She was too tired to counter his self-effacing put-downs this time.

"What'd the doctor say it was?" Alistair asked finally, withdrawing his hand from hers and opening a fresh pack of Players.

"Massive coronary," Helen answered, pulling herself up a little in the chair and rubbing her eyes. "Doctor said how his heart gave out before his liver was beyond him. Also couldn't understand why it was the heart and not the diabetes that got him. He said he was done for, no matter what. And you can't smoke in here."

"Right!" Alistair nodded, putting the cigarettes away. "How come you brought him back to the neighborhood to be waked? Aren't they going to bury him in Jersey?"

Helen nodded wearily. She'd had to explain this arrangement to at least fifty people already. "It was a compromise to keep Mom happy. Also, Paula and—and my brother didn't have too many friends in New Jersey, so we thought we'd get a better showing if we brought him back to Brooklyn. And the funeral mass will be at Mom's church, but then they're driving him back to the cemetery in New Jersey. Mom got hysterical over that, wanted him put in the family plot, but it was Paula's decision. We had a little hassle getting him brought across the state line twice, but Frank had a few connections through the Department, so that saved a lot of red tape. So tomorrow it'll all be over. Except for the bills. He owed everybody. He never made a will. The whole thing's a mess, and I don't want to talk about it anymore!"

"Okay," Alistair said, getting up. "Time I went inside with the body and comforted the bereaved widow."

"Stay!" Helen pleaded, putting a hand on his arm. "Keep me company so I don't have to talk to any of Mom's church friends. They're all here from the Rosary Society just like they were at Pop's wake, and I'm going to flatten the next one who comes near me!"

Alistair sat down again. "Where is your mother, by the by? I thought she was just avoiding me, but Frank says she won't be here all night."

"No, she won't!" Helen said, too harshly. "Because I got the doctor to knock her out last night and tonight, and I'll do it tomorrow if I have to, because I will not have any more dramatics!"

"She's home in bed, in other words." Alistair's voice was soothing.

"Yes," Helen said, collapsing back against the chair. "Johnny flew down yesterday. He and Vicki are over at the house keeping an eye on her."

"No kidding! Say, how is the little squirt?" Alistair grinned at the mention of Johnny's name, and still seemed to think of him as a kid.

"The 'little squirt' is twenty-six years old," Helen reminded him. "He's getting gray hair already."

"Oh, come on!" Alistair said, but Helen nodded in confirmation. "How about that? He'll end up one of those gorgeous white-haired Irishmen. Brother John. I can't get over it! Why is it the ones who don't need the good looks always get them?"

They laughed a little; it was the first time in three days

Helen had found anything funny. But she grew serious again. "How's Aunt Ag?" she asked. "I'm sorry, I should have asked you the minute you—"

Alistair shook his head. "Not good. She's no longer in the present. Rambles on about childhood when she can talk. Rest of the time she just sits. She's got to have someone feed her, take care of all the personal things. And she's got a strong constitution. Could go on for years, having these little strokes, living like a child. It's pitiful!"

"And you're taking care of her alone?" Helen was more than a little shocked. "You could hire a practical nurse. I know she had a lot of money put aside."

"No need." Alistair's words were clipped, as if several people had given him this argument and he'd memorized his defense. "I've quit work altogether. Me and a—friend—were sort of shacking it before Ag got sick, so now he's just moved in to her place with me. Matter of fact, I met him through Ag. He's a stockbroker. Handled her portfolio for years. Real three-piece-suit type. Never pick him for a fag in a million years. So now I stay home with Ag round the clock, and he earns the living for all of us. Just one big, happy family."

Helen stared at him throughout this narrative, amazed at how everything seemed to have fallen into place for him. One big, happy family, she thought. Exactly what Alistair's always needed.

"It's marvelous, what you're doing for Aunt Ag," she said sincerely, looking up at him as he strove to make his exit again.

"Don't go getting mushy on me," he cautioned, squeezing her hand and backing away toward the door.

"Don't be a stranger!" Helen called after him.

Alistair turned in the doorway. "Not anymore." He grinned.

Vicki sat stiffly in a straight-backed chair in her grandmother's room, tremendously uncomfortable but not about to move. Her grandmother's rhythmic breathing was hypnotic.

She would continue to breathe like this all night, whether Vicki sat with her or not. There was no reason at all why Vicki couldn't leave the old woman alone and go inside. No reason at all except Johnny.

Vicki had chosen the uncomfortable chair on purpose, even though Johnny offered to move one of the armchairs in from the parlor. Whenever he came by the bedroom door to see if she needed anything—and he came by often—Vicki pretended to be absorbed in her rosary and refused to answer his inquiries. When he passed on to the refrigerator or went back to the parlor, she let the beads drop into her lap, though she did not relax her painful posture in the chair. Vicki was doing a kind of self-imposed penance, because if she didn't exert absolute control over her emotions she was going to march into the parlor and put her fist through the television. And then, she thought, it was possible she might kill Johnny.

More conflicting emotions were screaming and tearing at each other in Vicki's breast at this moment than she thought she could possibly possess. What had started out as simple solicitude for her hapless grandmother, and the dreadful fear that Uncle Danny had died in a state of sin, had focused into rage, into pure murderous hatred against her beloved Uncle Johnny. Because Johnny was sitting in the parlor drinking beer and watching a baseball game, while his only brother lay in state in the funeral chapel only a block away.

This was only a small example of his overall disdain for the way things ought to be done. He had come down from St. John's on the plane wearing his clerical habit, but abandoned it the minute he arrived at his mother's house. He sat around in a pair of torn jeans and an Iona College sweatshirt, while the Rosary Society ladies, expecting a somber and pious young Brother John in full clerical regalia, were met at the door by an affable college kid in old sneakers. The Rosary Society ladies were universally scandalized, and so was Vicki.

She was scandalized, and worried, because Johnny wearing his habit was someone she could deal with: a member of a religious order, therefore a neuter and harmless person. Johnny out of uniform was a definitively male, hence alarming, person. Vicki did not know how to deal with men. She reacted to Frank by mothering him, knowing he favored Kathleen, but no longer resenting it. She dated boys from her college now and then, but always "safe" ones, the kind who didn't mind escorting her and footing the bill while she casually but firmly removed their hands from hers at dinner or in the theater. She would not allow herself to be threatened. Every man she knew must stand comparison with Johnny, and none of them could measure up.

So as much as she hated him at this moment, she was still drawn to Johnny, with a will-lessness that terrified her. If only he would wear his habit, define the distance between them. . . .

Vicki got to the end of her rosary somehow, and knew that her back could take no more punishment. She would have to find somewhere else to hide in the big, dismal railroad flat, but somewhere conspicious enough to force him to confront her, so that she could tell him off for his lack of decorum. Blessing herself and tucking the rosary into its little plastic case, which would in turn fit into a zippered compartment in her well-ordered purse, Vicki stood painfully. She gave her sleeping grandmother a dutiful kiss on the forehead and crept out to the kitchen, feeling somehow that she, not Johnny, was the transgressor.

She went to the refrigerator for a glass of milk. She found it—several days old and not quite fresh. Vicki winced when she tasted it, and contrary to her parsimonious nature, poured the contents of her glass and the container into the sink, then systematically checked to see what her grandmother was eating. There were perhaps a dozen bowls of nondescript left-overs: the stubborn regimen of someone unused to convenience foods or living alone, refusing to alter her life-style. Vicki gave up trying to determine what was in any of the bowls; she was naturally squeamish, and unless she was prepared to throw everything out, was really in no position to meddle. She would have to remind her mother to pick up some things after the funeral tomorrow. Besides, she was avoiding the inevitable, and she knew it. She must have it out with Johnny, and never mind taking inventory in her grandmother's refrigerator. Bracing herself for battle, she wended her way through the poor-smelling, unlit rooms to where the television glowed enticingly in the parlor. She reached the doorway in time to hear the crowd on the screen erupt wildly, and to see Johnny leap out of his seat with excitement.

"All right! Way to go!" he roared at the screen. He caught sight of Vicki out of the corner of his eye and became slightly subdued. "Hey, they did it! They're ahead by one run! God, how I've missed baseball!" He saw the look on Vicki's face—misinterpreted it. "Am I being too loud? I'm sorry! I'll lower it, if you think it'll wake her."

"Doesn't matter," Vicki said icily. "She'll sleep through anything tonight. And it's just as well."

"Yeah," Johnny said, his eyes drifting back to the screen. Vicki sat on the edge of the couch, seething, until the commercials came on. With the strength of martyrs to fortify her, she reached over and turned off the set.

"Hey!" Johnny objected, reaching past her to turn it on again. "It's only the top of the fourth! What's the big—"

"And your only brother is dead," Vicki hissed, blocking the control panel so he couldn't reach it. "Aren't you *ashamed?*"

"Ashamed?" Johnny echoed, then leaned away from the television and studied her. "Oh-ho! So that's what's been burning your cork all night. Why should I be ashamed? Was I responsible for his death? If you want to lay blame on someone, try putting it on Danny, or on a family situation that started before I was born, but don't try to pin anything on me."

"That's not what I mean," Vicki began, trying to be stern, but her usual clipped sentences were softening into something that made her extremely uneasy.

"Oh, I know what you mean!" Johnny said. "You expect

me to moan and wring my hands and shed a few manly tears
for the Rosary Society ladies to see, and then I'm supposed to
promenade around in my Sunday suit talking about God's
will and being generally ponderous. I'm sorry, Miss Victoria,
but I'm a Christian Brother, not an actor. Or a hypocrite."

Vicki started to splutter, but nothing coherent came out.
Johnny went on.

"You want to look at it from my perspective? All I remember of Danny from my childhood was an overweight bully
who farted a lot—mostly in my direction—and who got a
thrill out of pulling my hair or stealing a favorite toy to see
if he could make me cry. The thing is, I never would cry, and
that made him furious. By the time I grew up he was gone,
first into the navy, then married and out of the house. I never
had time to get to know anything but his bad side. He must
have had some good points, but he kept them well hidden
from me. So if I'm supposed to miss him, or feel somehow
bereft, I hate to tell you I don't. I'm sorry for Paula and the
kids, but I have a feeling that in the long run they're better off
without Danny. As for Mom—I know this is going to sound
heartless, but I've come to the conclusion that she's happiest
when she's most miserable. She hasn't had anything to cry
over since Dad died. And if she can't see her part in the mess
of Danny's life, then so much the worse for her. Maybe now
that her darling's out of the way she'll have a little time for
her other kids."

There was pain in his voice as he said this—even Vicki
recognized it—but he tried to talk it away.

"Besides," he said, wrapping up his lecture, "we're supposed
to be Christians. If we truly believe in the message of Christ's
death and resurrection, then we have to believe that Danny is
on his way to his eternal reward, and instead of moaning and
groaning we should drink and dance and rejoice. Do I detect
in your long face, Miss Victoria, a lack of faith in the message
of Christ?"

He was mocking her, and Vicki exploded. "How dare you

question my belief?" she flared. "I simply feel that out of deference for your mother and the rest of the family, you have an obligation—"

"To play-act deep sorrow at the loss of my dear, departed brother," Johnny finished for her, dripping sarcasm. "Sorry about that. I told you, I'm no actor."

He reached past her to turn the television on again, then changed his mind. He sat and stared at the thwarted and silent Vicki until she became absolutely uncomfortable.

"Avoiding all the old hens wasn't the only reason I volunteered to stay over here with you," Johnny said meaningfully. "I think it's time we had it out about your letters."

Vicki stumbled out a few words, looked embarrassed, tried again.

"I wasn't myself when I wrote that last one," she managed to say. He had not answered her last letter, written over three months ago, and Vicki knew why. "I . . . I don't know what happened. The strain of school or something. I didn't mean what I said in that letter. I was angry with you—wanted to make you react, I guess. I wish you'd give it back to me."

"What would you do with it if I did?" Johnny asked carefully.

"Burn it!" Vicki said vehemently. "Tear it into little pieces! Destroy it."

Johnny pondered a moment. "Scared yourself that time, didn't you?"

Vicki did not answer right away. "Yes," she said at last.

"Can I tell you something?" Johnny ventured gently, and waited for her to nod her assent. "This is going to sound like another lecture, but here goes anyway. Now, you don't need me to tell you that you are an intelligent, well-educated Catholic young lady. What you may not know—hey, let me finish—is that you're also very attractive, and shouldn't have any trouble meeting interesting young men, except that for some reason I cannot understand you always freeze up and block them out. Now, in spite of your torrid prose, I can't seriously believe it's because of me. I mean, you and I practically grew up together. If I were your actual brother, the incest angle would steer you off immediately, but because I'm your uncle it's once removed, so you think it's all right. I'm also under vows, which makes me doubly safe. Don't you see what you're doing? You aren't really 'in love' with me, no matter what you said in your letter. You're using me as a shield, to protect you from having to deal with men outside there in the real world. You're creating a hermit's cell for yourself, Vicki, and not a very comfortable one. You make up this fantasy about being in love with me because you know nothing will ever come of it, and then you don't have to deal with forming relationships and worrying about people's feelings, and sex—"

"Are you quite through?" Vicki's voice was like ice.

"I guess so," Johnny admitted, shrugging.

"Good!" Vicki said. "Because there is no reason why I have to sit here and listen to this filth for another min—"

"Oh, but I thought you wanted your letter back." Johnny grinned, turning on the handsome-Irish-boy charm. "Speaking of filth."

"Did you bring it? Do you have it with you?" Vicki was suddenly animated, all but tugging at his arm the way she did as a little girl, before she became so inhibited.

Johnny pulled something out of the pocket of his jeans and half-handed it to her. When she tried to snatch it from him he held it tightly by one corner, looking her straight in the eye.

"What is it?" he pleaded, allowing himself more genuine feeling than he could with anyone else. "What frightens you so? Can you tell me about it?"

Vicki withdrew. Physically, she let go of the letter and shrank back on the couch. Mentally, she was farther away than ever. Johnny watched her for some moments, giving her one last chance to come out of her hiding place; then he got up and left the room. The letter lay on the coffee table.

The funeral director was getting impatient. The parlor was supposed to close at nine o'clock exactly. The family in the adjacent chapel was already gone; the lights on that side of the building were off, the corpse left in quiet until morning. But the Manning party, at least the immediate family, was still here, and showed no sign of imminent departure, even though it was nearly nine-fifteen. The funeral director, son-in-law of the late Mr. Kelly who had managed Helen's grandmother's wake so long ago, kept clearing his throat and rocking on his heels in the foyer, hoping someone would get the hint. Helen roused herself from her reverie, realized how late it was, and got up to set things in order.

The place was virtually empty. The last of the Rosary Society ladies, the parish priest, and a boy who had been on Danny's football team in high school—now a balding real estate agent—had passed out the front door moments ago. Frank was nowhere in sight. It occurred to Helen that she had seen him sneaking out with Alistair, probably for a much-needed drink. He deserved that much, she thought, considering how much had fallen on his shoulders in the past few days. Her girls and Paula's, grateful to escape, had been sent to the bakery for cake. They would all go back to Helen's house for coffee once they got out of here. There was no one left in the funeral parlor except Helen, Paula, and—

And the unidentified man who had been monopolizing Paula's attention for a good part of the evening. They sat there now, in the shadow of Danny's casket, their heads close together, talking. Looking closer, Helen could see that his hand rested on Paula's knee.

He was distinguished-looking, graying at the temples, not yet fifty. A businessman. Danny's employer? A neighbor? Someone, at any rate, Helen thought, trying not to think of the obvious, who had come to comfort Paula in her hour of need. Helen was not about to get embroiled in this. At least, she thought wryly, if he was what he seemed to be in Paula's life, he might have enough money to put her kids through college without National Defense loans.

Standing in the doorway, Helen coughed softly. Paula jumped to her feet as if someone had stuck her with a pin, guilty. Helen simply pointed to her watch and slipped back out to the foyer, looking for the shoes she had kicked off when Alistair was there. In spite of her stupor, she couldn't help feeling a little smug. She had caught her sister-in-law with her guard down, and while she had no intention of doing anything about it, she knew she had the power to keep Paula guessing. That in itself could be most useful.

By the time Helen had found her shoes and was ready to leave, Paula's gentleman friend was gone. Paula stood uneasily by the front door, nervously twisting the short hair at the back of her neck.

"The girls went out for cake," she said, her normally strident voice tempered a little by the surroundings. "I told them to wait for us at your mom's. You coming with me?"

"In a while," Helen said, noting that Paula couldn't meet her eyes. "I'm going for a walk. Clear my head."

They stepped onto the sidewalk, much to the relief of the funeral director, who locked the door behind them, and stood on the corner.

"Are you sure you oughta?" Paula's voice was louder to match the outdoors. "I mean, all the Spics in this neighborhood—you could get raped or something."

"I'm not going far," Helen said, lacking the strength to correct Paula's prejudices, doubting it would do any good. "I'll stay near the church. You go ahead. I'll see you in ten minutes."

She crossed the street without giving Paula a chance to object and began to walk rapidly, her high heels clicking sharply on the sidewalk. She had to get away, had to be completely alone for the first time since her brother had had the bad manners to drop dead, had to escape from the decisions she must make for her mother and Paula and everybody else who was incapable of thinking in a crisis and who therefore leaned on her until she thought she'd sink right into the ground under their weight. She had to shake off the replay of Moday night's trip back to Brooklyn after they got word from the hospital that Danny was dead—the scene that had been running through her head, whole chunks of footage missing, since it had happened.

The blank patches frightened Helen. She could not remember how they managed to leave Paula and the girls alone and get into the minibus to go home. The next day Frank told her that Paula's older brother had come to look after her; Helen had no recollection of calling him, or of seeing him arrive. She could not remember how they convinced Kat to come home instead of sitting in Paula's living room wailing for attention, which was all she had done while Frank and Kathleen were at the hospital with Danny. Possibly Vicki had something to do with it. Helen vaguely remembered Vicki helping her grandmother onto the 'bus, her arms around the old woman's shoulder, her mouth at Kat's ear, ready with words of comfort. And, yes—a blank patch suddenly coming clear—Vicki and Kat had recited the rosary, over and over again between sobs, all the way home. Thank God for Vicki's peculiar brand of religion at such times, Helen thought. The droning of their voices had been part of the fabric of the journey home: the twins somber, and for once silent, in the back, Kathleen and Frank arguing, but inaudibly, in the front. Helen sat with Frankie on her lap, vaguely watching the underbrush whirr past on the lightless New Jersey highway, unaware that her silent tears were dripping down her chin and into the sleeping boy's grass-smelling hair. Frankie was not yet three, had not understood what had happened that afternoon, and now he slept, untroubled, his grass-stained bare legs swinging rhythmically as the 'bus jounced along. Helen cradled the sweaty, sweet-smelling warmth of him, trying to think that her brother Danny had once been something small and lovable

like this, long before he had somehow ended up as this afternoon's purple-faced monster. What was the weakness in the
male of the species, and how could she prevent Frankie—
slightly spoiled even now—from turning out like his uncle?
Helen cried into her baby's hair, frightened for the first time
in her childbearing life of what she might be doing wrong in
the raising of her children. Girls were easy, because girls were
recognizable, similar beings, but boys. . . .

And what had Frank and Kathleen been arguing about?
Helen had caught only a few words that night, disoriented
as she was, but now, in the clarity of the September evening,
as she realized she had walked as far as the Sons of Norway
hall some ten blocks from the church, she began fitting the
remembered dialogue together, understanding it.

"Aw, come on, don't gimme that shit!" Frank said, not
taking his eyes off the road.

"It's true though," Kathleen retorted, and there were tears
in her voice if not on her face. "If I hadn't called him a
drunk—"

"He woulda picked a fight with somebody else and croaked
just the same," Frank growled, taking a curve faster than
necessary. "You didn't kill him, so cut out the self-pity
routine. I don't buy that crap, so you're not getting any
sympathy outta me. Your Uncle Danny was in the process of
killing himself before you were born. You just happened to
be there on the day he picked to finish the job."

"But, Jesus, the look on his face!" Kathleen covered her own
face with her hands and was silent for a moment. "I don't
think I've ever seen such hate!"

"That was self-hate, kiddo," Frank said, chancing a sideways look at her face before squinting at the road again. "Let
me tell you something about that guy, something you maybe
didn't want to see because he was your uncle—someone you
were supposed to look up to and all that. He was a diabetic.

He knew that, but he wrecked his health anyway. He was overweight, and he never did anything about it. And the topper is he was an alcoholic. You care to know how many times he lost his job on account of that? And him with a wife— and I'm not crazy about her, but let's face it, she's got as much right to a decent life as anybody—and two kids to support. But the way he saw it, it was his life and he could do what he damn well pleased with it. For whatever reason (and your mother's told me some pretty hair-raising stories about the way they grew up) Danny never gave a shit about anybody but himself. The world was always out to get him. He had a lot of hate in him. And neither you nor anybody else was re-sponsible for that. So you had nothing to do with his croaking, Toots. You were what they call an innocent bystander."

They had crossed the bridge back into Manhattan during this speech, and the highway lights played wildly on Kathleen's silent, troubled face.

"I wish I could believe that," she said with a great shudder-ing sigh.

"Believe it, Toots," Frank said, leaning on the horn as someone tried to cut in front of him. "I know all there is to know about drunks. You got it straight from the source."

So there, Helen thought. She had it all straightened out now. She turned on her heel just before she got to the BMT subway tracks, and started the long trek back to her mother's house. She could look forward to a period of great difficulty now. Kat's melancholy would certainly not be improved with Danny gone. Johnny could take the weight off a little bit while he was home for the summer, but once he went back to New-foundland the burden would be all hers again. She thought of her childhood and her ever-present grandmother, tried to imagine what form of insanity would permit her to take Kat in to live with them. No, she decided, listening to the clatter of her own heels on the sidewalk. No house was big enough to hold three generations of *this* family. She could tolerate the daily phone calls and the almost-weekly crises, but Kat would stay in her own house and Helen in hers.

It was less than four months before Paula and her gentleman friend announced their engagement. A month later they were married. Helen and Frank went to the wedding out of politeness. Kat boycotted it, and ranted and raved for weeks. Within six weeks of the wedding, Paula gave birth to a son, Danny's posthumous legacy, whose existence she had not had time to announce on that chaotic Labor Day. Her new husband adopted all three children. Kat came to the conclusion, quite on her own and without any suggestion from anyone else, that the new baby was not Danny's at all, and a great deal of name-calling ensued. Paula and her new husband moved to another town without leaving a forwarding address, and Kat went to the storefront lawyer to have her will changed yet again.

"I've got a class at three," Kathleen said, getting out of bed first and collecting her clothes from the heap she had left them in on the floor.

"Can't you cut?" he asked, stretching, then tucking the sheet back around his waist, his hands clasped behind his head, relaxed.

Kathleen stood at the foot of the bed, her clothes bunched together in front of her chest, her sandals in her hand. "I could," she said, considering it. "But I don't want to. I *like* this class."

"Better than you like me?" He grinned, teasing her.

"Gerry, I've been here two hours," she said, irritated. "Enough already! I arranged my whole schedule this semester so the afternoons are free and you're still not satisfied. You I can see any time, but this class is something special."

She sailed off to the bathroom to get dressed, and he got out of bed, slipped into his shorts, and stood looking out the dirty window at the street. " 'Enough already,' " he imitated her. "It must be contagious."

Kathleen was running the water in the bathroom and couldn't hear him. "What?" she yelled, coming back into the room, zipping her jeans and frowning.

"I said you're beginning to sound Jewish," he explained, kissing the frown lines between her eyebrows.

"I wasn't trying to make fun of you, if that's what you think," she said, frowning harder.

"Is that what I said?" he asked. "You're getting paranoid."

"I'm sorry!" She put her arms around his neck and nuzzled into the hair on his chest.

"Hey, we gotta forget about this ethnic stuff and stick together," he said, stroking her hair. "I mean, we're all hippie commie weirdo freaks, no matter what our nationality, right? It's us against them, all the way."

"Gerry, you're weird!" Kathleen snorted, giggling into his ribs.

"Okay," he said. "So you'd rather hang out in school than stay with me. I can dig it. You better get your ass out of here or you'll be late. See you at the Peace Fellowship this afternoon or what?"

"I'll be a little late," Kathleen said, brushing the rats' nests out of her hair at the mirror. "Gotta sign out the mimeo machine for four, run off this week's newsletter. After that I'll get there."

"Right," Gerry said, sitting on the bed again. "But watch yourself with that machine. Hear you can get a nice high from the fumes."

"I should live so long!" Kathleen made a face at him.

"See? There you go again!" he said, shaking his head. "You're already half a convert."

"Fuck you!" Kathleen said affectionately. "Say, you think you people have a patent on the language or something?" She gave him a quick kiss. "Catch you later!"

"Not if I catch you first!" he called after her as she slammed out the door.

"Gerald. That's a fine Irish name," Frank said the first time Kathleen mentioned his name.

"He's not Irish, Dad," Kathleen said, jumping in, as usual, with both feet. "He's Jewish."

"Oh," Frank said nothing else for some moments. It wasn't easy. He was an honest man, had always been up-front about his prejudices. And no matter whom his favorite daughter brought home for dinner, he was apt to be disgruntled. "You're not—serious about him, are you?"

"Oh, hell no!" Kathleen lied, tossing her head nervously. Her father would probably kill her if he knew the truth. "We're just friends. We met at the Peace Fellowship symposium, and I enjoy talking to him, that's all. I don't have time to get married now. I've got a career to work on first. I just thought you might like to meet him. He's very intelligent, and I think you'd get some stimulating conversation out of him."

"Is this another one of your Convert the Old Warhorse projects?" Frank was bemused. "Sorry, Toots. You and your hippie friends can't make a dent in an old hawk like me."

"Never thought I could," Kathleen retorted; she enjoyed sparring with her father, even if she never won. "Anyway, if you saw Gerry on the street you'd take him for a Polack or a Kraut. Blue eyes, blond hair, and his nose is shorter than mine. No side curls, no yarmulke. You don't have to get uptight about the neighbors."

"Smart-ass!" her father said, grazing her jaw with his fist, glad to see she was no longer brooding over the events at her uncle's last summer. "I'm concerned about you, about making sure you get a guy that deserves you. As if you cared about the neighbors!"

"I don't," Kathleen said tersely. "I care about you."

It was Vicki who had to go and open her big mouth—Vicki

who worked at the college library and who was an incurable gossip. Vicki who always monitored her younger sister's activities because it was her Christian duty, and because her father favored Kathleen. Vicki did not approve of the antiwar movement; Vicki thought a true American ought to stand behind her country the way a good Catholic stood behind her Church—meekly and without question. Vicki especially disliked the hippies hanging around the college grounds, found their life-style threatening, and went out of her way to inform the college administration about strangers on campus. She had her eye on the blond young man in the Brooklyn College sweatshirt, had once engaged in verbal battle with him on the subject of pacifism and lost, and could not miss the vibrations between him and her sister. More than once she had caught them holding hands, laughing with their heads together. Something clearly had to be done. Wondering why she never saw Kathleen on campus in the middle of the day, Vicki went to the registrar's office. Checking the files, she discovered that her sister's class schedule had a gap every day from noon to three. There was only one reason why anyone would require such a long lunch hour, Vicki decided, and the following day she took her own lunch hour a little early. She tailed Kathleen at a safe distance as she left an eleven o'clock speech class for the subway station, got off the train in Flatbush, and entered a big apartment building. Vicki waited a few moments, and slipped into the lobby to scan the names on the doorbells, then hurried back to the library. That evening she made it a point to get home before Kathleen, and had a few words with her father.

Kathleen was in the theater club; there was a dress rehearsal that night and she did not get home until nearly one. The entire first floor of the house was dark when she got in, though there were lights on in some of the bedrooms. Her parents and little Frankie were no doubt asleep, she knew. Vicki stayed up reading until all hours, and the twins, Kathleen swore, could talk in their sleep. Creeping across the rug in the—she assumed—empty living room, she was frightened out of her wits by the sound of her father's voice.

"You lied to me." Frank's voice boomed off the walls in the dark room, calm but accusing.

"Holy shit!" Kathleen exploded, barking her shins on the coffee table and groping for the lamp. She switched the light on and nearly blinded herself, immediately on the defensive. Cringing slightly—what was he talking about? She, of all people, never lied!—she searched her father's face for meaning.

"You lied to me," he said again. He was sitting in his favorite chair, waiting. Kathleen straightened up, then deposited herself on the couch so she could be on the same level with him, and indicate she was not afraid.

"I never lie," she stated flatly, confident that it was true. "If you're freaked out because I'm late, I *told* you tonight was dress rehearsal. I *told* you I'd be out until all hours, and one of the guys drove me home so you don't have to wor—"

"One of the guys? Who, your friend Gerry?"

"Gerry's not in the theater club, Dad," Kathleen said, annoyed that her father couldn't keep her activist life separate from her artistic life. Suddenly she knew what he was talking about. "Uh-oh," she said, and then, "How did you—?"

"That's not important," Frank said, hoisting himself out of the chair and standing over her, ever so slightly threatening. He hadn't hit her since she was five or six, but that didn't necessarily mean he couldn't. "How I found out ain't important. Whether you're screwing around with one guy or six doesn't matter in the long run, because you're over eighteen and by law there ain't a damn thing I can do about it, except maybe kick you out of the house, which I'm not about to do. It doesn't even matter that the guy isn't Catholic, or that you couldn't wait until you got married—no, let me take that last one back, because that does matter. At least to me it does. I may be straightlaced, or an old fart, or whatever you want to call it, but I still believe a girl oughta save herself for the guy she marries. I know it's the style these days to fool around a little before you get married; in a way I can almost see that, considering the way people are getting divorced right and left these days. And I can see where my nose might be outta joint because you had to go and pick a Yid. All right, I'm prejudiced. But the thing is, you *lied* to me. You lied to *me*! You stood in this room with a straight face and you told me you and this guy had nothing going. And now I find out you not only got something going, but it's so hot you got it cooking five days outta the week! You *lied* to me!"

There were tears in Kathleen's eyes, and when she tried to swallow, her throat was paralyzed. She could not look at her father, but sat staring at her twisted, white-knuckled hands. What futility to try to explain that she had lied for the sole purpose of sparing him—and, yes, herself—this kind of scene! But her shame was fighting another emotion, a cold and vengeful anger against the person or persons who had finked on her, had told her father these things out of some unfathomable sense of duty. Who was it, and how had her father found out?

"You know what burns me?" Frank was saying, pacing now, doubtless to keep his anger under control. "What gets me is that you brought this guy around so I could meet him. And I found myself thinking, 'Jeez, if he'd get a haircut and lay off all this pacifist stuff I could almost forget he was a Yid. I could really get to like him. He's smart, he's got ambition. A guy wants to be an engineer—gets into MIT, too—that's nothing to sneeze about. Hell, if she decided to marry him I could almost be happy. She could do a lot worse.' I mean, when I think of some of the weirdos you been hanging around with! And then I remember that he sat at the dinner table and got along nice with everybody, and Frankie cried when you two left to go to the movies, and the guy sent your mother flowers the next day—that's a nice touch. I didn't think anybody did that anymore. A real gentleman, I figured. Only, now I keep thinking of the two of you horsing around every chance you get, and I keep thinking he was laughing at me. That both of you were laughing at me because I didn't know what was going on. . . ."

His voice trailed off. Kathleen could almost swear he was crying. He had slumped back into his chair, looking tired, older than she remembered him. Wondering with a sudden violence if it was her obligation to remain a virgin until her wedding night just to keep her father happy, she wiped the remains of her tears off her chin and made a decision. This scene was not her fault. The same man who had talked her out of feeling responsible for her Uncle Danny's death could, if he could be objective about it, admit that she was adult and her moral life was her own. Well, if she had lied—and Kathleen would admit, before witnesses if necessary, that she had—it had been out of consideration for her father. She had seen no reason to flaunt her life-style in his face; had resented, too, his reminding her that she was female, hence not entitled to the sexual freedom he would automatically afford a male child. Her father, of all people, had never insisted that she be a "lady." All those afternoons at the firehouse—all gone now, because someone had spoiled it. Someone had finked on her.

"Dad," she began miserably, "you're right. I lied, and I'm sorry. It's just that . . . just that there were so many things involved. I'm not screwing around with a lot of guys. It's just Gerry, and I am going to marry him someday. Only there are so many things in the way right now—"

"You *lied* to me," Frank repeated, a man obsessed, a man who had had hours to mull over the facts, and whose thoughts had worsened with every hour. "The two of you were sitting at that dinner table so damn smug because nobody knew your little secret. You were laughing at all of us."

"No!" Kathleen shouted, jumping up from the couch and all but flinging herself on her knees at his feet. "It wasn't like that at all. It's just that I didn't want to worry you. It's going to be years before we can get married, and I didn't want you all sitting around waiting for me to get pregnant, or waiting for us to break up and I'd be a fallen woman for the rest of my life, or whatever else—"

"So if you love each other why the hell can't you get married?" Frank bellowed, looking for a glimmer of hope. That was it; they could get married right away and the whole thing would be settled. His daughter's suppliant posture embarrassed him; he pulled at her arm. "Get up, will you? You look like some kind of jackass down there. Why can't you get married and cut out all this foolishness?"

"We will," Kathleen said, humble, getting up from the floor. "Only, Gerry got a low number in the last draft lottery, and he swears he's going to fight it even if it means a jail term. There's that. Then he needs at least three years at MIT, and I'll be doing grad work at the same time. If we got married now, one of us would have to work to put the other through school, and then the other way around. It doesn't make sense."

"But it makes sense for you to take *my* money for grad school and screw around behind my back?" There was bitterness in her father's voice. "Explain that one to me."

Kathleen hung her head, unable to rationalize it. "There's one more thing."

"Shoot!" her father said. "I'm all ears."

"Well, it's the religion thing," Kathleen said, relaxing a little, trying to be persuasive. "You know how I feel about religion, but I know it's important to you and Mom that I get married in the Church."

"You mean we want you to be really married," her father said aggressively. "Anything else don't count."

"Okay," she conceded, too unstrung to argue. "And Gerry and I have talked about it. He's willing to go along with it. But there's his grandmother. She's very old, and very religious, and it'd break her heart if her grandson married a *shiksa*."

"A who?"

"A Gentile, a girl who wasn't Jewish."

"Oh." Frank nodded. "So?"

"So, to be perfectly crude about it, she's eighty-five, she's got a bad heart—"

"And if you wait a couple of years—"

"Exactly."

There was a silence.

"So between now and then—whenever 'then' is—you two are going to keep fooling around," Frank said, not angry now, but needing to get the record straight. "Do I understand that part correctly?"

"Well, it won't be for long!" Kathleen said, torn between the need to satisfy her father and her own unhappiness. She and Gerry would be separated soon enough. "Gerry starts MIT in the fall—unless this draft thing messes him up—and I'll only get to see him whenever he's back in the city."

"And I'm supposed to sit here and keep quiet about this thing for—what—three years? And I'm supposed to keep coughing up the dough for your tuition, and—"

"Dad, I can't promise you anything!" She could no longer remain submissive, would have to stand up for herself. "I mean, am I supposed to take a vow of chastity or something? If you want, I'll move out, get my own apartment."

"Oh, no you don't!" Frank was on his feet now, his voice dangerously loud. "Your own apartment nothing! Next thing I know you'll be living with this guy full-time. No, ma'am! You'll stay in this house until you finish school."

"All right, if that's what you want," Kathleen said, something in his words puzzling her. "Does Mom know about this?"

"No, she doesn't," Frank said, calmer now, sitting again. "I don't see any point in getting her all wound up over it."

Kathleen took a deep breath. Her father had never found out about the incident with the birth-control pills, did not know his wife's true feelings about her daughters and premarital sex. She exhaled slowly. She had to ask him now.

"Who told you?" she asked with absolute calm.

"I don't think you need to know," her father said. "I don't want any bloodshed."

"I see." Kathleen nodded, knowing now why the light was still on in Vicki's room, knowing that if she ascended the stairs at this precise moment there would indeed be bloodshed.

With great deliberation, she rose from her chair and walked calmly to the foot of the stairs.

And as she walked—slowly, calmly—Kathleen heard something snap inside her head. All her life she had understood the distinction between religious pomposity and simple justice. All her life she had been honest, and the first time she had lied to anyone, out of simple compassion for him, she had been betrayed. She got to the door of her sister's room and let out a shriek like a wounded animal.

Frank stood at the foot of the stairs, listening. Sounds of scuffling, muffled screams, reached him, and he laughed in spite of himself, feeling in spite of what he knew to be right that Vicki was getting exactly what she deserved. It was only when he heard other voices and footsteps, and knew that his wife and the twins and even little Frankie were involved in the brawl, only when he was sure the neighbors would call the cops and was afraid Kathleen might actually do some permanent damage, that he betook himself with all reasonable speed upstairs to quiet things down.

But no matter what her reasoning was, and no matter that she eventually did marry her Jewish boy, the bond that had been between Frank O'Dell and his second daughter would never be the same.

"Should we tell her now?" Maureen whispered, knowing before she asked what her sister's opinion would be, and knowing that she would have to abide by it.

"No!" Mary Fran said emphatically, trying a new eyeliner and making faces at herself in the mirror. "Wait'll she's finished with this class-reunion thing. It's not that important."

"But it's been going on for months!" Maureen objected, always the alarmist of the two.

It was a rainy Saturday. The twins were supposed to clean their room before they went out. Maureen was busy—dusting, throwing things into the closet, untangling jewelry.

Mary Fran was experimenting with her makeup and pro-crastinating.

"So it can go on for another month before we have to bother Mom with it," Mary Fran reasoned, unruffled. "Listen, she said she'd take us for Pap tests when we turned eighteen. That's next week. We'll tell her then. Or tell the doctor and don't even bother her."

"I don't know," Maureen whined, picking the polish off one fingernail absently. By the time she was finished talking she would have peeled all ten nails, and would have to repolish them. "It's just so freaky, that's all. It's never happened before."

"Listen, I've got an idea!" Mary Fran began, but her sister silenced her.

"No!" Maureen snapped, reading her sister's thoughts. The psychic link they'd had since childhood had grown stronger since puberty.

"But if we go to the doctor first, then we can find out what it is and we won't even have to mention it to her," Mary Fran reasoned. "Maybe it's nothing serious. Besides, I already—"

"You didn't!"

"Yup. Made an appointment for the day after our birthday."

Maureen stopped to think about it, then got a bad case of the jitters. "Yeah, but—" she began, trying to find the right words. "I mean, like, we're still virgins. You don't think he'd do anything—"

"I asked Kath," Mary Fran said airily; she always had the facts at her fingertips. "She says he's very gentle. She says he told her every girl gets freaked the first time, even if she's had sex already."

"Really?" Maureen's eyes widened, but the fact that the doctor expected her to be nervous comforted her a little.

"Besides," Mary Fran added, scooping all of her makeup into her top drawer and trying to jam it shut, "at least we're in this together."

Maureen sighed, nodded, and rummaged around for her nail polish.

Helen put down the phone after the eleventh call and rubbed the back of her neck where it ached. For the first time in her life she was actually tired of talking. In the past two weeks she had called over two dozen girls from her high school class, inviting them to a twenty-fifth reunion.

Girls, Helen thought ironically. Some girls! We're all in our forties, and some of us are grandmothers already. How could we possibly have graduated twenty-five years ago?

She had dialed the phone numbers of women whose voices she no longer recognized, whose faces she still saw frozen at the dreamy age of eighteen in yearbook pictures; heard the puzzlement in their voices when she said her own name and the shriek of recognition as they remembered who she was. A thousand memories, not all of them pleasant, surfaced as she chatted with each woman for over an hour, even though she'd promised Frank to limit each call to under ten minutes. She could hear him gnashing his teeth in the background from time to time. After several such calls, it was difficult to return to the present.

And she could not locate Loretta. She would ask each class-mate in turn if she had heard from or knew the whereabouts of the girl who had once been her closest friend, but no one had heard from her in years. Helen finally found the courage to call Loretta's mother, who still lived in the old apartment she'd had when they were growing up. She was greeted with such a torrent of abuse about "that ungrateful slut" that she abandoned the search right there. If Loretta couldn't count to twenty-five, that was her problem.

"Whyn't you run an ad in the papers?" Frank suggested, grateful that the highly touted event was to take place the following weekend, so that perhaps the phone would have a chance to cool off. "You know, in the Personals: 'Loretta, call home. All is forgiven. We love you even without teeth.' What've you got to lose?"

"It's not funny!" Helen snapped, brooding over all the years she had let pass without speaking to her best friend. Loretta always sent them a postcard when she moved, but Helen never responded, and now she could no longer find the postcards. Now it was too late Of course, Loretta still had Helen's number, if she wanted to do anything about it. People changed as they grew older, and the passions that held them together at eighteen were not the same as when they—

The phone rang, so close to Helen's tired ears that she almost knocked it off the table in her fright. She grabbed the receiver before it could ring a second time.

"Hello," said a female voice—very soft, very far away. "Am I invited to this shindig or not?"

"Jesus H. Christ!" Helen gasped, borrowing one of Frank's expressions. "Loretta!"

"Just me, not Jesus," Loretta answered, the suggestion of a giggle in her voice. Helen could almost hear her punctuating her words with the snapping of gum, the way she always did.

"Well, for crying out loud, I've been going crazy trying to track you down! How'd you find out about the reunion?"

Loretta actually laughed this time. "It's the craziest thing," she said. "I mean, I haven't been within three blocks of a church in years—I mean *years*—and I got out of bed one Sunday feeling rotten and hung over and . . . well, to make a long story short—"

"Have you ever?" Helen interrupted, tears forming at the back of her throat. Memories.

"Have I ever what?"

"Made a long story short," Helen said warmly.

"Oh." Loretta seemed to consider it for a long moment. When she finally got the joke she laughed out loud. "Yeah, I guess you're right. I never did, did I? Anyway, this Sunday morning I was telling you about—as I say, I was feeling rotten, and I went down to the bakery for rolls, and then I picked up the *Times* (same thing I do every Sunday morning), and the next thing I know I'm standing in the back of the church, right in the middle of the late mass. I mean, I've lived in this neighborhood for years, walked past that church maybe a thousand times, and I never had the slightest desire to go in. I mean, I stopped going to church way back when, and my conscience was probably bothering me, but anyway—don't ask me how I got there, or even why I stayed, but there I was. I sat through mass, and then I started reading the parish bulletin, and the book with the songs in it, and then I went out to the vestibule and read all the notices on the bulletin board, and that's when I found this little announcement about Bishop's having this twenty-five-year reunion. And I got into this kind of a panic, and I thought, 'Jesus, the only one of that crowd I can still talk to is Helen, and please, God, I hope she hasn't changed her phone number,' and it took me until today to get up the courage to call you. So here I am."

She was out of breath, waiting for Helen to say something, but Helen was lost in thought. What had Loretta been doing all these years? Was she still alone? Why had she been feeling so distinctly "rotten," as she put it, last Sunday, or did she always feel rotten on Sundays, and other days of the week as well? Why had Loretta's life turned out the way it did? And why was she so excited about this reunion, so eager to return to the past?

"Are you sure you want to go?" Helen asked her finally. "To the reunion, I mean."

"Sure, why not?" She could see Loretta's usual careless shrug. If these things about her friend were still so familiar, could much else be changed? "Don't ask me why, but I figure, what the hell! Put me on the list, will you, kiddo?"

"Of course," Helen said, dutifully writing Loretta's maiden name down, without hesitation, knowing that Loretta had never married, would never marry. "You got all the information? The time and the date and everything?"

"Oh, sure. Say, I'll see you there, okay?"

"Okay. But listen, Loretta—" Helen said as she was about to hang up.

"What?"

"Why don't you come over here first? Over to my house. We're still in the same place. I'm sure Frank would like to see you after all this time, and you wouldn't believe how the girls have turned out. And you know about the other one, don't you? My little boy? He's five now, and I'm sure you'd get a kick out of him. If you come over a little early, we can—"

"I don't think so," Loretta said, quite calmly, but with a tone that brooked no debate. "I'll see you at the reunion."

"If that's the way you want it," Helen said, nonplussed, and Loretta hung up before she could say anything else.

Three days before the reunion, Helen came home from the daycare center to find the phone ringing insistently. No one else was home yet. It didn't matter. It was probably someone calling back to get final details on the reunion; she'd gotten one of those before she left for work this morning. She even heard phones ringing in her sleep lately.

"Change your shoes before you go out in the yard!" she shouted to Frankie, whom she'd picked up at kindergarten on her way home. Preoccupied, she reached for the phone.

The voice was male, which threw her for an instant. When she realized who it was, she was even more puzzled.

"Dr. Giraud?" Her gynecologist. What did he want? "I'm sorry, I didn't recognize you at first. What's the—?"

"I was wondering if you could drop by the office this afternoon," he was saying. "Now, if possible. There's something I think—"

Bells were indeed ringing in Helen's head. She had had her annual Pap test last month. She was at an age, and with all the years on the Pill, and if it wasn't uterine there was always breast cancer. . . .

"What's wrong?" she demanded.

"I don't want to alarm you." His voice was soothing. "It's nothing serious, but I'd rather talk to you in person than on the phone."

If it's nothing serious, Helen wondered, then why can't you tell me on the phone?

"Your two youngest girls came in to see me on their own this afternoon, and they're still in the office, and there's something I thought—"

That's why the twins weren't home, Helen realized, the only clear thought she could grasp at the moment. She automatically picked up the car keys from where she'd left them on the counter top, pushing the button on the phone without even saying she would come, then dialing her next-door neighbor to keep an eye on Frankie while she was gone. Dear God, she thought, what now?

A curious fact about Maureen and Mary Fran, aside from their celebrated telepathy, was that they always developed physical symptoms simultaneously. If one girl got a cold, the other began to sneeze. When Mary Fran sprained an ankle running, Maureen complained for days that she couldn't walk without pain. Their empathy was so total that they had both started menstruating on the same day just after their twelfth birthday, and they always got their periods at the same time for the next five years.

But within the past few months, as they told the doctor, their periods had become irregular, interspersed with bouts of mid-cycle bleeding that they'd never had before. These were the symptoms that had brought them to their mother's gynecologist, and this was the first thing he reported to Helen when she got to the office. Sending the girls to sit in the waiting room, he began to question her closely.

"You know, as soon as they came in, I tried finding your past-history file, but I couldn't. My predecessor had the screwiest damn filing system I ever saw. I've got no previous record on you prior to the time you came to me. That was when you were pregnant with your son—1968, wasn't it?—so you'll have to fill me in on everything that went before. I've meant to catch up on all my patients, but the work load. . . ."

Helen frowned, alarmed and puzzled. What did *her* medical history have to do with the girls' symptoms?

"You want me to fill you in on all my pregnancies, is that it?" she asked, and he nodded, pen poised over a note pad. "Well, my first pregnancy was in '50. That's Vicki. She was born in January. Two years later is Kathleen—November '51. Well, almost two years. Two years after her I had a miscarriage."

"What month?" he cut in, jotting it all down. "I mean, how far into the pregnancy were you?"

"About ten weeks," she replied.

"Please go on," he said, writing.

"Okay. About a year after the miscarriage (give or take a month) I got pregnant again. That would be up to nineteen fifty—"

"A *year* after a miscarriage?" the doctor echoed. "And you had two kids already? Weren't you overdoing it just a little?"

Helen shrugged. "I was a good little Catholic girl," she explained, trying to make light of it. Was it that simple, really? It was all ancient history; she could not possibly recall what had been in her mind so long ago. "I thought that's what I was here for. Having babies."

The doctor looked at her under his eyebrows, still writing. "And this time you had the twins?"

"That's right." Helen nodded. "After that I decided enough was enough, and I started the Pill. And the rest, as they say, is history."

"Okay!" he said, tossing the pen onto the desk and leaning back in his chair. "Now, tell me, was there anything unusual when you were pregnant with the twins? Were you told to stay off your feet, did you have any trouble with cramps or bleeding or threatened miscarriage?"

"Oh, not at all." Helen shook her head, then suddenly remembered something. "Dr. Allen put me on some kind of drug to prevent that kind of thing, and I never had any problems."

When she said "some kind of drug," the doctor's facial muscles twitched slightly, as if something he had suspected all along—something bad—had come about.

"Holy shit, another one!" he exhaled, grimacing. "You don't

happen to remember the name of this—drug—by any chance?"

"No."

"Do the initials D-E-S ring a bell? The name diethylstil-bestrol?"

Helen shook her head again. "No."

The doctor sighed. "That's probably what it was anyway. Jesus, this is going to be a pain in the ass!"

"Explain, please," Helen requested softly.

"DES is not a drug, but a combination of hormones that's been given to women over the past twenty-odd years to prevent miscarriage. What it also does, for some perverse reason, is cause spontaneous abortion if given in large doses during the first six weeks of pregnancy. It's what they give rape victims in the emergency room, in case you're interested. But the issue at hand here is that after twenty years of use they're discovering that this stuff has side effects, not so much on the woman who was given it, but on her female children."

"Side effects," Helen repeated.

The doctor hesitated. "I'm talking about a minority of cases, now. But symptoms such as mid-cycle bleeding, which your daughters have experienced, irregular periods, sometimes—*sometimes*—indicate abnormalities within the vagina, *some* of which are *sometimes* found to be malignant."

"Cancer," Helen said, sparing him the need to use the word.

"Very rarely," he said. "But it happens."

"You didn't tell the girls any of this?" Helen asked, strangely detached from the questions she asked and the answers she received.

"There's no need to until we get something conclusive," he said. "But I had to tell you, because they'll need tests. I've contacted a colleague at Brooklyn Hospital. They have a special screening center for this kind of thing. If the girls' tests come out negative, then you and I have gotten excited for nothing, and they never have to know what it's all about."

"But if they come out positive?" Helen pursued it relentlessly, ready to accept any answer, as long as she had the whole truth.

"I think we should wait until the prelim—"

"No!" Helen leaned toward his desk. "I need to know every possibility. Tell me the truth!"

"Listen, Mrs. O'Dell—Helen—may I call you Helen?" he asked, out of deference for her age.

"Certainly, Fred," she said, smiling momentarily, weakly. She felt sorry for him suddenly, seeing how concerned he was, how involved in the problem, whereas another doctor might be detached. She was picking on him for something that was not his fault. Helen calmed down, and sat back in her chair again.

"A lot of women experience a great deal of guilt over this kind of thing," he said. "Please let me assure you that you are in no way responsible, that none of us—and I've prescribed this stuff for patients, too—none of us had any way of knowing what a time bomb this would turn out to be. If we must blame someone, I suppose it's the drug companies. But for God's sake, those two beauties might not be alive today if you hadn't taken those hormones, babe. So don't sit there feeling guilty!"

"All right," Helen said. "I'm not blaming myself, or you, or anybody. But I've got to have the whole picture. Now give it to me straight. What happens if my two 'beauties' turn out to have cancer?"

"Then they'll need surgery," he said. "In most cases it's enough to remove some of the glands inside the vagina, and parts of the vaginal wall. They will still be able to conceive and carry a normal pregnancy, although they will probably have to be delivered by C-section. I've personally never had a case where a complete hysterectomy was necessary, but that's the opposite extreme."

"Oh, my God!" Helen cried, letting out her emotions at last. "They're only eighteen years old!"

She had no desire to go to the reunion after this, wanted to curl up in a defensive little ball and forget about everything else. But Frank made her go, pointing out that it did no one

any good to have her sitting home brooding over something
she could not control. The twins went for their preliminary
tests that Friday; when the results came back positive, Dr.
Giraud signed them into the hospital Saturday morning. They
would undergo a series of further tests over the weekend, and
surgery would be on Monday. Helen was told to go home;
she would accomplish nothing by hanging around the hospital.
There was nothing for her to do but get dressed and go to her
high school reunion.

But except for her conversation with Loretta, the entire
afternoon turned out to be pretty much of a blur.

Seeing Loretta for the first time in over ten years, Helen
could understand why her friend had been reluctant to come
to the house first. Loretta was an absolute wreck. She looked
older than her forty-three years. Her hair, which had grayed
prematurely and might have made her look distinguished if she
had let it alone, was dyed the wrong shade of red, and the
roots showed. She looked tired. There was a suggestion of a
bruise—perhaps a shiner?—under one eye, too carefully concealed with too much makeup. She chain-smoked; her voice
was hoarse. She was old.

Helen had expected to be one of the youngest-looking
women there. After all, for the mother of five kids (a momentary pang thinking of the two gigglers in their hospital room,
last seen flirting one on either side of a flustered young intern,
and improvising at Ping-Pong with cotton balls and tongue
depressors pilfered during blood tests) she was in excellent
shape. She had brought recent pictures of all the kids, and of
Frank, and had to stop herself from bringing the scrapbook
full of clippings about her hero/husband. And then, of course,
there was *her* career. . . .

The photographs were passed from hand to hand even as
Helen was admiring pictures of other people's kids, and she
was fairly glutted with oohs and aahs when she told people
about Frank, and the daycare center—and then she would
look over at Loretta, calmly lighting yet another cigarette and

making idle, acid chitchat with a former classmate whom she'd absolutely *loathed* twenty-five years ago, and the afternoon had a sick feeling to it. Helen wished she were home instead, or floating around the hall in the hospital waiting to buttonhole some doctor and find out what was happening to her daughters.

This day was empty, meaningless. These women with their recognizable faces and voices—older now, that was all—were strangers, had perhaps always been strangers, except that Helen had never had the sophistication to see it before. She tried walking through the halls of the school building, but the place was strange to her. There were echoes of incidents: the day she won an award in a Latin-translation competition; the day the art teacher, a mousy little nun who never spoke above a whisper, went absolutely berserk and ran down the halls tearing the crucifixes off the walls, screaming that they were bad art and ought to be destroyed; the day Loretta was caught smoking in the bathroom and suspended for a week; the day a girl in the senior class threw herself off the roof because she failed math; the day Berlin fell and the entire school erupted with joy, weeping and embracing and throwing old test papers out the windows—but all these were only echoes, not substantial enough to hold onto. The building itself was changed: refurbished, repainted. Classrooms were now called "audiovisual centers" and "media-access centers," and there was carpeting on the floors and desks were grouped in cozy little circles instead of regimented rows. The idea of a reunion was spurious, Helen thought, listening to the giddy laughter from the cafeteria, where everyone else was still gathered at the luncheon, and wondering why she was here. We cannot be reunited, because we are no longer the people we were.

She tried to get Loretta to leave early, hoping she could drop her at her apartment and then rush home, but Loretta insisted they go out for a drink. She needed to talk, she said.

"Quite a performance, wasn't it?" she started in at once, fortified with a couple of martinis and feeling belligerent.

"What?" Helen raised her eyebrows, fingering a daiquiri

she did not intend to finish. She should not be here. She should be home. She should at least call the hospital.

"Oh, come on! Don't tell me you didn't see what everybody was doing this afternoon!" Loretta sneered. "Miserable batch of overachievers, all of you, with your snapshots and your bullshit. Who has the most kids? Who has the most degrees? Who has the highest salary or the most important husband? Jesus Christ, I wanted to puke!"

"Or maybe the green around your gills was just envy," Helen snapped, infuriated. Why was she wasting her time here? "Just because you haven't accomplished anything in the past twenty-five years—"

"Oh, but you're wrong about that!" Loretta said, waving her finger at the cocktail waitress and pointing to her empty glass. "Maybe I never got married, and maybe I've still got a shitty job, and maybe my family's disowned me, but I'm still free. Nobody's got any claim on me. I've had more men than any of you, and more orgasms than the rest of the Class of '48 put together!"

"And more bruises as well?" Helen remarked quietly, looking her one-time friend in the eye.

Loretta's free hand moved defensively toward her face. "Jesus, is it that noticeable? I thought the makeup—He did it to me on purpose. When I told him where I was going today. He's only hit me one other time. . . ."

Her voice trailed off into a sob, and in a minute she was crying: big, familiar Loretta tears, her eye makeup running down her face. Helen let her cry for a moment without saying anything (it seemed to her she had seen this scene somewhere before), then reached for her purse and stood up.

"I've got to make a phone call," she said stonily. "I hope you'll be calmer by the time I get back."

She called the hospital. There was nothing new. All the necessary tests had been completed, and Dr. Giraud would be in tomorrow to assess them. Surgery, if needed, was still slated for Monday morning. The girls, it was reported, had last been seen loitering by the nursery, pestering the floor nurse to let them in to help feed and change the newborns. They were not in their room at the moment, and no one was sure where they were. Helen left word that they were to call her back that evening before the switchboard closed. She went back to the table, where Loretta had quieted down somewhat.

"Before I forget," Loretta began, touching up her eye makeup with the aid of a small mirror. "I wanted to ask you on the phone but I didn't think of it. How's Al?"

Helen frowned at her. "Al?"

"Alistair. I always called him that. I thought you knew."

"Far as I know you always called him 'the Blister,'" Helen remembered, sipping idly at her daiquiri. The ice had melted and the drink was watery, uninteresting. She put it down. "He's fine. You heard what happened to Aunt Ag."

Loretta hadn't. Helen filled her in, omitting any reference to Alistair's lover. She wasn't sure how much Loretta knew about that aspect of Alistair's life, if she knew at all.

"Gee, isn't it sweet of him to take care of her like that!" Loretta mused. "Most people would just ship the old lady off to a nursing home and forget about her. And she's not even his natural mother, I mean. Isn't that something!" She gave an odd little laugh. "Funny, but I always suspected he had a heart under all that tough-guy business. Maybe that's why I was always crazy about him. I still wonder what would've happened if he'd liked me, too."

Helen had a sudden urge to laugh. It might be the tension of worrying about the twins. It might be imagining the look on Loretta's face if she told her about Alistair's current lifestyle. Despite her real pity for this wreck of a human being, who had by her own admission spent years mooning over a love affair that could never have been, and throwing herself into others that should never have been, Helen wanted very much to laugh. She looked down at her placemat and tried to be serious. She thought about the twins again, and there was nothing in the world that was funny anymore.

"How does he manage without working?" Loretta asked suddenly, draining her third martini. "I know your aunt's got money, but the medication, and the doctor bills and everything else—"

If I tell her the truth, Helen thought wildly, she'll have to abandon her fantasy and begin to live in the real world. Or, knowing Loretta, she would do something crazy, like kill herself.

"Oh, um . . . Alistair has a friend who . . . lends him money," she faltered, wishing she could say she didn't know and leave it at that.

"Really?" Loretta stopped eating the olive from her drink and pounced on this information. "Probably some sexy chick he's been stringing along for years, right?"

"No," Helen said quietly, leaping into the abyss. "A male friend. He's . . . sharing the apartment with Alistair and my aunt."

"Oh." Loretta was momentarily puzzled, then a knowing look crossed her face. "So I was right about him all these years, wasn't I? I never wanted to say anything to you—you were always so naive—but I figured he was—how shall we put it? I know most of them hate the word 'gay.' "

"Yes," Helen said, relieved that Loretta's reaction was no more serious than this.

"Your aunt knows?" Helen nodded. "And she never tried to put him out or anything?" Helen shook her head. Loretta began to grow maudlin again. "Jesus, isn't that something!"

There was a silence. Loretta snatched the check as soon as the waitress brought it.

"This is mine! You can leave the tip if you want, but that's all." She was groping for her wallet when a thought occurred to her. "Say, do you think Al would like a little help? Someone to take care of the old lady so he can get away once in a while?"

Helen looked at her suspiciously.

"Hey, listen," Loretta said, conspiratorial. "You think I'm going to start a love triangle? I should live so long! I'm not going to mess up his life. Let me tell you a little secret about women like me. We always fall for men we can't have: married men, priests, homosexuals. That way we don't have to commit ourselves. We always have an out."

It was a confession, not an apology. Helen accepted it.

"Why don't you give Alistair a call, then?" she suggested.

"I may do that!" Loretta said positively, and they left the cocktail lounge.

Helen saw Loretta into a cab (she would not accept a ride home) and watched the cab pull away somewhat ruefully, wishing she had had a chance to unburden herself to Loretta about the twins, needing the solace of an understanding woman. But Loretta's problems always superseded everyone else's; it would have been useless to try to tell her anything. Helen walked to her car and started for home, knowing she had lost her best friend more irrevocably this afternoon than she had in the past twenty-five years. Reunions, she thought again, were not possible.

Dr. Giraud's complexion matched the color of his green surgical gown. He looked like a soap-opera doctor, the mask dangling picturesquely around his neck, except that he was saturated with sweat.

"Lousy morning!" His voice was raspy, barely a whisper. "Two hysterectomies (one of them malignant), an emergency C-section where we lost the baby, and then we had to do your girls." He shook his head. "I went into obstetrics because it's essentially a happy field. Nobody dies in obstetrics! I thought. Christ, it's days like this. . . ."

He had run out of words. Helen and Frank sat on the bench in the hall holding hands, looking up at him—silent, waiting. The doctor shook his head, realized he was being self-indulgent, and spoke to them.

"I'm sorry. You're sitting here waiting for me to tell you something—something you can hang onto—and I'm running

off at the mouth. Your two beauties are downstairs in Recovery. They should be coming out of it soon. Another hour
or so and you can talk to them. As for the surgery: Well, we
had to take part of the cervix in both cases, but the uterus and
ovaries are still intact. The one—God forgive me, but I can't
remember who's which—the aggressive one, the one with the
chipped front tooth—"

"Mary Fran," Helen said, so softly he couldn't hear her.

"She should have no trouble making babies. But the other
one—the blusher, the soft-spoken one—"

"Maureen," Helen whispered, shuddering a little and gripping Frank's hand. He had not said a word.

"We took the entire cervix in her case, and we may have
damaged the tubes. She might have trouble conceiving."

Helen nodded, accepting. She had been expecting the worst,
so even this sounded hopeful. Frank looked up from the
cracked linoleum for the first time—all this talk of female
anatomy embarrassed him—and spoke.

"What about the cancer?" he demanded, cutting to the
bone. This was a man who had given mouth-to-mouth to infants charred beyond recognition, who helped scrape up what
was left of those who panicked when the flames got too close
and jumped from sixth-floor windows. This was a man who
could look life in the eye without blinking. "Is it going to
spread any further? Will they be all right?"

The doctor appraised him before he spoke. "It's an unusual
kind of cancer," he said. "In almost every documented case,
it seems to limit itself to one area, with no recurrence after
surgery."

Frank nodded, knowing there was more. "But?"

"But all of the cases we've found have been within the last
five years or so. That's too short a time to be sure the cancer
won't come back. Twenty years ago we thought the drug was
safe. Ten years from now we may find out we didn't get
everything when we operated."

"This thing is like a time bomb, then," Frank said grimly.
"Is that what you're saying?"

The doctor shrugged. "I don't honestly know."

When the twins finished their first year of college, both en-rolled in nursing school. Mary Fran specialized in terminal pa-tient care; Maureen went into postpartum care. They worked in the same hospital. Both had occasional casual sexual liaisons, but neither would chance marriage for a long, long time. They needed to be sure their remission was permanent. Both were excellent nurses, both were still insatiable gigglers. But when they went for Pap tests every three months, they always went together, and asked that their results be mailed from the lab in the same envelope. Neither wanted to be the first to know.

". . . and the upshot of it is, I've taken him out of the school. He'll start fifth grade in private school this September."

Helen was on the phone again. She could swear she had spent more hours of her adult life with the phone receiver wedged between shoulder and ear than she had spent sleeping. She could not resist watching her mother's face—Kat was sitting at the kitchen table drinking tea with Johnny—when she made this last statement. But Kat either didn't hear or else she had lost none of her acting talent. The teacup never faltered on its way to her lips, despite the battle she and her daughter had waged over Frankie's schooling.

"What?" Helen asked the phone, momentarily distracted by her mother's flawless performance. "Yes, I knew you'd be proud of me. The point is, Sarah, I'm as much against abortion as the next person, but I don't like the way they go about brainwashing these poor kids. I mean, okay, they started with this mandatory 'Prayer for the Unborn,' and Frankie came home one day and said, 'Mommy, what's an unborn?' I guess he thought it was some sort of rare animal; he's very ecology-minded—knows all about the Save the Whale campaign and everything. He's very bright for a ten-year-old, even if I say so myself. Well, okay, I explain that 'unborn' simply means a baby that's still in the womb; he knew the facts of life when he was four, so that didn't faze him. But then the school starts showing films against abortion—*in the fourth grade*! I went absolutely insane. I called the principal and yelled at her; I yelled at the pastor. I said, 'You won't teach the children sex education, you won't tell them when and how a child is conceived, you won't even whisper the word "contraception," yet you'll expose them to these absolutely horrifying films!' It's as if they expect nine- and ten-year-olds to be out getting abortions! Frankie said some of the kids in his class actually vomited after they saw this film. And he's a pretty tough kid, but he's had nightmares where he says somebody's pulling him apart by the arms and legs and flushing him down the toilet. Do you believe that? Well, I couldn't listen to it anymore; he had me in tears. So I took him out of the school, and I told them why. I'll put him in Confraternity class and he can get his religious instruction there, without all this garbage about abortions!"

She spoke for a few minutes more, then said good-bye to her caller and hung up the phone. When she looked at Johnny, he was applauding her.

"Good for you!" he said, not caring if Kat disapproved. "About time somebody paid as much attention to the rights of the already born as they do to the unborn. Who was that on the phone?"

Helen poured herself a cup of tea and sat down; her throat was dry from all that raving. "One of my college professors. A very interesting lady. Someday I'll tell you about her. To make a long story very short, she had a stroke a couple of years ago—awful business! She recovered pretty much, but she didn't know how to read anymore. Can you imagine that? A college professor who can't read. But some of her former students and I helped her over the rough spots, and we still keep in touch."

"That's nice," Johnny nodded, eating sandwich cookies like a child, pulling them apart and eating the filling out of the inside before he ate the cookie. "Say, are you really taking the little champ out of St. What's-his-name's?"

Helen shot a glance at her mother before answering him; Kat was impassive. "It's the only solution," she said, watching Johnny take yet another cookie from the plate. "Hey there, Brother John, you keep eating like that and you'll go back to Newfoundland looking like the Goodyear blimp."

"Can't help it," Johnny mumbled, stuffing the cookie into his mouth all at once. "They don't have this kind in St. John's. I need a fix."

The Christian Brothers had sent him home for the summer to stay with his mother. In the fall he was being transferred to one of the mission schools, probably somewhere in the West Indies.

"Sure, when I was a girl down to Harmony Bay, we were after bakin' all our sweets ourselves." Kat spoke up for the first time in over an hour. "We never bought cookies in a store, then."

"That was a long time ago, Mom," Johnny said, not unkindly, his hand halfway to the cookie plate. Helen gave him a look and he stopped himself. He *was* beginning to gain weight.

"Sure, don't I know that!" Kat sighed, finishing her tea. "I'm seventy-four this October! Seems everything I'm after rememberin' is a long time ago!"

She got up from the table with great deliberation, and wandered into the living room. Helen and Johnny exchanged glances. When their mother was out of earshot, Johnny spoke.

"How's she been?" he asked quietly, the odd touch of a Newfoundland accent he'd picked up after all his years there clinging to his voice. "Seems like every time I see her she's farther away than ever."

Helen shrugged. "It could be her age. It could be the same old gloom getting deeper. The only thing she wants to talk about is religion, which is why she was ecstatic—in her own way—about your being down here for the summer. But all you talk about is baseball and the things you miss about Brooklyn, and when you do start on religion you disagree with her on everything. Your Catholicism and hers are miles apart. Oh, and you're turning away from her deliberately, she says. Just like I'm defying her by taking my son out of Catholic school."

"Now, wait a minute—" Johnny began, but Helen cut him off, exhausted with the subject.

"That's the way she looks at it," she said, going to pour more tea and finding the pot empty. She rummaged in a cabinet for tea bags, ran the cold water, put the kettle on the stove. "I'm sick of the entire thing. No one can talk sense to her anymore. I try to make sure she takes her blood-pressure medicine and yes her to death. It's like talking to a two-year-old. You want more tea?"

"No," Johnny said. "You got any beer?"

"On top of all that tea and all those cookies?" Helen got him one from the refrigerator anyway. "You're going to get sick!"

"I'm not a baby," he said, pulling the ring top, irritated.

"Aren't you? You eat like one."

He acknowledged the truth of that. "You're right. But it's a small vice. I'm not allowed any others."

Helen opened her mouth to say that similar small vices had already killed one member of the family, but decided it was useless. She had come to the conclusion that it was useless to offer advice to her mother, any of her five children, or her surviving brother. An incredible weariness had overcome her, insidiously, in the course of the past few years. It had nothing to do with menopause, which she'd managed to get through without being traumatized, but the actual cause of it eluded her. The only one who listened to her anymore was Frank, and Helen supposed she should be grateful for that.

"Has it been so bad?" he had asked her the other night. They were alone in the living room. The house had grown more silent in recent years. Kathleen had been married and gone for two years now; at about the same time the twins had coerced Frank into letting them get their own apartment, though he'd sworn for years that his girls would stay under his roof until they married. He had to make an exception in their case. That left Frankie, who was doing his homework upstairs or surreptitiously poring over a punk-rock magazine, and Vicki, who at the moment was attending a prayer meeting of the Third Order of St. Francis, the lay person's equivalent of a religious order and her latest obsession. Helen had a hard time getting used to the idea that she and Frank would one day be alone in this house, alone together for the first time in their marriage, since Vicki *in utero* had accompanied them home from their honeymoon. One day it would be just the two of them, with one lamp lit—Frank sitting at one end of the couch, Helen lying against the cushions with her feet in his lap. And he had asked her, that night, "Has it been so bad?"

And she couldn't answer him because of this dreadful, insidious melancholy, which had worked its way into the marrow of her bones. It had begun with the sense of guilt, of sick helplessness, that swept over her as she sat in the hall awaiting the outcome of the twins' surgery, the surgery that was the result of a disease *she* had given them by introducing an alien substance into her own body eighteen years before. It was easy for the doctor to say she should not feel guilty. She did, and had, for nearly six years. She would for the rest of her life.

Her guilt over the twins had been part of her depression, but Helen almost thought it would have happened anyway, without an external event to act as catalyst. Was she slipping into the abyss (harmless form of madness, but madness all the same) of depression that had engulfed her mother, and her mother's mother—and beyond that she could not tell, because no one knew who her mother's mother's mother had been—coloring even the most neutral happening with shades of blackish-purple, neutralizing happy moments into shades of gray? Why couldn't she give Frank an answer when the question had been asked half in jest and could surely be answered in the same way? Her only response had been to shake her head and burst into tears, tears which he had interpreted after thirty years of marriage as soundless joy rather than the hopeless confusion that they were. That had been a week ago, and Helen had found no better answer for him yet.

She arrived back in the present with a jolt. Johnny was staring past her out the kitchen window to the backyard, where the roses were beginning to open. He had not noticed her dreaminess.

"They're late this year," Helen said, and he frowned, not understanding. "The roses. Everything's late this year. All that damned rain. . . ."

"Up in St. John's the leaves are just coming out." Johnny grimaced. "And you can't grow roses. Too cold. You want to know what the national flower of Newfoundland is?"

"I didn't know they had one," Helen answered. "What is it?"

"Something called a pitcher plant. *Sarracenia purpurea*, if you want to be botanical about it."

"Sounds pretty!" Helen said vaguely. Any kind of conversation would do to keep the thoughts from crashing against each other in her head.

"It isn't. It's a weird, primitive tuber sort of thing, cousin to an orchid. Looks kind of like a small reddish orchid, too, only it's got these little cups at the base—those are the pitchers— that fill up with rainwater and trap insects. The thing grows in the marshes, and the soil's too thin to give it any sustenance, so it feeds off bugs. It's creepy!"

"Like a Venus-flytrap," Helen said, puttering around the room, filling the cat's water dish, searching the cabinets for the food for Frankie's gerbils. "Mary Fran was raising those for a while; have you ever seen them? They've got these little jaws—"

"Same principle," Johnny said, crumpling his empty beer can, aiming for the wastebasket, and missing. "And that's the national flower of Newfoundland. Got to tell you something about the natives, hasn't it?"

"Not necessarily," Helen said, retrieving the beer can where it rolled under a cabinet. "It just means they had to find an indigenous flower that only grew in Newfoundland, and that was probably the only one." She sat down again, wanting him to talk so she could pretend to listen, wishing really that he and her mother would go home instead of staying for supper as she'd offered them, wishing everyone would go away and let her sleep for a week or two or maybe even a year. Something she couldn't see seemed to be pressing her into the earth. "What're the people like? In Newfoundland, I mean. We've listened to Mom's stories for so many years I guess we don't have an accurate picture of what it's really like. It's as if time has stopped up there, as if it's one of those picture-postcard places where nothing ever changes."

"Forget about it," Johnny said, shaking his head. "It's nothing like what Mom remembers anymore. Some things haven't changed. Like the poverty, the lack of resources, lack of education. The picture-postcard world doesn't exist anymore. There are three Holiday Inns on the east coast—Gander, St. John's, and one in Pop's little town of Torbay. Incredible. The tourists outnumber the natives, and as usual they're making the place over to be like what they think it should be. I don't mean to make it sound totally negative. Some people have television, though there's only one channel and most of it's soccer, and the mail gets there faster, and they're building more hospitals. But the population's dropping like mad. It's as if once the young people discover there's a real world out there, they can't wait to get away."

"But it was always like that!" Helen objected, getting involved in his narrative in spite of herself. "Mom and Pop themselves, Aunt Ag, all their friends."

"It's more than that," Johnny said. "The ones that stay are all clustered in the big cities. The outports are disappearing."

"Not Harmony Bay!" Helen cried, a pang running through her for some reason, as if the little village she had never seen was such an integral part of her being, of her roots, that its destruction was part of her own destruction.

Johnny made a motion for her to keep her voice down lest their mother hear. "Even Harmony Bay. The first weekend the Brothers sent me up there—how many years ago was that?—

I borrowed somebody's car and drove up that way. The place is a ghost town; not a single soul lives there anymore. I couldn't find the house Mom lived in, if it still exists. Half the buildings have caved in. The wharf's washed away. The roof of the chapel's gone, and the churchyard's so given over to weeds I couldn't find any of the headstones. It was sad!"

"And Torbay?" Helen asked dispiritedly, grasping at his answer.

"It's still there, but it's all changed. The last of the diehards from Harmony Bay moved down there, but nobody fishes anymore. Everybody commutes to St. John's, or does seasonal work in the mines and papermills on the west coast. Fishing's all done by big refrigerator boats, all corporate-owned. Half the kids in town don't know how to row a boat."

"And Pop's store?" Helen asked. It was the last shred she dared hope for.

"Turned into a beauty parlor," Johnny said with quiet irony. "There are shopping malls now, supermarkets. Nobody needs an old dry-goods shop, not even for tourists. The woman who owned the beauty parlor said her father had bought it from the husband of one of the Manning girls—she couldn't remember her married name, and only knew she was a Manning because of the red hair—and she had no idea if any of them were still living. I contacted the convent where the one was a nun, but she died in 1968. When I asked Mom if she knew anything about that, she said Oh, yes, they'd sent her the obituary notice, but since it only served to remind her of her own dear, departed husband—you know the speech. The way of life is gone. I never went back up there after that, just stayed in St. John's and taught my knuckleheads their three R's, and tried to convince them that a college education might serve them better than a quick living in the papermills. I haven't been very successful at that."

He went to get another beer, while Helen just sat. The thing that had been crushing her before felt so heavy now she could barely move.

"Naturally I never told Mom any of that," Johnny said

meaningfully, coming back from the refrigerator with the beer in his hand. "Anytime she asks me I just make things up. When she starts talking about going back there I try to get her off the subject."

"Naturally," Helen echoed him, deeply troubled by all that he had been telling her. Why should it make any difference to her that the places her parents had come from, places she had never seen—rambling frame houses in villages too shabby and full of the stink of drying fish to be picturesque, houses clutching little patches of earth too barren to nurture anything but the itch to move on—no longer existed, if they had ever existed in precisely the form her mother remembered? Helen had never had the slightest yearning to visit these places before. Now that they no longer existed she mourned them, as if they were dear friends who had died. It made no sense to mourn them, to long for them. As well long for the unmarked places in Europe where her farthest ancestors had sprung from, or the distant planet in some other galaxy that would be home to her great grandchildren's great grandchildren. Why did she feel as if her entire past, up to and including the minute just preceding this one, had been pulled out from under her?

"Ma!"

A voice from that very moment, Frankie's pseudo-macho ten-year-old's artificial baritone, broke into her thoughts. He bolted into the kitchen through the back door, his hair damp, his clothing splattered with great blotches of damp.

"It's raining!" he reported, shaking himself all over like a wet dog. "Garage door's stuck again."

"Oh, shit!" Helen exploded, forgetting he was too young to hear her curse. She started for the door, then decided not to bother. Let the car and the bikes and the geraniums she hadn't had time to plant yet and the big sack of peat moss— "Let 'em get soaked! I haven't got the energy."

"Okay." Frankie shrugged, tracking wet sneaker prints across the floor and grinning unperturbably at her when she bellowed at him to take off his shoes and go find a towel.

When he came back with the towel, Helen rubbed his hair

with it, vigorously enough to make him yelp from time to time. Johnny watched idly, bemused, admiring the primal domesticity of the scene because he could be detached from it.

"What's in the can?" Frankie asked his uncle, though he knew perfectly well.

"Want some?" Johnny grinned conspiratorially, reaching the can across the table to him.

"Don't give him beer!" Helen shrieked before the can so much as touched Frankie's lips. The boy jumped violently. Her voice was so strident, her reaction so out of proportion to the occasion, that Johnny stared at her in alarm.

"What's the matter with you? You scared the crap out of the poor kid!"

"That's okay," Frankie said, embarrassed by the incident, anxious to escape. "I don't like the stinky old stuff anyway!"

When he was gone, Johnny repeated his question.

"Nothing's wrong with me!" Helen snapped. "But there was something wrong with Danny, and there's getting to be something wrong with you, and Frank's father was an alcoholic and I think Frank only holds on by his fingernails sometimes, and I'm damned if any of that's going to happen to my son!"

"Weakness in the male of the species," Johnny mused. "Interesting theory. But you won't solve anything by smothering the kid."

"It's none of your business!" Helen said, not even condescending to look at him. She went to the refrigerator and started taking things out of the vegetable compartment. Frank would be home soon, or at least Helen thought he might be, and at any rate she ought to get started on supper.

Frank had retired last year on full Fire Department pension, but found after less than six months that he had nothing to do. He was in his middle fifties, in perfect health, and while he had a whole lot of high-blown plans for his retirement, most of them didn't work out. He and Helen traveled a little, but she still had the daycare center, and they couldn't live on the road. He had tried trout fishing, but came home sunburned, fly-bitten, and bored. And a man could only go to so many ballgames. When he started hanging around the firehouse again just for old times' sake, Helen decided he needed something serious to do. She pointed him in the direction of the neighborhood volunteer ambulance company, and the rest was history. But while her husband had a new lease on life, she seemed to see less of him than she had when he worked for the Fire Department.

Of course, if she had him home all the time he'd only drive her mad, Helen decided, standing at the counter, her back to Johnny. She was going to make a colossal salad, and the rest of the meal would follow from that. Tearing up lettuce and running cold water over it, she was lost in thought for some minutes. Johnny got up and left the kitchen, coming back with a clear plastic folder containing a sheaf of typewritten sheets. Helen could not help being curious.

"This is the thing I wrote to you about," Johnny said. "What started out as a little amateur genealogy has practically turned into a history of Newfoundland. I ended up with more material than I could handle."

"What're you going to do with it?" Helen asked absently, grating carrots, remembering the countless weekends a much-younger Johnny had spent with her, reading aloud an English composition or a social studies report, hungry for praise.

"I'm not sure," he said. "I submitted this much to the St. John's Historical Society. They were very enthusiastic. Said they'd be willing to commission a full-length research volume, if I was interested. Royalties would go to the Christian Brothers, of course, but I get such a kick out of doing it. And I've done all the research already. Maybe if I take all my notes to the Virgin Islands or wherever they're sending me it'll take my mind off the climate. Can I read you some of it?"

"Sure," Helen said, pushing the hair up off her forehead with one damp hand, washing green peppers. "All of it, if you want."

"Okay!" Johnny grinned, flipping back to the beginning.

"Give you a small example of some of the fascinating characters hanging—literally—from our family tree: There was a Manning, first name Ed, which makes it plausible that he's our direct line (since that was Pop's father's name, and Manning's fairly common), who was tried under English law and hanged in 1790. Trouble is, I can't find out what the charge was, although in those days it could have been anything from stealing a mackerel to raping the British governor's wife. . . ."

Helen listened, mesmerized by his voice, not looking at him, smiling vaguely. He sounded not too different, this great intellectual, from the fourteen-year-old who two decades ago sat at this very kitchen table reading his term papers aloud for her approval. His words were well chosen, the subject matter fascinating, but he managed, as always, to stay at a distance from it. To Helen this was a chronology of living, passionate people—no matter that they were her ancestors, though that enhanced her emotion—but to her brother they were simply names, flat bits of data typed onto a page. Had Johnny ever had feelings?

Post-menopausal overreaction, Helen thought wryly, wiping a tear unseen onto the back of the hand that held the knife— its serrated edge a second before poised less than a millimeter from the surface of a nubile red tomato, prepared to plunge. I'm getting weepy over everything, she thought. And nothing.

Nothing, she thought. It is Nothing that weighs me down, Nothing that frightens me and wakes me up in the small hours of the morning, the big, fat Nothing that I anticipate as being the last twenty or thirty years of my life. I look at the way my mother is now; I remember how my grandmother ranted away the last years of her life, and I am afraid. Is this going to happen to me?

But no, my life is different from theirs, because I have not relied on home and babies to be my total fulfillment. I have the daycare center, my religious-education classes, my tutoring. I am nothing else if not busy. And my children are all mature, upstanding members of society; not one of them has turned out badly.

My children. Are they what bother me? Have I done what is best for each of them? Could I have done more if I hadn't had so many so close together? Would they have been better off if I had done less for them, left them to cope for themselves more often? What could I have done differently?

Vicki. Nearly thirty and still a virgin. Why couldn't you have been a nun, Vicki, so at least you could be among friends? Why do you shun the society of men? Was it something I did wrong? When I explained the facts of life to you, did I do or say something that frightened you, frightened you so much that you could not tell me? Was I too strict with you when you were small? Too lenient when you grew older? Victoria Mary O'Dell, are you happy with your life? Will you die a virgin?

Kathleen of the red hair and stuck-out chin. Scrawny premature bird six weeks a-roasting in an incubator. Is that where you learned your independence? Has anyone ever reached your heart? Rebel, smart-mouth, your father's favorite. If only we could have talked more often without hissing and spitting at each other! Do you still have nightmares? Will you and your Jewish boy ever give me grandchildren? And why do you bristle every time the subject comes up?

Maureen, Mary Frances—I must list you separately. Maureen: quiet one, smaller of the two at birth, speaker of half-finished sentences, sigher of profound sighs, collector of antiques, nail biter. Will you ever make a decision without automatically looking to your other for advice? If she were no longer in the same room with you, could you manage without panic? Had she never existed, would you have been any different?

Mary Fran: last of my girls, blabbermouth, mathematical wizard, bathtub soprano. Do you ever think before you speak? If you and your current boyfriend decided to get married, would you change your mind because of the hurt look on your sister's face? Will you always feel the necessity to pull her along with you?

And to both of you—can you forgive me for wanting you

so much that I put your lives in jeopardy? When you are both very old and one of you dies, will the other languish away right after?

Francis Xavier O'Dell, Junior—child of my middle years, baby. Am I nurturing in you, despite my best intentions, the potential to be like your uncle, overindulged and dying young? Can I break the jinx on the male of the species?

Do I deserve my children? Am I worthy of them? Am I worthy of all the generations before me, my ancestors, the people whose end product, really, is me. Brave people came before me—primitive people, true, but people of a courage, however eccentric and irascible, to claw an existence out of a hostile environment. Larger-than-life people, or are they made so simply by historical perspective? How tame we are by comparison: from my father, home from the sea and domesticated, to my mother who never left the shore, to the likes of me who travels in posh, air-conditioned airplanes without any sense of the distance I am covering, nor any effort employed in my propulsion. Are we—tame, sophisticated, literate—the reasonable conclusion of this race of tough and unschooled beings, or only the result of too much inbreeding? Are we merely victims of our genes, or individuals able to mold our own destiny? If there is a weakness in the male of the species, might there not be a dangerous strength in the female? Because my grandmother was driven, obsessive, manic and my mother is depressive, have I no other choice than to be manic-depressive? Are all of us, we women of dangerous strength, like the pitcher plant, clinging by main force of will to some cold and nurtureless bog, parasitic, trapping our nourishment out of the lives of others, out of the lives of our husbands and children?

Helen looked at the tomato in her hand—still inviolate, awaiting her verdict as she stood with the knife in her other hand. How long had she been standing here, suspended, half-listening to Johnny's narrative, lost in her own dreadful questions about genealogy, progeny, and her own helplessness? Irrationally, she looked at the tomato. Her mother had never seen one until she came to the States. Her grandmother had steadfastly refused to eat them all her life, firm in the belief that they were a deadly poison. Helen's children had grown them in the backyard the first summer they moved to this house, gorging themselves with them until they got stomachaches and diarrhea. Such was progress. Decisively, Helen sliced into the tomato, cutting it into wedges. Some of the juice squirted onto the back of her hand, and she licked it off just as Frank came in, slamming the back door.

Helen looked up at him. His face was grayish and he was out of breath.

"Christ goddamn!" he roared, punching the door frame, forgetting there was anyone else there. Johnny had stopped reading the minute the door slammed, and he sat watching, detached as always. Frank's color returned; he was in a rage. "We lost a guy this afternoon. I can't believe the way it happened! Worked over him for an hour and never got a heartbeat. Guy was as healthy as a horse, had a physical on the job a week before, everything's fine, and then—Wham! Heart attack. Just like that! Fifty-fucking-three years old! A year younger than me! Jesus shit *damn!*"

He punched the door frame again, then exhaled explosively and was calmer. Helen wiped her hands on the dishtowel and went to him. He stood with his forehead pressed against the wall, despairing. She put her arms around his waist, letting her face rest against his back. There had been so many of these horrors over the years, after fires with casualties—a baby lost to smoke inhalation, some derelict set aflame by neighborhood punks, an entire family incinerated by arson. Frank always took these disasters personally.

It wasn't necessary for Helen to say anything. She had only to be there. She held him, hearing his heart pumping angrily, knowing with a sinking feeling that someday she would lose him, because it was the destiny of most women to outlive their men, and because someday his big heart would simply have had enough. Helen pushed the thought out of her mind because Frank needed her now, at this moment, and there was no time to think about the future or the past.

"Has it been so bad?" he had asked her that night over a week ago. Tonight, when it was just the two of them, she could give him her answer.